VEINS OF MAGIC

EMMA HAMM

Copyright

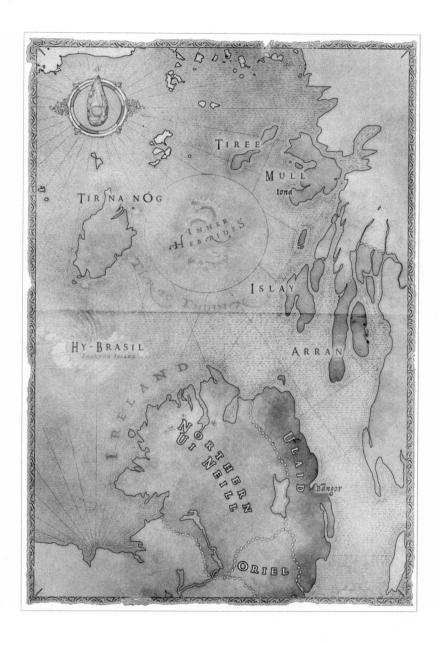

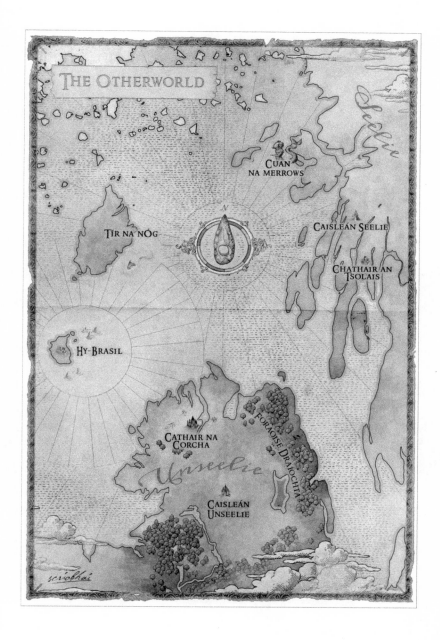

Glossary of Terminology

Tuatha dé Danann - Considered to be the "High Fae", they are the original and most powerful faerie creatures.

Seelie Fae - Otherwise known as the the "Light Fae", these creatures live their lives according to rules of Honor, Goodness, and Adherence to the Law.

Unseelie Fae - Considered the "Dark Fae", these creatures follow no law and do not appreciate beauty.

Danu - The mother of all Tuatha dé Danann and considered to be an "earth" mother.

Nuada - The first Seelie King, often called Nuada Silverhand as he has a metal arm after losing his own in a fearsome battle.

Macha - An ancient Tuatha dé Danann who is known as one of the three sisters that make up the Morrighan. Her symbols are that of a horse and a sword.

Redcap - A troublesome faerie, frequently found in gardens harassing chickens.

Máthair - "Mother"

Will-o'-the-wisps - Small balls of light that guide travelers into bogs, usually with the intention for the humans to become lost.

BROWNIES - Friendly, mouse-like creatures who clean and cook for those who are kind to them.

PIXIE - A winged faerie whose face resembles that of a leaf.

CHANGELING - Old or weak faeries swapped with human children, usually identified as a sickly child.

GNOME - Generally considered ugly, these small, squat faeries take care of gardens and have an impressive green thumb.

DULLAHAN - A terrifying and often evil faerie who carry their heads in their laps.

BEAN SIDHE - Also known as a banshee, their screams are echoing calls that herald the death of whomever hears them.

HY-BRASIL - A legendary isle which can only be seen once every seven years.

MERROW - Also known as a Mermaid, merrows have green hair and webbed fingers.

MERROW-MEN - The husbands of their female counterparts are considered horribly ugly with bright red noses, gills, two legs, and a tail.

BOGGART - A brownie who grows angry or loses their way turns into a boggart. They are usually invisible, and have a habit of placing cold hands on people's faces as they sleep.

POOKA - A faerie which imitates animals, mostly dogs and horses.

KELPIE - A horse like creature who lives at the edge of a bog. It will try to convince you to ride it, at which point it will run underneath the water and drown the person on its back.

SELKIE - A faerie which can turn into a seal, as long as it still has its seal skin.

Prologue

Once upon a time, a rose fell in love with a stag.

She was nothing more than a seed when he first passed. She saw him and spread her roots deep into the ground. Small buds appeared the next time he walked by, and she bloomed so that he might lean down to smell her sweet scent. Her leaves unfurled and her thorns shrank so she would not frighten him.

But roses weren't meant to grow on salty shores. He bid her climb upon his antlers, where he could carry her. And though roses were meant to settle in soil, she tangled her roots around his tines.

He carried her for a time. She turned her petals towards the sun and danced in the rays. She grew thirsty, but did not tell him for fear he might put her down. She was the happiest she had ever been in her short life.

Waves crashed toward their home and threatened the stag's well-being. Although he did not tell the rose, he worried for their safety. A stag could swim for shore.

A rose would surely drown.

Then one day, when the waves were at their peak, a raven flew by. The stag called out to him and begged the raven to take the rose in his claws. "Bring her somewhere safe," he pleaded. "Somewhere she can stretch her roots again."

The raven took her gently, ignoring her sad cries and petals reaching for the stag. "You're going home," he said. "A rose cannot grow where there is no soil."

They flew across land and water, sea and surf. The salt spray burned her roots and knocked all the petals from her blooms. By the time the raven put her down in the forest, she had given up.

The old oak sighed, "You are not a rose. You have no thorns."

"I am a rose, though my thorns are dull."

The birch tree swayed. "You are not a rose. You have no petals."

"I am a rose, though my petals fell off."

The ash tree wept. "You are no longer a rose, but you can become something more. Sleep in my roots for a time."

When the rose awakened, she found that the ancient trees were right.

Branches grew from her hair and bark covered her skin. Roots tangled in her feet, but she was not the same as the trees. Her body was curved, her mind clear, and she could move far from their side.

"See?" The ash said. "You aren't a rose after all."

The Rose And The Stag

"**S**orcha, my face itches!"
"Sorcha, my stomach hurts!"
"Sorcha, I can't breathe!"

Sorcha blew a tangled curl away from her face and stared into the rafters as if she could see her sisters through the floor. They claimed the plague had rendered them useless and refused to move from their beds, no matter how many times Sorcha reminded them that they weren't dying.

Yet.

Laundry obscured her vision, piled so high she could barely see over the edge, making her biceps shake with the weight. This was the first load of many that she would need to bring to the river. She was the only family member who wasn't infected by the plague, and the only one the villagers allowed to leave the brothel.

"Small blessings," she muttered before calling out, "I'll be right there, dearest sisters!"

"But Sorcha!"

"I know your discomfort is great, but I beg you, have patience! I need to put the laundry away."

"Is the laundry more important than us?"

She rolled her eyes. Her sisters had always been superb at convincing their father how ill they were. It was a shame they couldn't convince their healer sister.

Sorcha reminded herself that they were gravely ill. The blood beetle plague wasn't something to brush aside. It was a silent killer. But she couldn't shake off the feeling they could at least be attempting to help. Even Papa got out of bed for dinner. He didn't make her carry plates all the way upstairs and bring them back down.

A cool breeze brushed her sweat stained nape. Its touch was welcome and pleasant though surprising considering nails held the windows shut tight.

Lifting a brow, she set the laundry on the floor and nudged the kitchen door open. Her father sat feeding a small brown bird on the windowsill, wooden planks leaning against the wall next to him.

Sorcha leaned against the doorframe and crossed her arms over her chest. Papa nudged the seeds forward. Patient, he let the bird peck and eat before setting more down. Closer and closer until the tiny nuthatch hopped onto his hand and ate from his palm.

"You have a rare talent," she said.

He glanced up with a smile. "I learned this from you."

"Did you?"

"When you were little you used to say, 'Papa. Birds are scared of you because you're big. If you make yourself small and quiet, then they will like you as they like me.'"

"I don't think you've made yourself small."

"Well, I've never been good at shape shifting."

The nuthatch shook its feathers and took one last bite, flying out the window on silent wings. Papa watched it with a melancholy expression.

"You miss the outdoors," Sorcha said.

"More than anything. What season is it now?"

"Spring is coming. I think we've seen our last snowfall."

"So soon?"

"It doesn't feel soon," she chuckled. "But we're all still here. And that's a blessing."

"All of us?"

"Yes. Who else are we missing?"

Papa turned on the window seat and gave her a measured look. "I may be ill, but I am not blind. You left something behind."

"Everyone leaves something behind after a long journey."

"Even when it's another world?"

"Yes."

Sorcha took a seat at the long kitchen table, pulling the stained kerchief from her head. A mane of red curls sprang free to billow around her. It still felt strange that nothing had changed in her childhood home.

The wooden table held the marks she had carved into its edges to distract herself from family quarrels. Herbs hung over the fire to dry, filling the air with the scent of basil and rosemary. A cauldron bubbled with soup for dinner.

The same and not. She noticed details that never would have bothered her before. Dust around the edges of the hearth. Cobwebs in the high peaks of rafters. Drafts of cold air that never seemed to disappear.

She blew out a breath. "Do you want me to tell you more stories of Hy-brasil?"

"Your sisters were calling for you."

"Yes, they were."

"You don't want to tend to them?"

"Not really." Sorcha plunked her elbows onto the table and cupped her head. "Does that make me a bad person? I should want to help my sisters. They're ill, and they deserve all my attention and care."

She heard her father stand and shuffle towards her. The bench creaked as he sat down next to her. His thin hand rubbed her spine. "You've been so dedicated in keeping us all alive, I thought something terrible must have happened."

"Why?"

"No one works with such fervor unless they're trying to forget something. Or someone."

"And I am."

"I know."

She turned her head to peer over at the man who had saved her life countless times. New wrinkles had appeared on Papa's face. Crow's feet deepened into folds of skin, his forehead lined with worry and pain.

"It's still hard for me to grasp how much time passed," she said. "A year and a day? Really?"

"I can say it over and over again, Sorcha. We thought you were dead."

"I'm sorry to have caused you worry."

"Stop saying that." He reached forward and pulled her hand away from her face, holding it in his tight grip. "You experienced an adventure that none of us could ever imagine. You tell us stories every night that fill our dreams with wondrous things. It is a blessing you have returned to us."

She couldn't think of it like that. Sorcha didn't want to think about Hy-brasil at all. The haunting memories of ocean eyes and crystal skin plagued her dreams. The hole in her heart tore wider with each passing day. She didn't know how to stop the ache, so she soothed it with family. But even their comforting presence did little to fix what was broken.

Sorcha squeezed Papa's hand. "I'm glad to help. It's good to be home."

"But it's not where you want to be."

"No."

"You want to be with him."

"Yes," she breathed. "Very much."

"Then you must go back to him."

"I can't."

Papa frowned. "Why not? You can go to the Otherworld, can't you? You can find a pixie to help guide your way."

"It isn't like that. Pixies will let the king know I have returned, and he will track me down. I don't even know if Stone is still alive."

She had resorted to calling him by his nickname, for fear the wrong ears would hear his true name. Humans weren't likely to get involved with faerie politics, but one could never be too careful.

Her heart throbbed. She hoped he was alive. His vigor and strength were such that he may have won the first battle with his brother, but she had seen the golden army and feared the worst.

"Does your heart say he's alive?" Papa asked.

"Yes."

"Then he is alive."

"Ever the optimist. Did the bird tell you he still had breath in his lungs?"

"Birds tell us many things. This one told me you have not been yourself."

Sorcha's lips twitched. "Did it?"

"You know it's the truth, dear one. You haven't even visited the shrines."

"I don't want to."

"Since when?" Papa dropped her hand and slammed his fist down on the table. "Those shrines meant the world to you, even as a child. What has changed?"

"I no longer believe they are useful."

"You're lying."

She remembered how the faeries tasted lies on the air. Perhaps her father had more faerie blood in him than she did. Sorcha arched a brow. "You think so?"

"There's a hard edge to you now. You break your back taking care of us, but I don't think you want to anymore. There was a time when I thought you would work yourself to death just to save us. Now, I wonder if you even care."

"Of course I do."

"Then where is your faith? Where is your request for faeries to come and aid you? Have you grown so arrogant that you think you can do it on your own?"

She shoved away from the table. Her legs needed to move, her mind racing as she walked the kitchen end to end. "I am afraid! Is that what you want to hear? I did not fulfill my half of the bargain, and as such, I broke a faerie deal. I cannot go to the shrine because I do not know what awaits me there."

"You think they will kill you?"

"I don't know!" Sorcha threw her hands up, catching an herb on her fingers and tossing it to the ground. She sighed and stared at the ceiling. "I'll go get the broom."

"No." Papa lifted his hand. "You will not. You'll leave this house and go to the shrine."

"What will happen if I don't come back? Who will pull the beetles out of your bodies and keep you alive?"

"We managed for a year on our own."

"Because I made that part of my deal!" Her shout rose into the rafters and a pigeon took flight. She sighed and rubbed her temples. "I'm sorry, I didn't mean to shout. I don't want to see you die, and I do not trust the village healers."

"Neither do I. But, I think the faeries still have plans for you. We're alive for a reason." He stood and pulled her hands away from her face. "You're a talented healer, Sorcha. But you aren't the only reason the beetles haven't killed us yet."

He was right. She had noticed how quickly they healed from her surgeries. The beetles weren't multiplying inside them as they were in her other patients. In fact, the entire brothel seemed stuck in a single point of time. They remained ill, with the same amount of beetles, but the sickness did not grow.

"I have nothing to bring them," she mumbled. "No sugar, no cream, no flowers from our gardens."

"Then you will bring them your apologies."

"Faeries don't care for my guilt. They care for offerings."

"Perhaps they will forgive you. I remember a time when people used to go to the shrines just to be with the faeries in nature. I don't believe everything is about giving them something. Sometimes, the giving is in being there."

"When did you become a philosopher?" she asked with a wry grin.

"About the same time I looked death in the eyes and he told me that my daughter saved my life."

Tears stung her eyes. "Oh, Papa."

"Don't you 'Oh, Papa' me. Get on with you girl, and pick some of those lovely greens on the way back."

"Dandelions?"

"I don't care if they're a weed, they taste delicious and they do my old bones good. Say hello to the faeries for me."

She cast a critical glance at the laundry and shrugged. "Why don't you come with me? You've never greeted them before."

"They wouldn't want me to start now. They'd see an old man stumbling towards them and think I'd lost my way. It's far easier for them to connect with a pretty, young woman. Now, off with you!"

Sorcha didn't wait for any further arguments. Her sisters would yell again, and then her opportunity would disappear. She raced from the kitchen, wrapped her cloak around her shoulders, and plunged outside.

Cold air sank into her lungs with fine, claw-like points. It made her gasp, charging her blood with electricity. She came alive when she left the brothel.

She had changed so much.

Papa wasn't wrong when he pointed out her lack of care. She'd missed her family dearly, but the distance had provided her with experience and perspective. Her sisters couldn't stop talking about trivial things, men, cleanliness, food and drink. Her father only spoke of his travels, though at least that was slightly entertaining. And none of them had the magical qualities of the Fae who she held dear in her heart.

The old fence door squeaked as she opened it. One of these days, she would fix the rusty hinge. She needed to fix the window shutters, the rotting holes in the roof, clean up the backyard... The list went on and on.

Perhaps she resented this life. For a time, she had lived in a castle, waited on hand and foot. Now she was the one who waited upon others.

"Have I fallen so far?" she questioned and cast a glance towards the silhouette of her home. "Do I resent them for being ill?"

Yes. The answer was a resounding yes that echoed in her head like a scream in a canyon.

She gripped the fence in her hands, glaring up at the house as if *it* was the problem.

"Sorcha! It's too cold to be outside." The smooth masculine voice made the hair on the back of her neck raise.

Plastering on a fake smile, she bared her teeth. "Geralt."

He strode toward her with all the grace of a dancer. Tight pants hugged his legs, accentuating what he believed to be his best feature. A grand cloak of black wool swept the ground behind him clear of fallen snow.

"You'll catch a cold, Sorcha, and who will take care of you while you take care of your family?"

"I manage quite well on my own."

"But you shouldn't have to." He stripped the leather gloves from his hands, finger by finger. "Please, allow me."

"I'm not taking your gloves, Geralt."

"You most certainly are! What kind of gentleman would I be if I let you wander without proper clothing?"

He reached forward and took her hand, pressing the gloves into her palms with a smile that made her want to smack him. She let the leather fall to the ground.

"Is this how you usually treat women? As if they don't understand when they need to take care of themselves?"

"They shouldn't *have* to take care of themselves."

"What if some of us want to?"

"Why ever would you?"

Sorcha snorted and rolled her eyes. "You'll never understand."

"Nor do I wish to. I enjoy taking care of those who are dear to my heart—"

"Don't." She lifted a hand to interrupt him. "I have no interest in hearing what you have to say. I have places to be, Geralt. Now, if you don't mind."

"I'll walk with you. Are you going into town?"

Certainly if a single woman were traveling, she must be going to town. Sorcha tried not to roll her eyes, and failed horribly. Where else would a single woman be going but to town? Ridiculous man.

"I'm going to the shrine."

"What shrine? At the church?"

"No. In the forest."

"Ah," he said and frowned. "You would never have admitted that before your disappearance."

"People change."

"Apparently so."

Her boots crunched through the snow, leaving the faintest hint of footprints in her wake. She wouldn't stand around and listen to him say anything else about her life. She had no interest in speaking with a man who wanted her to bend to his will.

"Where were you anyways?"

He didn't know when to leave well enough alone.

The hills were all white around them. No trees sprung up from the earth, only small mounds where stone walls stood. Even the sheep stayed close to their barns this time of year. No one wanted to wander too far from the safety of a fire.

Sorcha tucked her cloak tight against her body and ducked her head. Perhaps, if she was lucky, Geralt would leave.

"Did you hear me? I asked where you went."

She sighed. "You've asked me that same question a hundred times over."

"Yes, I have. And you have yet to give me any kind of answer."

"I'm not sure why I'm required to answer you at all."

"You aren't. I wish to know."

"Why?"

"I care for you, Sorcha. You know this."

If she rolled her eyes any harder, she'd see the back of her head. "You care for the *idea* of me! You don't know me."

"I do! I've known you since you were a child."

"You rode past me with your father a few times. That hardly counts as knowing."

The tromping sounds he made through the snow grated on her nerves. Didn't the man know how to be quiet? She wanted a peaceful walk to the shrine! Was that really too much to ask?

"I've been talking to Briana through the wall, and she told me where you think you were. The faerie world, isn't that the story you've told?"

"Briana talks too much," she grumbled.

"You know faeries aren't real, don't you Sorcha?"

She cast a sidelong glance towards him and stopped walking. He had no right to tell her what was real, and what wasn't. This man pushed too much, thought he knew far more than a simple woman, and she grew weary of men who thought so highly of themselves.

"Geralt, is the sky blue?"

"Yes." He hesitated as he answered, looking at her as if she had lost her mind.

"Is the grass green?"

"Yes."

"But it's white right now."

"Well, there's snow on it."

"Then how do you know there is green underneath?"

"Because I've seen it."

"And if you hadn't?" She gestured towards the fields. "If you had never seen green grass before, how would you know what color it was? Would you not think grass was white?"

"I'd move the snow."

She kicked her foot, toeing the ground until it revealed the yellowed dead grass underneath. "You'd be wrong then, wouldn't you?"

"What are you trying to teach me?"

"You haven't seen the faeries, but you seem to think you know about them. Before you judge the hills to be green, I suggest you attempt to see them first. Faeries won't like you entering their shrine without permission. I really must go alone."

His jaw dropped, and she didn't wait to see what he might do next. Geralt had tried for far too long to woo her. And as much as he would make a good, traditional husband, he would not be a good husband for her.

Women were two-dimensional to him. They fit into a little box of his own making so he could explain their reasoning and actions. Sorcha stunned him every time she opened her mouth. Perhaps that was why he found her so intriguing. But she thought it more likely that he wanted to tame her.

That would never happen.

Snow crunched behind her.

"If you keep walking towards me Geralt, I will put you on your back in the snow. Leave me be."

"You've changed!" he called out.

"Yes," she said. "I have."

Her father wasn't the only one to notice. The bitterness in her heart had spread so far that she couldn't control it. Pain made her angry, and this wasn't a physical pain she could mend with herbs or medicine.

Bran had been wrong. He said she'd put herself back together, find meaning in saving lives.

She had done exactly the opposite. Bitter anger festered in her soul until she looked at the blood beetle victims as weak creatures. Sorcha didn't like the changes in herself, but she didn't know how to stop them.

The forest appeared in the distance. A snow squall headed her way, small enough that it wouldn't touch her once she ducked beneath the trees. Snow-laden branches touched the ground. They looked as though they were bowing to her as she stepped into the shadows.

If only they were. She wished the trees could hear her, that a man might step out of their bark and beckon her forward. "Come to us," he would say. "Find our hidden secrets and faerie rings.

She shook her head. The villagers claimed she lost her mind. A strange man must have kidnapped her, done horrible things, and the poor dear had broken. Why else would she speak of faeries as if they were real?

"Forever misplaced," she grunted as she ducked beneath a branch. "Always the one believing in the wrong things."

The woods were quiet. Too quiet.

No branches pulled at her hair, warning her to hide her anger. No birds sang their songs. Only stillness and the muffled thump of snow falling from the trees.

Where were the faeries? Where was the wind that brushed through her hair?

Brows furrowed, she stepped into the well-known clearing with anxiety twisting her stomach. There was something wrong.

"Is it me? Have I offended you, Macha?"

Even the light had disappeared from this sacred place. No water burbled in the stones. The triskele carvings turned dull with age, no magical glow giving them life.

She hadn't thought this was how they would punish her. Silence was worse than the threat of death.

"Are you never going to let me see you again?" A tear slid down her cheek. "You can't hide from me. I can see through your glamour!"

No giggles danced on the wind. Nothing but silence.

"You're just going to cut me off?"

She wanted to scream. She wanted to rage at the faeries who thought she deserved this, but the truth rang in her head. They could never see her again and it wouldn't hurt them at all.

They ripped magic from her life and everyone she held dear.

Sorcha lifted her chin, locking her knees so she would not fall and embarrass herself. She would remain steady. Tears dripped down her cheeks, but she refused to admit that was a weakness.

Only those strong enough to feel let tears fall.

"I will not apologize," she pleaded. "I was gone longer than expected, and I did not leave willingly, but I had to take care of my family. It was not a slight against you or your kind that I did not keep this shrine alive."

A sharp pain dug into her ankle, twin points of agony that ground against the delicate bone. She gasped and glanced down. A bright green snake, as long as she was tall, rose out of the snow.

Its mouth closed around her ankle, impossibly wide with silver fangs that dug deeper and deeper into her flesh. It coiled, looping its thick ropey body around her shin.

Pain and numbness spread from the viper's fangs. It stared up at her with glittering cold eyes.

"Impossible," she slurred. Snakes couldn't move in the winter. Snakes like that didn't live in Ui Neill.

She tasted nightshade on her tongue. Her tongue thickened, lips growing numb. She knew the signs of poison well.

⚅⚄⚅

Eamonn lifted his face to the blistering cold wind. It whistled through the crevices on his cheeks, sinking deeper and deeper into his being. The freezing edge of winter was as much a part of him now as the exaggerated limp and useless right arm.

"Master!" Cian shouted through the shrieking wind. "We cannot keep going!"

"We must!"

They could not stop in the storm. Snow blew against them, pushing jagged edges of ice underneath their clothing. Relentless and angry, the Otherworld appeared determined to destroy them.

He pulled the hood of his fur cloak lower and tilted his head down. He would beat back the wind himself if it meant they would reach their destination.

There weren't many of them left. His brother had ridden onto the isle with single-minded intent. Destroy everything in his path and leave nothing but smears of blood and ash.

"M-Master!" Oona coughed the words, her lungs weak from days in the frigid tundra. "I can't go any further!"

"We have to keep going."

"I—"

The wind swept past his ears, drowning out any words she might have said. Anger heated his blood. The crystals around his neck flared with bright violet light.

"Oona, I don't have time to argue with you. We continue on towards the dwarven stronghold! It's the only place where we might find sympathetic faeries."

They didn't respond.

Growling, Eamonn spun on his heel. His cloak flared around him and cold air buffeted his chest. It sank deep into the crystal wounds lacing his body.

Oona sat in the snow, shoulders slumped and heaving. Cian knelt beside her with his hand on her shoulder, his expression one of complete loss.

They were all bundled up in whatever they could find. Fifteen people left from the hundreds who had lived on the isle. A mother and her child hung near the back, the tiny pooka still healing from an injury a midwife might have tended.

Boggart hung near the back, her thin frame quaking with every breath. She was too thin, too small for such a journey.

He imagined he could see an outline behind the faeries. A pillar of shadows that shifted and moved. Red curls hung about her face, vivid even in the ghostly form.

She stood behind them, watching over each staggered movement. She haunted his footsteps with the echoes of her voice.

"Take care of them," she whispered on the wind. "They need you."

Eamonn sighed and rubbed a hand over his face.

"We'll stop awhile."

"The dwarves?" Cian asked.

"Nowhere to be found, my friend. We're going in the right direction, but they don't want to make themselves known just yet."

"Damn dwarves. They'll let us freeze to death and rob the clothes from our back."

Oona whimpered. "I remember dwarves. They were kind creatures with hearts made of pure gold. They could sing magic that would let women spin gold from straw."

"You're delirious," Cian grumbled. "That wasn't the dwarves."

"You've never met a dwarf."

Eamonn didn't have time to listen to them quarrel about yet another faerie species. Rolling his eyes, he pointed towards the few who remained on their feet.

"You, find something for kindling. You, help me create a bank out of snow to give us some kind of shelter. You, gather up clean snow for water so we can boil it. You—" he pointed at the mother. "Take the extra furs and bundle him up."

"I couldn't, m'lord. The others need them just as much as us."

"Your boy's lips are turning blue. Let him have a turn with the furs first, and tuck Boggart in with him. We'll pass them around later."

Gods, he tired of the cold. He wished for a warm ale in his hand, an able-bodied woman on his lap, and the cold to disappear forever.

None of which were likely to happen. He had sent away the only woman he wanted in his lap, there was no ale, and frost was gathering around his lips again. He grunted and shook ice spikes from his shoulders.

The others quickly set up camp. They'd had enough practice over the weeks of travel. He looked back at them as he set his back to work, pushing the snow into some semblance of a shelter.

They huddled together for warmth and comfort. Not a single faerie kept a hand from each other. Even Cian reached out to smooth hair from a forehead, touching fingers to lips, whispering words of encouragement in ears.

He ground his teeth. They wouldn't offer anything to him. He was the master, the invincible Tuatha dé Danann who held the sky at bay.

If only that were the truth. He shook his head and pushed the snow until a thick, tightly packed wall sheltered them. Wind dashed over the top, blowing flecks in his face as he stood. It would do for the night.

The selkie looking for kindling returned, shaking his head. "There's nothing, master."

"Of course not," Eamonn grumbled. This cursed land was trying to kill them.

He raised an arm against the biting storm and charged towards their supplies. The sled made for perfect kindling, and it would be drier than whatever was buried underneath the snow. They could carry the food and water in their packs.

"Master!" Cian called out. The gnome was just a head traveling through the drifts, his body lost in the mass of white. "We need that!"

"We'll put everything in the packs."

"We can't carry any more on our backs!"

"We need to stay warm."

"Then we'll huddle in the shelter you made."

"Without a fire, we'll all die, Cian. It has to happen."

Cian reached his side, jumped, and grabbed Eamonn's arm. The weight pulled him to the side. "We cannot carry any more."

Anger surged through his veins, so strong that he saw red.

"Then I will carry it myself!" he shouted as he loomed over the gnome. "I will lose no more to this fucking cold!"

The storm raged on. Bitter cold winds pummeled their bodies, digging into their furs, and leaving ice crystals on their bare faces. Cian stared at him with a frown.

"We will lose people, master. It is inevitable."

"Not if I can stop it."

Eamonn turned and pulled the remaining packs from the sled. He set them with the others, marking their location in his mind so he could find them tomorrow. The snow would bury them.

The sled had served them well, and now it would do even

better. He lifted the six foot frame and snapped it like a twig between his hands.

Cian sighed. "Well, you'll be wearing those."

"I said I'd carry them."

"It's a lot of weight. That's most of our food and water."

"Enough, Cian."

"I'm just trying to look out for you, master. You certainly aren't doing it."

"I don't need someone to look out for me," Eamonn growled. He cracked the remaining pieces and tucked them under his arm. "Let's go back and get the others fed."

They trudged through the snow. Cian spat into the wind as they reached the higher drifts, the wad froze before it hit the ground.

"What are you planning to say to the dwarves?" Cian called out. "They don't like your kind!"

"They'll like what I have to say."

"And if they don't?" The gnome hopped up to catch a glimpse of Eamonn's expression. "They aren't the most amiable lot."

"They don't have to like it; they just have to do as I say."

"Right, because that has a history of working so well with dwarves."

"They like my brother even less than they like me."

"That's not because he's your brother or even that he's the king. They don't like Tuatha dé Danann. They might not even let you in."

"Then we can all be thankful that I'm this large. I'll force my way in."

"Through solid gold doors?"

Eamonn lifted a crystal fist. His hand had been injured in the fighting, the bones turned to a solid mass of violet. He could still move it slowly, but it took practice. He considered it a small miracle and tried not to fear the change.

Cian audibly swallowed. "Point taken, master."

It took only a few moments to get the fire started in the center of the bank. Magic assisted to dry the wood, and soon a merry crackle sang over the howling wind.

Eamonn set himself apart from the others. He was furthest from the fire, allowing the others to soak up the warmth. Their small bodies needed it more than he did. Oona roasted vegetables with a pan from Cian's pack and a large packet of herbs, honey, and milk.

"Master?" she asked. "Will you join us?"

He shook his head and flashed a mouthful of dried venison.

They huddled together in a lump of Lesser Fae. The boy tucked himself so close to the fire that Eamonn worried he'd set himself alight. They were all exhausted, cold, and hungry.

He could do little more than shoulder the heavier burdens. He chewed his food, ignoring the worried glances Oona cast over her shoulder. The gnome must have told her about their conversation.

Worry ate at his mind. He didn't want to tell them the extent of his injuries. His hand was the least of his worries. Valleys and crevices stretched across his body in all directions.

He barely felt the cold. The numbing ice sank into his crystals and only barely slowed his body; it didn't affect him like the others.

It was worrisome.

Eamonn had never pushed the affliction as far as it could go. He didn't want to know what would happen when he was more geode than man.

He hadn't told them that Fionn's blade had caught him by surprise. Eamonn could still see his twin as he rode from behind and lifted his blade. Eamonn had felt him, like a cold wind that danced down his spine.

He turned, and the blade followed the same path their father's sword had. It dug along the dip of flesh and bone through his eye.

Eamonn took care not to show the others. He didn't want them to see the fractured half of his eyeball, the crystal splitting the orb. He touched it now and then, musing that he didn't even feel the touch. All the other wounds were sensitive, but not this one.

If he closed the other eye, he saw the world in fractured pieces. A few faeries turned in hundreds. Fire became a blaze that stretched all around him. He wondered if this was what madness felt like.

"Master?" Oona called out one last time. "We're going to rest. Join us?"

"No."

"It's warmer by the fire."

"Sleep well, Pixie. I'll take the first watch."

She grimaced. "The only watch."

"Indeed."

"You have to sleep sometime, Eamonn."

"Not tonight. We're too close to dwarven territory. I'll not be caught off guard."

He ignored the tears that welled in her eyes. He couldn't fall prey to her emotions, no matter how tired he was.

Soldiering was what he did. Their travels brought back memories of a time long ago when he had pushed his men towards armies of Unseelie Fae. They had scattered before his great sword, running from the Untouched Prince.

He had never seen the Otherworld with snow like this. The drifts were nearly as large as he was in some areas. He guided the faeries around the mountain-like structures and hoped it wouldn't tire them out too much.

Obviously, he had been wrong. They all fell asleep within moments of laying their heads down on the ground.

The fire crackled. The wind howled. And Eamonn remained so still that snow gathered on his shoulders in small lumps. Hours passed but his mind never quieted.

He didn't need the fire, for a fire lived in his memories. Sorcha, the one woman who had captivated his thoughts since the moment she burst into his throne room. She danced in his mind's eye, swaying to and fro with the fire. She wore the green dress, the one he was particularly fond of, and the flared skirt fanned around her like ocean waves.

Gods, how he missed her, but this was no life for a woman like her. He hoped she had gone home, found her family, and maybe a good man to give her children and warm nights.

The crystals on his throat throbbed. Any man who dared touch her would find himself at the end of Eamonn's blade. Perhaps it would be better if she were alone.

A shadow moved in the corner of his eye. Short, stout, and far too narrow to be a gnome, the dwarf slipped past the sleeping faeries.

Dwarves were shifty folk. They had sticky fingers, and no one could find them in the winding tunnel systems that made up the dwarven strongholds.

The shadow shifted again, but Eamonn did not move. Still as stone, he willed his body into complete silence. He didn't even breathe as the dwarf slid over a mound of snow and made his way towards their packs.

At least, Eamonn thought it was a he. The beard suggested "male" but one never knew with certainty until they spoke.

Eamonn stood and silently made his way towards the thief. His footsteps made no sound, and he did not reach for his sword, knowing Ocras would sing for blood.

His face twisted into a snarl as he darted forward. The dwarf had no chance, Eamonn's hands closed around its shirt.

"Oy!" the dwarf wriggled violently, trying to slide out of the jacket.

Eamonn twisted his fist, crunching crystals through the fabric, forcing the dwarf to remain still. "You're going nowhere."

"Le' go!"

"I don't let go of thieves."

"I ain't a thief!"

"You were stealing from our packs."

The dwarf stilled its struggles, narrowed its eyes, and shrugged. "I was just looking at 'em."

"Why?"

"Thought they might 'ave something interesting inside."

"But you weren't planning on stealing?"

"No, sir."

Eamonn arched a crystal brow. "Let me get this straight. You were just going to look at the packs?"

"Sure was."

"Just to see if something interesting was inside."

"That was the plan."

"And if you found something you fancied, you would leave it."

"You got it, mate."

"Even if it was a valuable sword?"

The dwarf's eyes dipped to the red gem on the pommel of Ocras. "Well, that might 'ave been a different story."

"You would have taken that."

"A pack of hungry peasants don't 'ave any need for valuable objects."

"So you would steal something worth money?"

"I wouldn't call it stealing," the dwarf quipped.

"You'd leave something behind for it?"

"Sure would."

"Like what?"

Eamonn could see that the question stumped the dwarf. It wiggled its feet and shrugged again. "I'd 'ave found something."

"Do you have any food on your person?"

"No."

"Any water?"

"Just snow."

"Then you have nothing worthy of trade. That's called stealing," he said as he leaned closer to glare into the dwarf's gaze. "And do you know what I do with dwarves who steal from me?"

The soft creaking of a bow being drawn carried on the wind. Eamonn stiffened and listened for the telltale rustle of feathers as an arrow was notched.

"I think you would say that you gave thieves whatever they wanted and let them go in peace," the heavily accented voice rumbled. "Now put the girl down."

Eamonn cocked his head to the side and looked the dwarf in his grasp up and down. "Girl?"

"What?" she pinwheeled her arms at him. "You couldn't tell? Come 'ere I'll show you what a girl looks like up close!"

The dwarf behind him barked, "Put 'er down."

"I don't think so," Eamonn twisted his hand until the girl yelped.

"Now."

Eamonn glanced over his shoulder at the dwarf who planted his feet into the snow. His bow stretched higher than his head, and Eamonn was certain this one was male. His grey beard fluttered in the wind and silver-plated armor decorated his body.

Their gazes locked and Eamonn gave him a feral grin.

Oona stirred, waking from her slumber to blink at the standoff. "Master," she murmured. "Perhaps you should do what he says."

But he was already angry. So angry that he wasn't thinking straight and frustrated that the dwarves were already pulling weapons. What had he done to earn their hatred? They didn't know who he was. They had no right.

He twisted the girl's jacket until she grasped the neck and wheezed.

"Shoot the arrow," Eamonn said. "Show us the true nature of dwarven hospitality."

The dwarf didn't hesitate. He loosed the arrow that cut snowflakes in half and struck Eamonn right over his heart. The metal tip bent as it struck flesh and then crystal. Wood shattered into splinters that decorated the snow in tiny shards.

Eamonn felt nothing. He cared for nothing. All he knew was that the dwarf had attacked.

Cocking his head to the side, he dropped the girl onto the ground and snapped the metal tip from his crystal. "You cut my jacket."

The dwarf dropped his bow into the snow. "What are you?"

The smaller dwarf at his feet scuttled backwards. "Cursed."

"Monster," the other echoed. "You are not welcome on dwarf lands. We will drive you and your cursed people out."

"You can try," Eamonn growled.

Oona scrambled to her feet, holding out her hands. "No, please. He's no monster!"

"Explain what he is then, because the dwarves do not abide by black magic."

"He is your king!"

The wind whistled through his crystals and Eamonn stared the dwarves down. The little girl climbed towards the male, ducking behind him as if that would keep her safe. His hand hovered over Ocras, but he did not pull her free. Not yet.

"King?" The dwarf shook his head. "There is only one king."

"You are correct," Oona warned. "You stand before the High King of the Seelie Court. The firstborn son of Lorcan the Brave."

"Who, the Untouched? He's dead."

"I'm not dead," Eamonn said. "Far from it."

The dwarf shook his head. "Well, pull my beard. If it's really you, the lord under the mountain will want to see you."

"Wait just a minute," the female dwarf grumbled. "'Ow do we know it's really 'im?"

"You don't," Eamonn said.

Oona shuffled forward, hesitating when the dwarves backed away. "I am Fae, just as you. I cannot lie."

"You could believe that he's the high king, and he might lead you astray."

"I cared for him as a child. I sang songs to him when he slept, and I watched while they hung him. This is the eldest son, the one spoken of in song."

"And what do you want with the dwarves?" He directed his question to Eamonn with a nod.

He shifted, placing his hand against Ocras. His furred cloak parted in the breeze and revealed his crystal fist and misshapen torso.

"I wish to speak with the lord under the mountain regarding an army."

"For what?"

"For war against Fionn the Wise."

"You want to take back the throne?"

Eamonn shrugged. "I wish to see my brother's head on a stake."

"You have no desire for the throne?"

"We shall see how the story unfolds. The rest is for your lord's ears alone."

The dwarves turned their back on Eamonn and the rest of his crew. They wrapped their arms around each other and mumbled. One of their heads would raise to meet his unwavering gaze before they ducked back down.

Finally, they turned as one. "We'll take you underground."

"You'll feed and wash my people."

"We take only you."

"You take everyone." Eamonn's hand flexed on the pommel of his sword. "Or I'll insist upon justice for the attempted theft and find myself another dwarf."

"You'd never find another."

"If you think I cannot tear this mountain apart, then you do not know my reputation."

The male dwarf snorted. "Come on then. The lot of you."

Eamonn turned his back on them and gestured at Oona. "Wake the others. We're going underground."

The Medicine And The Blade

S orcha couldn't breathe, couldn't think, couldn't feel. Black sparks obscured her vision as poison coursed through her veins. The snake sunk its fangs deeper into her ankle.

Blood dripped from the twin punctures onto the snow where it sizzled and sank to the earth. Swallowing hard, unable to feel her own tongue, she glanced down and watched seedlings grow from the perfect red circles. The snow melted around their fragile stems.

She blinked and the powdery white returned, its blood-stained imperfection swallowing the seedlings.

The snake squeezed her leg, unlatched its mouth, and wound its way up her body. The smooth scales rasped against her skin as it looped around her neck and opened its mouth wide.

Venom dripped from each fang. She felt the poison land on her cloak, burning through the thick fabric and sticking to her breast. It burned, but she couldn't lift her hand to brush it away.

Her gaze caught the slitted eyes of the snake. A low hiss vibrated through her skull and the air turned hot. She panted, but could not inhale enough air. Not while the creature swayed, tightening around her throat.

It looked away from her, pointing its flat head towards the forest beyond.

Delirious, she stared at the trees and watched the snow melt. Leaves unfurled and moss grew upon the trunks, so thick and lush that it rivaled any she had seen before.

The trees moved. They did not pull up their roots or bend. They parted like a wave as if the world ripped in half and a new path formed.

Sorcha furrowed her brows, struggling to stand and watch the phenomenon. The snake hissed in her ear and it sounded like words.

"Walk forward," it said. "Walk towards your destiny."

But she couldn't walk. She couldn't even lift a foot as the venom that tasted like nightshade froze in her veins. She was cold. So cold.

Snapping jaws closed around her jugular, sinking deep into the corded muscle of her neck and pumping more venom into her body. She felt it. Cold like ice and hot like fire all at the same time. It unthreaded from her neck and stretched in splintered pieces throughout her body.

"Go," the snake hissed again. "The trees know the way."

A tear slid down her cheek and she stepped forward. Whispers echoed in the trees. Not faeries, for she knew their voices well. The deep grumbles came from within the earth, tangled in the roots of trees. They groaned out legends, myths, and stories about a rose garden that grew between great oaks.

Sorcha listened as she walked through their path. Her vision warped, and she saw people in the shadows. Not faeries, not dryads, but figures wearing leather with their faces painted blue.

The sun set, and the moon rose at the end of the path—a full moon though she was certain it had already passed. Her head tilted to the side, baring her neck to the snake which hissed in her ear. The moon was dripping silver.

Fat droplets fell towards an altar at the end of the path. Sluggishly, they dripped into the basin. The water turned silvery-white, like milk with rainbows dancing upon the oiled surface.

"Drink," the viper hissed. "Drink and join the others."

"What others?" Sorcha asked, her words slurred.

The snake didn't answer. She heard her ragged breath mingling with the steady thrum of her heart. It sounded like the beat of drums.

It was drums, she realized, drums beaten by those standing among the trees. They weren't there, she thought. They couldn't be there because she could see through them. They held swords and spears in their hands. The sound came from striking blade against shield.

"Drink the moon?" she slurred. She could already taste the heady flavor. The cold ice water that would wash away the nightshade as she swallowed.

"Drink," the viper hissed again.

Sorcha stepped forward and dipped her hands into the altar. Underneath the milk white water, her flesh melted away. She flexed her skeletal hands, whimpering because there was no pain. Only a blank space where feeling should be.

She wondered how she was meant to hold the water in these hands. But as she scooped it in her palms, the flesh returned. She lifted the moon to her lips and drank deeply of its essence.

It slid down her throat like a balm. The physical effects of the poison washed away. Closing her eyes, she reveled in the return of sensation.

The viper's jaw snapped.

Sorcha opened her eyes and stared at the moon. Blood dripped from the top and turned it red.

"A bad omen," she said.

"Not for us," the viper hissed. "Never for us."

"Us?"

The phantoms stepped forward. Their hands trailed down her sides until Sorcha could no longer tell what was a hallucination and what was really happening. She could feel their fingers clutching her flesh.

They lifted the snake from her neck and stripped the clothing from her body. They plucked at her hair, pulling strands from her head. Their fingers were cold.

Shivering violently, she wrapped her arms around her nudity and stared at their painted faces. They warped, changing from man to beast.

To nightmares.

A woman stepped forward, twigs tangled in the long length of her wild hair. She was nude as well, twin circles painted around her breasts and runes carved into her skin.

"Welcome, sister." She placed a crown of ivy on top of Sorcha's red head.

"Sister?"

"We're all sisters," another voice rasped in her ear. "And now you have finally returned."

"I've never been here before."

"You have."

"No," Sorcha shook her head. "I would remember this place."

They traced circles on her skin, leaving blue paint in their wake until runes and markings she did not recognize covered her body.

Hands pushed her forward, towards another altar she had not noticed.

"Lie down," the voice behind her cajoled. "Lie down and join us."

"I don't know what is happening."

"Come home," they chorused. "Come home and finally be free."

"Free?" Tears gathered in her eyes, although she could not explain why. "I want to be free."

They pushed and pulled, stretching Sorcha out on the altar. The red light of the moon bathed her skin, its rays nearly as warm as the sun.

She heard the vines slithering over the stone altar before she saw them. Leaves softly rustled as they tentatively touched her legs and wrapped around her calves. They twisted around her arms and coiled in her hair.

"What is happening?" she moaned. "What are you doing to me?"

"We're waking you up," a voice sang. "It's long past time for you to join your mother."

"My mother is dead."

"Your mother is always alive."

Sorcha's mind spun as the painted women chanted. They linked hands and rocked back and forth. They spoke in a language she did not understand, but that didn't matter. The moon was shining, its rays red as blood.

She thought the moon had cured her of the viper's venom but she had been wrong.

The snake's scales rasped over her hipbone. It traveled up her belly, between her breasts, and arched until it loomed over her and obscured the red moon. It opened its mouth.

The women stopped chanting. All fell silent as a fat drop of venom landed upon Sorcha's chest.

"It is time," the women cried out. "Will you join us?"

"Yes," she found herself saying. "Yes I will join you."

The snake lunged forward and sank its fangs into her neck.

Sorcha jolted forward. She landed on her knees in the snow, curling her fingers in the cold. She patted her body down, feeling only her woolen cloak and thick layers of skirts.

"What?" she mumbled.

It wasn't possible. She had been in that forest glen with chanting women and a snake digging its fangs... She felt her neck for puncture wounds.

Two perfect scabs left raised edges on her neck.

"Hello, granddaughter." The voice came from the edge of the clearing. It sounded like the whisper of tree leaves and strangely familiar.

She glanced up at the man. A leather thong pulled his silver hair back. Furs covered his body, and he held a staff made of silver wood she did not recognize. He stared at her with a gentle expression and recognition in his green eyes.

She knew his eyes.

"You have my mother's eyes," she observed.

"That is because she shared mine. Just as you do."

"Who are you?"

"I am your grandfather."

"What happened to me?" Sorcha gestured at her neck. "Was that real?"

"In a way. The things that happen in our minds always have meaning and are not always simply in our heads."

"What was it?"

"An ancient ritual no longer practiced by our kind."

"Our kind?" She shook her head. "I'm sorry, I don't understand. Who are you?"

He strode forward and held out a hand. "My name is Torin. I am your grandfather."

She stared at his hand. Fine wrinkles stretched from the palm out to his fingers. They would have meant nothing to her before coming to this clearing, but she read them easily. A long life. A lost love.

Sorcha slid her fingers into his. "You are my mother's father?"

"I am indeed." He pulled her to her feet. "And you look exactly like her."

"You knew her?"

"I did."

"I did not."

"An unfortunate mistake I take full blame for. She should never have been allowed to leave when she was insistent upon staying so close to the Fae."

"Why did you let her?" Sorcha's heart clenched. "If you knew it was dangerous, why did you let her go?"

"She wanted to take you into the wilds of the world. Brigid was never afraid of anyone."

"Brigid," Sorcha repeated the beloved word. "You knew my mother."

"She was beautiful, like you."

"I am not beautiful."

He reached forward and tucked a wayward strand of hair behind her ear. "How do you feel?"

"Like myself."

"Not new?"

Sorcha flexed her fingers. "Perhaps a little new. What should I feel like?"

"Changed."

"Why?"

"You took part in the ceremony. You are not the same person anymore."

"Why can I not be the same person as before?"

"You gained much knowledge."

"And knowledge changes a person?"

"It does."

Sorcha wracked her mind for any differences, but she could feel none. She shook her head. "I feel the same."

Torin frowned and held out his staff. "Take this."

She took it.

"It's well made," she observed.

"Does it feel warm to the touch?"

"No."

"Hm," he pulled it out of her hands and pointed towards the forest. "Look at the forest. What do you see?"

"Trees."

"And?"

"Leaves."

"Hm," he grumbled again. "And listen to the air. What do you hear?"

She closed her eyes and exhaled. She tried to listen, but couldn't focus. Her hands were shaking, her heart beating so rapidly she forgot how to breathe.

Had she really been in the forest glen this whole time? Had the snake been in her mind? The women too?

He hadn't answered her questions. Instead, Torin had spoken in veiled truths and strange riddles.

Who was he?

She found it hard to believe a relative appeared out of nowhere. Her mother's family had never tried to contact her before. Nor did she remember her mother ever speaking of them. It was as if they didn't exist at all.

"Child?" he asked. "What do you hear?"

"The wind," she shrugged and opened her eyes. "I hear the same things as before."

"Try again."

"I fail to see what you are doing. Why do you want me to listen, look, and feel? What good will this do?"

"I'm trying to see what kind of druid you are."

"I am me." Sorcha lifted her hands palm up. "I am Sorcha of Ui Neill. I am a healer and a friend of the Fae. That is all."

"A druid is always something."

"Then I shall be the first to remain who I am."

"Your mother was one of the Banduri. A legendary healer and seeress."

"My mother was just a healer," she corrected. "A friend of the Fae, as am I."

Torin scoffed. "You can ignore your legacy all you want, but you are one of ours. You accepted it in the ritual and now you must learn."

"I don't take kindly to people telling me I *must* do things."

"You will learn!" He struck the staff upon the ground, and an echoing strike slammed against her ears. "You have no choice!"

"You will be silent, old man!"

Her scream echoed through the forest and shook snow from the leaves. A cry echoed hers, the aching grumble of a troll awakened from its slumber.

"Oh," he said. "So you are one of those."

"What did you say?"

"We call your breed of druid a 'Weaver.'"

Sorcha shook her head. "What are you talking about?"

"A Weaver's purpose is to tie together the lives of druid and Fae. To link those of us who keep watch over the land and its people. It is a rare gift."

"What do you want from me?"

"I want nothing from you." He flexed his hands on the staff, leaning against it with a soft smile. "I want to help."

"What can you possibly help me with?"

"Curing the plague. Returning home to your lost love. Finding the faeries and affecting the course of time."

Sorcha blinked.

What was he going on about? Did he really think he could change all those things with a little druid magic?

"The druids are long gone," she said. "How do I know you can do all you say you can?"

"Trust me."

"I find that trust has grown far more difficult to earn."

"Yes, after all you have gone through, I imagine it is."

"What do you know of me?"

Torin nodded towards the remains of the faerie stones. "I have watched you since the beginning. I know you went to Hy-brasil, that you fell in love with the high king. I saw him force you to leave the isle so he could battle his brother without fear you would fall."

Sorcha's heart leapt in her throat. Eamonn's image danced before her eyes. "Is he well?"

The question fell from her tongue like a drop from the moon. She wanted to suck it back in, to not ask at all for fear of what he would say. Her heart hadn't healed yet. It couldn't be torn open again so soon.

"He lives," Torin said.

Her knees buckled, and she fell back onto the ground. "He lives?"

"He fights for the throne."

"I told him to," she sighed. "I don't know if that was right or wrong."

"He will save his people, but you must save him."

"Why?" She looked up at her grandfather and saw an eye painted in the center of his forehead. Memories swam in her mind, images of a fearsome beast and her husband. "You work for the Unseelie Queen."

"I have contact with her, but a druid works for no one."

"Why am I so linked with the fate of the Fae?"

"You are his." Torin smiled. "And he is yours. The end does not happen without both sides of the coin."

"And his fate decides that of the Fae?"

"Precisely."

"Oh, Eamonn," she said quietly so that Torin would not hear the faerie's real name. The forgotten prince was so intertwined with the future and he didn't even know. "I should be there with him."

"Yes, you should. But not now."

"Why not now?"

"There are people you must save."

Sorcha threw her hands into the air. "Why does everyone keep telling me that? I cannot save anyone at all! The blood beetle plague is worse than before. I need a cure."

"Then you must ask for one."

"Why? Because you have one?" She scoffed. "No one has the cure. All I can do is watch people die and wish I knew how to help."

"I have the cure."

Sorcha froze. He had a cure? There was no possible way he could have a cure, but he didn't appear to be lying.

She rose to her feet and pointed at him. "You have the cure?"

"Yes."

"The faeries said they had it."

"The Fae you spoke with knew I had the cure. They would

have traded that knowledge after you'd completed three great deeds."

"And you'll give it to me?"

"Yes."

"For what price?"

"Druids do not ask for payment. It is a gift to my grand-daughter."

Sorcha shook her head. "No. Nothing is free. What do you want from me?"

"Our seers have looked into your future, and we wish for you to remember us kindly."

"Why?"

"You did not want to see your future when the Unseelie Queen provided you the opportunity. Have you changed your mind?"

Had she? Sorcha wasn't certain. So many other people seemed to know her future. Why shouldn't she?

"No," she conceded. "I do not want to know my path before I walk it."

"Then I give you this gift, granddaughter."

He reached underneath his cloak and pulled out a small vial. Gold filaments wrapped around the glass, leaving a melting texture on the outside of the orb. It was not of this realm, although she did not think it was from faerie either.

"This contains waters from the Cauldron of Dagda. They can give any human immortality, or heal any grievous wound. Make your choice wisely."

She took the vial and held it to the weak sunlight. Fracturing rainbows danced upon its surface, like the water of the moon. "I would never consider keeping it for myself. There are so many people this could help."

"Precisely why I feel no worry in giving it to you."

She clutched the vial in her hand and sighed. "And returning to the Otherworld?"

"The Fae banished Druids from their shores long ago. I cannot assist you in returning. But if you create miracles as you travel, the faeries will find you themselves."

"One drop of this will save a life?"

"And it will always replenish itself."

"You believe Macha herself will find me?"

"I believe there are many ways to get to the Otherworld, and you will find at least one, if not many, in your travels."

Sorcha blinked. "Travels?"

"Do you want to just save your family? Or do you want to save the world?"

She thought about the question long and hard. Long ago, she would have said the world. She would have given up everything she had just to journey and have that appellation stamped onto her name. Sorcha of Ui Neill, the healer of the blood beetle plague.

Now? She shook her head. "If I could give it to another, I would. As soon as I find a way back to the Otherworld, I will hand off this burden to another."

Torin nodded. "I thought as much. You feel very strongly for him, don't you?"

"I do."

"Why?"

"I have no answer for that. He earned my trust and showed he is an honorable man. That is enough for me."

"Do you love him?"

Did she love him? Sorcha knew she wasn't herself without him. That she missed him so much her heart ached, and a great crater grew with every passing day. She could survive without seeing his face. She just didn't want to.

Sorcha sighed. "What is love but burning passion and fleeting moments? I knew him for a small amount of time and I cannot say if I love him or the idea of him."

"He loves you."

Her heart stopped. Her stomach clenched and her hands began to shake. She tucked them underneath her armpits and shook her head again. "What?"

"He loves you. Faeries do nothing by half, and he admired you greatly."

She wanted to go back to Hy-brasil. So much that she could barely breathe. But it wasn't there anymore. Her home, her people, all destroyed by a beautiful king and his golden army.

What could she do? There was nothing left for her there but a faerie who wanted his throne and whose brother wanted him dead.

She sighed. "I wish we had longer together, but I cannot go back. How would I even find him?"

"I have faith in you."

Sorcha turned to leave, but hesitated at the edge of the clearing. This place was always where her life changed. Glancing over her shoulder, she looked at her grandfather. A man who should have been in her life since she was a child.

"What can a Weaver do?"

He flashed a grin. "They're the reason the druids were banished from the Otherworld and hunted until we nearly disappeared forever. They knit the Fae together with humans, but they can also control them."

"They can control the Fae? They must need the faerie's name."

"Druids have a drop of faerie blood. Some can control nature, some change the shape of objects or themselves. But Weavers? Weavers can command the Fae without knowing their true name."

She clenched her hand around the vial that would save her people. Eamonn's face flashed before her. The ruined crystals of his body glinted in the light of his brother's sword. She remembered the mistreatment of faeries by the Seelie Fae and the corrupted castle of the Unseelie Queen. Their pain and anguish called out to her.

She could leave this clearing and never return. She could heal her people and be renowned across the land. She didn't need the faeries' help. Sorcha could forget them entirely as they had so clearly forgotten her.

Her hands trembled, and she turned towards her grandfather.

"Show me."

⚜

A HARSH STRIKE OF A HAMMER SLAMMED AGAINST THE BACK OF Eamonn's knees, and he fell with a grunt, crystal cracking against stone. It annoyed him to hear the harsh sound that no normal faerie would cause. There was no pain, no discomfort, not even the smallest twinge from his knees.

How far gone was he that he couldn't even feel pain?

"So this is the high king?"

The deep voice of the Lord Under the Mountain rattled him. It was a voice Eamonn recognized, though one he had never expected to hear again.

Glancing up, his eyes caught upon the throne. The dwarf seated on the giant gold monolith was tall in comparison to the rest of his people. His beard was short, trimmed rather than left in a long braid. His hair hung to his shoulders which were free of armor and covered only by a sleeveless shirt. Black tattoos swirled in circular patterns from his shoulders down to his fingertips.

"Angus," Eamonn said. "How fortuitous."

The dwarf behind him shoved at his shoulders. "You'll treat the lord with respect!"

"I'll treat him with respect when he gets down off that throne."

The Lord Under the Mountain snapped his fingers. "Have you no care for the head that resides upon your shoulders? At any point, I can order the guards to remove it, and they will not hesitate."

"I'd like to see you try." Eamonn tilted his head back to reveal his ragged neck wound. "It's already been attempted a few times."

"Aye, I remember you swinging up there."

"I remember you dragged away in chains."

"Tis a shame neither of us won our freedom that day."

The dwarf behind him inhaled. Eamonn thought it rather pathetic that he didn't realize sooner the two men knew each other.

Eamonn straightened his shoulders and placed his hands on his thighs. "Are you going to make me kneel for the rest of this conversation?"

"I rather like you on your knees."

"Just so you can finally look me in the eyes?"

Angus snorted and hopped down from the throne. His heavy boots echoed as they struck the ground. He paused in front of Eamonn, planted his hands on his hips, and shook his head. "Shame that you're right. You'll have to lose your legs just so you can't look down on me."

"As if you'd ever let me."

"All right, since you're so handsome. Stand up."

The dwarves surrounding them gasped as Eamonn rose to his full height. He slapped a hand against Angus's shoulder and grinned. "You're lucky I recognized you, otherwise we might have come to blows. You've changed, old friend."

"And what would you have done if you didn't? We'd have swarmed you."

"Unless you've got your pickaxes handy, I don't think it would have done much."

"No," Angus shook his head with a trouble expression. "It's gotten worse."

"It will only continue to worsen."

"It's no curse then?"

"No."

"Shame." Angus turned towards his people and waved his hands. "Off with you. I can take it from here."

"But sire—"

"I said no, Cait." He addressed her with affection. "You've done your scouting duty well. Return to your training."

She huffed and joined the others, glancing over her shoulder before leaving the throne room.

Silence echoed in the large underground hall. Eamonn's own people were tongue tied, staring at Angus and he as if they'd conjured magic out of their palms.

Cian was the first to break the silence. "What the bloody hell was that?"

"This is Angus," Eamonn turned with his hand on the dwarf's shoulder. "An old friend from my days serving the previous king."

"When you were fighting the Unseelie?"

He nodded. "Angus was one of the few dwarves who willingly joined the fight. He was a remarkable warrior."

"Still am," Angus quipped. "Don't you be questioning my capabilities."

"In my experience, sitting on a throne does little to sharpen the blade."

"You have little experience sitting upon a throne." Angus's voice took a hard edge. "That fool twin of yours is hardly an example of a good king."

"In that, we agree." Eamonn gestured towards the faeries he brought with him. "Food and lodging?"

"Absolutely."

While Angus called out for his people, Eamonn prepared his. "They'll bring you food and water. I don't know what kind of hospitality they'll offer, but I assume they'll at least provide beds. Get a good night's rest."

"I'll stay with you, boy." Cian straightened his cloak with a grimace. "I don't like the idea of you here without one of us by your side."

"Angus is trustworthy."

"And you don't always make the right decisions when you aren't thinking straight."

"This is my battle to fight, my friend." Eamonn clapped a hand on his shoulder. "It is appreciated, but I'll need you healthy for the rest of this journey."

He grumbled, but followed the tiny dwarf woman who led them all from the throne room.

Angus perched on the arm of his throne, looking Eamonn up and down with a critical glance. "You look like you've been rolling with the pigs."

"I've been on Hy-brasil."

"Same thing then."

"You could say that." Eamonn held his hands out at his side. "I came in peace."

"Ocras is out in the open. I'd dare say that wasn't your intention."

"One can never be too careful with dwarves."

"Now that is the truth." Angus bounced his knee before blurting, "Why are you here, Eamonn?"

"I want to kill the king."

The silence that followed was deafening. Eamonn clenched his fists and forced himself to remain still. Angus would not refuse him. It was sheer luck he had become Lord and not one of his many brothers. Angus knew first-hand what Fionn could do to the Seelie Fae.

The dwarf pulled a blade from his hip and dug it underneath his nails. "You're going against blood? Since when?"

"Fionn has crossed the line."

"He didn't cross the line when he tried to hang you?"

"Don't focus on my misgivings. He is my brother, Angus. I had no desire to turn my back on the only family I have left."

"So I ask again, what changed?"

"He attacked my home," Eamonn growled. "He attacked my people."

"Not that I don't appreciate the change of heart, but it doesn't sound like you. You've never cared that much. He played you. What the hell changed to make you go soft?"

He saw red hair stirring in the breeze, trailing over freckled skin so white it was nearly milk. Dirty fingernails with blood caked underneath from helping heal his people, even though he didn't want her to. Eamonn heard her name dance in the air and tasted sunshine on his tongue.

"I gained perspective."

"You met a woman."

Eamonn glared.

"In my experience, that's the only reason a man would change his entire outlook on life. She must be a stunning faerie to have convinced you to return home."

"She's not Fae."

"A human?" Angus's knife slipped and cut his thumb. Fat drops of blood dripped to the floor, but he didn't react. "You fell for a human?"

"I fell for no one."

"A human, Eamonn? One of the unwashed creatures who swarm their world and destroy everything in their path?"

"She's not like the others."

"Oh, none of them are like the others. That's how all the stories go until they turn on you and go back home. Just how badly do you hate yourself?"

"She wouldn't leave," he growled. The large hall suddenly felt tiny as the walls closed in on him. "Be wise, Angus, and still your tongue."

"I don't see her in your crew, thus I am correct. She left and now what? You want to take back the throne so she'll return to your arms? Grateful a king would want to place her on the throne next to him?"

A slow warning growl rumbled through Eamonn's chest. "Choose your next words carefully, friend."

"You'll attack me over a woman? How the tables have turned." Angus hopped from his throne and tucked his knife back into his waistcloth. "I cannot provide as much help as you'd like. Your brother has attacked the dwarves too many times."

"All I ask is for a few men to fight by my side."

"I don't have even a small number. I have enough to keep this stronghold safe while still helping out the other tunnels. You'll have to make due with five."

Eamonn grunted. "Five men? You want me to kill the king with five men?"

"You were a great general once. Think like that man again."

Angus had lost his mind. There wasn't a flaming chance that

Eamonn could pull off the greatest assassination their people had ever seen with five dwarves, a gnome, a boggart, and a pixie at his disposal. No matter how renowned he was in battle, Eamonn would fail.

"I go to war," he gritted through his teeth. "And you say I should fight with five men?"

"I didn't say I wouldn't help in other ways." Angus rolled his eyes. "Easy there, Untouched. Your quick temper hasn't changed in all this time I see. Follow me."

"Where?"

"Ocras has served you well, but she won't be a match for thousands."

"And you have a sword that will be?"

"It's not just any sword. I have the sword of Nuada."

Eamonn's heart jumped into his throat. The sword of Nuada was a legendary blade, passed down through his grandfather's line. No one had seen it in hundreds of years. All the relics of the original Tuatha dé Danann had disappeared long ago.

Until now.

"You have the sword of Nuada?"

"I do."

"And you told no one until now?"

Angus scoffed. "Just who would I be telling? Your brother?"

"Why are you telling me?"

They descended a stairwell from the main throne room. Living space gave way to a giant cave system with networks of halls that disappeared deep into the earth. Pulley systems lifted dwarves up and down the great mines, all lit by a channel of lava that poured out of vats from above.

"Of all the royalty in the Seelie court, you're the only one I'd trust not to use this blade against my people."

"Why's that?"

"I fought with you, Eamonn. I've seen what you can do with a sword and I've seen how you treat the Lesser Fae. You didn't see us as base creatures." Angus's reflection in the polished stone walls revealed his grimace. "I hope I can trust your opinion to be the same now."

"It's been a long time. I fell into the affliction carried by my brethren."

"No longer?"

"You can thank the little human for that."

"Oh?" Angus's voice lifted in curiosity. "What's she got to do with all this?"

"She saw them as equals, even when I could not."

"I think I would like this girl."

"Most do."

"But still so foolish that she left you?"

Eamonn growled. "That was my doing."

"Ah." Angus maneuvered them around dwarven miners who stared up at the beastly man walking among them. Most shied away from meeting his gaze although a few glowered as they passed. "Then it is not she who is the fool."

He couldn't agree more. He had been a fool to force her to leave, but there had been no other option.

Eamonn refused to put her in harm's way. His brother would try to use her as a pawn. The Seelie would fight to capture her, to tear her from his side and do unspeakable things just to make her talk.

She was innocent. She did not know the ways of the Fae, nor did she know how to protect herself. Of all people, he would preserve that innocence with his last breath.

As they passed another group of dwarves, he flexed his crystal hand and told himself this would all be over soon. If he had the sword of Nuada, others would surely follow him. The dwarves may not fight, but there were many more creatures he could call upon.

They would follow the High King of the Seelie Fae to the pits of hell. Or he would force them.

And once all this was done, he could find her again.

Eamonn sobered at the thought. Time passed differently in her world. She may be an old woman, with wrinkles and frail bones.

He'd never seen an aged human before. They weren't often found in the Otherworld.

"In here," Angus grunted. "And try to keep your wits about you, Eamonn."

The dwarf was right. Eamonn forgot too easily where he was. The dwarven strongholds were mazes that even the most intelligent of Fae could get lost in. He needed to pay attention to where they were, in case Angus left him in the dark.

Angus reached up and pulled a lever. The pail attached to it dropped, pouring lava into a trough that spilled out into the most incredible treasure room Eamonn had ever seen.

Gold stretched as far as the eye could see. Mountains of coins, gemstones, and armor piled atop each other as if they didn't matter in the slightest. These items should be displayed, placed in a setting of honor. A crown caught his eye, diamonds glittering in the solid metal.

"What is this place?" he asked.

"The place we put things we want to forget."

"You put the sword of Nuada in this room?" Anger raced through his blood, hot and hard.

"I *hid* the sword of Nuada in this room. Great beards! Would you calm down?"

He had never controlled his anger well. Long ago, when war was in his blood and rage flickered at the edges of his vision, he had rode the waves of anger like a captain guiding a ship. He'd gotten too good at convincing people he wasn't a split second from tearing out their throat.

"Just get it over with," he growled.

"Eager to get your hands on the weapon that could change the tide of war?"

"It is my grandfather's sword, and I still don't think you have it."

Angus arched a thick brow and plunged his hand into a mountain of treasure. Gold fell in an avalanche all around him, trickling down in great waves that sounded like dripping water.

Each clink grated on Eamonn's ears until he could barely stand it.

He watched with rapt attention as Angus pulled his arm out of the pile and brandished the most beautiful blade in all of history.

Claíomh Solais. The Sword of Light.

Red stones glittered in the pommel of the sword, each like a tiny drop of blood. The gold hilt tapered into the open mouth of a wolf that swallowed the rest of the blade. It was a beautiful blade. Light glinted off the sharpened edge, runes scribed into the flat edges spoke of the battles it had survived. And won.

Angus pulled it back when Eamonn reached for it. "Not so fast. You know the legends of this sword?"

"Yes."

"Then you know what it can do."

"It carries the power of manipulation, controlling the minds of others once the blade is drawn. Yes, I know, Angus."

The dwarf grimaced. "I'm handing you a very powerful weapon, Eamonn. Please take this seriously."

"Do you know the legends?" Eamonn's lips split into a feral grin. "That blade will only work in the hand of the high king."

Angus pointed the tip at Eamonn's belly. "Kneel."

"No."

"Walk away."

"No, dwarf."

"Remove yourself from this mountain and never return."

"Are you quite done?"

Angus shrugged. "I wanted to see if you were telling the truth. Do you want to see if you're really the high king?"

Did he? Eamonn wasn't so certain. He'd spent a majority of his life avoiding his birthright.

He licked his lips and held out his hand. "It's far past time I accepted my heritage."

"You're certain?"

"Give me the sword, Angus."

Although Angus's face twisted in worry, he extended the hilt towards Eamonn.

Licking his lips, Eamonn reached forward and grasped the wolf head. Cold metal struck frigid stone, and fire raced through his blood.

He gasped and staggered backwards, holding the sword with both hands now in fear he would drop it. The wolf's mouth opened and closed in a frenzy as it tried to swallow the blade. The desperate thumping of his own heart echoed until Eamonn's eyes burned.

A pulse of magic filled the room, lifting the gold coins into the air and dropping them all with a boom that shook the walls of the cave. He clenched his fists around the haft of the blade and willed it to still. It would bend to his will.

The wolf exhaled and blue fire licked up the sword of Nuada. Twisting and hot, it burned the tips of his fingers. Crystals formed on the palm that had not yet been ruined.

Through it all, Eamonn gritted his teeth. He would bear it. If this was the price the blade had chosen, then he would pay it. His physical form would withstand the pain because he refused to break.

He heard the growl of a wolf in his ear and the pleased chuckle of his grandfather.

"Well met, grandson. Take the blade; it is yours."

Another blast of magic fluttered his cloak, and all fell still. Fire cooled. Wind quieted. All he could hear was the ragged breath of the dwarf and the creak of crystal as he peeled his hand from the sword.

"What kind of cursed magic was that?" Angus spat out.

"That was my grandfather."

"So, you are the High King of the Seelie Fae?"

"It appears so."

"I will not bow."

"I would not expect you to," Eamonn said. He pointed the

blade towards the dwarf and growled, "What other relics do you have hiding in this place?"

Angus struggled, clasping a hand around his throat while his face turned bright red. His body twisted and crumpled to the ground as he fought against the blade's magic. "I will cut out my tongue before I tell you," he choked.

"Then be free, old friend."

Eamonn dropped the blade. Angus fell limp, panting as he stared up at Eamonn with a shocked expression.

"You've changed," the dwarf observed.

"Time is not on my side. Now, we will talk about the army you have hidden in this mountain."

"I don't have an army hidden."

Eamonn pointed the sword once more, arching a brow when Angus gulped. "Twisting your words will not deter me. We both know you aren't telling me the whole truth."

"I will not put my people at risk."

"Don't make me force you, Angus."

"The man I fought beside would never stoop so low."

Eamonn swallowed hard and cast his gaze from his oldest friend. "Then I suggest you choose wisely. There is no other choice I can make. Fionn must fall."

"The dwarves have no army."

"Then I suggest you find one. Quickly."

The Dreams Of Witches

The hovering drop of liquid fell from the vial, splashing against Papa's tongue. He was the last she treated and the most stubborn. Sorcha had argued with him night after night, but he refused. He always put his girls first, even though he had suffered the longest.

She didn't want to heal them all at the same time. Who knew what was really in the vial that her druid grandfather had given her? She didn't want to risk their health on the word of a strange old man.

Briana was the first, the bravest and most tired of being ill. A single drop on her tongue, and they waited. For days and days they waited until Sorcha finally cut into her sister's back.

She pulled out each beetle and stared in shock at the dead insects. They didn't move, they didn't struggle, they didn't even twitch.

The cure worked.

Sorcha treated the rest of the household one by one, then pulled out the beetles remaining underneath their flesh. The miraculous substance in the vial baffled her and never seemed to diminish.

Her father swished his mouth and swallowed. All his healthy daughters clustered around him, staring with rapt attention. They prayed that Sorcha was right and hadn't gotten lucky with all thirteen of them.

He looked into their expectant faces and shrugged. "They don't seem to be moving anymore."

Rosaleen shrieked and jumped into his arms. "You're cured! You will live, Papa!"

The other sisters leapt forward. They all clustered together in a great circle around their father, tears streaking their cheeks and laughter bubbling from their chests.

Sorcha smiled, tucked the vial back into its small case, and stepped back from the revelry. They would all live. It was a miracle that should fill her soul with happiness.

But she was still so empty.

She stirred the soup above the fire and let them have a moment. They deserved to be happy. Their lives unfolded in blank pages they could write upon, though they would hold scars for all eternity.

When had she become so cold? Was this a normal reaction for someone after coming home from the Otherworld?

She imagined it was. This place, these people, they all seemed so dull compared to the life she had seen. They didn't understand magic or the wondrous things it could do. Their minds were so focused upon themselves, rather than each other. The plain wood walls, dirty stone floors, and drafty rooms made her heart heavy.

Sorcha missed the faeries more now that she knew they lived. Now it wasn't that she had lost them. They had chosen to leave her behind.

She blew out a breath and pushed her hair back. Hy-brasil had taken everything she knew about herself and obliterated it. Now, Torin was trying to give her back some semblance of self.

Who was she now? Who was this woman who saw faeries, healed the blood beetle plague, and felt her heart grow colder by the day?

"Sorcha?"

Briana's voice snapped her out of her thoughts. Smoothing her sweaty palms against her skirts, she turned with a false smile. "Yes?"

Her family stood together and stared. Worried expressions crossed all their faces, except her father's. His crestfallen expression warned Sorcha that he could read her thoughts.

"What?" Sorcha asked. "What is it?"

"You won't be staying with us, will you?" Briana asked.

"No."

"You'll do the right thing and heal all those people who need help?"

"Yes."

"You're leaving us?" Rosaleen's lower lip quivered. "We just got you back!"

Briana stepped forward and cupped Sorcha's face in her hands. She searched Sorcha's gaze. "Did we ever really?"

She should have cried. She should have at least sniffed because her sister was right. Sorcha was physically here, but she had left her heart in the Otherworld.

"No," she said so quietly that only Briana could hear. "I fear you did not, sister."

Briana leaned forward and pressed their heads together. She smelled like herbs and sickness. Not the way Sorcha remembered her, but the scent that would forever stick in her mind.

"You were never happy with us, no matter how hard we tried."

"I wasn't meant for this life."

"You were meant to run with the faeries." Briana leaned back and pressed her lips against Sorcha's forehead. "My little changeling sister."

Their father stood. Sorcha caught his eyes over Briana's shoulder and flinched when she saw the tears gathering. "We've already packed your things and took the liberty of adding another pack with what little we've had saved up."

"I'm not taking your money."

"You're saving people by leaving us, child. We want to help in any way we can."

"I should help remove the beetles—"

"We've watched you, and Papa has already agreed to allow us to remove them without your help."

She frowned. They were all misty eyed, wanting to give her their hard earned money and leaving themselves at a disadvantage. Shouldn't she feel something?

"Thank you," she said. "I will return as soon as I can."

"Don't." Briana squeezed her arm. "We always knew we only had you for a short amount of time, and it was selfish of us to keep you this long. Go be...whatever it is you are."

She should hesitate.

She didn't.

Sorcha hugged Briana and the rest of her sisters. She pressed her palms against her father's cheeks and kissed him soundly on the cheek. "Thank you."

"Visit us."

"I will do my best." She whirled around and rushed towards the door, wanting to leave as soon as possible.

Her father's voice made her freeze with her hand on the door.

"And go back to him."

Her hands clenched. "I will try."

She fled her childhood home with two packs slung under her arms. She looked back only once as she walked down the street towards the sick-house. Her sisters waved from all the windows and her father propped himself up at the door.

They were good people. They would be all right without her.

She spent weeks in the sick houses of her small town. The healers called it a miracle. That God himself sent her to purge their people of the plague.

Sorcha let them give her whatever name they wanted. She fanned the flames of rumors hoping that one of the Fae would come investigate.

None did.

Geralt stopped her a few times, his cheeks red and concern running like river through his veins.

"Sorcha! Stop for a moment would you? You will run yourself into the ground!"

"I have people to help, Geralt," she shook his hand from her arm. "Let go."

"When was the last time you slept?"

"Days ago."

"Sorcha, I know you want to help these people but you're no good to them if you're dead." He pushed back the lock of hair that always fell in front of his eyes. "Let me help you. Go eat, sleep, and come back with clear eyes and clear mind."

"I'm not handing this vial over to anyone."

"Where did you get it, anyway?"

"The faeries," she lied as she checked the temperature of a patient, pleased that this one was still alive. The man had been so emaciated she thought he would die long before the beetles were extracted.

"There are no such thing as faeries!"

"You can believe what you want, Geralt. But right now, you're in my way."

She put her shoulder against his and shoved. He stumbled backwards, landing on a bed where she piled the beetle corpses.

His shout of disgust was music to her ears. She did not offer him help, nor did she turn to look at him no matter how much she wanted to see the shocked expression on his face.

Geralt gave up after that. His incessant declarations of love ceased, and he disappeared back to his family manor. He shouldn't have been around the plague victims anyways. He was more distraction than help.

Sorcha cleared her town of those infected and moved onto the next. She waded through healers crying out their remedies, through priests blessing the infected, and walked directly into the sick houses.

Everyone she touched healed.

Her patients spread stories of the red-headed woman who walked among them. They saw her pointed ears and said she was one of the Tuatha dé Danann casting pity upon their people. Others said she was a bean sidhe guiding their souls from the land of the living.

When asked, Sorcha merely smiled and inquired about their health. As cold as it seemed, she wasn't interested in getting to know her patients. This was a means to an end. Healing was a stepping stone to the next point of her life.

She got her patients down from hundreds to ten. Those who had been sick the longest no longer suffered from the blood beetle plague, but from the after effects. Their lungs were weak, their bodies frail, and she would see this through until the end.

"Sorcha?" the little girl she tended asked. "What's that sound?"

Laughter and shouting echoed down the halls of the sick house. Frowning, Sorcha stood and smoothed her apron down. "I don't know."

A bang on the front door, followed by laughter, was the last straw. No one had any right to disturb the ill.

Temper in full blast, she raced towards the door with her hands curled into fists. Another shout, female this time, fueled the flames of her anger further.

Throwing the wooden doors wide, she glowered at the group of men hovering over a bundle of rags.

"How dare you?" she shouted. People milling through the streets hesitated. "Have you no respect for the wounded?"

"Ah, hush healer," one man replied. "We're just having a little fun!"

"You are disturbing my patients. Get away from here."

"Or what?"

Sorcha reached into the shadows behind the door and pulled out a knotted staff. She had found it during her travels, and it felt right in her hands, settling between her fingers with the perfect weight. She used it to knock the riffraff off her steps.

The men chuckled. "Come on now, Red. You won't do anything with that."

"Won't I?" She charged down the step and swung. She held the end in her hand, letting the weight of the staff do the work her arm could not. The bulbous end struck the vocal man on the temple. He dropped like a stone.

The others gaped at her.

"Well?" She jabbed the staff at them. "I don't have all day, boys. Get off my steps!"

They picked up their friend and raced away laughing.

"Damned fools," she grumbled. "Too many of them in the city."

"You can say that again."

Sorcha started and looked down at the pile of rags. Or rather, the woman wearing the most disgusting clothing Sorcha had ever seen. Bits and pieces of fabric fluttered in constant movement as the woman stood.

Her black hair was so tangled, Sorcha would have shaved it all off. Dirt smudged across her face and underneath her nails. She speared Sorcha with her gaze. Mismatched eyes, one blue and one brown stared straight into her soul.

"Pity for the poor?" the woman asked. "Or rather, penance for the unworthy?"

"What are you going on about?"

"Have you a spare farthing?"

"I have no money to give."

"Pity." The strange creature spat upon the ground.

"Why were those men accosting you?"

"They claim I am a witch."

Sympathy flooded through Sorcha. The emotion startled her as she had not felt it in such a long time. She reached out and smoothed a hand down the woman's arm. "They have called me the same."

"Sure they have, healer. But they're right about me."

Sorcha drew her hand back with a gasp. Her hands shook with the desire to cross her chest. "What?"

"I'm a witch, and I willingly admit to consorting with the Fair Folk. I call upon them, and they listen to my desires."

Sorcha lifted a brow. "Really? You call upon the Fae and they do whatever you tell them?"

"Of course."

"Faeries don't do that."

"Perhaps not your faeries."

"Are you making deals with them? Over and over again? You're selling your soul doing that." Sorcha shook her head and turned back towards the sick house.

"You think you know the Fae?" the woman called out.

"I know I do." Sorcha paused at the top of the steps. "I spent more time in the among the Fae than you could imagine. Making deals with faeries is dangerous."

"Hey!"

The woman's shout echoed as Sorcha closed the door. Let her follow if she wished, but Sorcha would not argue. There was little she could do for a woman up to her neck in debt that would eventually be paid.

The door slammed open and footsteps echoed down the hall towards her. "I said, hey!"

"I heard you."

"Then why didn't you stop?"

Sorcha grabbed a towel from one of the racks. "I'm a busy woman."

"You've spoken with the Fae?"

"Yes."

"You lived with them?"

The woman was leaving dirt smudges on the floor that Sorcha would have to mop up. The other cleaners had fled when she said she had no more use for them. They likely ran from memories of the sick and dying, the tragic souls who lingered in torment.

Pursing her lips, she pointed towards the small kitchen. "That way."

"Why?"

"You want food and water?"

She didn't have to say anything else. The ragged woman spun on her heel and charged into the kitchen.

Sorcha leaned against the doorframe and watched the crazed witch rifle through her cupboards. She pulled out bread and cheese, tossed sugar onto the window sill, and clunked down a tankard of water.

Little manners, but she might have been pretty if she cleaned up. Sorcha could tell a beautiful woman hid beneath the grime. She couldn't tell her age, although it would have been hard even if she was clean. People who led hard lives always had haunted eyes that aged them.

"What's your name?" Sorcha asked.

"Aisling."

"Pretty name."

"I'd say you could tell my mother that, but she's dead."

"Any other family?"

Aisling paused with a mouth full of food. "No."

"Well, you can stay here then if you help out."

"I'm not asking for handouts."

"You just asked if I had money," Sorcha said.

"Didn't say I was going to work for it."

"You are incredibly rude, aren't you?"

Aisling flashed a toothy grin. "Dealing with the Unseelie will do that to you."

Sorcha sat down and watched the witch eat. What had driven her to make deals with the Fae? Was she so foolish that she didn't care for her own safety?

Perhaps Sorcha would never know. Aisling finished her food in record time, leaned back, and patted her stomach.

"You never remember how good food is until you go a few days without."

"You haven't eaten in days?"

Aisling shrugged. "Some weeks the good folks want more than others."

"You peddle witch's wares?"

"I speak to the faeries for them. Like you, apparently."

"The faeries don't speak to me anymore," Sorcha said as she shook her head.

"They cut you off?"

"Seems so."

"Is that why you're making a name for yourself?" Aisling leaned back and propped her feet up on the table. "You're trying to go back."

"In a way."

"You're trying to piss off the faeries so bad they take you back to punish you. You're really that crazy."

Sorcha blinked. "Crazy?"

"Faeries aren't kind to the ones they want to punish. If you mess up enough here, they won't take you back to the Otherworld and let you go your merry way."

"I have to get back."

"There's hundreds of ways to get to the Otherworld, and this is your choice?" Aisling leaned back and shook her head. "Not a good plan, healer. Find another way."

"What would you suggest?"

Aisling turned and stuck her hands into the folds of her clothing. She had pockets, Sorcha realized. Although she wasn't certain which flaps were pockets and which were just random bits of cloth.

The witch pulled out a worn leather book and held it out. "There's probably something in here."

"What's this?"

"Something I stole from the Otherworld. Maybe you'll be able to make some sense of it."

Sorcha took the worn journal and thumbed a page open. The blank parchment quickly filled with inked words. A signature she recognized, *Scríobhaí*, appeared at the bottom of each page.

"Wow," Aisling exclaimed from over Sorcha's shoulder. "It never did that for me."

Sorcha's eyes danced over the words, skimming through the

dark magic spells that required sacrificial animals and the like. One word stood out above all others.

Portal.

She snapped the book shut and held it to her chest.

"Hey!" Aisling yelped. "I was reading that!"

"It's not for you."

"How do you know?"

"Because it didn't reveal the words to you. I know druid magic when I see it, and those were not for you."

"They looked like interesting spells."

"Every spell does, I'm sure."

Aisling yanked her rags and gave Sorcha a critical glance. "I don't know what you've gotten yourself into, healer, but it doesn't look like something you're prepared for. When you want to open that portal, call me."

The witch whirled around and sulked away. She held a stolen apple in her hand as if she dared anyone to tell her to put it down.

"Sorcha," Sorcha called after her. "My name is Sorcha."

Aisling's shoulders shook as she began to laugh. "Sorcha? Of course you're her. The entire Otherworld is abuzz with your name. I'd be careful if I were you, Sorcha of Ui Neill. The Fae are mad at you."

She watched the other woman slip out of the sick house, laughing the entire way.

What did the witch know that Sorcha didn't?

Worried, she tucked the book under her arm and went to complete her rounds. The patients didn't care she struggled with new information nor that her future suddenly became brighter. They wanted her to feed them, roll them off their sores, and empty their bedpans.

Sick houses were never short of work. She stowed the book away for later viewing and tired herself out. The sun had set by the time she completed her rounds.

She was weary down to her bones.

Sorcha stumbled into her room and washed herself thoroughly.

Although the blood beetles no longer threatened her life, she had to worry about every other sickness.

Eamonn's voice whispered in her ear, "Humans are so fragile."

The memory made her smile. He did not understand how fragile humans really were. She had watched children die because they fell into a lake at the wrong time of year. Women fell ill because their corsets were too tight, and men died from a simple cut on their leg.

Death followed humans like a well-known lover. Sorcha could almost feel him breathing down the back of her neck, waiting for the moment when she made a mistake.

She eased her dress over her shoulders. Bruises covered her spine and back from the savage slaps and kicks some of the patients gave her. She was prepared for them to be violent. She would have been, too, if there were only a single window for her to stare out of while she waited for weeks and months to heal.

They designed sick houses for death. Sorcha swore that people died faster here than if they were outside. Although she left the windows open, the private rooms had none. The air grew stagnant and cold.

Her dress fell to the ground with a soft sound, and she finished washing. Each drag of the washcloth made her bite her lip. What she wouldn't give to slide into a warm bath and have Oona wash her back for her.

Sorcha stumbled to the bed and fell asleep almost instantly, praying no dreams would wake her. She was far too tired.

But the dreams came. Dreams of the most unusual origin.

She blinked her eyes open. Fog swirled in coiling billows and staircases led into a never-ending mist and disappeared. This wasn't a normal dream, nor did she feel the strange lightheaded quality of sleep.

Sorcha was awake, or at least aware, in the dream she wandered through. Frowning, she spun around.

A fine dress covered her legs. It wasn't something she ever

would have chosen for herself, her first indication that a faerie meddled with her dreams.

Red velvet poured over her shoulders like blood. Bell sleeves touched the tips of her fingers and the wide skirt flared over her hips, so heavy and large that she felt the entire dress move as she shifted.

Her hair swirled as it piled on top of her head.

"Ah," a smooth voice said. "Look how pretty you are."

"Fionn," she growled.

"You remember me? How flattering."

Sorcha spun in a circle, trying to find him in the billowing mists. "How could I forget the King of the Seelie Fae?"

"You've grown bold."

"I've grown desperate."

A hand touched her waist. Strong and achingly familiar, she spun around in his arms to stare up at the beloved face. Eamonn looked back at her, vibrant blue eyes blazing. But it wasn't him, not really.

She flinched back from the mask Fionn had placed over his face. It was a macabre imitation of his brother.

"What's wrong with you?" she growled. "Why would you wear that?"

"Do you not like it? I thought it would be rather agreeable, considering how you favor my twin."

"You are a sick and twisted man."

"You and my twin are of the same mind when it comes to that." He pulled her into his arms. "It is good to see you again, midwife."

"Healer now."

"Of course. How could I forget? The little midwife who saved everyone from the blood beetles."

"You sound disappointed."

"I am. I always thought you would do more important things than save humans. There was an edge of greatness to you when we first met." He shrugged. "Either way. Won't you dance with me?"

"Dance?"

Sorcha felt the brush of fabric against the back of her dress. Gasping, she craned her neck to see hundreds of other faeries had joined them. Each more beautiful than the last, the Seelie Fae had joined their king in the dream world.

Music burst into the air. Violins and harps twining together to create a jig that no one could have sat still through.

She hated it. She hated it even more when he pulled her closer, placed her hand on his shoulder, and propelled her into the crowd.

"What do you want?" she growled.

"Can I not wish to spend time with my favorite human?"

"You hate humans."

"I don't hate you."

She glowered at him as they spun wildly among the other Fae. "You want something from me."

"Can you not enjoy the night before finding your way to politics?"

"I will not be stuck in this dream forever."

His expression changed, twisted into something awful. Something she recognized far too well. "You are too intelligent for your own good, midwife."

"You have told me this before."

He spun her in a wide arc around a tree that grew in the center of the room. Its roots groaned as they passed. "Where is he?"

"Who?"

"Don't play coy. You know of whom I speak."

"I couldn't even fathom a guess."

Fionn pulled her towards him. She struck his chest hard enough to knock the wind from her lungs. He squeezed her, painfully tight, in warning. "You know where he is."

"If I knew where he was, don't you think I would be with him?"

"He sent you away. He pushed you out of the castle and back into your life where you live in grime and ruin. Why else would you want to go back to the Otherworld? The human world is far too plain for you."

The cajoling expression was back on his face. If she were any other woman, he might have convinced her to stay here with him. He was painfully handsome, all high arched cheekbones and a dazzling smile.

Fionn had a dangerous edge to his looks. It was behind his eyes, she thought. Something behind those vivid blue eyes had twisted to hatred.

Her thoughts turned to the first night she had met Eamonn. To a throne room cast in shadows, and a slash of light across glittering eyes. He had the same eyes as his brother back then, filled with darkness and anger.

She reached up and feathered her fingers over the crest of Fionn's cheekbones, just underneath the azure rage. "You're so much like him."

The emotion in his eyes boiled, but he smiled down at her. "I can be anyone you want me to be, little midwife. Just ask."

"You can't be him."

"Why not?"

"Eamonn has learned something you have not."

"Which is?" he growled.

"He has learned how to let go of his anger."

Fionn tossed his head back and laughed. She shook in his arms, each rumbling chuckle pulsing through her body. The faeries dancing around them paused and joined in his laughter.

"Oh, little midwife. You are thoroughly entertaining. You think my brother has let go of his anger?" His smile warped into a menacing grimace. "Let's see how wrong you are."

He spun her around in his arms, yanking her back against his chest and twisting his hand in her hair. He used the rope of her braid to secure her. Pulling her head back, he petted the long column of her throat.

"Look."

She jerked, not caring that her hair pulled at her scalp. He had no right to contain her in such a way. She squeezed her eyes shut as a flicker of light burst through the fog, revealing images.

"Look, midwife. See the choices your lover makes."

Sorcha didn't want to open her eyes, but temptation clawed at her stomach. Fionn lied. Whatever he showed her would be a lie, so there was no harm in looking.

She peered into the fog. Swirling light and colors accosted her senses, and then sound filtered through.

Clanging strikes of steel against steel. The harsh crack of a whip, and the song of the wind as it whistled through crystals and stone.

A sword sliced through the thick layer of mist. Eamonn stepped from the whirling colors of fire and brimstone like a warrior victorious. Blood splattered across his armor and dripped through the valleys of his wounds.

But he was alive. And he was well.

Sorcha breathed a sigh of relief that was short lived as he advanced towards her. Fionn held her still as Eamonn brandished his sword and snarled.

He charged towards them with an unfamiliar blade glinting in sunlight she could not feel. Sorcha gasped and screwed her eyes shut as he lifted his blade, flinching against Fionn's shoulder.

"Oh no," he murmured in her ear. "You don't get to close your eyes for this. Watch."

His fingers dug into her cheeks, forcing her to turn for the last moment when Eamonn plunged his blade into her chest. The ghost sword sank through her torso and she gaped up at the man she loved. His face twisted into a grimace of cold, calculated hatred. There was no pain, for dreams did not have pain, but he stared down as if she were nothing more than an animal.

"He sweeps through my armies, killing hundreds of good men with families waiting for their return," Fionn growled.

She stared up into the glittering eyes and wondered what had happened. He had been so against death, at least when she left him. Crystals were digging into one of his eyes, freezing it in place until all it could do was stare with cold rage.

"He doesn't care about our people. He only cares about the throne and his personal vendetta."

"That isn't him." She shook head head. "He cares about the Lesser Fae. He cares about them all."

"You are so sweet. So naïve. Do you see that sword in his hand, little midwife?"

Eamonn pulled the blade from her chest. A wolf's mouth swallowed the steel, glittering red eyes staring at her as he pivoted away from the faerie he had just killed.

"Yes, I see it."

"That is my sword. My rightful sword from our grandfather."

She knew who their grandfather was. Had seen Eamonn kneeling at an altar, asking the ancient Tuatha dé Danann for guidance. "That is the Sword of Nuada?"

"It is. And only the true King of the Seelie Fae can wield it." His grip tightened on her waist, squeezing until she whimpered. "And I am the true king."

"Apparently not."

"You dare threaten me so?"

"I am so tired of faeries saying that to me," she growled and wrenched herself out of his grasp. "I am no weak maiden who fears you. You would be wise to fear *me*, would be King of the Seelie Fae."

He tossed his head back and laughed again. "And why should I?"

"I know your true name, Fionn the Wise."

He froze, glaring at her as if she had done the unthinkable. "Using that name brings you down a dangerous path."

"I have used faerie names before, and I will again. Now release me from this dream."

"Tell me where he is."

"I will not. Fionn, let me go."

She could feel him fighting against her words. The weight of his will fell over her shoulders as if he were pressing down upon her.

He grinned. "You have to mean it, midwife. You have to really mean to strip my own thoughts from my mind and force yours in their place."

"Let me out of this dream, Fionn."

"Again!" All the faeries surrounding them echoed his laughter. "Again, little girl. Maybe with more practice you will control the King of the Seelie Fae!"

"Now, Fionn. I bend you to my will. Let me go!"

"No!"

He spun on his heel and advanced. His hand fisted in her hair, twisting the strands until she yelped and her knees gave out. She landed on her knees at his feet.

His handsome face twisted with cruelty. His lips touched her cheek as he leaned down to whisper in her ear, "You will never control me. Now tell me where my brother is."

Sorcha winced as he pulled hard on the long tail of her braid. "I will never tell you."

"That's fine," he chuckled in her ear. Magic swelled around them, pressing upon her shoulders and into her mind. "Then tell me where you are, sweet midwife."

Sorcha fought against the desire to tell him everything he wanted to know. She struggled in his grip to no avail. Panic welled in her belly until all she could do was tilt her head back and scream.

"Fionn, let me go!"

She lurched up in bed, her hair a tangled mess around her and the scent of stale sweat filling the tiny room she slept in. The fire had died down. Shadows danced in her visions as the faerie magic dissipated.

Sorcha pressed a hand against her chest and tried to catch her breath.

"I did it," she gasped. "I controlled him."

But had she? She wouldn't ever really know, although she suspected he wasn't finished with her yet.

Her pillow suddenly seemed less inviting. Nightmares waited down that path, and she wasn't certain she had it in her to battle

Fionn again. The King of the Seelie Fae was much stronger than she'd given him credit for.

Shivering, she pulled the blankets around her shoulders, left her bed, and stoked the fire back to life. Light would banish the nightmares from her mind. Sorcha threw open the window for good measure, hoping the sickly sweet scent of fear would leave on the wind.

What battle had she won? And what was Eamonn doing?

"He needs me," she said as her heart clenched.

He needed someone to remind him that there was good in the world. That he needed to be that good for others, or he would find himself walking the same path as his twin. But she couldn't do that from Ui Neill.

Her gaze caught on the leather-bound book the witch had given her.

"No," she told herself. "You will not stoop to dealing with the Unseelie. There are other ways to get back to the Otherworld."

None that were so quick, however. Sorcha chewed on her bottom lip and stared at the easiest solution to her problem. Eamonn didn't have much time, and neither did she. The Seelie king was coming for her. She needed protection and Eamonn needed a conscience.

Grumbling, she tossed the blankets from her shoulders and picked up the book. Magic hummed against her fingers as if the book knew she wanted to use it.

She flipped it open and ran her fingers down the center seam. Words appeared on the blank parchment, words she shouldn't understand but somehow did.

This was dark magic, not just faerie favors or spells that might heal. Witch words appeared, calling upon powers that Sorcha could never understand. Nor did she want to. Runes, chicken blood, sacrificial lambs, and more danced before her eyes until her stomach rolled.

As if the book knew she had seen enough, the pages fluttered and settled upon what she wanted.

69

The portal.

"I'm just reading your pages," she muttered. "I'm not using you."

A voice whispered in her mind, "*Not yet.*"

Shivering, Sorcha ran her fingers over the words and tried to decide whether it was worth it. Shadows danced just out of her reach as Unseelie Fae slipped into her room.

She could see them out of the corner of her eyes. Twisted and warped, the goblins hunched over each other and held their breath. Would she do it? Would she take the deal offered in the form of stretched skin and ink?

The spell was rather simple, but it required more than one person. Sorcha couldn't drag one of her patients into this mess. She didn't even want to make the deal herself.

Another spell appeared on the edge of the page. A spell to find someone. A spell with a name already written in blood.

"Aisling," she muttered.

It was cruel, perhaps, to involve the witch in even more deals. But who better to assist opening a portal to the Otherworld than someone already up to their neck in debt?

Sorcha snapped the book shut and ignored the triumphant screams of the Unseelie Fae.

She had a witch to catch.

The Hangman And The Portal

Eamonn swung his blade over his head, the metal singing as he brought it down onto the nearest elf. The unnaturally beautiful creature danced backwards and the sharpened edge traced a scraping line down his breastplate.

The elf grinned. His helmet covered only the sides of his face, leaving his eyes and mouth free.

"You won't win, beast," the elf crowed. "You can only fight for so long!"

"Haven't you heard the legends? I will fight until the last of you is dead."

"I'd like to see you try."

Unable to bear the creature's prattle for a second longer, Eamonn rushed forward. His opponents never expected him to come within range of their swords. Some were forward thinking enough to lift their blades, hoping they would cut through Eamonn's impenetrable skin.

They were always wrong. His crystals sliced through metal until it was nothing more than dust.

This elf was not intelligent enough to even try. He cried out, held up his hands, and froze when Eamonn caught him by the throat.

"Wait," the pretty creature gurgled. "Mercy."

"I have none for your kind."

Eamonn squeezed his fist until gore and meat covered it. Only then did he let the body drop to the ground.

The battlefield was a horrendous place to be. In the many years since he had been a general, Eamonn had forgotten what it was like. The true fear and crazed stares as men fought. The screams of the victorious mixed with those who clung to life, refusing to die quickly.

The Sword of Light hung heavy in his hand. It drew him down in a way Ocras never had. The runes written upon every inch of metal vibrated with power, stinging his palms and heating the crystal of his hand. He didn't like it, but it was effective.

A dwarf ran past him. Young, perhaps too young to be fighting, and screaming as an elf cut him down. Blood splattered into the air, filling it with iron and red mist.

Anger simmered just beneath Eamonn's skin. What right did they have? The High Seelie Fae were no better than the Lesser Fae. And yet, he saw the glee in the elves' eyes. They wanted to kill the dwarves. They wanted to see their blood on the ground but refused to lower themselves to allow even a speck to touch their armor.

The sword in his hand throbbed. Energy, like nothing he had ever felt before, surged through his arm and straight to his heart.

Claíomh Solais knew what to do. The runes glowed as its power flexed, pushed against his mind, and begged to be let free. The sword could make them pay. It could destroy them all.

Eamonn let it take over his entire being, lift his arm, and draw the blood it desperately wished to drink.

The blade carved through air and flesh. He dimly heard screams that rang in his ears, piercing and echoing with pain. A stream of blood dripped down his chest and underneath his armor, creating a river between his abdominal muscles.

How much blood covered him now? He didn't know.

He didn't care.

The sword cleaved through flesh and bone, separated limb from trunk. He stabbed through the lines of Fionn's army over and over again.

Time slowed. He did not know where he was, who he was, nothing other than the repetitive motion of his body. Parry, block, swing the blade along with his body. He was no longer a man, but a weapon.

Belatedly, he realized he had been fighting for a very long time.

Eamonn swore as he cut down the last of the elves. His shoulders ached from swinging the heavy blade that fought for control with each movement. His body wanted to rest after hours upon hours of battle. The Fae did not stop when they started a fight. They would continue until everyone was dead.

He swung too hard and the Sword of Light split through the last elf's torso. He stared into the man's eyes as he fell, clutching the gaping wound on his belly.

Shouldn't he feel something? Eamonn shook his head and stumbled backwards.

He only felt exhaustion. There wasn't room for pity in the empty spaces of his mind.

"Master?" Oona called out.

Why was she here? Eamonn spun, sticking the sword's point into the ground to balance himself. Bodies lay upon the battlefield, strewn like fallen red leaves in autumn.

He frowned. Had he done all this? Who had fought with him?

"Eamonn!" Oona's voice became frantic. "Answer me!"

"Here," he mumbled. "I am here."

A tiny winged body crawled over a mound of fallen soldiers, her expression melting into relief when she saw him. "Oh, my boy, we thought we lost you!"

"I'm fine."

"I can see that, but how?" She clasped her hands at her chest and gazed up at him, purple wings vibrating in fear. "Dearie, how did you do this?"

"Do what?"

"The dwarves retreated hours ago. You've been alone."

He glanced down at the sword. "I don't know."

"Sweetheart... Are you all right?"

"I don't think so, Oona. I am not myself."

She breathed out a relieved sigh. "Come with me, dearie. Let's get you cleaned up."

He stared down at her hand. Could he touch her? After he had spilled so much blood, was he worthy to touch the woman who had raised him?

"Eamonn," Oona gently said. "Let go of the sword and let me guide you from the battlefield."

Did he want to? Eamonn couldn't decide whether he wanted to put the sword back in its scabbard or if he wanted to run it through the pixie.

She closed her hand over his, so tiny and small compared to the crystalline structure of his fist. "Rest easy, my boy. The battle is done."

The battle is done.

The words rang in his ears over and over again until he sighed and thrust the sword into its sheath. "My apologies, Oona."

"I know blood lust runs in your veins, dearie. I've been raising those in your line since your father was a boy."

His father had suffered from what he called a blood rage. Eamonn knew the back of his father's hand much better than the front. He had never wanted to become that man.

He clenched his fists. "I have no wish to follow in my father's footsteps."

"And you won't. Come with me, Eamonn. Come and see your kingdom."

"My kingdom?"

"We're at the foothills of Cathair Solais. It is far past time for you to see the castle of your childhood."

"Has it changed?" He didn't know what he would do if it had changed. If the world had grown better in his absence.

"Only a bit."

Oona placed her hand on the small of his back as she guided him away from the carnage. He couldn't help but look down, attempting to force his mind to remember. What did their faces look like? What terror had they felt as he plowed through them?

He couldn't remember anything. Only a red mist that swallowed his view. Anything that walked through the mist, he had killed. Plain and simple.

"Where are the dwarves?" He slurred the words as he said them.

"They retreated."

"Why?"

Her fingers flexed against his spine. "They didn't want to get in your way."

"Smart."

"Has this ever happened before?"

Eamonn shook his head, then lifted her up and over a large pile of men. At her confused glance, he shrugged. "I don't want you touching them."

"So sweet, even after all of this." She patted his cheek. "It will be all right, you know."

"It has to be."

"I know you'll try."

They walked away from the battlefield and over to a cliff edge. The dwarves remained as far away from him as possible, he noted. Perhaps they knew when a beast walked among them.

He heard the whispers as he walked by. "The Red Stag...it's really him."

"I thought he was dead?"

"So did I. But there he is in the flesh. Did you see the way he carved up those elves?"

"Chopped them up as if they would be his dinner, he did. That blade of his wouldn't stop moving! Couldn't even see it."

Eamonn blocked them out, shaking his head and clearing the echoes of screams. He wasn't the same as he used to be. He didn't remember this red fog, and he certainly had never forgotten the faces of those he killed.

They plagued him for centuries. But now? He had to force himself to look at their faces, and even then couldn't care less that they were dead. They fought for the wrong side.

"Come here," Oona reached out her hand for him. "See your kingdom in the light."

His kingdom.

Eamonn inhaled deeply, took the offered hand, and stood to stare down at the Castle of Light.

It gleamed as only the golden castle could. Sunlight bounced off its smooth surface, but also absorbed into it. White and gold, the high peaks and pristine towers had never been dirty. They sparkled and blinded those who looked upon their surface.

The grounds had changed. A colorful garden stood in place of the maze he had run through as a child. He could see faeries walking through it even now, oblivious that a battle had taken place just above them.

He couldn't attack the castle. Not yet. There was much to plan, and his brother couldn't know how close he was.

Soon, he would return home.

"Let's go," he said.

He needed to address the dwarven army. Men fighting for Eamonn couldn't be afraid of him. He didn't want to rule like his brother.

He climbed off the rise and let the image of his home fade. The castle would wait for him; no army would destroy the legendary Castle of Light.

The sword at his hip bumped against his thigh, reminding him that there was much more at play here. As the high king, he had certain abilities his brother did not have. As long as he could figure out how to use them.

Dwarves huddled together in small family clumps. They

weren't happy about fighting for him. They weren't happy about fighting for anyone but each other.

Cian rushed towards him, holding up a hand. "They aren't pleased with you, master. I'd go so far as to say they're frightened of you."

"I'm not surprised."

"I wouldn't be addressing them any time soon. Let their fear settle."

"What else would you have me do?"

"Walk?"

Eamonn glanced around them and lifted his arms. "Where do you want me to walk?"

"Pick up the bodies then. They're frightening everyone."

"What did they think they would find in war? Sunshine and flowers?"

Oona tugged on his arm. "Come with me, we'll go for a walk. It'll be good to ease your muscles."

"I don't want to walk."

"Master," she pulled again. "Please."

He recognized the panic in her eyes. She had worn the same expression when Fionn rode up to the castle on his white steed. She was hiding something from him.

Eamonn turned around and felt his heart freeze in his chest. Now that his mind had settled, he recognized this place and the rotting platform tucked into the side of the mountain.

He waded through dwarves that scattered as he approached. His booted feet touched the edge of the platform as he stared up into the blank space where a pole once stood and a rope had swayed in the breeze.

He lifted a hand and pressed it against his throat. The crystals pulsed with light, ancient pain vibrating through his body.

The breeze ruffled his hair. His long braid swayed, but his body remained still as stone.

Voices whispered in his ear from long ago.

"That's the monster."

"That's the one who betrayed us all."

"Look at him! He's so ugly now."

"I can't believe I ever let him touch me."

They had forsaken him. Not just the people who had professed to love him, but his own family.

He would never forget the haunted gaze of his mother who pressed her fingertips to her lips and said nothing. Did nothing. Watched her eldest son swing from the end of a rope with tears in her eyes, immobile and silent.

The crowd behind him held their breath as if they thought something remarkable was about to happen. The banished prince, the ugly man who had fallen from grace, stood before the gallows which had started it all.

He lifted a foot and placed it on the rotting planks. They held his weight as he ascended the stairs. Oona sobbed out a breath, the only sound in what remained of the battlefield.

Why did he suddenly feel so old? His bones ached almost as much as his soul. He tilted his head back to the sky and remembered ravens pecking at his eyes. He experienced every memory he had kept buried deep within his person so he would not feel this pain again.

But now he felt it. He lived every second of the days he swung from the end of that rope. The biting pain in his neck as the crystals sank ever deeper. The worry that perhaps he might never die, and they would leave him here.

He had survived. And so had his purpose.

Eamonn clenched his fists and turned towards the crowd of dwarves and the remains of his people.

"You all know my story," he began. "Some of you were there to watch while my own family condemned me for my face."

The temporary army stared up at him with shock, some with awe. To the younger faeries, he was a legend. A myth that parents told their children at night. The Untouched prince who carved his way through armies without getting a single wound.

"It was never my intention to come back here." He looked over the battlefield and shook his head. "It was never my intention to start a war. But someone reminded me that my people were being mistreated."

Oona sniffed and pressed a hand against her mouth.

He jabbed a finger behind him. "This is the very place they tried to take my life. They saw me as a monster, but more than that they saw what I stood for. If the royal family could be marked as 'flawed,' then the Lesser Fae were not half beasts. You are Seelie Fae, just as much as they are. I survived, and I know now that my purpose was to return here, on this day! To guide you back to your homes, to your people, to the rights stripped from you."

A few of the dwarves stood up.

"I will not allow my brother to destroy this land any further. You and your families deserve the recognition you are owed. I will place my life on the line for you as I did on the battlefield today. Stand with me, brothers and sisters of the Fae. Let me be your sword, for I will strike down any who threaten you. Let me be your shield, for I will weather you through this storm. Let me be the biting cold of winter and the blistering heat of summer, for I will cut through the forces of Fionn the Wise and bring you home!"

A thunderous applause shook the ground as the faeries all stood and stomped their feet. They screamed up at him, anger and rage fueling the flames.

He would bring them home. Or he would die trying.

❦

"Don't get too comfortable," Sorcha grumbled. "I only asked you here to help because the spell requires two people."

"We both know why you asked me here, and it wasn't for that." Aisling grinned and tossed one of her new coins in the air. A full bag jangled at her waist, the last bit Sorcha had to her name.

"Just..." Sorcha blew out a breath and placed her hands on her hips. "Quiet. Please. I'm trying to concentrate."

"You're not doing a good job of that."

"And that is entirely because you won't shut your mouth."

"If you'd listen to me, then this might go faster."

"What!" Sorcha threw her arms to the sides. "Where am I going wrong then? What could you possibly have to say that the book can't tell me?"

Aisling hopped down from her seat on a nearby stump. Mud caked her bare feet which slapped against the cold wet ground as she hunched over a nearby rune. Tangled hair covered her face, twigs and leaves knotted into the heavy mass. She reached out and touched a ragged nail to the tail of the rune.

"This is wrong."

"That's exactly how it looks in the book," Sorcha grumbled. "It's not wrong."

"The Beacon cannot be curved. The lines must be straight for the rune to stay lit." Aisling moved, her hunched body crawling over the circle of runes Sorcha had carved into the ground. "Your Elk rune is quite good, but the Birch Goddess is missing its top."

"You're saying words I don't understand."

Aisling arched a brow. "And you want to be a druid?"

Sorcha's cheeks burned. She was horrible at this—at magic—at rituals foreign to her. How was she supposed to figure this out when no one was here to teach her?

And the witch before her seemed to know so much. Aisling said there was no druid blood in her lines, nor faerie for that matter, but she was innately capable when it came to spells. She crouched over the runic circle and pivoted, fixing all of Sorcha's mistakes.

"Thank you," Sorcha said. "I appreciate your help."

"Say that more often, and I might keep you alive."

"I already said it!"

Aisling looked over her shoulder and bared her teeth. "Then say it again."

"Thank you, Aisling, for helping me return to the Otherworld."

"And for keeping you safe."

"I fail to see how you are doing that."

"If you make this portal wrong, it will chop you in half when you step through." Aisling clapped her hands together. "Just like a cleaver on a fish head."

Sorcha's neck ached in response. She nodded. "Point taken. Are we certain it's fixed then?"

"Oh, now you're worried. Ridiculous. Just trust me, would you healer? This is what I do."

"How do you even know how to do this?"

"Grew up with it."

"You grew up with a druid?"

Aisling drew straight lines to link the runes together. "Sort of. I lived with a traditional witch. The old hedge witch type that made money off love potions and other lies. She had these books though, like the one I showed you. Books that spoke to me, and some that didn't."

She had to have druid blood. Sorcha couldn't believe anything else. If the books were revealing their secrets, then it seemed all too likely.

"They're druid books?" she asked nonchalantly.

"Guess so. If the one you have now is druid, the others are pretty much the same." Aisling leaned back and puffed out a breath. "It looks about right."

"About right doesn't sound as if you have much faith it will work."

"It should work."

"You're not giving me any confidence here."

"Well, I've never done this spell before, have I?" Aisling glared. "The goal is to get you through alive. That's the best I can offer."

Sorcha nodded. She didn't want to interrupt the witch too much, but her legs bounced and her palms slicked with sweat. Just how much time had passed in the Otherworld? Would she even be able to find him?

Him. She could feel the bumps and grooves of crystal against her fingertips just from the thought of him. The soft sigh he let out whenever she leaned on his shoulder, or touched his hand without flinching.

Something deep inside her knew he needed support. Fionn's dream had solidified that, but she had known long before the dream. She had known the moment she left the isle that she took a piece of his soul with her.

"That will do," Aisling stepped carefully out of the circle. "We'll see once it's activated."

"That's it?" Sorcha stared down at the ground. "It doesn't look like much."

"Did you think magic would be all flashing colors and pretty lights? Of course it doesn't look like much. This is natural magic, not the crap those traveling peddlers pass off." Aisling held out her hand. "Now give me something of his."

"What?"

"We have to find him in the Otherworld, and the only way to do that is to have something of his. Don't you have a lock of hair?"

Sorcha wrinkled her nose. "I don't keep people's hair."

"Amateur. You should always have hair from everyone, just in case."

"Do you have mine?"

"Yes," Aisling said and patted the folds of fabric over her chest. "But don't worry. I have no desire to curse you."

"Not yet."

"You're learning. So you have nothing of his?"

Sorcha shook her head.

"Blast. This suddenly became a lot more difficult."

"It said nothing in the book about needing something of his," Sorcha said. She pulled the journal out of her back and leafed to the page with the portal drawing.

"I'm not surprised. That's just a way to *get* to the Otherworld. But it will put you down wherever it decides, and we need to make sure it's where you want to go."

"Then was this all a waste?" Sorcha snapped the book shut. "I cannot go anywhere in the Otherworld, I'll never be able to find him."

Aisling tapped a finger against her chin. "Just how close were you to this faerie?"

"Very close."

"Close enough that he might be thinking of you?"

"Time passes differently in the Otherworld. I don't even know how long it's been since we've last seen each other."

Sorcha rubbed her chest. The thought he might have forgotten her made her skin itch. What if he didn't want her back? He had sent her away to stay safe, but there was always the chance he sent her away because he was done with her.

"I can find someone that's thinking of you," Aisling muttered. "Are you ready?"

"Now?"

"Now."

Sorcha nodded, though nerves made her stomach rise into her throat. Too many things could go wrong. Bad endings ran through her mind over and over until she questioned the sanity of this. She didn't even know this witch!

Kneeling at the front of the circle, Sorcha scooped up a handful of dirt. "By earth, I open this portal between our world and the Otherworld."

Aisling crouched at the top of the circle, leaned down, and blew upon the next. "By air, I break the shields that separate our kind."

Sorcha spat on the next rune. "By water, I lift the veil and create the way into the Otherworld."

The witch hesitated only for a moment, a feral grin splitting her features. She lifted a hand and snapped her fingers. Fire danced upon the tips, crackling with unnatural energy. "By fire, I open the portal."

Aisling tossed the fire onto the last remaining rune which burst into flames. The circle melted into the ground as the elements combined. A glassy surface spread before them, and Sorcha stared down into the Otherworld.

It was just as beautiful as she remembered. Green grass so perfect that her eyes watered. Sunlight and faeries flying past the portal without even glancing up at the two women staring down at them.

Aisling sighed. "It never gets old, does it?"

"No. It doesn't at all." She missed it so much. Just seeing the land and the faeries made her soul squeeze. "Now what?"

"Now we find someone who's thinking of you."

"That could take a while."

"It most likely will. I can't imagine there's hundreds of faeries thinking of you all the time. No offense, healer."

"None taken."

Aisling spread her hands over the portal and hummed under her breath. "Spirits of the air, aid me. Seek the one who dreams of a red-haired lass, who whispers the name Sorcha of Ui Neill. Breathe into this portal your guidance and bring us to the place where they rest."

The surface rippled and zipped across the landscape until everything was a blur. It seemed to hesitate in some spots for a few moments, but then continued searching for a person thinking of Sorcha.

She blew out a breath. "Come on. One of you, please think of me. Please."

Surely she hadn't been gone that long? They couldn't have forgotten her already.

And then the mirror stilled, settling on a small patch of moss in the center of a forest. Emerald green and dotted with dew, the meadow was a small slice of heaven.

"Better go now," Aisling said. "I don't know how long it will hold, and if it's moving while you jump then you'll be tossed into the air."

"I just jump down?"

"That's all."

"Will it hurt?"

"I don't have a clue. Never been through a faerie portal before. Never even seen someone try it until you."

The flashing grin she gave Sorcha was not comforting. There was something about the woman that was strange and unusual. Not her looks, Sorcha had seen a fair bit of women who were rough around the edges. It wasn't the way she moved, or spoke, but something innate that hovered just out of reach.

Sorcha sprang into movement and tossed her pack over her shoulders. "How old are you anyways?" she asked.

"Me?" Aisling put a hand on her chest. "It's rude to ask."

"I find it hard to believe you're worried about my manners."

Aisling stood, placed a palm against Sorcha's spine, and shook her head. "I'm younger than you. Eighteen years to my name, and I already know more than most people find out in their entire lives. Say hello the faeries for me."

"You're how old?"

The witch shoved, hard, and Sorcha tumbled through the portal. She landed on her hands and knees, cushioned by moss. The jolt still knocked the breath from her lungs.

"Aisling!" she cried out. "I'm not done with you yet!"

Sorcha rolled onto her back and stared up at the portal which was steadily shrinking. A bird's nest covered head poked over the small window and waved. "Have fun!"

"How do I get back?"

The portal closed before the witch could answer.

"Blasted witch!" she grumbled. "I need to get back, eventually!"

She rolled back onto her hands and knees, pulling out the leather bound book. There had to be something within its pages that could help. The portal page flew past, but there were no inked words after that.

Plenty of spells appeared, all to protect herself against faeries and their ilk. Nothing that would help her get home, or even find the creature who had been thinking of her.

Sorcha rolled over, her curls spilling over her face and tangling in front of her. No faeries stared back at her. No birds sang in the trees, and no bugs flitted through the air.

All was still and silent.

She was home. Sorcha breathed in the clean, sweet air and felt the missing piece inside her slide back into place. This was where her soul belonged.

Tears stung her eyes and she couldn't catch her breath. She felt as if a lifetime had passed since she'd last walked in this wondrous land. Her fingers sank deep into moss that shimmered with dew.

There was someone here thinking about her. Someone she must have known, for who else would think of her in this place?

She swallowed. "Please don't be Fionn."

Sorcha rose to her feet, nearly stumbling. Should she call out? Should she let whomever was here know she'd arrived?

It was the only option. Although it seemed foolish in place like this, Sorcha knew it was the right choice.

"Hello?" she called out. "Hello? Who's there!"

A twig broke to her left.

"I'm not supposed to talk to strangers." The voice was young and made her sag with relief.

"Pooka," she breathed and turned. "It's me."

"Who are you?"

"You don't remember me? It's Sorcha, Pooka."

The boy had grown so much since she last saw him. He stood nearly as tall as her. He hadn't taken the form his mother chose, the patchwork woman had been uncomfortable to look at. Instead, Pooka had chosen a thicker form that leaned heavily towards canine features.

He squinted his eyes. "I don't know a Sorcha."

"I put your arm back together when you were little." She pointed at the appendage. "I told you stories of Macha to keep you quiet and said you were a brave man for handling so much pain with nary a peep."

She watched him rub the arm, exactly where he had broken it.

She held her breath and prayed that he would remember. How long had she been gone? He was so different than she remembered.

"If you're really her, then what are you doing in the Otherworld?"

"I came to find your master."

"He doesn't need to be found."

"He does."

"Why?" Pooka gave her a suspicious look. "Are you going to stop him?"

"Stop him from what?"

Another voice interrupted, calling out, "Domnall! Where are you, boy?"

Pooka turned bright red. "You didn't hear that name."

"I wouldn't have used it against you anyways."

"Domnall! I thought I told you to gather mugwort, not to wander off into the forest and-" Oona stopped talking and halted behind Pooka as she caught sight of Sorcha. Tears filled her eyes. "Oh."

Sorcha's words stuck in her throat as all the emotions bubbled up. "Hello, Oona."

Tears dripped down her leaf-like cheeks as Oona launched herself into Sorcha's arms. "Oh my dearie! My girl, you are here!"

"It's been so long."

"Longer for us." Oona squeezed her so hard that she could barely breathe. "Oh my dear, sweet girl. How we have missed you!"

"Are you all right? You made it out of the castle?"

"Just barely."

"Cian?"

"Alive."

"Boggart?"

"Still with us."

"Good," Sorcha mumbled against Oona's shoulder. "Good."

"I cannot believe you're here!"

"Neither can I!"

Oona pulled away, framing her face and touching every part of Sorcha she could. "You're real."

"I'm real."

"How?"

"There's so much to tell you. But only once everyone is together. Where is he?" She watched Oona's face fall. The knot in the pit of her stomach clenched hard. "Oona?"

"Oh, dearie. It's been a long time since he sent you away."

"What happened?"

The leaves rustled behind them. Cian blundered towards them, shaking leaves from his shoulders. "I can't leave you two alone for even a second! You wander off like you have nothing else to do—"

He looked up and froze.

Sorcha waved. "Hello, Cian."

"What are you doing here?"

"I'm glad you survived the battle."

He huffed. "Yeah, well. You picked a bad time to come back."

"Why?" She looked around at the beloved familiar faces. "Why is this a bad time? What's happened?"

"The master," Oona said. "He's...not the same as he was when you left."

"What do you mean?"

"The king's forces seek us out. Somehow, Fionn caught wind that Eamonn was building an army. We have been fighting our way through the Otherworld to get to the Castle of Light."

"I'm sorry, why has this changed him? He's always been a warrior."

"You've never seen him like this, dearie."

"I've watched him kill for me. Have you forgotten I was there? I was with him when the battle started. He killed five elves and didn't even flinch. They couldn't touch him!"

Oona winced. "They're touching him now. I don't think he cares anymore if they touch him."

"What?"

Cian shuffled his feet. "What the pixie is trying to say is that he's falling to pieces. Solidifying more after every battle because the crystals strengthen him."

"He's throwing himself in front of the blade," Sorcha gasped in horror. "That won't make him stronger."

Oona played with her fingers, twisting them to and fro. "We've been trying to convince him of that, but he won't listen. He's certain he'll get his throne back and save everyone. But now you're here! Maybe you can convince him otherwise."

"I can try," she whispered. "But I don't know if he'll listen to me. How long has it been?"

"Five years."

She rocked back on her heels in shock. "Five years?"

"Five long years filled with fighting and hardship."

Pooka snorted. "And hunger."

"Have you been traveling all this time?" Sorcha asked.

"We haven't stopped since the battle."

She exhaled and tried not to think of their struggles. There would be time for that. She had all the time in the world now to be with them. But, there was something she had to do. And she couldn't wait any longer.

"Where is he?" Sorcha asked.

Oona pointed. "Through the woods in the glen."

"You're certain?"

"Yes."

Sorcha handed off her pack and smoothed her hands down her simple, blue skirt. "Please take this back to your camp. I'll join you later."

"You're going to him?"

"I am."

The Reunion And The Throne

Leaves fell from the trees, green and bright. They smelled so sweet compared to the winter she had left.

Her hands trembled as she walked through the forest towards the glen where Eamonn stood. Would he even want to see her again? Had he missed her as much as she'd missed him?

Tiny orbs of light burst into the air from their haven atop the leaves. They trailed after her, landing in the curls of her hair and nesting deep within the coils. Perhaps they felt the rapid beat of her heart and heard the whispered promise of a story coming to life.

The forest was so quiet. Sorcha picked her way through the moss, avoiding every twig or stick that might give her away. She didn't want him to know she was coming. She needed just a few more minutes to control her breathing, feel the tingle in her fingers, and face the fear of rejection.

She brushed aside a tangled length of vine and there it was. The glen that glowed gold in the sunlight.

And him.

Eamonn sat on a stump in the center of emerald ground. An unfamiliar sword laid across his lap, and he stared down at it.

He had changed. The crystals had spread, but it was more than that. He was in the sunlight without a cloak, without fabric covering his face. Eamonn was bare to the world, and he did not flinch away in fear.

She placed a hand against the nearest tree to balance herself. The dream Fionn had shown her was true. He had truly become more crystal than man, and yet he was still *hers*. She could feel it.

He must have been deep in thought, because he did not look up. She stepped onto a twig and let it crack beneath her heel.

"I asked for solitude." His deep voice sent shivers down her spine. "I need no company, Oona."

She couldn't speak. He sounded the same, even though time had passed. It was still him.

His shoulders hunched forward before he growled. "Oona, how many times do I have to tell you?"

Sorcha watched him stand while holding her breath. He turned around, and their eyes met. Lightning danced between them. The wind rushed into the glen, whipping the tail of his braid that was longer than she remembered.

But it was his eyes that held her. Like a physical touch, a whisper, a promise.

"You came back."

"Of course I did."

"After all this time, you came back."

He took one step towards her, a lurching step before catching himself as if he didn't know whether he had the right to touch her. She let out a choked sound, and then they were running towards each other. She didn't know which one moved first, but it didn't matter.

His arm wrapped around her, one hand lifted to cup her face and press her forehead against his, breathing her in.

"I thought I'd lost you forever." His breath fanned against her lips.

"How could I stay away?"

"You aren't safe here."

"Is life worth living if we are not together?"

Eamonn bent, lifting her by the hips until he could kiss her without straining. They poured their frustrations, their longing, their heartbreak into a single kiss that wiped those emotions away.

She wrapped her legs around his waist and dug her fingers into the grooves of his shoulders. He was solid and real, the man she had desired for so long. Finally, she could clasp him to her chest and breathe him in.

Her back hit a tree, the bark digging through the fabric of her dress, but she didn't care. Sorcha traced the angular curve of his jaw, down the strong column of his neck, into the deep crevices she didn't remember.

Eamonn kissed her as if he were a drowning man. Each lingering pass of firm lips and biting crystal healed her fragile heart. He didn't just take her lips, he devoured her.

He drew back for a second, pressing a raspy moan against her throat. "I should let you go."

"Please don't. I only just got you back."

Her words snapped the tether of his tight control. His hands were everywhere. Splayed open against her spine, pressing her closer to his body while sliding up the smooth length of her thigh. Her dress parted and warm air danced along her calves.

Every nerve ending in her body fired until all she could feel was him. He licked a trail of fire down her throat and across her shoulders.

This time was different than the first. He didn't hesitate or draw back, he did not allow her to take control. Somehow, she understood this moment was not about how much they missed each other. This wasn't just a reunion or a heartbreaking moment to remind each other they existed.

He wanted to brand her with his touch because he'd come so close to losing her.

The fabric of her bodice tore as he moved too quickly. Sorcha gasped and arched her back.

He licked a trail from the hollow of her throat to her breasts.

She forgot how to breathe as he drew the tight pebbles into his mouth. Their first time had been so sweet she hadn't been able to think.

Now she felt as though she were adrift at sea and he was the only raft in sight. She clutched onto his shoulders and rocked on the waves they created.

His hand slipped underneath her skirts, slid up the back of her thigh and clenched the globes of her bottom. He pulled away from her chest, breathing into her ear, "I have missed you."

"Stop toying with me," she ground out. "Now, Eamonn."

"We've hardly gotten started."

"I will learn every inch of your body again, but I cannot wait any longer!"

He leaned back and arched a brow. "I forgot how demanding you were."

Sorcha yanked his braid so hard that his head jerked backwards. "I'm insulted you forgot anything at all."

"I didn't forget your taste." He leaned forward and licked her lips. "Sunshine and strawberries."

He fumbled with the clasp of his belt to free himself. Sorcha braced, knowing it had been a long time and that he was a considerably large man. But then, he hesitated.

Eamonn brushed her curls from her forehead and pressed a kiss against her temple. "Are you sure? There's plenty of soft moss to cushion your back, and time before the others find us."

This was why she adored him. Sorcha's eyes drifted and a smile burst free. "Yes, yes this is what I want."

"Thank the gods."

Her thighs clenched hard around his hips as he plunged inside her with one swift stroke. She had dreamed of this moment so many times but no dream could replicate the feeling of his hands so gentle on her hips. The crystals slashing across his abdomen rubbed against her belly with each grind of his hips against hers. He whispered endearments in her ears with each flex of his muscles.

"My sunshine," he groaned. "My light."

She framed his face and brought his lips to hers in a kiss so delicate it was painful. "Yours."

There was no way to get closer to him, and yet she wanted to. She dug her nails into his back, catching on new wounds. So much pain laced across his skin, but she could provide him a haven.

Her toes pointed, her head tilted back to brace against the tree.

"Eamonn," she gasped.

He traced his palm up the arch of her spine. Cupping the back of her neck, he pressed his lips to hers again. "I can't lose myself in you."

"Who says you can't?"

The groaned response was little more than noise, and he quickened his strokes. Each time, he came closer and closer to touching her very soul.

Unexpectedly, light exploded behind her eyes. The orgasm happened so fast she hadn't felt it building. Stars fell from the sky and burst free from her skin in one clenching moment that had her holding her breath.

He growled and buried his face in her shoulder as he found his own release.

Panting, she tightened her hold on him. He wrapped his arms around her, holding her so tight she could barely breathe. As she stared up into the dappled green leaves above them, she wondered how she would ever let him go again.

Her thighs clenched hard around his hips, drawing him ever closer. She couldn't shake the feeling that the moment she let go, he would disappear again. Tears pricked her eyes.

"Please let this be real." She pressed the words against the crown of his head. "Please tell me this isn't a dream and you won't disappear the moment I look at you again."

"Let us both hope this is not a dream for I would surely not survive the waking."

"Don't say that. Not so soon after you almost died."

"I cannot die."

"You aren't invincible, Eamonn."

"I am with you at my side."

He pulled back, and she looked upon his beloved face with fearful love. She traced his wounded brow.

"Your eye," she gasped.

"It is nothing."

"Does it hurt?"

"No more than the others."

Sorcha could see the pain in his eyes. He was afraid she would reject him for his differences. And she had forgotten how much his past influenced his future.

She leaned forward and pressed a chaste kiss against his brow. She hoped the butterfly touch would heal the scars on his heart.

"I am sorry for your pain."

His fingers flexed against her sides. "Mo chroí."

"Eamonn, don't get mad at me for what I'm about to do."

"How could I grow angry with you now?"

She drew back just enough to cock her arm back and slap him across the face so hard that the crystals on his cheek sliced through her palm.

He flinched and lifted a hand to his cheek. "What was that for, you mad woman?"

"Don't you *ever* force me to leave your side again!"

"There was a battle! You would have died if you stayed!"

"And that is not your choice!" Her shout echoed through the glen. "If you get to risk your life for me, then I get to do the same. And if you try to do that again I will find a way to put a sword through your heart."

He blinked at her in shock. "Did you just threaten me?"

"Never take away a woman's choice to stand by her man. Do you hear me?"

"I hear you."

"Say it again."

"I hear you, my fierce druid priestess." He traced the outline of her lips with his thumb.

"I mean it, Eamonn. Never again."

"I will always put myself as your shield. I have to protect those I cherish. And you are my heart, Sunshine."

His words dug into her ribs, wiggling their way through the icy exterior she had erected. "Then let me walk beside you and heal every wound."

Their lips clung together, breath mingling until all her tongue stung with mint.

"I am so glad to have you back."

"As am I."

He pressed his forehead against hers, rolling back and forth until the crystals made her wince. Only then did he step back, lowering her legs to the ground gently and holding on as her balance reset.

Moss sank between her toes. When had her shoes fallen off? She glanced around, looking for the worn slippers that had kept her feet warm all winter.

"Looking for these?"

Eamonn held them dangling from his fingertips.

"Yes," Sorcha said while holding out her hand.

"They're so tiny."

"I imagine they would be to you, I'm a lot smaller than most Fae." She hopped, trying to grab them out of his hand.

He let the slippers drop into her waiting hands. Sorcha marveled at how easy it was to slide back into this life. She had thought it would be harder, more difficult to connect with him.

It was as if she had never left.

Hopping on one foot, she pulled her shoes on. "What's happened while I've been gone?"

"I could ask you the same question." He waited until she was standing again before pulling her into his arms and carrying her to the stump.

Eamonn settled with her in his lap, his hands playing with the dip of her waist. She couldn't stop touching him either. Every new cut needed exploring, and she couldn't see all of him.

She sank her fingers into his hair and pulled hard. "What happened on the isle?"

"Fionn overran the castle. His men cut through most of ours, beloved people fell because they didn't have sword or weapon."

"How did you get out?"

"I don't know." He shook his head, dislodging her fingers from the crown of his head. "I don't remember it. Oona says I drew Ocras and took care of the problem, but will not tell me any more."

"Blood lust?" She had heard of such a thing in the legends, but hadn't thought it was real. Worry knotted her stomach as if a fist closed around it.

"Far worse than that, little sunshine. He retreated to the edge of the isle, but was obviously gathering his forces for another attack. There were so few left we fled into the Otherworld. There were many hard months as we struggled to find a new home."

"I thought our people couldn't return to the Otherworld? You said banishment is forever."

"It is, until the High King of the Seelie Fae decrees they are absolved."

Sorcha stopped breathing. She hadn't thought it possible such a thing was possible, although she was ashamed she hadn't thought of it herself. He was the eldest son, the rightful heir to the throne.

"You took a great risk," she said while shaking her head.

"I knew I was meant to be king from the moment I first took breath."

"You chose to forsake that life."

"That doesn't mean I cannot take it back."

His palms smoothed down her spine to calm her. But her brows furrowed all the same, and her gut twisted. "Eamonn, it will not be easy to take this path. Your brother won't give up, your people will be confused. You're suggesting splitting your people in two."

"I know that very well. I've spent the last five years fighting to regain independence and my throne."

"How has that worked for you?"

"I'm still in a forest, without throne or crown."

Sorcha had thought as much. She wracked her mind for an idea, something she could say to help. But she was thoroughly out of her element. A peasant girl from Ui Neill knew little to help a faerie king.

She cleared her throat. "What steps have you taken thus far?"

"I have an army of dwarves, and the few gnomes who have come to help the cause." He shook his head, lips twisting to the side in disappointment. "It is a very small army with little ability to fight Tuatha dé Danann and elves. Luck is not on our side."

"You're meeting them head on?"

"How else would you have me fight?"

She toyed with his braid, pulling it over his shoulder and rubbing the silken strands between her fingertips. "I wouldn't have you fight at all. You're a king, should this not be solved through the courts?"

"This is not something my brother and I can talk about."

"Why not?"

"He will not give up the throne."

She rubbed the fine strands between her fingers again, trying to remember all the legends and myths of the Fae. Sorcha had never been the storyteller. She much preferred using her hands to listening, and tended to doze off when the ballads were sung.

Sorcha wracked her mind for any story which might fit, settling on a legend she'd heard long ago. Cormac Ulfada, a wise High King of the human race, and his many intelligent decisions to keep his throne.

Her eyes glinted as an idea formed. "He doesn't have to."

Eamonn tilted his head to the side and regarded her with a curious expression. "What do you have brewing in that mind of yours?"

"These are your people, Eamonn. You have proven yourself to

be the high king. Fionn has no real claim to the throne. Why should you have to fight for what is yours?"

"That is what we do. We fight for what is ours."

"But what if you didn't have to fight? What if your people made the choice for you? They will follow you without a war, without blood, without death. All you have to do, is give them the option to follow a more worthy leader."

He blinked at her in shock. "Just how much did you learn while you were gone?"

"Learn? I have been home with my father and my sisters."

"Are they well?" Eamonn stroked her chin, worry painting fine lines across his forehead.

"They live."

"You cured the plague, didn't you?"

The proud expression on his face filled her heart near to bursting. He believed in her when her own family hadn't thought she could make miracles happen.

"How did you know?" she asked.

"I always knew you would."

"With no help from you."

"Did you need my help?"

Sorcha shook her head. "No, apparently not."

He traced a finger down her forehead to the tip of her nose. "You have never needed me to cure the plague. You're perfectly capable of saving your own people."

"Am I supposed to say the same thing to you?"

"It would be appreciated."

"I don't agree with you, Eamonn. All this death seems unnecessary. How many people have to die before you trade thrones?"

He sighed and buried his face in her neck. She felt the hard press of his lips against her collarbone. "This is not something a human could comprehend. Tuatha dé Danann do not give up, and Fionn has desired the throne his entire life. He's not going to welcome me into his castle with a smile."

"Have you tried speaking to him?"

"Enough, Sorcha. Let me enjoy having you back in my arms for a few moments before you try to heal all my wounds."

She hugged him closer, her mind whirling with thoughts. Fionn had obviously been concerned about Eamonn's whereabouts. If he was invading her dreams, then he had an inkling his twin was closer than he wished. But just how close was Eamonn?

"Are we near the Castle of Light?"

He heaved a sigh. "Right above it, mo chroí. So close to my family home I can feel its magic in the air."

"What are you planning, Eamonn?" Her heart beat hard in her chest, so rapidly that he tapped his finger on her skin in time to the beats.

"Another battle to end all battles. I cannot keep fighting him like this. He has an endless amount of soldiers and they continue to draw closer and closer to our location."

"Then you need to find a stronghold."

"A stronghold?" He leaned back and stared into her eyes. "First you declare I must speak with him, and then you suggest a stronghold?"

"What about the Castle of Light makes it so special?" she asked. "Is it powerful? Are there people there who would aid you? Or is it merely the familial ties?"

"There is nothing special about the castle."

"Then let us find a new castle. A new place where those who have been wronged may flee." She scooted up in his lap, plans already forming. "If you refuse to speak with him, then build your army out of those who willingly fight for the cause. Spread word that you exist. That the high king wants to return to the throne."

"You are suggesting a coup."

"I'm suggesting much more than that," she said, excited as the idea formed. "I'm suggesting you create a second throne. A higher throne."

"I like the way you think."

"Not every man would listen to a woman."

"I know better than to ignore the wisdom of women. Though I

do not always agree with you, mo chroí, I will never dismiss your opinions."

Her heart swelled with happiness.

Eamonn smiled, wolfish and full of mischief. "Now, why don't we stop thinking for a while?"

He tilted her back until her spine hit the soft moss. Prowling after her, he settled between her legs and smiled.

She grinned back, happiness bubbling in her chest. "The moss is comfortable."

"I wouldn't put you anywhere else."

"The sun is warm."

"It sees you and smiles."

"You feel so familiar," she said in wonderment and lifted a hand to touch the new crystals near his eye. "And yet, so different as well."

"No more talking, mo chroí."

She didn't for a while as she found each new wound and left her mark on his body once again.

❦

"Here you are, dearie."

"Thank you, Oona." Sorcha took the offered bowl filled with rabbit stew. The mere scent of it made her stomach rumble. She couldn't remember the last time she had eaten, but that was what came with the job of healing.

They all sat around a small fire. Boggart sat in her lap, Cian and Oona bickering over the right way to cook rabbit. Sorcha had grieved with them when she first arrived. They had lost so many. Now, they all gathered to eat and forge their bonds all over again.

Small fires crackled in the shadow of the mountain range around them. Clusters of dwarves formed around each flame, little mingling occurring this late at night. Family groups, Sorcha guessed. The dwarves were silent folk and weren't interested in speaking with her.

Although, they were far more intuitive than the other faeries she had met.

A small female dwarf stumbled into Sorcha as she arrived, snorted, and muttered, "Now there are druids 'ere too?"

Sorcha had stared after her in shock.

They stayed away from her after that. She didn't know if dwarves were among those that banished her people in the first place, but she guessed it was likely they were a part of the decision. Druids were fearsome creatures to the Fae. Humans capable of magic defied all logic.

She tucked into the stew and tried to find Eamonn in the crowd. He slipped into his warlord visage as soon as he set foot in the camp. All of his attention poured into catching up with the dwarves he called "generals." She thought it more likely they were heads of their families.

Boggart tugged on her sleeve and pointed.

Sorcha followed the direction of Boggart's jabbing finger, finding the same female dwarf at the edge of the shadows. She didn't look frightened, but something else entirely. She was watching Sorcha with a hard gaze.

"Can I help you?"

"I don't think so."

"Are you hurt?" Sorcha asked. "I'm a healer."

"Druids don't 'eal dwarves."

"You have a problem because I have druid blood?"

"Your kind makes poor decisions. I remember the stories of when you 'ad free access to the Otherworld. Stealing magical objects. Using them against each other until you accidentally killed an important faerie. I know all of it, and I don't trust you."

"Well," Sorcha put her bowl to the side and hugged Boggart tighter in her embrace. "Perhaps it would set your mind at ease to know I do not follow the old ways. I was not raised a druid, and magic is very new to me."

"Is it?" The dwarf nodded at her bowl. "Then why did you leave a bit of food?"

"I'm no longer hungry."

The little woman crossed her eyes and flicked her beard over her shoulder. "Go on. Do what you want to do with it. I'll watch to make sure you aren't up to any funny business."

"I don't want to do anything with it."

But that was a lie. The dwarf was reading her mind, Sorcha realized. Her fingers itched to pick the bowl back up and throw the remnants into the fire. She had always done that, even as a child. She always tossed leftovers into the flames, even food someone else might eat.

Words bloomed in her mind like the ink that appeared on the papers of her books. Baring her teeth in a grimace, she picked up the bowl and flicked the remaining food into the flames of the campfire.

"Feast, ancestors of old. I thank you for the food you have provided and the safe haven you offer for my soul. I honor your memory with this simple food. Blessed be."

The flames spun up into the air, and Sorcha saw people in the dancing spikes. Faces she did not recognize, but made her relax all the same. Each wore the blue woad the women in her vision had worn.

She clenched her hands into fists.

The dwarf tsked. "See? Druids never fall too far from the tree. You're lucky I'm not my grandfather, or I would 'ave already taken your 'ead from your shoulders."

"Why hasn't anyone else then? I see waves of dwarves as if I looked into the ocean, and not one of you has raised a finger towards me."

"Because we're all dying out there." The dwarven woman jabbed a finger at her family. "And if you can stop that, put an end to all this madness, then that means you get to live. Otherwise? Stay out of our way."

Darkness swallowed up the tiny woman as she fled back to her own campfire.

Sorcha shook her head. "Are they all like that?"

"They are when it comes to protecting what is theirs. Are you really a druid, dearie?"

Oona's eyes were massive. The moon reflected in their iridescent depths, twin limpid pools that Sorcha thought were all too hopeful for her liking.

"Yes. My grandfather found me while I was home."

"Family? From your mother's side?"

Sorcha hummed, Boggart's soft snore vibrating against her neck. "I don't know how much I trust him. He seemed to know far too much about my life, but didn't appear to care for my choices. It was all very odd."

"It's good to have people who understand you."

"He doesn't understand me. He doesn't seem to understand the world." She snorted. "I'd trust the witch more than him."

"Witch?" Oona startled. "Witches are dangerous creatures."

"Don't I know it. But she helped to get me here, and I think it's more likely that she has a little druid blood in her."

"The druids are returning then." Oona's voice took on a strange quality, a whisper in the wind. "It is as it should be. The Otherworld is returning to its previous state. The high king takes his throne. The druids walk back through the portals. The Lesser Fae join their families and leave their lives of hardship."

"We hope."

Cian plopped down on the other side of the fire. He shook himself and water sprayed from his rolls of flesh. "That boy won't listen to a damn thing."

"Eamonn?" Sorcha asked.

"Aye. He's got it in his head we'll be moving. A whole army! Moving from the nearest point to the castle we could be."

"Where are we going?"

"Ask him. He won't say a word to me."

Sorcha stood, searching for Eamonn across the campfires that dotted like stars.

"He's there, dearie." Oona pointed towards what used to be a solid platform, but now had rotting holes like gaping mouths. "In the place where all this started."

She didn't comprehend the words until she realized where they were. A platform, a great column of wood, and a man whose throat bore the mark of the noose.

"No." Sorcha shook her head. "No, it cannot be."

"He chose to remain here. To remind himself day after day why he is fighting so hard."

"This is where they hung him?"

"We're standing in the same spot his family stood all those years ago. They watched him swing from a rope for hours before going back to their castle and falling asleep." Oona sniffed. "I still don't know how they did it. They made me go back with them, and nary a one had even a nightmare. Their boy was left out to the elements, unable to breathe, and with all the beasts of the Otherworld chewing on him. And they didn't seem to care."

Sorcha couldn't bear it. Her feet moved her towards the platform where Eamonn stood staring up at the sky. No one was looking at him.

They were looking at her.

She was graceful as she picked her way through the crowds. Her skirts glowed in the moonlight, turning them silver and white.

"A ghost," someone muttered.

"A bean sidhe."

"No, a druid."

Her hair stirred in the breeze. Curls fluttered across her face as she stared at him. He didn't respond to her approach. The muscles of his back tensed, his fists curling in on themselves.

He knew. He always knew when she was walking up to him. And she was certain he knew she was about to argue with him.

Silently, she walked up the rotting stairs and placed a hand against his spine.

"Eamonn."

"You will not change my mind."

She smiled. "Why would I even try? It was my idea, mo chroí. We leave this place?"

"I will not stay upon this cursed land for a moment longer."

"Wherever you go, I will follow."

"It will not be an easy journey."

"Then it is good you have a healer who will help you along the way."

A great sigh rocked his shoulders. He turned to her then, pulling her into his arms and bending to rest his chin on her forehead. "I didn't think it possible to miss another person as much as I missed you."

"I would miss losing a limb. And that is precisely the way I feel when you are not with me."

"Thank you for standing by me."

"I will convince you to speak with your brother, Eamonn."

"You can try, but I will never yield."

She shouted in her mind words of encouragement. Not for him, but for herself. Sorcha knew, deep in the pit of her gut, that the only way to end this war without further bloodshed was for the two of them to talk. They had to understand there was only so much more war this land could take.

But for now, she would wrap herself in Eamonn's arms and pray that he understood.

He straightened, tucking her underneath his arm. "Men and women of Underhill!"

The dwarves all stood. Sorcha looked out over their ranks and wondered just how many they had lost. Five years of battle? Or was it five years of Eamonn fighting, and these people had only been here for a few weeks?

Old scars and new decorated their faces, worn armor weighed them down. Rust outlining the edges and chips marring the pristine surfaces.

"We have fought for a long time. You are a hard and true people, but now I must ask another boon."

A rumble of worry echoed.

"We leave this land tomorrow. I will not risk our troops and our lives any further. We go to our family's homeland. To the castle of old where the Tuatha dé Danann first touched the ground."

"Where?" someone shouted.

He squeezed Sorcha against his chest. "To the castle of Nuada Silverhand!"

The resounding cheer at these words could likely be heard all the way to the Castle of Light. They were going to Nuada's sacred home?

She glanced up at Eamonn. "Is that wise?"

"Where else would we go?"

"Anywhere. I do not wish to anger your grandfather."

"Neither do I." He released her, holding her hand and guiding her down the stairs. "But there is no other choice. As you said, the battle can only go on for so long. I need a new throne until I take mine back."

❧

THEY TRAVELED FOR DAYS ACROSS THE WIDE EXPANSE OF THE Otherworld.

Sorcha began to recognize mountains and hills. The peaks she had climbed over as a child, now covered with sparkling glitter, traversed by faeries, and far more vibrant. Flowers reached for her with their leafy hands. Grass tangled around her ankles if she stopped for too long, stroking whatever skin it could find.

Eamonn set a blistering pace that left the entire company exhausted. He did not come to see Sorcha again, although she understood why. The dwarves took much of his attention.

The more she watched them, the more she wondered how he had gathered such an army. They didn't *like* each other, let alone him. Small squabbles quickly turned into giant brawls. Taking care of them sapped his energy.

He hadn't forgotten her, she was certain of that. After all this time, she was finally in the Otherworld. He was busy, not distant.

Sorcha kept repeating the words in her head. It became a poem, a hymn, that repeated over and over again in her mind until it stuck.

After all this time.

She turned to look back the way they had traveled. A long line of dwarves trailed down the mountain like a river. It was a rare day of sunshine that turned the fields to rolling waves of green grass. Stone outcroppings jutted from the earth, mimicking frothy white peaks.

Oona and Cian stayed close to her, the others from Hy-brasil not far behind.

Stones crunched behind her, but she didn't need to look. Pooka was far younger than the rest of them. His boundless energy sent him running ahead and back with updates on where they were going.

"We're stopping," he sullenly reported.

"Is that a bad thing?"

"Might be, depending on what you think of this journey."

The wind picked up and blew Sorcha's long strands like a banner in the wind. "What do you mean by that?"

"We've arrived."

"And so soon."

She looked back at him, crouched on a rock with a frown on his face. When had he gotten so old? She saw the worry lines that marred his expression and knew he had a reason to be afraid.

"Go help the others," she said. "We will need them all with us when we reach the castle."

"You want them in the front?"

"I think it would be wise to have his family near him."

"You think he considers us family?" Pooka shook his head and hopped to the ground. "You got a lot of big ideas in that head of yours, but you still don't understand Tuatha dé Danann."

"I think holding onto prejudices brought your kind to this point. Now go get them all and meet me at the front. How much further is it?"

"Far."

She pinned him with a censoring gaze. "Domnall."

"Over the rise," he grumbled. "You'll see it before you get too close. He stopped everyone so they could look at the castle before we go anywhere."

Oona huffed and puffed up to them. "Are we stopping?"

"No, sorry."

"Ah well, it was a hope anyways. Do we know when he wants to stop for the night?"

"He's reached the castle." Sorcha looked up at the jagged edge of the mountain they climbed. "It's on the other side of this crest."

"We best be going then."

"Pooka, how many times do I have to tell you to go help the others?"

"You don't get to order me around."

Sorcha turned on her heel and grabbed the boy by the ear. His yelp sounded eerily like that of a wounded puppy. "I tell you what to do because you need to learn how to respect your elders. Go get the others before I leave an imprint of my boot on your behind."

"You wouldn't dare."

"Try me, pup."

He glared for a few moments before his shoulders rounded in defeat. She gave his ear one more twist before setting him off.

Oona chuckled. "You'll have him fawning over you in no time."

"The boy needs to listen."

"The boy is halfway in love with you, and you hardly cast him a glance."

"Of course I don't." Sorcha rolled her eyes to the heavens. "He's just a child!"

"I wasn't suggesting you encourage him."

The two women started back up the mountain. Sorcha held out her arm for Oona to take, although she knew the pixie wouldn't admit to weakness. They linked together and clambered over the rocky path.

Oona was out of breath. Sorcha could feel her lungs burning. It was a shame she was so tired, for the landscape was beautiful, and she would have liked to pause and enjoy it.

The mountain was foreboding. Sheer cliffs dropped off into nothing, with no path to mark their direction. No one had been here for a very long time.

They passed a few dwarves who sat themselves on stones and pulled out their water skins. Red cheeks and sweat-stained faces revealed how hard Eamonn had pushed them. Too hard.

"Why does everyone seem so nervous?" Sorcha asked.

"It is said the castle is haunted."

"Nuada's castle? Why would it be haunted?"

"You know of the Fomorians?"

Sorcha had grown up on the stories of the beastly men who'd battled the Tuatha dé Danann. Centuries of war had thinned the numbers of both, although there were plenty of romantic stories in between. It seemed the two cultures loved to fight each other just as much as they loved to break the rules.

"I know of them."

"The human legends never said they crossed over into our world, but they did. Nuada's castle was the first they took, and they reigned there for a good century before they lost everything. So many people died there." Oona blew out a breath. "It is said that ghosts walk the halls with the heads of goats and bodies of men."

"So it's abandoned?"

"Far more than that. It's cursed. Even the Unseelie will not traverse its battlements."

"Wonderful. And what about a haunted castle sounded like a good idea to Eamonn?"

Oona tightened her hand on Sorcha's arm. "Nuada Silverhand was the last High King. You haven't put it together, have you? A king can be anyone in name. People will kneel before anyone with a crown. But the High King of the Seelie Fae is something else entirely. He is the true ruler recognized by the land itself. There can be many kings. There can only be *one* High King."

Sorcha blew out a long breath, forcing the tension in her body to ease. It made sense that Eamonn would be the high king. He was the first born son and did not bend to the old ways. He saw things in a way that would benefit the whole of his people.

What had she gotten herself into?

They crested the top of the mountain and Sorcha nearly fell to her knees. Nuada Silverhand's castle was built on the peak of the nearest mountain. Walls stretched from the cliff edges, supporting the ornate towers above. Tattered banners fluttered in the wind. Stone outcroppings melded into the castle, making the castle appear as if it grew out of the mountain itself.

The only way to enter was a crumbling bridge dripping stones like water. Crows sat upon it watching the meager army appear over the rise.

"It is terrifying," Sorcha observed. White birds rose from the castle battlements and circled overhead.

"I fear it will be even worse inside."

"How long has it been since anyone has lived there?"

"Centuries."

Sorcha sighed. "Then it will be falling apart."

"An army does better when there is something to do. He is smart to bring us here while waiting for more to come."

"Will they?" Sorcha glanced down at Oona. "It was an idea I had, but I do not know the ways of the Fae. Will it be likely that others will follow him?"

"I believe they will have no choice. The High King of the Seelie Fae commands us all."

Sorcha's eyes strayed across the crowds of dwarves. Standing like a mountain in the center of a field, Eamonn stared at the castle. She could see the determined set of his shoulders, the way his long legs stood strong and braced. Wind buffeted him, but he did not move, didn't react even when the dwarves set down their clanking packs.

He was just as worried as she was.

With a gentle squeeze, she released Oona and made her way

through the throngs of faeries. This time, they did not whisper that a druid was among them. They merely watched as the strange redheaded woman moved among their ranks.

She stood next to Eamonn, tiny compared to his great height, and watched the strange birds circling overhead.

"We've made it," she said.

"Against all odds."

"It's far larger than I imagined."

"Long ago, this castle housed thousands of faeries."

"I can see how it would be possible." She reached out tentatively, unsure whether he would want her support. It didn't seem likely that he would want her hand. Instead, she linked her pinky with his. "Are we going in?"

"I don't know how dangerous it will be."

"Then perhaps just the two of us should go first?"

He shuddered as if the mere suggestion made him uncomfortable. "You will not go into that castle until I have made certain it is safe."

"I thought we already had this conversation."

"We have, and I say it again. This is not a safe place for humans, Sorcha. Remain here so I don't have to worry about you while I clear this castle of any remaining evil." He slid a finger under her chin and nudged until she looked directly into his gaze. "Do you understand, Sorcha?"

"When did you get so domineering?"

"About the same time I took being a king seriously."

"I don't like it."

"You don't have to. You just have to listen." He let his hand drop and headed back towards the dwarves. "Don't even think about it, Sorcha!"

Sorcha was damn well thinking about it. He should know by now she hated anyone telling her what to do. All she wanted was to set a foot on the bridge to see his reaction.

She glared at the missing stones and moss covered parapets. It would be so easy to pick her way across that and explore the massive castle. And really, what was he going to do? He wasn't even looking at her.

Part of her knew this was a bad idea. She could feel in her bones that something horrible might happen.

But her pride wouldn't let her forget his order. She gnawed on the idea like a dog with a bone until she blew out a breath and shrugged.

She'd have to go fast. The bridge didn't look like it could hold a lot of weight, but if she hopped between the large gaps, it should hold up. Lifting her skirts, she jumped from the nearest gap to the center of the bridge.

It groaned so loudly that she was certain it would break. The clouds beneath her weren't likely to catch her when she fell.

"Sorcha!" Eamonn's shout seared her to the bone.

The stones underneath her feet began to crumble. Heart beating, lungs heaving, she flew across the falling bridge. Each step she took felt as if it would be her last. The crashing of stones striking the ground beneath her echoed through the canyon.

The bridge in front of her quaked. Did that mean what was behind her had already fallen?

"Don't look," she muttered as she leapt from stone to stone.

Looking would only solidify how much danger she was in. She had to focus, had to get to the other side of the bridge or fall to her death.

Sorcha planted her foot on a stone that was already falling. She shoved, leaping into the air and rolling onto the other side of the bridge. Air exploded from her lungs and she shoved herself over.

Hair fell in front of her eyes, but she could still see him. Her massive faerie prince who raced across a bridge that crumbled to dust behind him. Eamonn's face was twisted in anger and concentration, sunlight sparkling as it struck the crystals of his body.

She held her breath as he let out a powerful roar and the bridge fell away beneath him.

"No," she breathed. It couldn't be. He couldn't fall and die now. Not because of her foolish mistake.

Wisps of smoke and debris puffed from the ground. It swirled like ghosts, the movement strange and unntural. Would he haunt this place with all the others?

A crystal hand latched onto the remaining edge of the bridge. His human hand followed, fingers gripping the stone so hard that it dented.

"Thank the gods," she muttered as she crawled over to him.

Sorcha leaned over the edge to flash a relieved smile. Eamonn did not appear amused.

"It's not over yet, sunshine."

She grabbed onto his forearm and blew her hair out of her face. "Never doubted for a second you'd make it."

"Let go."

"You're hanging off the edge of a cliff, let me help you."

He released the hand she grabbed and shook her off. "Back up, Sorcha."

For once, she realized it was probably a good idea to listen to him. She slid backwards on her bottom to give him enough room. With one great heave, he yanked himself up and over the bridge, rolling to her side.

Eamonn dropped a hand on his chest that lifted rapidly with each breath. "Don't do that again."

She leaned over him, her hair creating a curtain around them. "You didn't have to follow me."

"Of course I did," he said as he smoothed a thumb over her cheekbone. "Are you done risking your life for curiosity?"

"Doubtful."

Eamonn groaned, rolling to his side and onto his feet. He waved at the dwarves that stood in a line at the edge of the cliff. Oona and Cian piled on top of a large rock, teetering dangerously at the edge as they waited to see whether they were all right.

They were lucky. Sorcha's stomach clenched as she saw the damage to the bridge. There was nothing left but the skeletal bones reaching out into the abyss of nothing.

"Would you look at that," she said. "Seems like we're stuck here for a while."

"The dwarves will fix it in no time. Once they figure out that they want to follow, they'll speak to the stones."

"Speak to the stones?"

"Did you think they tunneled through mountains?" Eamonn turned to her, his crystal eye glittering. "They ask them to move, and they do."

"Ah," she nodded. "As with everything here, I suppose I have to say that makes sense and move on. Are we going to the castle?"

"Absolutely not."

"But it's right there!" She gestured at the looming dark stone and high parapets.

"I can see that, Sorcha."

"It's where we were planning to go anyways."

"And it is dangerous. Faerie-cursed land is never friendly to humans."

"I've already been to Unseelie," she said, planting her fists on her hips. "You're telling me that this castle is more dangerous than the Dark Castle? If it is, then perhaps we should find somewhere else to bring your army."

"You've been where?" His eyes blazed with anger. "I'd forgotten about that."

"Yes, well, the Queen was awful." Another flock of birds burst into flight. The wind billowed around them, clearing out the dust from the collapse and revealing the decrepit walls. "Are you certain you don't wish to go in?"

"We're waiting here until the dwarves complete the new bridge."

"How long will that take?"

He waved again at the dwarves. She could see their mouths moving, but their shouts wouldn't carry over the deep valley between them. "As soon as they start building, it shouldn't take long."

Sorcha snorted. The dwarves were setting up camp for the

night, and she didn't blame them. They would likely start building as soon as the sun rose again. Eamonn set a grueling pace and they were all exhausted.

They deserved a bit of rest.

She shook her head and started up a path. There were buildings all around the roads that splintered out from the bridge. She imagined these had once been homes as it seemed unlikely that anyone other than royalty and their immediate staff would have lived in the castle.

Ivy crawled up the walls of the buildings and the protecting battlements that surrounded the entire town. Gothic swirls and dramatic rooftop peaks suggesting this had once been a home for artists and craftsmen.

"Sorcha? Sorcha! What did I say?"

She rolled her eyes. "You said you would stay and wait for the dwarves. I don't fancy sleeping on a cliff's edge."

"Get back here!"

"No."

She heard his growl of frustration and the skittering of small stones as he followed her towards the central courtyard.

"I don't like ghosts," he grumbled when he caught up with her.

"There's no such thing as ghosts."

"We're in the Otherworld. Anything is possible."

"Then I should like to meet them."

"Please don't say that."

Sorcha grinned. "Is there someone following us, Eamonn?"

"No."

"I'm quite certain I can hear a third set of footsteps."

"Stop it!"

The Ghosts Of The Castle

Paint flecked from the rotting wood of the railings once grand stairs overtaken by moss and vines. The doors were easily twice Sorcha's height, terrifying and imposing in their grandeur and age.

"Is this what it felt like?" Eamonn asked.

"What?"

"Walking up to the main door of the castle on Hy-brasil and wondering what was behind it?"

"Yes," she replied. "This is exactly what it felt like."

"I don't give you enough credit for your bravery."

"Or for my foolishness," Sorcha added with a grin. "I was just as impulsive when I walked into your throne room."

She placed her hands against the wood and shoved. Surprisingly, her hands didn't puncture the door. The echoing creak danced down her spine, but it swung open without falling off its hinges.

It was a start.

She peeked through the cobwebs and tangled vines. There were shadows dancing upon the walls, ones she didn't think came from the plants. Could they be goblins? They looked faintly similar to the hunched creatures she had seen in the Unseelie castle.

Eamonn's hand landed on her shoulder and nudged her behind him. "Let me go first."

"I thought you were afraid of ghosts?"

"Not so much that I would let you put your life before mine." His lips tilted to the side. "Have a little faith, sunshine."

"I never doubted you."

His scoff echoed as they walked into the great hall.

King Nuada Silverhand's castle was as grand as she imagined it. Stained glass windows framed the hallway, and colored lights danced on the white and black checkered floor, which was missing a few pieces of marble.

Vines grew over the walls, and giant blue hydrangeas poked through cracks and crevices. Gold glinted on the wall nearest to her. Sorcha stepped closer, shifting ivy to the side and stumbled back with a gasp.

Eyes stared back at her.

Eamonn caught her against his chest. "It's a painting."

"I thought it was... It looked so..."

He spread his hand wide against her belly and leaned down to chuckle in her ear. "Who is afraid of ghosts?"

"Apparently both of us. Whose bright idea was it to come in here when the sun was setting?"

"I believe it was yours."

"Right, queen of bad ideas."

"Come on, Sorcha. We've only stepped a few feet into the castle."

"Now you want to explore," she grumbled and detached herself from him. "What are those shadows?"

"The glass."

She glanced up. The stained glass high above them revealed outlines, human and faerie in nature, created by smoke and black tar. "Strange."

"An intimidation tactic most Fae recognize."

"I didn't think the Seelie Fae would be all that interested in marring such beauty."

A shadow passed over his face, his blue eyes piercing her with their intensity. "That wasn't created by the Fae."

"The Fomorians then?"

"Likely."

He turned and marched through the hall as if he owned it. And in a way, he did. As a direct descendent of Nuada, he was the only person remaining who could claim this haunted place.

He always seemed to end up in forgotten places, she mused. Their feet left slashing marks against the dust ridden floor. Some of the large blue blooms picked up their heads as she walked past, tiny vines stretching for her.

"The plants don't do that with anyone else." Eamonn narrowed his eyes at the offending greenery.

"Sure they do. They just want attention."

"From you."

She picked her way over a tree which had fallen through the wall and landed atop a stairway leading up. "They don't do it to faeries?"

"No."

He paused in front of a plant that had grown so large it covered the entire wall. "Come here."

"I don't know if I want to. They seem more interested in me than the other plants."

"I want to try something."

"I don't."

"Sorcha," he growled.

She gritted her teeth and let him grab her hand. "What do you think will happen? They're just plants!"

"They aren't just plants. They're guards." He furrowed his brow in concentration, holding her hand just above the nearest hydrangea. "These flowers aren't native to the Otherworld, and yet, here they are."

"You think I have something to do with that?"

The plant reached out a thin vine and wrapped it around her finger. Smooth and warm, it slithered to her wrist, gently stroking the sensitive skin.

"I think there's something behind this wall of plants," he murmured.

"Why do you think that?"

"The stairs stop here."

"They also keep going behind us. This could just be a wall."

"You said you have druid blood. Ask the plants."

Sorcha rolled her eyes. "Ask the plants, he says. As if that's possible."

The vine tugged hard on her wrist. Eamonn caught hold of her hips and pulled her back against him, but the plant did not let go. Another vine lashed out and wrapped around the other arm, this one significantly thicker and stronger.

She stared in shock as the leaves parted and green eyes met her gaze. The rustling wind brushed past her ears, but she could not feel it.

"Eamonn?" she gasped. "There's another painting."

"I don't see anything, Sorcha."

"Please be another painting."

The eyes crinkled at the edges in a smile. She had time to let out a small whimper before the vines pulled her arm even harder. Eamonn's hands slipped, crystals digging into her soft skin before the plants enveloped her.

"Sorcha!"

She stumbled out to the other side of the plants, which placed tiny leaves against her bottom and pushed hard. Wildly, Sorcha spun in a circle, praying the opening would still be there. She wasn't fast enough and couldn't catch even a glimpse of Eamonn through the tightly wound plants.

The wall rippled, leaves twisting and turning, flowers pushing through to stare back at her. Unnerved, she glanced over her shoulder.

"The throne room," she said in awe.

What else would the flowers guard?

Roses crawled over the walls, sinking thorns into stones, red sap oozing down the cracks like blood. Threads hung from the ceiling — remnants of once grand curtains — each strand humming as her gaze passed over them.

"They're your ancestors." A voice drifted out of the darkness.

"Torin?"

"I never strayed far from your side, granddaughter."

He stepped out of the shadows, his staff thunking against the cracked stone floor. Robes hung from his broad shoulders and braids twisted through his long grey hair. He looked different here. Stronger and more confident.

"What is this place?" Sorcha asked.

"Our ancestral home."

"This is the castle of Nuada Silverhand. I have no claim here." She hoped. A small part of her clenched, hoping he wasn't about to tell her she was a descendant of the great Fae.

"That is where you are wrong. You have more claim than Nuada did when he entered this place."

Torin circled her, his staff echoing in the chamber. The roses turned with him, twisting and twirling in the air, following his every movement.

"This is a Seelie castle."

"It used to be, but it was Fomorian before that. And afterwards as well."

"How is that possible?" she asked. "The Fomorians and Fae have never lived side by side."

"They did here for many centuries."

Her eyes widened. "The Fomorians and Fae lived in harmony?"

"They did."

"But that's not possible. All the legends say the Fae and Fomorians hated each other."

"The legends were wrong. It was here our people first started."

"Are you claiming druids came from the Fomorians? I thought we had Fae blood."

"We didn't come from the Tuatha dé Danann." He stopped in front of her and smiled. "It is why we're connected to the land, to the sea, and to the sky. A faerie and a human can make a faerie or a human child. Fomorians and faeries made something else entirely."

"They made druids," she said in wonderment.

"Indeed."

"Why did you wait so long to tell me?"

"Would you have believed me?"

Sorcha tossed her arms out to the side in disbelief. "I'm having a hard time believing anything lately. Why am I here, Torin? I might suggest this was your plan all along."

"Yes, I wanted you to return to this castle."

"Why?"

"You should be with your family."

"My family is back home. I left them to come here, so you must give me a better reason than that."

He stepped back, gesturing at the roses which bent to his will. They slithered away from each other, scraping across the floors and walls until they revealed a giant stained glass window in the shape of a sun. It was so big she thought it would rival a tree. Six men's height, or taller, spindly pieces all fitting together to create a masterpiece of art.

Light splintered through the room, revealing two thrones at the center. One blackened by fire and jagged, the other covered in roses and thorns.

"What is this?"

"These are the thrones of our people. Many have sat upon them, Nuada, Balor, kings and priests. But it is not the first king who shaped our world." Torin walked towards the blackened throne, placing his hand upon a knife sharp point. "Nuada Silver-hand created an empire of Tuatha dé Danann. He fought, he battled, and he ruled as a good man." He placed his hand on the vines of the other. "Ethniu, his wife, was a Fomorian who gave up her world to be with him."

"Ethniu?"

"The daughter of Balor, king of the Fomorians. She left every-thing she knew because of her love for Nuada. And as his first wife, she gifted him children the like of which the world had never seen. Children who became the druids. She feared him, loved him, and sat upon this throne to spread goodness and light."

Sorcha swallowed. "This is too familiar to me, grandfather."

"As it should be. Time repeats itself over and over again. Stories, legends, myths, they're all happening even now as we speak."

"You want me to be queen," she blurted. "Queen of the druids."

"Queen of the Seelie Fae."

The words sounded ludicrous even to her own ears. Her? Queen? Of all people, Sorcha was the last person to ever desire a throne.

"I am not royalty," she argued. "I am a midwife, and I am happy as such."

"You searched your entire life for something more than squalling babies, screaming mothers, and a brothel."

"That doesn't mean I want to be a queen," she growled. "It's ridiculous to even consider the thought!"

"You would make a good queen for the Fae."

"He'll never ask." Her heart shattered into a million pieces, but she meant every word. "He will be the greatest king they have ever seen. He will take a Seelie faerie as a bride and forget all about me. I will help his people, I will guide his thoughts, but he will never make me queen."

"He already has. He's brought you before his people, made speeches with you by his side, planted his seed inside you. What more could you want?" Torin slapped both hands down on the thrones.

"The words," she said. "I want him to say it. I want him to ask me to be his queen. Otherwise, I'm forcing myself upon him."

"Sorcha. Do this for your people."

"Who are my people?" she cried out. "Please, tell me grandfa-ther. To whom should I show my allegiance? The human family who raised me as a child? The faeries who took me in and showed me kindness? Or the druids who appear in my life unexpectedly and ask for impossible things?"

"You go with your heart. I can read you like a book, child. You want to belong somewhere, and I tell you now, you belong with us."

The words soared through her veins and took root in her soul. "Us?"

"Did you think we left you? Or that we brought you to a place that was not as much yours as ours?"

People stepped out of the vines. Each flower, each leaf, each stalk revealing a soul hidden in the shadows.

"We've been waiting for you," Torin said with a smile. "Centuries have passed since the last druid walked these halls. And now, you can take the throne. Nuada is not your ancestor, Sorcha, he left his wife to the mercy of the wilds. But Ethniu with her gracious wisdom, and her kind heart, married another. You are her descendant."

"You want me to walk in her footsteps?"

"I want you to take up your blood right. This place, this castle, these people are all yours."

"They are his!" Her shout echoed and a few of the spirits blasted back.

The throne of Ethniu shivered. Leaves quaked and buds pushed forward to bloom into bright red roses.

Torin gestured towards the movement. "This place is no longer that of the Fae. It can be something far more than that, and you are the only one who can take this step. Join us, my sweet girl."

"What would a Queen look like?" she asked. "What kind of ruler would I be? All I can do is control them."

"What do you think he plans to do?"

"To help his people."

"With Nuada's blade? That sword controls all who stand within its path. He destroyed an entire army on his own because they stood still and let him cleave their heads from their shoulders."

She swallowed. So that was how he had won. All this time, she wondered just how far he would go to gain back his throne.

Now she knew.

"The queen tempers the Seelie King," she repeated the words Oona had told her so long ago.

"She always has. But now is not the time for a tempered queen. Now, when the worlds are shifting and time is unraveling, we need a Queen who will speak for us *all*." Torin stepped forward and held out his hand. "Speak for the druids, for your people. For those who have a right to the Otherworld just as much as the Fae."

Sorcha stared into his eyes, wondering just how much of this was truth. He might be her blood, but she didn't believe for a second he wouldn't lie to her.

Torin had his own agenda. His words tasted bitter and dangerous. Would she go against Eamonn by taking her grandfather's hand?

He smiled. "I'm not trying to trick you, Sorcha. Few druids draw breath, and I would not see our people die out."

Something wasn't right. Brows furrowed, she reached for his hand and watched as hers passed through it. "You aren't real."

"I am real to you, to our people."

"But you aren't here."

"Didn't they tell you the castle was haunted?" The corners of his eyes wrinkled. "Druids are connected to the earth, tethered by their souls. We are not quick to fade from this realm."

"So you are all..." She looked around, catching the gaze of each druid lingering by the ivy. "You're all dead."

"Yes."

"Your souls are in the plants."

"And the dust, the glass, the mortar of this castle."

Sorcha's eyes filled with tears as she realized the magnitude of this decision. These weren't just trapped souls, they were her family.

"If I do this, will you be released?"

"No," Torin shook his head. "That is not what we want. We

want to be here, with you, and give meaning to all the sacrifices we've made."

Sorcha lifted a hand and pressed it to her heart. The shifting spirits blinked in and out of existence. Torin wavered in front of her and the throne glowed. "None of this is real, is it?"

A few of the spirits spoke, their words like the rustling of reeds in fall.

"This is very real."

"No it isn't. This is the same as the altar, as the snake, as everything else you've shown me."

Spirits sank back into the greenery at her words. Torin's teeth flashed bright in the white of his beard. "You have never ceased to impress me, granddaughter, but in this you are wrong. The altar was real. This is real. Whether or not what you see is physical, does not make it any less important."

"Then if I take the throne?"

"You do so in the physical world as well."

She blew out a breath and weighed her options. Queen was a heavy title to bear, and not one she'd ever intended to have. She hadn't considered what a relationship with Eamonn would turn into, hadn't wanted to. His choices were his own, and she couldn't control him.

Sand tipped through the hourglass of her mind and she saw their time together dim.

Torin placed a hand back on the throne. "What kind of king will he be without you?"

"A better one."

"Do you believe that?"

She didn't. She had already seen what he could do, had heard of his battles, and seen the mark of each sword slash upon his skin.

Sighing, Sorcha picked up her skirts and walked towards the throne. "I never thought I would agree to be queen with a dirty hem."

"I wouldn't expect anything less from you." The cold touch of his hand passed over her forehead. "But there is far more symbolic regalia for you to wear."

Magic shimmered down her body like a cold splash of water. Gasping, she looked down to see her dress had disappeared.

Thick green wool swayed around her hips with golden threads embroidered in the shape of leaves falling to the ground. A leather corset hugged her ribs, ending just below her breasts. The long sleeves of the green underdress hooked around her middle finger, triangles of fabric leaving her hands warm and green.

A magnificent silver fur covered her shoulders, soft and infinitely warm. She tossed her head, red curls falling freely to her waist.

Arching a brow, she looked up at her grandfather. "Furs and wool?"

"The regalia of our people."

Thank the gods he hadn't put her in a faerie outfit. She turned with a sigh. All the other druid souls watched her, their faces painted blue and their eyes hopeful.

What was she getting herself into?

"You walk in the footsteps of Ethniu," Torin said. "This throne does not make you a Queen, but your actions from here on out. Do you accept this title?"

"I do."

She lowered herself onto the throne with a troubled mind. Was she ready for this? Sorcha could say with near certainty she wasn't. Responsibilities already weighed heavy upon her mind. And now she had even more people to take care of.

A great cheer lifted in the throne room, but she hardly heard it. Vines closed over her wrists, thorns dug into the sensitive skin of her biceps.

"Torin?" she called out. "What's happening?"

"Now, we test your lover."

"What? No! Stop!"

Leaves stuffed into her mouth and roses bloomed over her eyes. She pulled against her bindings, flexing her arms and wiggling her legs until thorns dug into her skin. Blood slicked across her biceps as the vines tightened and pinned her down.

"Eamonn!"

⚬⚬⚬

"SORCHA!"

The vines dragged her through the wall and he could do nothing about it. Her warmth still heated his palms.

He growled, lifted his blade, and hacked at the green leaves. They did not move, nor did they break as the sharpened metal slid across them

"Magic," he spat. "Where have you taken her?"

No one responded. Instead, the leaves bounced as if someone behind them chuckled. Tilting his head back, Eamonn roared as fury turned his blood to fire. How dare they? Ghosts with no form had no right to still be on this land, let alone steal what was his.

He clenched his fists and stilled his breathing. There had to be some sound, some hidden chink in the armor of this place. No faerie had ever built a castle without leaving secrets behind.

The plants snapped vines at him, each thorn dripping green poison. He jerked backwards, holding his blade up as a shield. They left a slick, shiny residue on the Sword of Light. Disgusted, he slid it back into its sheath.

He would have to find another way. He turned and ran his hands over the walls. If it were his castle, he would have put some kind of stone that would shift, opening a door or secret chamber. No magic was completely controllable. Faeries always had an escape plan.

Giggles erupted behind him.

Eamonn froze, hand immediately reaching for his blade. "Where is she?"

"Here."

"She's not here."

"Then she's there."

He turned on his heel. The space behind him was empty other than the shadows which danced upon the walls. Eamonn's lip curled. "Unseelie. Show yourself."

"No."

The Sword of Light sang as he pulled it free again. Its sharp edge glinted as he raised it over his head and pointed directly at the shadows. "I command you to answer me."

The giggles grew louder and one of the shadows pulled off the others. It was human in shape, but he knew how deceptive these creatures could be. When it noticed his gaze, the shadow waved.

"No."

"I command you."

"Oh how lovely. He knows how to use a sword." The shadow twisted into a plant which shook in laughter. "Shame he doesn't know how to deal with ghosts. Turn around."

He spun. There was no longer a wall behind him, but a moor filled with fog and will-o'-the-wisps.

"What trickery is this?"

"Welcome home, brother," a masculine voice spoke in his ear. "Just how long did you think you could avoid me?"

Eamonn twisted, slashing his sword through the air. It passed through Fionn's throat without leaving a single mark.

He narrowed his eyes. "Are you some kind of mirage?"

"Oh, much worse than that."

There was something wrong with Fionn's eyes. Eamonn had seen anger, madness, and fear reflected in those eyes that were eerily similar to his own, but he had never seen such glee.

"You thought you would come here and....what? Take a new throne? Eamonn." Fionn tsked. "That is so petty. What's wrong with mine?"

"I have battled you for five years."

"And you want me to believe you're finished?" Fionn's hair slid over his shoulder, a graceful waterfall of movement and gold. "That's quaint. I know you aren't done. So what are you really up to?"

"Our people have bled long enough."

"That's not why, either," his twin snarled. Leaping forward, Fionn blasted through Eamonn's form in a shower of icy pain. "What are you doing here?"

"I've told you already," Eamonn stumbled to the side and stuck the tip of his sword against the ground. What had Fionn done to him?

"You're still hiding the truth. Half-truths, brother, only succeed in making us both angry."

"I am not angry."

"But you will be." Fionn reached for him, fingers curling in the air just before he touched Eamonn's face. "You and I were close once. As only twins could be. What did you do to us?"

"You know this was not my choice."

"Wasn't it? You were always the favored son, the firstborn. While you were out battling, and killing, and maiming our allies, I was fixing all the bridges you burned along the way," Fionn snarled. "Tell me again, brother, how this was not your doing."

Eamonn's palms slicked with sweat and the pommel of the Sword of Light slipped in his grasp. He didn't have a response to his brother's accusations. They were all true. Eamonn had filled his youth with poor decisions and war. Fionn had spent his learning how to be king, and filling his head with old, outdated prejudices.

"We're both at fault, are we not?" Eamonn finally asked. "I was a poor brother, but you were the one who stabbed me in the back and let me hang."

Fionn rolled his eyes. "We're going back to the 'poor pitiful Eamonn' card again?" He disappeared, reappearing directly behind Eamonn. "You deserved to hang."

"I did nothing wrong."

"You are not fit to be part of this family. Monster."

"I am a good man. I have always been a good man, and I will not allow you to take advantage of our people any longer."

"If you want it that bad, take it." Fionn's hand lifted over

Eamonn's shoulder and pointed towards a jagged throne. "Take your new throne, become king of the weak and foolish."

And there it was. The throne of Nuada, blackened by years of warfare. The metal tips curved and split away, sharp enough to slice the throat of anyone who got too close.

It was perfect for Eamonn. That throne had been through more than Fionn could even imagine, more than Eamonn had suffered.

He felt the imprint of his brother's hands upon his shoulders for a brief second before he disappeared. Eamonn glanced once over his shoulder. Mist and fog obscured any shape from his vision. Shivers danced down his spine as he felt the gaze of someone, or something, watching him.

Should he take the throne? In this place, he wasn't sure what would happen.

He worried that he would become someone else. Someone darker, more dangerous, closer to his kin than he wished to be.

His boots struck the ground, solid and comforting in the weightlessness of the bog. The throne was his birthright, and the symbol of everything he had fought for his entire life. He would take it, no matter the cost.

But, as he expected, the spirits were not done with him yet.

The instant his foot touched the first step to the throne, a soft voice echoed behind him. "Eamonn?"

"No," he groaned. "Not that. Anything but that."

"My son?" Queen Neve, the most beautiful Seelie faerie to ever exist, walked out of the mist. He stared at her, pain splintering through his chest as if someone had run a sword through his heart. "My beloved boy."

"Please don't do this," he moaned.

"What are you doing in this place, my shield?"

The childhood nickname made him squeeze his eyes shut. "You aren't real. You aren't here with me now."

"Eamonn, of course I am." He flinched as her hands touched

his cheeks, gently tracing the outlines of wounds that had smoothed with age. "What have they done to you?"

Though he knew it was a trap, his resolve shattered. With a ragged sound, he folded around his mother and drew her into his arms. She was so small, so delicate, in his strong grasp. He worried he might break her.

"My shield," she said as she stroked his hair. "Hush now, Eamonn. I am here."

"This is impossible, Mathair. You cannot be here in this twisted place."

"I came as soon as I felt your presence. What are you doing here?" She pulled back to stare up at his face, and something inside him healed when she did not flinch away.

"Fionn must be stopped, Mathair."

"Your brother is doing his best. It is all we can ask of him."

"His best is not enough."

"So you come here? Of all places?" Neve looked around, worry lines forming between her eyes. "I never understood your obsession with your grandfather. He and I never got along."

He remembered. Their arguments were quiet, as his mother had always been, but powerful enough to push everyone from the room. She had kindness bred into her, but she was one of the Tuatha dé Danann who supported the old ways.

"My grandfather was a good man and brought about much change for our people."

"Until we removed him from the throne," she replied. "Eamonn, don't do this."

"I must."

"If you take this throne, how long do you think you will stay upon it? You will show our people it is possible to dethrone a king. They will do it over and over again until the Otherworld is reduced to ruin. Let things stay as they are. It is safer that way."

Eamonn's lips twisted to the side. She had said the same things to him long ago before his twin had carved the future into Eamonn's flesh.

Her hands upon his jaw turned him back towards her. He drowned in her pity, in the sadness of her eyes. "My son. Do not sit upon that sullied throne."

Every word she said cut him to the bone. He pulled her close and pressed his lips against her forehead. Squeezing his eyes shut, he said against her, "I love you so much. Memories of you kept me alive for so long after I was banished. I remembered you brushing my hair as a child, singing lullabies, whispering stories in the dark after father had grown angry. I wish I could tell you all this in person."

"You are."

"You aren't really here." He squeezed her. "But whoever you are, you will need to do a lot better than this."

His mother dissolved into thin air.

Eamonn ground his teeth together and spun in a circle. Spreading his arms wide he called out, "What else? What further evil do you have planned?"

Fingernails clicked as they wrapped around a spike of the dark throne. Ready to pull his blade, to run it through whatever phantom they called upon, he turned on his heel with a snarl.

He fell silent as Sorcha stepped around the throne.

They had clothed her as a princess of his people. Fine feathers slid across her curves, each dipped in gold and carefully sewn into the dress. Flakes of gold stuck to her fingers, tangled in her hair like stars, and dotted across her shoulders.

She was so beautiful.

His expression crumbled, and he twisted away from her. This was worse than his mother, worse than this twin. These spirits had no right to twist her form like this.

"Eamonn?" Sorcha asked. "Why do you turn from me?"

"You are not Sorcha."

"Is this not to your liking? This is the form you desire most, is it not?"

He almost groaned. Her hands stroked his biceps, circling him until she stared up at his face. This was a truly talented trickster. She looked exactly the same.

"Eamonn," she tilted her head to the side. "Kiss me."

"No."

"Do you no longer want me?"

"You know that would be impossible."

"Then why won't you kiss me?"

"Stop this." His voice was little more than a croak. "Why must you torment me?"

Her hands smoothed over his chest, dipping into the crevices and circling the numerous wounds. "Sometimes tormenting is fun. Come with me, my love, let me show you."

Her love. He bared his teeth in a grimace. "You aren't playing fair."

"I never said I would." She looped an arm over his neck and pulled him down. "Come, my love, my life, come with me from this awful place."

"You are not my Sorcha."

She couldn't be. Every person so far had not been the person he expected them to be. Why his mother and Sorcha were solid, he did not understand. But he knew this stunning phantom was not the woman his heart beat for.

"Let go of me," he growled.

"Why? Don't you want me?"

"Where is she?"

"Who?" Sorcha tilted her head to the side. "Don't you mean me?"

"You are not Sorcha."

"I could be, if you wanted. I would grovel at your feet, press kisses against your lips and worship the ground you walk upon."

"That is not what I want."

"Isn't it? Why else would you choose a human woman? If you wanted an equal, you would have chosen a faerie." She tsked and stepped back, smoothing her hands down her chest and stomach. "You wanted a druid, a forbidden creature to taste and sample until

Sorcha grew old and frail. Leave the weak girl behind, Eamonn. Take me instead."

"Never."

"Why not?"

"She is not a weak woman, nor is she less because she is druid," he snarled. "Her name on your lips is blasphemy."

"You claim to care for her?"

"Her bravery, courage, and unwavering loyalty to my people captured my heart from the moment she first washed up on Hybrasil."

"Prove it. Prove that you care for her, more than anything else."

"How?" He would do it. He wouldn't hesitate to prove that she was the reason he drew breath.

"Choose." She lifted a hand and pointed towards the throne. "Which future do you want, Eamonn?"

Another throne appeared next to his. Tangled vines and thorns stuck out in all directions from the roses blooming, but it was the shape that held his attention. Red hair peeked through the gaps of greenery, streaked with blood and sap.

A choked sound slipped off his tongue. He stumbled forward, but hesitated when he remembered that everything had been an illusion thus far. "Is it really her?"

"Of all the things you've seen, that is the only truth." The other Sorcha leaned against his side. "You have two futures before you. One as king, seated upon your throne knowing she is safe and sound. Beside you, yes, but also kept safe from all you fear. The other future is that she is free to wander on her own."

"Why wouldn't I choose the second?"

"You can't control her if she wanders free. Sorcha will continue to grow into her own power, finding her history, her family, her culture. Everything you love may change and grow into something else." She traced a circle on his chest. "Just how much do you want to ensure your future, High King?"

To be certain she was safe would be a pleasure he had never

considered. Consorts of kings had suffered worse, at least she would be alive.

"Can she see?" he asked, voice cracking.

"No. She is awake, but not. Dreaming without sight, sound, or touch."

"So she isn't really alive under all that."

"An offer for you, Eamonn of the Seelie Court. If you leave her here, she will join with the rest of her ancestors. She will live among the roses for all eternity at your side."

For all eternity, the words echoed over and over again. She wouldn't die. He wouldn't have to watch her grow old, crumbling to dust in his hands. Centuries of loneliness spread out ahead of him without her. He could keep her safe and preserved.

But it wasn't his choice. She was a fiercely independent woman and Eamonn had no right to make these decisions for her. He could only keep her safe for so long.

"No," he said, shaking his head. "She is not mine. She is her own being and I will not take that from her."

The Sorcha beside him flashed a feral grin. "Then go to her, High King. Free your bride and remember that we told you not to take this throne."

"Why?"

The thing burst into shadows and rushed away, giggling so loud that the halls echoed with its screeches.

Halls.

Mist and fog disappeared. Eamonn stood in the same place he had when Sorcha disappeared through the wall.

He spun to the wall of roses, seeing only an open space where the plants had once stood. Charging through, he rushed into the throne room with the giant glass sun while shouting, "Sorcha!"

Two thrones stood at the end of the hall. One black, the other covered in red roses. She sat upon the queen's throne, bound into place by the very beauty that set her apart.

He blew out a horrified breath and ran to her. His eyes did not stray to Nuada's throne, to his birthright, to anything other than her.

She needed him.

Falling to his knees, he ripped at the thorns that tore his flesh. Crystals flashed into view, peeking through tiny holes in his hands. The fine bones of his wrists creaked with stone that sent shivers of magic pulsing through his veins.

"Hold on," he growled as he pulled at the plants. "I'm here, Sorcha. I'm here."

The sound of her exhalation was music to his ears. He yanked her hands free and pressed them against his face.

"Can you hear me?" he asked.

She did not respond.

Frantic, he stood and ripped vines away from her head. The flowers shrieked as they pulled away. There were leaves in her mouth, he realized.

He scooped his fingers between her lips, pulling handfuls of plants out. Over and over again, he yanked leaves and vines away until she let out a moan and then gasped.

"Eamonn!" she cried out.

"I'm here," he pulled her out of the throne and wrapped his arms around her. His soul settled, peace finally easing the tension in his neck. "I'm here, mo chroí. I am so sorry."

"This was not your fault," she coughed as she spoke. "This was mine."

"Do not blame yourself."

"I should never have brought us here. You were right, this is a dangerous place."

"We will find another castle." He pressed his lips against her forehead and tightened his hold. He had almost lost her. Again. "We will leave this cursed place and never return.

"I cannot."

"We can, Sorcha. This is not the only option for us."

"I cannot, Eamonn!" She pulled away, her green eyes dark and haunted. "This castle echoes with the souls of my people. Druids, like me. I told them I would stay, I took the throne."

"You did what?"

He stumbled backwards, looking at her as if he had never seen her before. He had fought against the demons of his past, denied his birthright, and she had taken the throne?

"Why are you looking at me like that?" she asked. "Eamonn?"

"They told me not to take the throne."

"Who?"

"Your people."

She licked her lips. "These are the thrones of Nuada and Ethniu. They wish us to walk in their footsteps, following the path they carved together."

"Does that future not belong to me as well?"

"It was a test," she said. Her eyes were as large as the moon. "They were testing you, Eamonn."

"And what was the test?"

She believed the words she said. He could see the truth in her eyes and taste it on the air. But what could such a test prove? That he had a weakness?

Another voice joined them, deep and unfamiliar. "A test you passed, my boy."

The man was old. He wore a wrap of fur and balanced upon a cane, but Eamonn was certain the ancient exterior hid powerful magic.

"Did I?" Eamonn asked. "And what was the test?"

"That you would take care of my granddaughter."

"Granddaughter?" Eamonn looked from Sorcha to the new man. "I see no family resemblance."

"Then you are far less capable than I thought you to be. She is mine, and if you wish to take her, then I needed reassurance you would treat her well."

"Have I not thus far?"

"You have ignored her. You have fostered a fear of her own magic and controlled your people while not listening to her words.

You are a Tuatha dé Danann. You must excuse me, High King, but I do not trust you."

Other words echoed underneath the deep tones. Suggestions of punishment should Eamonn make a mistake. But something else as well. Something older, and so powerful that it resonated in his tones.

Eamonn narrowed his eyes. "Just how old are you, grandfather?"

"Old enough to know when a boy is trying to back me into a corner."

Sorcha reached out and touched Eamonn's arm. "His name is Torin."

"This is the druid who found you in the glade?"

"I am," Torin replied.

"You are not what you appear."

Eamonn pulled Sorcha into his arms, tucking her behind his broad back as he pieced the stories together. "How many generations have passed since you were her grandfather?"

"Seven."

Although surprised Torin would respond so easily, Eamonn recognized the game. "You said you were a druid?"

"Yes."

"Were you something else before?"

"Yes."

Sorcha pulled against his arm. "What are you doing, Eamonn? He's my family!"

"That is Ethniu's throne behind you, is it not?"

Torin lifted a brow and placed a hand upon the back. The roses twined around his wrist as he nodded. "It is."

"And you sat upon that throne yourself, didn't you?"

"Clever boy," the ancient man chuckled. "Take care of her."

A blast of air pushed them back as Torin disappeared from the room. The thrones remained, symbolic but still pulsing with power.

"You know who he is," Sorcha exclaimed.

"I do."

"Who?"

"Ethniu's father, King Balor."

"I thought he was dead?"

"We all think the ancient ones are dead, but they exist in some manner." Eamonn glanced down at her, brows furrowed in worry. "You are King Balor's granddaughter?"

"And you are Nuada's grandson."

He had grown up with the legends of Balor, the Fomorian god. His third eye would open and cast destruction wherever it looked. He had been the only one capable of defeating the original Tuatha dé Danann on the battlefield. A great king, a horrible enemy, and the father of the druid race.

And now, he looked upon the fearsome creature's granddaughter with new eyes.

"Do you fear me now?" she asked. "I did not know who I was."

"No, mo chroí. I am in awe of you."

"Good. I would not want you to see me differently because of this."

"Come here." He yanked her forward and pressed his lips against hers. "We will weather this storm, as we have all others."

"Is this a storm? Who my family is?"

"It is a sign. We bring together families, people, races that have never existed side by side before. We are the beginning of a new age, Sorcha. Together."

He swept her into his arms and carried her from the haunted place. Spirits fled from his shadow as he brought them into the light. And in that moment Eamonn made a vow to himself that he would protect her from everything.

Even herself.

The Sword Of Light

Faeries filled the banquet hall, their laughter and joyous shouts echoing from the rafters. They had made it to the castle. A new home, a new future, and the promises of new hope.

Rows lined the hall, each sturdy table filled to the brim with whatever food they could scavenge. Oona was in her element, bustling to each person who lifted their empty goblets, asking for more drink.

The wine cellar was still full. The dwarves had returned with their arms full of elixir, chortling at their find.

After all they had been through, Sorcha thought they deserved a few nights of merriment.

She sat with the others of her new family. Pooka leaned over the table and reached for bread, his hands already sticky with honey.

A dwarf passed by and handed off a cup to Cian. "It's not the usual."

Cian grinned and downed whatever the new drink was. "My thanks!"

The merriment was contagious. She could hardly hear a word

over the din, and loved every second. How could she not? These were her people, and they were so happy after their struggles.

She ducked as a chicken flew by, its feathers bursting into the air. Oona waved her hands and raced after it. The clucking squawks only added to the laughter.

There were many colors, people, and vibrant sounds. She hadn't seen such a gathering since the Samhain festival. Sorcha leaned her elbow against the table and watched their antics with a grin.

The door to the banquet hall slammed open and silence rang louder than the laughter. A cup dropped to the floor, shattering with a crash.

Shadows crawled in from the hall. The candles beyond had long since burned down to their bases, blinking out any light which might have shown.

She recognized the silhouetted figure. Eamonn, their fearless leader who had brought them all this way. Sorcha wondered where he had stolen off to.

It was difficult for him to be here when there was so much merriment. His thoughts grew clouded, responsibilities, family, and centuries of solitude distracting his mind.

The faeries were silent. They did not cheer for him, nor did they stand. They seemed to be holding their breath.

Sorcha waited until she could no longer stand it. He stood in the doorway with his hands loose at his sides, conflicted and incapable of movement. She would not stand by while his own people rejected him.

She stood and passed each of the faeries who acted as if they were stuck to their benches. Her footsteps were soft, but they seemed loud to her ears. Each step was a choice. A confirmation that he was hers, and she was his.

She held out her hand for him to take. "Welcome, king."

The shadows obscured his relieved expression from the others, but she could see it bright as day. "Good evening, Sunshine."

"Have you come to join us?"

"If I am welcome."

"You are always welcome among your people."

He took her hand and pulled her closer. The shadows enveloped her, along with his strong arms. "Are you so certain of that?"

"Come and eat with them and we shall find out."

The crystals at his throat bobbed as he swallowed hard. "I have no wish to ruin their dinner."

"You never did while we traveled."

"A general is something entirely different than a king. They should be afraid of me on the battlefield, and they will take orders from anyone who will bark at them. But now? This is different."

"How so?"

Eamonn squeezed his eyes shut. "They want a man, now. A king who can sit at the table and be regal. The king who inspires courage and honor, settles the worried mother and calms the wounded soldier. I am not that man."

"That is not who they expect you to be." She reached up and stroked his cheek. "They know who you are, Eamonn, that is why they follow you. If they wanted a king to sit at a table and look nice, then they would pledge their allegiance to Fionn."

"They are here."

"Exactly. They don't want you to change! So come eat with us, drink with your men, and tease your women. They are your people, now. Not his."

The tension eased from his shoulders and his expression softened. "Lead the way, my queen."

Shivers danced down her spine. His queen. Did she want to be? His yes, but all the others?

She wasn't so sure.

Sorcha tangled her fingers with his and drew him into the banquet hall. The dwarves watched with wide eyes as the dangerous warlord who had led them through battle calmed at the touch of a druid woman.

Sharp eyes caught the moment when Eamonn reached out and

hooked a finger through one of her curls. The long length swayed at her waist, and coiled around his finger as if it knew he needed its strength.

They made their way to one of the remaining tables where only a few sat.

Eamonn tugged on her hand, "Why here?"

"Let them come to you," she said as she sat down. He let her draw him to her side.

"Will they?"

"I watched a master horseman break a stallion once. It had spent its entire life wild and free, but this man never gave up. He sat in the pen with the horse for hours upon hours so it would grow used to his presence. No whips, no shouting words, no ropes to ensnare it. The horse grew to love him merely because he was there."

"You think the dwarves are like horses?"

"I hope they are," she said with a soft smile. "It's how I'm hoping they will come to like me."

"Then let us both eat our meals and perhaps they will join us."

He leaned forward, piled food on his plate, and tucked in. Eamonn did not look at the others, nor did he waste any time waiting for them.

As if he felt the weight of her stare, he looked up at her. Mouth full, he paused. "Everything all right?"

"Yes."

"You sure?"

"I am."

He gestured at her plate. "Are you eating?"

"I've already eaten a little, but I'll pick at this."

"And it's to your liking?"

"Yes."

She had missed this, Sorcha realized. Eating with him, talking to him. The mundane things that meant so much.

He saw the change in her eyes. The softness that seeped through from her soul into her eyes. Eamonn reached out and took her hand, his thumb smoothing over her knuckles. "I missed you, too."

Warmth sparkled through her veins like falling stars. She sighed and squeezed his fingers, words impossible to find.

Oona bustled towards them and slumped down onto a bench with a huffed sigh. "My goodness! I didn't think it was possible for faeries to drink so much!"

"They're dwarves, Oona," Eamonn said with a chuckle.

"And they need to worry about their addiction!"

"They deserve to have some revelry after all the fighting."

"That they do." Oona pulled her skirts up and swung her legs underneath the table. There were so many layers of skirts, Sorcha couldn't decipher where they stopped and the faerie started. "Are we to be staying here then?"

"I don't see why not," Eamonn said. He shoveled more food into his mouth and gave Sorcha a look that suggested she continue the conversation without him.

"It needs a little bit of love," she rushed to fill in. "But I think it has the possibility of being a home for us all."

"The dwarves included?"

"Of course," Sorcha moved the food on her plate around in a circle. "I think they'll be useful in the coming months. I cannot imagine sending them away."

"Sending them home, you mean."

"I'd rather call their families here." The idea had seemed impossible as it left her lips, but Sorcha saw the merit of it. Bringing women and children here would only make it more of a home.

There would be maids to help with the cleaning, children to help with the farming. Eamonn looked up at her, a question in his eyes.

"Families?" Oona asked.

"Yes. Spread the word that the dwarves are welcome to bring their people here. The intent of this castle was to create a stronghold for those who stand against Fionn. That means making it a haven for all, not just soldiers."

"Can we support that many people?" Eamonn asked.

Cian lumbered over, his bulk pushing aside a few dwarves who had stood. "That we can. The gardens are wild after so many years untended, but they're still producing enough to feed many. We've got quite a few hunters here, and even more who'd like to learn."

"And bedding?" Sorcha leaned forward, excitement rushing her words. "We have to put them somewhere. I know the castle needs a lot of work, but what about the surrounding buildings?"

"I can send a few people out to check on them tomorrow," Oona said. "There's a few women interested in cleaning the place up. The outbuildings are in better shape than the castle."

"Then this is possible?" Eamonn glanced at the three of them. "Are we prepared to add another potential hundred mouths to feed?"

"Hundred?" Sorcha laughed. "Eamonn, your army is easily over two hundred men and women. Their families are likely an additional three people, if not more than that. We're considering many more than a hundred people."

His stunned expression made her grin. Sorcha reached out, pressed a palm against his cheek, and chuckled. "When you started this journey, you knew you would become a king."

"I did not think that would include so many people."

"You're planning to rule all of Seelie. Starting with a small empire is not a bad thing."

"Empire," he repeated and shook his head. "What have you gotten me into?"

"Exactly what you wanted." She looked over at Oona and Cian. "Is this something we can start soon?"

"Yes."

"Do you think the dwarves will be interested?" Her worries dug at her hope with sharp claws. "I know there is always a concern about bringing family to war, but I would like to make this place more than just a place to feed an army."

"I think the dwarves miss their families just as much as we would," Oona replied. "They will be happy to have their spouses and children at their sides."

Sorcha thought about children running through the halls of this haunted place. She glanced around and saw all the cracks where plants grew and the shards of glass that littered the ground.

It was not a safe place yet, but it would be. This castle would shine before she would let any children wander around. She imagined maids rushing through the banquet hall with brooms and washcloths. Men with large beams on their back walking amongst them, ready to fix broken walls and cracked floors.

This castle had been a home to her ancestors once, and now she would make it a home for her people again. She wanted to hear the rooms filled with laughter, the kitchens filled with the aroma of cooking food, and the grounds brimming with marketplaces.

They could do it. This was just the first step.

"Let us begin then," she said. "Oona, Cian, spread the word amongst the dwarves we are making this castle our own. Bring their families and all those who wish to work for their keep."

She met Eamonn's gaze and blushed at the awe she saw in his eyes. She reached out and took his hand.

"Are you ready for this?" he asked her.

"Absolutely. It's time to make this place our home."

৩৯৩

SORCHA LOVED WATCHING THE DWARVES SING STONES TO LIFE. They lifted their hands in song, palms raised to the sky, and let their voices fly free. The land listened to them, as she had never understood before.

Boulders shifted, rolling gently into place. Carefully carved statues pieced themselves back together and sealed old wounds with quiet grumbles. Brick and mortar rose into the air and glided back into their places.

She had explored as much as she dared. There was something sinister about this place, far more than Hy-brasil had ever been.

Sorcha worried all the rooms would be dangerous until she found a hidden corridor and a quiet place. The plants didn't move when she walked by, the stained glass windows were still intact, and moss covered the cold ground. Sorcha enjoyed the cushion against her weary feet.

She worked with the others when she could. She gained peace from helping, even though the dwarves were loath to let her anywhere near them. The tiny bearded woman who'd first spoken to Sorcha was not the only one who held prejudice in her heart for the druids.

The giant window let her watch them without interfering with their work. They would likely stop if she stepped outside, similar to how the other faeries had reacted to her presence.

Now, she knew how to coax them into liking her.

"I thought I might find you here."

She smiled. Eamonn always knew where to find her, no matter how she tried to hide from him.

His arms wrapped around her shoulders, pulling her back against his warm skin. She brushed her fingers over his forearm. The smooth crystals were not the same as she remembered from so long ago. She found herself touching him more now, familiarizing herself with this new version.

"Did you sleep well?" she asked.

"Better if I had woken up with you beside me." He planted a kiss on top of her head. "Why are you not in bed?"

"I wanted to watch them."

"You enjoy the dwarven songs?" He snorted. "It is early for them to be up."

"I think they want to finish as soon as possible. The rains have slowed them far more than they wish."

She let her head tilt to the side as his fingers tangled in the curls above her ear. He frequently pulled on the coils, letting them bounce back into place before doing it again.

She thought he enjoyed seeing something so vibrant in his life.

Blue light splashed over his forearm, the stained glass window giving new colors and life to all the light touched.

"Come back to bed," he said with a chuckle.

"We have much to do today."

"We?"

"Oona has asked me to help clean out the kitchens."

"You are the lady of this castle. You don't need to clean."

"I want to," she said. Spinning in the circle of his arms, she planted her hands against his chest. "It's important for me to be useful, Eamonn."

"I will never turn you into a royal, will I?"

"Why would you want to?" She smiled up at him, stretching for the kiss she knew he would give her. "I'm just fine the way I am."

"Fine isn't the word I would use," he said, pressing a kiss against her forehead.

"No? Then how you would describe me, High King?"

"Well," his lips feathered over her cheek, moving over her nose to the other. "Exquisite. Thoughtful. Kind."

He tilted her chin with gentle fingers, pressing a chaste kiss against her lips.

"Those are good words."

"There are not enough in the world to accurately describe you, mo chroí."

"Your nobility is showing," she replied, playfully tugging on his ear. "When you speak like that I can see the king in you."

"Only then?"

Sorcha rolled her eyes and pulled away. "What would I know? I've never met a king before you!"

"You've met my brother."

"Are we calling him a king now? I was unaware."

"Sorcha," he growled. "Come back here."

"I'd rather not."

"Now."

A delightful shiver ran down her spine. She loved it when his voice took on that hard edge. The grating sound that suggested he was a hair's breadth from losing control.

She bit her lip and shook her head.

The crystals in his throat glowed a mere moment before he lunged forward. She let out a happy shriek and leapt over the bench behind her. Skirts tangled in her legs, the distraction giving him just enough time to reach out and snag the back of her dress.

He tugged, a warning he had caught her, and then let her go. He wanted the chase, her warrior king.

Spinning, she held her hands loose at her sides and darted her gaze around the room.

"Are you looking for an escape?" he growled. "There is none."

"There's a particularly strong looking vine behind you."

"You plan to climb it?"

"I plan to tangle you in it. That will give me enough time to slip out the door and find a far more suitable place to set up camp."

"High ground," he advised. "If you're battling an opposing army, you always want the high ground."

"The towers then."

"And then what? Do you face me and fight?"

"No," she muttered as she looked around for a better escape. "You are much larger than me, so I do not face you. I look for anything I might throw or distract you with."

"While?"

"While shouting for someone who is more skilled with a blade to come and help. They will arrive from behind if we are on the tower stairs, and then we will flank the enemy."

"Good," Eamonn nodded. "Now come here."

Sorcha stooped and upturned the nearest bench. It crashed against the floor and gave her enough time to sprint past him.

But he was no green warrior, and she was an untrained human. He snagged her arm, spun them so he wouldn't hurt her, and lifted her up into the air.

"I have taught you well," he said as he pressed his lips against her collarbone.

"That was the point, wasn't it?"

"You're a quick study."

"I have a good teacher."

She brushed his hair back from his face, smiling down at him. Her heart was light in moments like this. When a smile crinkled the edges of his eyes, and his lips twisted with no sarcasm. He truly was a handsome man when he wasn't so severe.

His expression fell. "I have to go."

"Go? Are there more buildings to plan?"

"I have to leave the castle grounds."

"What?" She shook her head in confusion. "Why?"

"Our city is growing, and there are many more mouths to feed. I am taking a small battalion to hunt."

He let her slide down his body. Each inch scraped over grooves underneath his clothing she had not noticed. Armor.

"Eamonn," she grumbled. "I thought we agreed you wouldn't fight anymore."

"I am not looking for a battle. Even you cannot disagree that there are many more people to feed."

She sighed. This was an argument she knew well, and she understood why he was so antsy. Eamonn was a man of action. The many years on Hy-brasil hadn't helped that. Now that he was home, he wanted to do everything he could to help his people.

It was grating on her nerves.

"We should focus on bringing more people here. You can turn the Seelie Fae away from your brother without bloodshed. Force his army to see you are the better king. The one who will take care of them, their families, their livelihoods. You don't have to do that by spilling more blood upon the ground."

"I'm not going to," he said with a chuckle. His finger slid underneath her chin, tilting her gaze to his. "I am getting food, so we might bring even more people to this castle. I'd like to see more Fae than dwarves."

"You won't fight?"

"I will not look for a fight with Fionn."

She searched his eyes for the truth. There was something off-putting about the way he spoke. As if he was hiding something.

Faeries couldn't lie. She had to trust he wasn't twisting his words, and he'd given her no reason to feel wary.

A slow smile spread across her face. "I rather like the dwarves."

"No you don't."

"I do! They're steadfast and hard workers. That's something rather difficult to find these days."

"They ignore you."

"So did the other faeries," she said with a shrug. "There's nothing I can do about that. They don't trust me. Yet. I'm working on it."

"I have no doubt they will fall in love with you." He pulled her into a tight hug. "I won't be gone long. Only a few days."

"Be careful."

"I should say that to you."

"I'm safe behind castle walls. You'll be avoiding your brother's army, all while trying to hunt down enough food to feed a large village."

He chuckled and released her from his hold. "Do me a favor? Don't speak to any ghosts while I'm gone."

"I don't plan to sit on the throne either."

"Good girl."

She watched him leave the room and told herself the pit in her stomach was foolish. He would be fine. He didn't leave with a fight on his mind, nor was his plan to confront his brother's forces.

But she couldn't shake the feeling that he wasn't telling her everything. Troubled thoughts dug at her.

Eamonn wasn't the type to wander. He was clearly mad about her, far more than any of his people had ever seen him before. Sorcha didn't worry that a tiny dwarven woman had caught his eye. And if she had, then good for the dwarf.

The only thing remaining to worry about was that he still

wanted to fight. That battle ran through his veins and he was sneaking off hoping Fionn might find him.

She hoped not. Five years of war had been enough, his people grew tired of fear and hardship. There were only so many deaths that the Seelie Fae could sustain. Birth was difficult for their kind, and she feared she was the only midwife in the Otherworld.

Worry made her mind wander. She stood in the same place, she did not know how long, staring at the door as if he might return.

"Are you going to stand there all day?" A rough voice barked. "Or are you going to do something?"

"Excuse me?" Sorcha looked over her shoulder at the female dwarf who had berated her soundly. "Who are you?"

"'Course you don't remember me."

"No, I remember you from the campfire. That doesn't mean I know *who* you are."

The female dwarf tossed the tail of her beard over her shoulder and crossed her arms. "Well? Why 'aven't you done it yet?"

"Done what?"

"You're a druid. They always do something sneaky to get out of situations like this. So go on. Do whatever it is you do."

"I'm a Weaver."

The dwarf snorted. "As if. There aren't any more of those left, we killed 'em all when we sent your lot off. I bet you talk to plants. I've seen 'em reach out to touch you."

Sorcha narrowed her eyes at the rude dwarf. Bravery such as this was foolish. She didn't know what Sorcha was capable of, and she still provoked as if there was no danger.

Stinging from Eamonn's abrupt departure, Sorcha focused on the dwarf.

Weaving had become easier here in the Otherworld, even more so in this castle. Druid souls fed her power, their ghostly hands stroking her arms and guiding her mind.

Plucking the name out of the dwarf's skull was almost too easy. She pulled just the slightest amount and a strand of shimmering light hovered just above the dwarf's ear. No one could see it but

Sorcha, and perhaps the druid souls who whispered excitedly in her ear.

"Yes," they said. "That's it. Pull it a little bit, don't let her notice."

Sorcha sighed. "That is enough, Caitlyn."

The thread hummed, revealing that the dwarf preferred the name Cait.

The dwarf crossed her arms. "That's a good trick. Guessed that one, did you?"

"No. It's what Weavers do."

"And I'll tell you again, we killed the lot of them in the last war. There ain't any Weavers left. You'd be wise not to call yourself that, there are dwarves 'ere who would want to kill you."

The fine thread of patience Sorcha clung to snapped. She tugged hard, words spilling from her lips like fine wine. "They would kill me? Then perhaps I should be more prepared. What other names do you have stored in that little head of yours?"

Another swift tug of her mind revealed a few names, but nothing important.

"Hey!" Cait shouted. "Get out of my head!"

But she wasn't quite done yet. Sorcha pulled once more, smiled, and tilted her head to the side. "There it is. You were a lucky girl to be taken in by Angus, the man who would become king of the dwarves."

"That's not your name to have." Cait growled.

"And my life is not yours to take."

They stared each other down, neither wanting to let go of the anger that burned behind their eyes. Sorcha's tension eased when Cait shrugged and sighed.

"Fine. So you've got a little bit of fire in you. That's not a bad thing. Now, how do you plan on protecting yourself?"

"Against who?"

"Everyone. The dwarves. Faeries who don't want a human in the Otherworld. Your lover's twin who obviously wants you gone,"

Cait ticked off fingers as she spoke. "Seems to me like everyone wants you dead."

Sorcha blinked. The dwarf flitted from emotion to emotion so quickly that even the heat of the air changed. "Why do you want to know?"

"Because it's important that people know how to protect themselves. And you've proven to me that you plan on keeping yourself alive, even though that little escapade with the king was embarrassing to watch. What do you know?"

"Eamonn has been teaching me to fight from the high ground."

"Fight? With what?"

She repeated what she had told Eamonn only moments ago, slowing as Cait shook her head. "What? Why are you making that face?"

"What do you do if no one comes to help you?"

Sorcha didn't have an answer to that. "I fight them myself I suppose."

"And what happens if they grab you?"

"Then I struggle."

"With what?"

"Kicking and screaming until they let me go."

"Right," Cait snorted and crossed her arms. "Let me tell you how that will go. You'll scream, they'll slap you so hard you taste blood and then once more just to make sure you see stars. Then they'll pin you down, and you won't be able to move. You'll be lucky if they kill you at that point. So let's start again. How are you going to fight?"

The dwarf had a point. She had argued a similar fight with Eamonn, who refused to even entertain the idea that he would be so far away he couldn't protect her.

And then he left her here alone.

She straightened her spine. "I don't know."

Cait snapped her fingers and pointed at Sorcha. "That's the right answer. Come on then."

"Where are we going?"

"I'm going to teach you how to fight."

A part of Sorcha hesitated, wondering why the dwarf would helping when she obviously didn't like druids. But another part wanted desperately to know how to protect herself.

Perhaps that was the druid coming out. She had only felt the strange yearning in her heart a few times, but each instance was a powerful one. There was a creature inside of her that longed to be stronger than ever before.

"All right," Sorcha said. "When?"

"Right now, unless you want to stare at the door for a little while longer."

She didn't. Sorcha narrowed her eyes and said, "No. We can go now, if you are prepared to teach me."

"Come on then, out into the yard with you. What weapon do you 'ave experience with?"

"None."

They moved past dwarves singing to their stones. Not a single one faltered in their work, but their gaze burned against her back. Perhaps they were merely curious about who she was. More likely, they wondered why she was walking with one of their own.

Cait shoved a dwarf aside that stood in their path. "That won't do. Swords?"

"I don't own one."

"Can't make you one any time soon in this pit. Knives?"

"Just the kind that carve food."

"That's a start," Cait jabbed at the air as if she were stabbing a person. "People are a little bit like meat. A little more sticky. We can work with that, and every woman should have a 'idden blade. Bow and arrow?"

The mere thought of stabbing someone made her queasy. She had dedicated her entire life to helping and healing, not harming. "I used to hunt with my father when I was young."

Cait perked up, bouncing. "Did you ever get anything?"

"No."

"Oh. Well then you don't know how to shoot a bow."

"I was a good shot."

"You could hit still targets you mean. Moving ones are a lot different."

She imagined they were. Sorcha treated such wounds before, and knew that an arrow stuck in bone sometimes. She shuddered at the memories.

"Don't get squeamish on me now," Cait said with a chuckle. "We'll get you ready for anything that might come our way."

"I have to ask again, why are you interested in helping me?"

"The way I see it, you're right on the way to becoming our queen. I already don't like the man who's trying to make himself king. The last thing I want is two royals who have little sympathy for my people."

"Eamonn cares," Sorcha said. She skirted past a dwarf who stepped in her way, his song deepening for a moment in disapproval. "That's why he's working so hard to take back the throne. To give your people a voice."

"Funny, that's not how we see it."

"Then how do you see it?"

They walked into a training yard. Only a few dwarves lingered in this area, most of them choosing to work with stone rather than practicing their battle skills. Sorcha found it strange for an army to not train every second they could.

Cait kicked a bale of hay as they passed it. "How do we see it? Just more of the same. Another noble who thinks he can make a difference because his ideas are a tad different than the last one's. Nothing ends up happening, no matter who is on the throne."

Sorcha had seen a very similar situation in her own world. The peasants, those who worked all day to make their living in life, had never cared who was king. They did what they wanted, worked hard, gathered food and water for their families, and the royals lived entirely separate lives.

"That's disappointing," she said. "It is similar in the human world. Royalty has no connection to the people. I always wished they did, but those of us who lived hard lives never even saw them."

"You want me to believe you ain't royalty?" Cait snorted. "Right."

"I'm not. I was raised in a brothel and became a midwife to heal my sisters and prevent them from filling the brothel with children."

"You were raised with whores?"

Sorcha winced. "It's a rather cruel word, but yes. My sisters made a good living and kept us all alive. I value them greatly, no matter their choice of employment."

The more she spoke, the further Cait's jaw dropped. "You don't care at all that they sell their bodies to whomever will pay the most?"

"Not in the slightest. What they do with their own flesh is none of my business."

"And you don't judge 'em for that?"

"Not unless they get with child, and that would only happen because they didn't take the tea I gave them. If they were foolish with their bodies, their hearts, their minds, then yes. I would judge them. But they are highly intelligent women. I have never once thought less of them for their choices."

"You know, I could like you."

Sorcha's jaw dropped. "That's all it took?"

"Guess so."

"How?"

Cait turned and rummaged through a few of the sacks lying on the ground. "Dunno. Guess you're more of a person now then you were before."

"I wasn't a person?"

"Royals ain't people. They don't know how to be people."

"Fair enough."

Sorcha glanced around the yard that the dwarves had repaired. A short knee wall surrounded three sides, the remaining side abutted the cliff peak which stretched up two men's height.

Targets leaned against the wall, not yet set up or used. She recognized a few of the straw dummies. Eamonn had used them in his own training yard.

Hay littered the ground, not yet disturbed by footprints. Everything was pristine, perfect, exactly how it would be when they were first made.

"Are you not practicing?" she asked. "Everything seems to be untouched."

"We ain't an army, that's why."

"What?"

Cait walked over and handed her a bow taller than she was. "Dwarves don't have an army. We don't like to fight, other than brawls in pubs. That we'll do. Now take the bow, 'ere's your arrows, and shoot that target."

"What do you mean dwarves don't fight?"

"Shoot the target."

Sorcha could hear the iron in the dwarf's voice, and didn't know how to take it. Faeries didn't lie. There wasn't any reason for Cait to twist the truth. But what did she mean that dwarves didn't have an army?

What had Eamonn done?

She took the offered arrow, notched it, and lifted the bow. She could hear her father's voice in her ear. Breath out before the arrow is released. Sight the target with one eye. Keep the arm straight.

She exhaled and released the arrow.

It sang as it shot through the air and struck the edge of the target. Letting out a whoop, she turned to Cait with a grin. "I hit it!"

"Well that's just great, princess, but if that had been the size of a person then you'd have missed them entirely. There's a giant red dot on that target for a reason. Again."

"I thought that was all right for someone who hasn't picked up a bow in years."

"I don't care if you're all right. Just aim again, would ya?"

Sorcha grumbled and lifted it to her eye. "Are you qualified for this, if you aren't a soldier?"

"I can teach a person to fight. Not to be in an army and march in a line towards their death. Dwarves fight to stay alive. That's how you should fight too."

She exhaled and let her next arrow fly. This one was closer to the center, although it stuck weakly in the bottom, drooping towards the ground.

Cait tossed her hands into the air. "Well this will take all day. Again!"

⚜

SORCHA MET WITH CAIT EVERY DAY, SETTING UP LUNCH IN THE training yards and eating in the dirt. At first, the dwarven woman seemed nervous and uncomfortable around the consort of a would-be king. But, the more Sorcha showed she didn't care about the state of her skirt, the quality of her hair, or getting mud on her hem, the more the dwarf loosened up.

On the third day, she arrived in the courtyard with her bow already strung, Cait pointed at her dress and shook her head. "That won't do."

"What won't?" Sorcha looked down. "It doesn't matter if I get it dirty. There are hundreds of these musty things in the castle."

"Skirts will only trip you up. I already talked with Oona, she's waiting in the kitchens."

"In the kitchens? With what?"

"Your clothes." Cait hopped up onto the fence of the training grounds and tossed her beard over her shoulder. "Go on then. I'll wait."

Sorcha narrowed her eyes and pointed. "You'll let me braid your beard?"

"Why would I ruin a good beard by doing that?"

"Agree, and I'll wear whatever clothes you want."

"Fine. Just hurry up, I don't 'ave all day to waste training you."

"That's exactly what you've been doing!" Sorcha called out with a laugh.

She left her bow and arrows with the dwarf, racing to the kitchen with laughter ringing in her ears.

Of all the time she had spent in the castle, these few days training had been her favorite. She missed Eamonn and even Cian, who had gone with him. But there was something so refreshing about learning new things, using her hands and body as they were meant to be used.

Her hands were already strong from healing, her arms larger than most women. Every night she went to bed with aching muscles and a smile on her face. She wasn't a delicate creature, nor had she ever wished to be.

Banging open the kitchen door, she sauntered in, calling out, "Oona!"

"Here, dearie!"

Sorcha brushed aside a large sheet hanging up to dry. The pixie was elbow deep in soapy water, but grinning from ear to ear.

Sorcha smiled. "There you are. Cait said you had something for me?"

"It's long past time you accepted the faerie way of dress!"

"Please tell me it isn't made of spiderwebs, I'll tear it the first second I put it on."

"Oh no, dearie. It's much better than that." Oona nodded towards a table. "I think you'll be able to figure it out, but let me know if you need help. I'll dry my hands off!"

Sorcha stood stock still when she saw the clothing laid out on the table. Leather leggings, so smooth and supple that they were perfect. A loose tunic, split over her hips for ease of movement, and a leather corset. Twin wrist guards sat atop the small pile.

"These?" she asked.

"I know they're considered men's clothing in your world, but they're much more comfortable."

"You wear skirts."

"I'm no warrior. I work in the kitchens and I'm not expected to do anything other than that. You need speed on your side, whether you're working as a midwife or fighting. It'll make your druid ancestors proud."

Sorcha could feel it was true. Hands smoothed over her shoulders, tightened on her bicep, and pushed her forward.

"Grandfather?" she asked.

Fingers tapped on her shoulder in agreement before pressing down on the cloth, leaving a handprint behind. Even the druids wanted her to wear the outfit.

Sighing, she gave up her sense of propriety and took the clothes with her to change. Sliding the leather leggings over her skin brought a strange sense of self-reliance. She shed the dresses and petticoats with relief, and became a new woman dressed in men's clothing.

Smiling, she walked into the kitchen and gave Oona a small twirl.

"Well would you look at that," Oona said with a giggle. "What a pretty faerie you would make."

"Don't my ear tips qualify me as one?"

"Doubtful, but we'll let it slide. You really are beautiful, dearie. Eamonn won't know what to do with himself when he returns."

Sorcha's smile dimmed. "It's been quite a while."

"It can take a bit to find the deer. Don't you worry that pretty head of yours, I'm sure nothing has happened to them. Now off with you."

Sorcha saw the worried expression that Oona carefully hid. A part of her wanted to push, to see whether her newfound power could force Oona to speak. The faerie was hiding something.

They all were. Shaking her head, she wandered back out to the training grounds where the dwarf sat.

"What's the matter?" Cait asked immediately.

"Nothing."

"You look like you just watched someone kick a child. Don't give me that bullshit."

Sorcha let out a frustrated groan. "I feel as if everyone is hiding something from me! No matter how much I try to get everyone to give me a clear answer on why it's taking Eamonn so long."

"Oh well that's easy."

"Is it?"

"They don't want you to know that he took out a whole troop of dwarves to find more people to force into his army. And if they happen to find some of Fionn's forces along the way, well, that's all the better."

Stunned, she blinked a few times. "Thank you for the honest answer, but you can't possibly be right."

Eamonn couldn't have lied to her, could he?

Cait gave her a look that suggested he could. "Fine, if that's what you want to believe. I'm just training you."

She released arrow after arrow, her mind a turbulent sea of crashing waves. She didn't want to believe he had bent the truth. They had only just found each other again, and they had agreed this was the best course of action.

There wasn't another choice. Fionn had to be stopped, but the real concern was the people of the Seelie Fae. They didn't need to go through another war. It had been five years already, and that tactic hadn't worked.

Eamonn had understood her point of view. He'd agreed with it, acted as if he was relieved. Was he that good at deceiving her?

The sun arched overhead and dipped down to kiss the horizon. Still, she didn't stop. A frown furrowed her brows, her biceps trembling from the stress. Her tongue swelled, mouth dried, body ached for water.

Her mind wasn't done yet. She wasn't done processing that he might have betrayed her. That he might still think she was a foolish little human girl who couldn't understand Faerie politics.

"Sorcha!" Cait's voice cut through the fog of her mind. "You're still here? Enough!"

She couldn't —wouldn't — stop until he returned. Until she could look him in the eye and accuse him of all the wrongdoings Cait said he had done.

"Enough!"

The bow flew out of her grasp, clattering across the stone ground and scattering the hay. Breathing hard, Sorcha whirled to glare at Cait.

"I'm not done yet."

"Yes, you are."

"You have no right to order me," Sorcha pivoted and reached for the bow.

"Stop it! You're bleeding, can't you see that? You've practiced enough today."

She could see her hands now. Fingers raw and blistered, blood dripping from beneath the nails and landing in fat droplets atop the discarded bow. When had she begun to bleed?

Pain seeped through her skin. The gut-twisting ache immediately stiffened her fingers, locking them in place.

Crying out, she fell onto her knees and held out her hands. Foolish, she berated herself. Now all her training would go to waste.

Cait reached out, at eye level now that Sorcha sat upon the ground. The dwarf grasped her hands and winced. "I should have known it would upset you. I apologize, Sorcha. This wasn't the time, nor the place, to voice my concerns."

"Was it true?" She looked at the dwarf with hope in her eyes. "Please, tell me it was just rumor."

"You'll have the ask the king for the truth."

"Then you don't know?"

"I know where the men went, and why they packed their armor. I know they all expected to meet an elven army on the road because the path chosen is a known trade route. Can I say that the High King chose this with full knowledge? No. I cannot read his mind."

Sorcha's shoulders slumped forward in defeat. "He knew."

"How can you know? Can you read faerie minds, druid?"

"He wouldn't go, otherwise. Eamonn is meticulous in his decision making. He knew."

"I'm sorry," Cait said. She patted Sorcha's arm with a firm smack. "I know it's not the easiest thing to hear, especially when you thought you knew him."

When you thought you knew him.

Did she? Sorcha wasn't certain anymore. They had spent many hours together, but all of them superficial at best.

Was it even possible for a human, so limited in years and knowledge, to understand the full breadth of a faerie life?

"Chin up. You'll have your moment to ask him for clarification soon."

"What?" Sorcha glanced over the dwarf's shoulder, towards the castle gates. "They're returning?"

"We could see the trail of dwarves an hour ago. I called out to you, but you weren't responding. I figured it was best to let you go rather than interrupt."

"I can't see him like this."

"Good thing dwarves are always prepared."

Cait pulled a small jar from her pocket. She smeared the salve over Sorcha's hands which miraculously healed before her eyes. The cuts sealed, blood dried, and the bruises faded to yellow.

Holding her hands up to the dying light, she shook her head in wonder. "Remarkable."

"Useful, ain't it?"

"Why doesn't everyone use it?"

"Because it's dwarf magic, and not everyone has access to it." Cait nudged Sorcha's shoulder. "Go on with you. Go and greet your man."

"I don't know if I want to."

"He'll know something is wrong if you don't."

"Then I'll remain here."

Cait shuffled. "The others will know there's something wrong as well."

"And?" Sorcha looked down. "They don't care for me."

"You're growing on us. The consort of a king plays an important role in the well-being of the Fae. If you're upset, we'll likely be upset."

She wanted to say then so be it. Eamonn could deal with an upset group of dwarves on his own. But the other half of her said it was her duty to comfort the others.

Sorcha had never spread fear before, nor had she perpetuated it. She would not start now.

Squaring her shoulders, she rose to her feet with a groan. "That salve wouldn't be good for muscles, would it?"

"You're on your own with that. Good luck."

She would need it. Sorcha trailed across the training grounds, hardly noticing her feet touching the stones. Her heart raced, her palms grew sweaty with the mere thought of confronting him.

Would she scream? She certainly wanted to. Words built up at the back of her throat, pushing against her tongue, longing to spray acidic anger. Her palm already stung in anticipation of a resounding smack.

She climbed the steps up to the battlements. Wind whipped her hair loose from its tie until it tangled around her arms and shoulders.

There they were. The long tail of dwarves, not together as they should have been, but loosely spread across the mountain. They had not yet reached the bridge, their pace sluggish and weak.

White banners of makeshift bandages spread among the crowd. Some wore the fabric around their heads, others their waists and hands. The anger drained from her body as she saw a few litters, bodies lying limp upon the rickety frames.

They had fought, and they had lost.

Her gaze caught on the tallest figure. Eamonn picked his way over craggy rocks and sparse heather. His torn cloak revealed new crystals, wounds and slashes decorating his skin.

He glanced up and their gazes caught.

Many emotions sizzled between them. Relief he was alive, even though so many were dead. Happiness they had returned, for she had missed them all. And disappointment he had lied to her.

One of the dwarves on the wall hummed. His voice carried on the wind like the steady beat of a drum. Others joined in, their haunting call a hymn to their fallen brothers and sisters.

A hauntingly beautiful voice soared overhead. Tenuous at first, then growing in strength, Cait's voice carried the souls of the dwarves from their bodies deep into the earth.

Tears dripped down Sorcha's cheeks as she counted the fallen. Eight litters. Eight men who had died because Eamonn had not kept his promise.

The dwarves looked to her, their gazes solemn. What would the lady of the castle do? How would she treat the returning warriors?

It was the first time she had to make a decision worthy of a queen. Druid souls pressed against her spine, their hands supporting her when she might have faltered. They drew her straight, pulled her shoulders back, tipped her chin up.

"Good," a voice whispered in her ear. "That is how a queen stands."

Sorcha squeezed her eyes shut for a moment. She could do this. She could walk in the footsteps of so many women before her. Druid women who had made such a decision hundreds of times before.

Cait's voice trembled and fell silent. The deep thrumming bass silenced until all that remained was the wind whipping in her ears.

Her eyes found Eamonn's again, his begging her forgiveness. He wanted her to understand his decision. Try as she might, she couldn't.

Heart breaking, Sorcha turned her face from him and the warriors who had drawn their blades. She stepped back down the stairs, refusing to look back.

"M'lady?" Cait called out, the first time she had ever given Sorcha a title of respect.

"They know their way home." Her voice was icy and iron hard. "Tend to the dead, but let the wounded see to their injuries themselves."

"Are you not our healer?"

"I am." She glanced around to find the dwarves had followed her off the battlements. No one remained to greet the returning soldiers. "Hear me now! I will not lift a finger to help anyone who has dedicated their lives to bloodshed. There will be no more *war*."

Cait pushed to the front of the crowd, her eyes brimming with tears. "We cannot go against the orders of our king."

"You all have a difficult decision before you. Follow your high king, and lose your healer. Follow me, and lose your king."

She headed towards the castle, stones crunching underneath her feet. She would not look back, would not see whether he made it across the bridge in time to see her leave.

☙❧

THE BRUSH SNAGGED IN HER CURLS, CATCHING UPON LEAVES AND tangles that were always in her hair. She had changed out of her new clothing and tucked the articles away in a drawer she wasn't certain she would open again.

He hadn't seen her in them. Now, she wasn't certain that he deserved to.

Her white nightgown was another relic found in a treasure chest. Simple, plain, and sturdy, it serviced her desire to feel something from home. All the velvets and silks made her head spin. She wanted was something simple, and the only thing she could find was a nightgown.

She tugged hard on the brush, stoically bearing the angry sting of her scalp.

Night had fallen long ago. The rest of the castle residents settled into bed, their snores and quiet dreams angering Sorcha further. He hadn't come up to their room yet.

He had a right to be nervous. She still wasn't certain what she would say, or how she would say it. Anger simmered underneath her skin like the ragged edges of claws.

He was likely drinking. She had heard that soldiers did that after returning from war. The alcohol would wipe their memories of blood and death, and then they would return to their wives.

"Not me," she vehemently told her reflection in the mirror. "I will not be that wife who will service a man making foolish decisions. He has no right!"

He should have *listened* to her! Did he think her incapable of forming a plan that would adhere to faerie politics? Or did he think her incapable of anything in the realm of Fae?

The door creaked open just enough for shadows to creep in. He paused, frozen as soon as the spear of her candlelight slashed into the hallway.

"Eamonn." It was not a question. She knew who lingered at her door.

"You're still awake."

"I was waiting for you."

He sighed and pushed the door open the rest of the way. She wanted to berate him, to scream and shout and throw her brush at his head.

But bruises spread across his cheeks, a ragged edged crystal slicing down his neck. It spread from the old wound, and she knew someone had tried to take advantage of the weakness. They wouldn't know it was his strength.

She sighed and put the brush down.

"You're going to yell," he said. His shoulders squared as if he were preparing for the worst. "I deserve it. It was a horrible idea, and I didn't listen to you."

"Yes, it was."

"We lost good men out there, because I thought we were prepared. I was wrong."

"Yes, you were."

"Our people saw you turn from me. The army is already on the verge of deserting, and seeing your reaction certainly didn't help. I'm not saying it wasn't the right thing to do. It likely was."

She stared back at him, silent in her regard.

"Why aren't you yelling yet? I can see you have plenty to say."

"I don't need to yell at you, Eamonn. You're already doing it for me."

Her words broke something within him. A low breath hissed through his teeth and he rushed towards her, dropping to his knees at her feet. The tension drained from his body, shoulders falling forward in defeat.

He placed his head in her lap, wrapping his arms around her waist with a low moan. "Yell at me, mo chroí. Be angry, break pottery and statues. Do something other than this, I beg you."

"What good would it do?" she said, stroking his head. "You know what you did, and how wrong it was."

"I am lost." He pulled the length of her nightgown up to her thigh, breath whispering over her skin as he pressed crystal lips against her. "Everything I thought I knew is wrong. This world is one I remember, these people familiar faces, but I cannot find the man I once was."

"You don't need to find him. The warrior prince is no longer who you are, nor what this land and people need."

"Who do they need?"

He looked up and their gazes locked. She wanted to say that the world needed him. They needed the kind soul that existed inside who wanted to help his people. But the longer she was here, the more she realized that faerie culture was beyond her.

"I do not know," she said. "I might have once said they need a kind king."

"And now?"

"They are looking for someone to lead them, but also for someone to understand them." She thought of the dwarves and their steadfast ways. They didn't want to fight, other than the occasional tussle, yet here they were. "They trust you, in their own way. But they fear you will follow in your brother's footsteps."

"Blood calls to blood."

"No." Sorcha dug her fingers into the crystals of his cheek. "You will not become Fionn."

"How can you be so sure? I can feel it, the old ways sinking underneath my skin."

"The old ways are not the best ways. You were the first to believe that, Eamonn." She stroked a thumb over his lips. "No more of this. No more fighting, blood, and death. Your people deserve to rest."

"I cannot stop." The torment in his eyes nearly shattered her heart. "He will come here next, and he will not stop. Fionn has no care for our people or how many people must be sacrificed to make his point."

"Which is?"

"I am not worthy to be king."

"No man ever is," she said with a soft smile. "You can only try your best to be a good king. You will never win over the hearts of every single one of your people. But you can provide for them, ensure their lives are rich, and their bellies full."

"How do you know this?"

"I was one of those people wishing that my king only knew that we were hungry." She stood, pulling him with her until he rose to his great height. "Have you bathed?"

"No."

"Has anyone tended to your wounds?"

"There is no need. My wounds do not bleed."

Sorcha winced. She wanted to remind him that not all wounds were external, that sometimes a person could heal through physical touch. His gaze caught hers, holding her locked within blue crystals as sharp as a sword and deep as the ocean.

He knew, she realized. He knew what she wanted to tell him and still he did not want her to say it.

"Come with me." She held out a hand for him to take.

"Sorcha..."

"Take my hand, Eamonn. Let me tend to your wounds."

"I don't deserve your forgiveness."

"I have yet to meet anyone who didn't." She let her hand hover in the air, waiting for him.

He fought with himself. She watched a battle rage behind his eyes until he finally sighed and took her hand.

"I don't deserve you."

"No, you don't. Now come into the bath and let me show you what the dwarves have created."

The room behind their bed was a modern work of art. The dwarves had brought to life an old washroom by tapping into the geothermal vents underneath the castle. A slight twist of a knob, and hot water rushed into the large iron tub they had carried up the stairs.

Sorcha had already used it more times than she should have. Her practices with Cait had made her muscles ache and her body tremble. The warm water had soothed those aches, as she hoped they would for Eamonn.

He stopped in the center of the room, and she ran her hands across his shoulders. Standing on tiptoe, she reached for the clasp of his cloak and let it fall to the ground. The soft sound echoed in the tight room.

"You don't have to do this," he said, searching her gaze for an answer she did not have.

"I do."

As angry as she was, Sorcha needed to feel his ribs expand under her fingertips. Life coursed through his veins, strong and violent as a churning river. He had been wounded, but survived.

It was all that mattered.

A sigh slid through her lips as she tucked her fingers underneath his tunic and lifted the fabric up. He stooped to help her slide it over his head, sinking to one knee.

Again, she curled her fingers over his hair. Snarls tangled and tugged, but she patiently worked each and every one loose.

"Stand, warrior."

He looked at her as if she were his world. Eamonn rose to his feet, powerful chest broad and scarred.

Sorcha hooked her fingers at his breech waist, tugging until he was completely bare. She pressed a kiss against the newest scar. It was an angry thing, ragged and raw with crystal so sharp they pressed against her lips.

"Let me take care of you tonight, Eamonn. Tomorrow, we will wage a battle of our own."

৯৯৯

SORCHA COULDN'T SLEEP. HER MIND WHIRLED WITH possibilities and the screams of dying men.

War flickered to life behind her eyes. Memories that were not hers, but those of druid women. Blood coated their hair, bodies painted blue as they screamed out their rage. She couldn't understand the power of their anger. It bubbled over their soul until they became a beast, no longer human.

Eamonn shifted behind her. His arm slid from her waist and he rolled onto his side. Distance. It kept growing between them, further and further until she wondered if they slept in the same bed at all.

She swung her feet over the edge of the bed and slipped from beneath the furs. Glancing over her shoulder, she waited until he settled again.

Did he know how beautiful he was? Eamonn was a vision of power. Crystals glinted in the moonlight, decorating his skin like thousands of stars.

It hurt to look at him when she was so angry.

She couldn't yell at him for making a decision that felt right. He had made his choice, and they fundamentally did not agree on how to handle this war. She only wished he would listen more carefully.

The floor was cold against her toes, bitter and icy. Her white nightgown suddenly seemed flimsy against the cold night air that wiggled beneath the door and sank claws into her skin.

She pulled the fur from a nearby chair and slipped out onto the balcony.

The full moon smiled down at her. Silver light gave mist a

magical quality as it swirled through the courtyard below. The dwarves had built a pattern into the stones they replaced. A triskele, she realized with a smile. They honored the old ways.

"Shouldn't you be in bed?" The warm voice was recognizable, and one she had not heard in a very long time.

"Bran," she replied, warmth imbuing her voice with happiness. "It has been a long time."

"Yes, I suppose it has."

"Where have you been?"

"My life is not all about meddling in Seelie affairs."

She grinned and turned towards the raven man. "Just recently?"

He looked exactly as she remembered him. The strange dark feathers that smoothed along his cheekbone and forehead. A raven eye filled one socket, too large in comparison to the other and restless in its movements. One side of his head was still shaved, although a new growth filled in the pale skin of his skull.

"You look well," she said.

"As do you. Something has changed within you."

"I discovered I am a druid."

"No it's not that." He leaned forward and lifted a lock of her hair. "You appear more confident."

"I am."

"You're carrying yourself far more regally than before."

"I have learned to do so."

"But you're still dressed like a peasant." He let his hand drop. "Eamonn has not yet beaten his brother, I take it?"

"Do you really think I wouldn't dress like this if I was Queen?"

Bran shook his head, a severe look marring his handsome features. "No, you are far too connected to the earth to be swayed by jewelry and silk."

"I wouldn't be able to keep it clean."

"And how would you fight?"

She frowned and leaned back against the banister. "You've been watching me."

"I have not."

"You cannot lie, so what are you omitting? You would never know that I was training to fight."

"A raven has many paths to fly across. If I saw you training with that fiendish little dwarf, that was merely by mistake. A traveler sees much, but does not watch others specifically to gain knowledge."

"You've been practicing that for centuries, haven't you?"

He chuckled. "I have."

Sorcha gestured towards the stairs leading from the balcony. They ended at another protrusion, this one far more precarious than the first. The dwarves had yet to add railings or safety to it. Still, she was quite certain it would hold their combined weight.

Like the gentleman he pretended to be, Bran gestured for her to go first. Pulverized stone coated her fingers as she glided them down the railing. Settling on the very edge of the rock, she let her legs dangle high above the ground.

Bran sat down next to her. "Your mind is troubled."

"Is that why you took human form? Bran, I'm touched."

"What happened?" He nudged her shoulder with his. "Regardless of the fact that I dislike rules, nor do I follow any form of law, I still prefer to know what others are doing. And I find myself growing fond of you."

She blushed. "Eamonn is still battling Fionn for control over the Seelie throne."

"And is this a bad thing?"

"His people have had enough dying. They deserve at least some kind of break."

"It hasn't been that long of a war."

"It's been five years!" Sorcha exclaimed. "How much longer should it go?"

"Faerie wars last centuries. We fight, that's part of living in the Otherworld."

"Don't you ever tire of that?" Sorcha could hear the exhaustion in her own voice.

And she was tired. She didn't want to see the horrified expression on the dwarves faces. Oona had aged greatly. Cian resorted to kindness just to make people feel better. It was unnatural for any of these creatures to undergo such stress.

Bran watched her, his raven eye spinning. "You want to care for them."

"Don't you?"

"No. Faeries look out for themselves, and if they can't, then they are not training the next generation to be hardy."

"What if you didn't have to be hardy anymore?" Sorcha turned towards him and grasped his hands in hers. "What if you lived in a land where war was nothing more than memory? Where food and water was abundant, and people worked for their own living. No more slaves. No more lesser Fae."

"It would be a utopia."

"It would. It would be a beautiful place to live, and one that was inclusive and kind to all who lived there."

He tapped her nose with a claw tipped finger. "That is not the Fae way."

"Why can't you change?"

"We have changed much in the many centuries since our people began. But we are not human, Sorcha. You continue to give us human traits, and forget that faeries are more beast than man. We want to fight. We want to argue and meddle. These are parts of us you have to accept if you want to remain here."

"Why are you so intelligent?" she asked. "Every time I ask a question, you not only have an answer but find a way to make me look like a fool."

"You are not a fool. You are an extremely kind hearted woman who wants to save the world. It's admirable."

"He's forcing them to fight." She looked down at the ground. It was so far away and obscured by the shadows of night that she could almost imagine it wasn't there at all.

"Forcing?"

"I don't know how. Cait, the dwarf you called fiendish, told me that the dwarves no longer wish for war. They did not make the choice for battle and they are tired. I don't know how he's convincing them to continue if this is true but..." She shrugged. "How could it not be true? Faeries cannot lie."

Bran leaned back on one hand and stroked his chin. "You think Eamonn is coercing them or forcing them?"

"I hope neither."

"And yet, you are still talking about it."

"Something isn't right."

"Do you think it will make everything better for these dwarves to no longer fight? Do you think without an army, Eamonn will stand a chance against Fionn?"

"I don't know." She looked over at him, her shoulders slumped in defeat. "Do you?"

"Fionn is unpredictable. He sees the world in black and white, right and wrong, the classic definition of Seelie Fae. It's why he's made a relatively good king."

"Good?" Sorcha's jaw dropped open. "How is enslaving his own people and perpetuating class structure considered a good king?"

"It's always worked for the Seelie before."

"You cannot honestly believe that."

Bran held his hands up. "I believe nothing. I think the Seelie race in general is a waste of breathing space. Even your lover, whom I consider a friend, would better the world by not being here."

"What are you getting at, Bran?"

"Eamonn and Fionn are two very different men. One favors the old ways, which certainly puts a grouping of faeries at a disadvantage. But, the others brings a large amount of change. That can be just as dangerous as not changing at all."

"You're speaking in riddles."

"That's what faeries are good at."

She rolled her eyes and looked towards the sky for guidance. He was right, in a way. There were so many ways this could go wrong. But could she stand by and watch others die?

No. She couldn't. It went against every fiber of her being to allow a war as senseless as this one to go any further.

"I know Eamonn will make a good king."

"Why is that?"

"Because I will be at his side."

The words vibrated through her with enough power to weaken her knees, if she had been standing. Sorcha sucked in a breath. She had meant it. He would be a better king because she would never let him be anything else.

"Good," Bran said. "That's exactly what I wanted to hear."

"What?"

"These lands have been without a Queen for too long. Faeries are volatile creatures. We have a lot of emotions, but rarely show them until they are overpowering. It's why we love with all our being and why we fight wars until everyone is dead.

"A King encourages faeries to be who they are. He teaches the younglings to protect themselves, tells the old to pass on traditions. His role is important, for his is judge, jury, and justice.

"The Queen is different. She is the gentle soul that passes through the lands, healing injuries, and breathing life into wombs. She is the softness in a world that is as hard as steel. Without that gentle mother, our people quickly descend into chaos."

Sorcha exhaled. "There's nothing I can do to help. I will not lie with Fionn, and Eamonn has not yet been successful at taking back the throne."

"I think you're doing all the right things."

"And Eamonn?"

Bran chuckled and rose to his feet. "He's doing his best. It's been a long time since he's been home. There's an adjustment period."

"Is there any way I can help him?" Sorcha looked up at the dark man standing before her. "Is there any way I can help his people?"

Bran hesitated for a brief second, and in that moment she knew. There was something he wasn't telling her. Something that could stop all this madness.

"What do you know?" she asked. "What is it that you have discovered?"

"Do you trust that Eamonn will be a good king?"

"Without doubt."

"And you believe that Fionn will not come and find him with an army?"

"There are more secrets in these castle walls than you know. An army would have a difficult time finding us."

Bran licked his lips, fingers twitching as she shifted side to side. "I shouldn't tell you."

"I thought you liked to manipulate the story." She toyed with his natural desire to meddle. It was a cruel trick, but one she thought necessary.

He blew out a breath. "It's the sword."

"Which sword?"

"The Sword of Light, midwife, what else could it be?"

"Nuada Silverhand's sword?" She gaped at him. "What does that have to do with this?"

"It's how he's controlling the army. That sword controls anything that it points at. Eamonn is ordering the army to fight for him, and if he gets the chance, he's likely ordering Fionn's army to kneel."

"Then why hasn't he stopped everyone in their tracks? He could have avoided all this entirely if he simply ordered the men to return home."

Bran shrugged. "That's not the Seelie way. Honor demands that he defeat them without the help of magic. It's likely that Eamonn is ordering the dwarves to fight, but giving both armies a fair fight."

Sorcha's mind raced. Her hands shook as she realized what Eamonn had done. "Cait was right," she whispered. "They really don't wish to fight."

If he was forcing the dwarves to become his army, then what else was he capable of? It was no wonder that he carried so much guilt on his shoulders. He had done the unthinkable and took the choice away from his own people.

"How do I stop it?" she asked.

"Destroy the sword."

"I suppose you meant that to sound easy. Destroy the sword of Nuada? Just how do I do that?"

"I'm sure your little friends will help," Bran said. He winked at her with a roguish grin. "The druids always knew how to destroy faerie objects."

"Bran."

"I'm not telling you anymore. You said to meddle with the story, and now I have. You're a smart woman. I have full confidence you'll figure this out."

A rush of wind swirled around his body. Clothing fell to the ground and dissolved. Feathers sprouted from his skin as his form shrank into that of a raven with one human eye. Bran cocked his head to the side, croaked at her, then spread his wings and flew away.

"Destroy the sword of Nuada," she grumbled. "That's the only way to stop this?"

Warm air surrounded her. Hundreds of hands pressed against her shoulders and legs, no longer strange or discomforting. They were her family, her past, and her future. The druids would assist if they could. They wanted the war to end just as much as the faeries.

Sorcha wished she knew why.

The Wisdom Of Ethniu

Sorcha sat at the head table with Eamonn and marveled over the changes the dwarves had wrought in such a short time. The banquet hall was far more than the ruin it had once been. They even repaired the stained-glass windows, although she was not certain how.

Simple chandeliers hung from the ceiling. Candles stuck to their metal rings, melted and glowing merrily. They lit the entire space with ease. Wall sconces glimmered at the edges of her vision, giving light to even the darkest of shadows.

The tables were sturdier now that the dwarves had built them to last. There were a few extras, though many of the dwarves no longer ate in the hall.

Hundreds of dwarves had arrived in swarms. They refused to swear fealty to Fionn, and as such, left their mountain abodes to seek shelter from the coming winter. Each family chose where they wished to live, and the rest gathered by trade.

It was quiet and peaceful among the dwarves.

Sorcha wished it was in her life as well.

She clutched the spoon in her hand so tightly she worried the metal might bend. He hadn't said a word to her since their late night when he returned from battle.

Eamonn made himself scarce. He fought, trained with the dwarves, ate dinner, and then disappeared during the nights. She did not know where he went.

"Eamonn," she began.

He lifted a hand to silence her. "All is well."

"We have not spoken in some time."

"I have dedicated myself to repairing the castle. There is much work to oversee."

"And at night?"

"There are secrets within these walls I need to uncover. I will not rest until I am certain this castle is safe for all who live within it."

"The ancestors have assured me that everyone is safe." They whispered secrets in her ears when she could not fall asleep. Stories of the old days, recipes for spells and magic. Anything that would keep her mind occupied while she waited for him. "You need not worry."

"I do not know your ancestors, nor do I know the world they came from. What is not dangerous to druids may prove deadly for the Fae."

"They would tell me if it was."

"Would they?" He glanced towards her. "The druids have never been fond of my kind."

"I am."

She watched him struggle to find the words to respond to her. He knew she wasn't lying. She had proven herself time and time again to all the people of this castle. Sorcha was a trustworthy woman who wanted to help them.

He knew that. He understood it as well, but he still held prejudices against the ghosts of her past.

It was a shame he couldn't trust her.

Sighing, she stirred her soup and slowly nodded. "So, that is the way of it then."

"Sorcha, I'm not angry with you."

"No, I suppose you are not. But you are still distant. You have been since I returned here."

"I don't know how to change that."

"Spend time with me."

Eamonn tossed his cutlery to the table with a loud clatter. "I have so many things I have to do, I'm hardly finding time to sleep. And you want me to find more time to spend it with you? I am only one man, Sorcha. And there is only so much time in the day."

"Then include me. Give me something to do, so I might report my successes. Then at least we are working together!"

"I—"

The banquet hall doors opened, cutting off Eamonn's exasperated words. Cian made his way through, arms pumping as he raced towards the head table. "My lord! Visitors!"

"Who?" Eamonn stood.

His shoulders squared and his legs spread wide. He crossed his arms over his thick chest, muscles bulging as he pressed them forward. Sorcha shivered as he changed from her lover to the high king who fed off the energy of war.

"I do not know." Cian gulped. "They are not familiar to me."

"Let them pass."

"And if they mean harm?"

"Then let them come."

She watched Eamonn place a hand against the Sword of Light. It rarely left his person although she had noticed it disappeared while he was assisting the dwarves on their repairs. She simply didn't know where he left it.

Sorcha reached out and caught the fist resting upon the pommel of the blade. "No violence."

"If they come here intending to harm, I will not stop."

"You will. These people may seek shelter, and they do not know you. Your reputation as the man who kills precedes you. Do not give them reason to spread such a rumor any further."

"They should be afraid of me."

"Only in battle. When you are in your home, peace must reign."

She waited until his fingers relaxed and released his hand.

A small troop of faeries entered the room. Their foreheads were overly high, eyes so large they reflected the light, their bodies thin and lithe. Twig like hair smoothed back and hung in dreadlocks down their backs. Moss grew upon their shoulders and arms while leaves covered their bodies where clothing might have been. Flowers bloomed on a few of them. The females, Sorcha assumed.

"Peat faeries," she said in awe. "I didn't know they still existed."

"They don't in your world. Humans killed them off, along with the will-o'-the-wisps. Their kinds have warred for centuries."

"They're beautiful."

"They're dangerous. Too many of their kind have turned Unseelie."

"That is a personal choice, so you've said. It's not bred into species whether they are Seelie or Unseelie. They make a choice to uphold the honorable ways, or they do not."

"That does not mean they are trustworthy."

She glared at him and stood. Turning towards the faeries who hesitated before their table, she forced herself to smile. "Hello, and welcome travelers."

"Thank you, lady," one of the flowered faeries said. She stepped forward, large eyes blinking rapidly. "We come seeking shelter."

"From whom?"

"That of the king. We no longer wish to have our homes trampled by the High Fae and their ilk."

She had suspected this would happen and was pleased to see she was correct. News had spread fast that the High King had returned and was taking his subjects back one by one. To prove a point, she asked, "How did you find this place?"

"The legends speak of a Stone King who provides shelter for those who seek it. We have journeyed far to understand the truth of this legend." The woman's eyes dipped towards the ground. "I see the rumors of his ferocious nature were not exaggerated."

Sorcha glanced over her shoulder to see Eamonn's hard expression. He was trying to scare them and succeeding. Rolling her eyes so only he could see, she turned back to the faeries. "He is fierce on the battlefield and unparalleled by any warrior. But he is also a protector of his own."

"We would like to swear our allegiance to him."

Again, she looked back at the large man standing behind her. Lowering her voice, she asked, "Is this what you wish?"

Eamonn replied directly to the peat faerie. "Your people have feuded with many. There will be no fighting amongst mine."

"We have no wish to fight any more than we already have."

"I will hold you to that. The first person who lifts a finger in anger will be measured by my judgment."

A shiver raced through all the faeries. Their leaves turned over, revealing silver veins underneath the vibrant green. "We understand and acknowledge your warning."

"Good. Then you may stay within the castle walls."

"With all due respect," the faerie said, "we would prefer to stay in the peat bogs on the other side of the bridge. We are happy to sound an alarm if anyone approaches."

She could see Eamonn was considering it. "It may be of use," she murmured. "There is merit to knowing when someone is arriving, rather than when they get to the bridge."

"Every faerie here has a use," he declared loudly. "If you will provide us with a watch, then we will gladly provide your food. My dwarven army will also provide you safety should any issues arise."

"Thank you, High King." The peat faerie and her kin dipped into low bows. "You are most gracious."

"Do not forget my warning, for I will not."

"Thank you," they said in unison again.

They turned to leave the hall on trembling legs. Sorcha stared at their backs with a troubled expression.

"What?" Eamonn grumbled as he sat back down. "I know that expression, you think something is wrong."

"I don't think you should rule through fear."

"How else should I rule?"

She shrugged. "I've never been a queen, I do not know."

"Then sit back down, Sorcha. I'm doing my best."

"That's all one can ask." Her words trailed off as her eyes caught upon a bright, vibrant color laying upon the floor.

She left the high table without thought. Her feet whispered across the stone floor and the din of the crowd fell silent as she walked to the center of the room. She felt the eyes of a hundred dwarves on her back like a physical weight.

Kneeling, Sorcha scooped up the bright pink blossom that smelled like sunshine and sweet wine. Its oversized petals drooped over her fingers, limp and forgotten.

One of the peat faeries would miss this, she knew it in her heart that a flower was as much a part of them as their vines. She cupped it as gently as possible and rose to her feet.

A soft sound made her look up.

The smallest peat faerie stood before her, wringing its hands and staring at the flower.

"Is this yours?" Sorcha asked.

The tiny female nodded.

"You don't have to be afraid, I don't plan to keep it." Sorcha held it out for the faerie to take. "It's the most beautiful flower I've ever seen."

"Thank you, druid."

At the word, Sorcha's vision skewed. She could see all the threads that tangled around the peat faerie. Golden loops that tied her back to her family and far beyond Sorcha's vision. A thread that Sorcha could tug so easily, and secrets would spill from it like water from a basin.

She did not tug, instead, choosing to leave the faerie privacy.

"You are safe here," Sorcha said. "All of you are safe."

"That is all we have ever desired."

"It is what all of us strive for every day. If you have need of anything, please reach out to me."

"Thank you, lady."

She watched the peat faeries leave. The small one affixed the flower back to her person, just above her heart. The head female patted her on the head and glanced back at Sorcha with a soft smile on her face.

All would be well, Sorcha could feel it deep in her bones.

Turning back to Eamonn, she sighed at the scowl on his face. There would be many more battles to fight with him. The faeries were still dangerous to her and to his people. But he needed to understand that this was the path towards growth.

He would come around, she decided.

She walked back to their table and sat down. "They will be a good addition."

"Are you so certain?"

"Yes."

He lifted his goblet to his lips and nodded. "Then they will stay."

"Just like that?"

"You are the one with the golden heart, mo chroí. I trust your judgment even more than my own."

She relaxed. "You made me worried."

"That I would not accept them?" Eamonn shrugged. "The more you speak, the more I see the light. You have taught me much, Sunshine, and I would be a fool not to listen."

THE CLANG OF HAMMERS STRIKING STONE ECHOED THROUGHOUT the castle. Sorcha's head pounded, pain blooming in the center of her forehead and radiating out in pulsing circles.

"I have to go," she said to Oona. "I can't stand this incessant noise any longer."

"Are you ill, dearie?" Oona reached forward and pressed the back of her hand to Sorcha's forehead. "You feel a touch warm."

"I'm fine."

"Have you been sleeping well? I know it's been a stressful time for all of us."

"Really, I am well. I just need to get away from all this noise."

Otherwise, the headache behind her eyes might explode. She couldn't stand the constant movement of the castle, the watchful eyes of the faeries, the dwarves who made constant jokes. They were wonderful in small doses, but Sorcha desired a single moment of pure silence.

"There's a garden behind the castle which needs tending," Oona said. "I'm uncertain anyone has looked at it. The vines have created quite a mess, and the thicket is large enough to hide a human."

"Thank you." Sorcha's chair squeaked she stood up so fast.

"I understand the desire for freedom, dearie. Get yourself off and enjoy the quiet."

"Do you need anything before I go?"

Oona gave her a bright smile, lifted two oversized pieces of cotton, and stuffed them into her own ears.

That would certainly do the trick.

Sorcha grinned and slipped out of the kitchen, heading to the one place where she might find a little peace. She knew which garden it was. They had all seen the ominous, overgrown area. It was impenetrable, axes couldn't hack through the tangled roots and weeds.

There was a small path leading into the center. A few of the younger dwarves had dared each other to race to the center. Sorcha had watched them jostle around, but none had actually attempted the frightening adventure.

Now, it was her turn, and she refused to hesitate.

The ancient castle door shrieked as she pushed it open. The wild scent of autumn air bit at her arms and lifted the hairs. She had missed this most of all. Sorcha enjoyed being outside, away from the stifling, thick air inside of the castle.

Rustling leaves filled her ears with music while chirping

crickets overpowered any remaining hammer strikes she might have heard.

"Thank goodness," Sorcha said, relieved by the cool touch of silence.

Finally, she could hear herself think. She appreciated the little moments when she could be alone.

Brushing aside tangled ivy, she peered into the shadows. It was a perfect place for a lover's tryst, or for a Fomorian to hide.

Twigs crunched underneath her feet, snapping and cracking as she trod over their fallen limbs. Light disappeared as the thorns and vines arched overhead. The thicket was dark even when the sun was at its peak.

A hand pressed against her back, ghostly and smoother than any she had felt before. It was a comforting touch.

Sorcha wasn't certain the exact moment she had grown used to the druid souls that clustered around her at any given moment. They were as much part of her daily life as the dwarves. She was just as grateful for their presence as the faeries who toiled throughout the castle.

At the center of the wild garden, a natural altar grew. Purple amethyst and quartz crystals jutted from the land. Each peak was hewn flat, creating a table bare of offerings.

Her heart thumped painfully. No altar should be left untended. It reminded her too much of the faeries her own people had forgotten, and how much the land had suffered.

The gentle hand pressed against her spine again and smoke swirled around her. "Honor the dead," a calm voice whispered. "Wake them."

She didn't hesitate. Sorcha walked up to the altar and sank to her knees.

Her fingers curled into the dirt at the base. "I ground myself through the earth," she began.

She tilted her head back and breathed in the crisp, clean air. "I fill my lungs to clear my mind."

The brittle thorns shifted, letting a spear of sunlight play across her features. "I connect with the fire of the sun and link it to my own."

A single drop of water fell from a rose that bloomed above her head. "I heal all wounds with the water of life."

Her soul settled. Each word pieced together a part of her she hadn't known she was missing. Sorcha had gone to her own forest altar at least once a week, more if she was feeling stressed. That part of her life had disappeared, and now, returned.

The rituals made her feel whole.

"Well met, daughter." The warm voice from before was one she did not recognize. "See what your offerings have begat."

Sorcha blinked her eyes open and stared up at the altar. The crystals had changed form. They grew and stretched towards the sun, creating a figure who was more beautiful than anyone she had ever seen.

The woman wore a druid ceremonial garb. Furs graced her shoulders, a tunic touched the tops of her knees, and a headdress made of deer antlers sat atop her head. But it was her face that captured Sorcha's attention. It was beautiful, perfect in every way and form.

"It is a fair likeness," the voice said. "Although I always think they are too kind."

Sorcha glanced over her shoulder at the real life version of the crystal woman.

Beauty, so overwhelming that it was painful to look upon, made the newcomer all the more otherworldly.

Dark hair curled in waves down to her shoulders. Her face was pointed at the chin, delicate with perfect, smooth skin. Vibrant green eyes, so close to Sorcha's own, glittered with a smile.

"Ethniu?" Sorcha asked.

"Yes, granddaughter. It is I."

"You're alive? Or are you dead like grandfather?"

"I am neither. I exist in a world between life and death, a place where you could never find me." She reached out and brushed a hand over Sorcha's head. "But I am real enough to touch you."

"How is this possible?"

"You look very much like your mother," Ethniu said. "She was one of my favorite students. So talented, bright, capable, the kind of woman who could take the world by storm."

"She honored the old ways."

"And they burned her because of it. Humans can be unnecessarily cruel."

"They dislike what they cannot understand."

"To horrible ends."

Her grandmother wandered over to the altar and pressed her hands against the smooth surface. The ancient Tuatha dé Danann did not hesitate to show themselves to her, now the Fomorians also spoke with her.

"We visit our grandchildren," Ethniu said with a chuckle. "Even Nuada has visited Eamonn."

"Did you read my mind?"

"Being ancient has its perks. Druid minds are fragile, easy to peek into."

"You found nothing that disappointed you?"

"How could I?" Ethniu smiled at her, brilliantly white and blinding. "You are everything I ever desired. The druids were meant to be like you. Kind creatures who looked out for the humans in our absence."

"Were they not?" Sorcha heard the sadness in her grandmother's voice. "The old druids?"

"No one can control their creations. We didn't expect the druids to be so unpredictable, but they are two races with anger and pride in their blood. The Fomorians, my people, were beastly and cruel. The Seelie Fae, Nuada's people, are thoughtless and rule with iron fists."

"And the combination made druids dangerous. They desired power," Sorcha replied. She had heard the legends from the other faeries.

"They did," Ethniu agreed. "And some, like you, were wondrous. They did great things, created empires, healed small creatures, and then they died quietly along with the small miracles they wrought."

"Witches."

"Druids. Men and women connected to the earth as no human had ever been before. I am glad you became exactly what I meant for your race to be. The druids were banished from the Otherworld because they wanted to rule. They survived in this castle for a few hundred years, but eventually the faeries overran them. Banished to the human world where the druids nearly disappeared. They were burned at the stake or unable to pass along their knowledge to children capable of great magic."

Her grandmother reached out, hands hanging in the space between them.

Sorcha took Ethniu's hands. "I do not know what you wanted me to be. I can only continue to live by my own morals."

"Healing?"

"And spreading love."

"This is why your mother was my favorite. She, too, thought the world could change just by a little healing energy sent out the window every night."

"I remember that."

Tears welled in Sorcha's eyes as a memory long forgotten surfaced in her mind. Her mother used to hold her hands out the window as if she were cupping hands full of water. When Sorcha asked, her mother would laugh and say she was letting happiness drip through her fingers.

Eventually, she would toss her hands into the air as throw good feelings out into the world. Sorcha used to find it a rather odd, but entertaining ritual.

Now, she knew it was real.

"Why are you here?" Sorcha asked. "I have not had luck with Tuatha dé Danann telling me things they want me to do."

"Ah, but I am Fomorian, and I want nothing from you."

"Then why are you here?"

"I wanted to meet my granddaughter, face to face."

"Just as Balor did?" Sorcha's voice grew hard as stone. "I do not trust him, and you must forgive me for having difficulties trusting you as well."

"My father is a difficult man to trust. He has caused so much heartache in this world he no longer knows how to prevent himself from doing so. You should not trust him, but ask the right questions."

"Why?"

"The Fomorians are a proud people. We gather knowledge as the Fae gather art. I sometimes wondered why they are so enamored with beautiful things when there is so much more out there. Knowledge is a power that can be turned against anyone. Beauty is merely a talent."

Sorcha arched a brow. "A talent? Or a gift from birth?"

"Anyone can be beautiful if they love themselves, but not everyone can be intelligent. Which do you want to be?"

Sorcha didn't know the answer to the question. When she was younger, she would have chosen beauty. Making men fall to their knees because she was the most beautiful woman in the world made her knees tremble.

But then the knowledge of every living creature and thing would provide her with everything her soul needed. Beauty was fleeting, but intelligence meant that her name would remain on people's lips for thousands of years to come.

"Knowledge," she answered. "I would choose knowledge."

"Why?"

"If I measured my worth in beauty, I would live a life full of riches and happiness. If I am valued for the knowledge I impart on the world, then I live forever."

The smile that bloomed on Ethniu's face warmed Sorcha's soul. "Yes, you are correct, my granddaughter. I am proud that you are of my blood."

"And I thank you for it. I did not come to this grove to meet you, but I am glad that is the path my future took."

She leaned forward and pressed her forehead against Ethniu's.

They leaned against each other, fingers linked atop the crystal altar and the remains of a once great empire around them.

Sorcha breathed in the magic that crackled around her grandmother like lightning. Ethniu was beautiful in a hard way. Perfect, lovely, but so smooth that she seemed made of stone. It was fitting for a creature who had come from a difficult familial line.

"Sorcha," Ethniu breathed, "There is so much to say. I would give you wisdom if you will listen."

"Always."

"Nuada and I did not have an easy life. We made decisions that angered each other and changed the course of the Otherworld. There are things I have done that I regret. But I never feel guilt for staying true to what I love, and the people I hold in my heart."

Sorcha understood what she was trying to say. Love came in many forms and underwent much stress throughout the course of time. She stayed silent as Ethniu continued.

"I know what it is you seek. The Sword of Light has changed many people's lives. Though it can bring an army to its knees, destroy an entire race of people with a single word, it can also do much good. My husband used it in such a way, and I would not see you destroy it."

"I have to. How else can I prevent Eamonn from turning into his brother? He's hurting his people because he is so blind to his own rage."

"Then hide it. Leave it in the waters of the ocean, throw it from the cliff and give it back to my capable hands. Let the sword sink to the ocean floor where it will remain until the next generation has need of it. But do not destroy a relic that is one of the few remaining pieces tying our people to the original race."

The words dug into her heart and twisted. These people had lost enough over the centuries. They wanted to hold on to whatever they could from the old days, the good days, the ones where they had ruled over everything.

Now, their children continued to fight and quarrel like vultures picking through bones.

"I want no one to use it," Sorcha admitted. "In my generation or the next. No one deserves the power to control."

"Like you?"

"I will not use my power against the Fae. I do not want to control them, and I see no reason why I should. They are intelligent creatures with the capability to love greater than any other."

"You want to appeal to their good senses," Ethniu said with a chuckle. "You know that won't work."

"It has to."

"Fionn has no reason to give you any time to speak. He will listen to your pleas and then he will strike you down."

"I won't let him."

"By controlling him?" Ethniu leaned back and squeezed her hands. Vibrant eyes stared into hers with more knowledge than any person should hold. "You've already controlled him once, Sorcha. He knows what you are capable of and that is why he is so frightened."

"If he truly knew what I was capable of, then he would not be afraid. I will not hurt anyone."

"Throw the sword off the cliffs of the castle, and I will hide it in a place where it will not surface again."

"Where?"

"I will give it back to my husband. The Tuatha dé Danann have no desire to change the course of this story. We're enjoying watching you. Druids are unpredictable in their choices, and you far more than the rest."

"There are others?" Sorcha blinked, her heart squeezing as hope lifted her chin. "Are there are other druids who live?"

"Yes, although you are all spread out. I do not know if you have ever met another, but I feel as though you may some time in your life."

"Will you take me to them?"

"That would meddle with the story, and unlike your Unseelie friend, I dislike meddling."

Ethniu stood, the furs on her shoulders touching Sorcha's

hands. They were impossibly soft, smooth, like that of a rabbit rather than a sheep. But Sorcha had never seen a rabbit large enough to create a seamless shoulder piece.

Where was this giant woman from?

"Thank you, granddaughter, for sparing a relic of the Tuatha dé Danann. For that, I will look after you in the coming days."

"What is coming?" she asked.

"War. Violence. Death. All the things you have feared, they follow your lover's footsteps like a loyal dog."

"Is there any way to shake him free from that grasp?"

"Not that I know of," Ethniu breathed. "But I believe you may find a way."

Sorcha closed her eyes as sorrow coursed through her veins. She wanted this to end. Everything. Every bit of hatred and anger that spread through the Fae like wildfire through a dry forest. They deserved happiness.

She deserved happiness, and it wasn't fair they weren't allowed to have it. After all she had been through, after all she had given up, she was still stuck here waiting for the moment when her life would begin again.

"Ethniu," she called out, "I need your guidance. He is so much like his grandfather, warlord more than politician, that I do not know what his next step will be."

Silence was her answer. Sorcha opened her eyes and glanced around the grove which had fallen so quiet. Ethniu had disappeared.

A cricket strummed a tentative tune, growing louder when it realized nothing would speak again. It was as if the meeting had never occurred.

Cold air brushed across her skin, lifting the tiny hairs until Sorcha rubbed at her arms. The Fomorian had been far more unsettling than the Tuatha dé Danann.

What did that mean? Was she so unsettled by her own people?

"Yes." She let the word fly into the wind, in case Ethniu was listening to her thoughts. "I am."

All she knew was there was now a step to take. A beginning to the end in the form of a sword and a cliff.

She had to find it.

⚜

"I'M NOT TELLING YOU, GIRL. OFF WITH YOU!"

"I healed you, Cian! You must pay with something."

He blew air at her, flabs of skin turning bright red in anger. "If I had known the payment for healing would betray my master, then I would have gone elsewhere!"

"You're not betraying him! Stop being dramatic."

"I am! You don't want that sword for just anything, I know you girl." He waggled a finger at her. "You're up to something."

"I am not."

"Yes you are."

"I'm sorry, did you somehow learn to read minds while you were off on your adventure? If I tell you I'm not up to anything, then I'm not!"

Oona opened the door to the kitchen with a loud crash. Her arms were full of carrots, so large they piled nearly above her head. "Are you two arguing again?"

"Bartering," Sorcha corrected. "Do you need help?"

"No, dearie, I'm just dropping these off before I go back out. Those dwarves grow the most impressive vegetables!"

She dumped her armload in the corner of the room with a loud bang. Dusting her hands on her skirts, she turned back to them and shrugged.

"Do they?" Sorcha asked. "Strange, I thought gnomes were renowned for gardening."

Cian hopped up to smack her shoulder. "We are!"

"You made nothing so impressive. I wonder if size difference matters?"

"Excuse me?"

She'd never seen the gnome look so angry. His face turned tomato red, and every roll jiggled as he held himself in check.

Peals of laughter filled the room. Oona leaned against the table and wiped tears from her eyes. "Do you think it's because he's so small, dearie?"

"Well the height difference certainly makes me consider that the dwarves, with a few extra inches, may have a significant advantage."

"It's a good thing to be closer to the earth!" Cian shouted. "That's where all the plants are!"

"I'll stop teasing if you tell me where it is."

"Absolutely not."

"Oona? Have you ever heard the joke about the gnome and the dwarf who met the same lovely elven lady? She said she would only sleep with one, but that it all depended on how large the faeries was. So, both men turned and pulled down their trousers—"

"Enough!" Cian shouted.

Oona looked as though she might burst. Giggles shook her form until her wings rattled. "What is it that he's hiding from you, dearie?"

"I want to know where Eamonn is keeping the Sword of Light."

"In the treasury, love. It's the safest place for it."

"Oona!" Cian shouted. "The girl is up to something! Don't tell her where it is!"

"Thank you, Pixie." Sorcha dropped a kiss to her cheek as she passed. "That's exactly what I wanted. Cian, if you follow me I will drop you in a bin you won't be able to climb out of."

"You wouldn't dare!"

"Try me. I'm all too happy to see what happens when you stuff an angry gnome in a barrel."

"Fine then! You can handle Eamonn when he finds you."

She absolutely would. The man might be intimidating, but he knew what she was like when she wanted something. Sorcha didn't know how to stop.

She left the kitchen with a smile on her face. One step closer to her next goal. Life was turning around.

In the cold quiet of the hall, she took a deep breath and reached deep into the well of power inside her. It still felt unnatural. Almost as though there was something else inside her, a woman she didn't quite know yet but could feel.

"Ancestors?" she asked. "I need to know where the treasury is."

They didn't answer her immediately. The longer she remained in the castle, the more they saw fit to leave her alone. Sometimes she went days without feeling their hands on her skirts.

The ghosts were kind, but odd. They didn't react to things the way normal people did. A tea kettle shrieked, and they flew out of the room in a panic. Swords striking against each other would invigorate them to beg Sorcha to train. Horses pawing the ground almost made the ancestors visible.

She had yet to discover the key to what frightened them and what they liked.

The halls were quiet this time of day. Every dwarf in the area dedicated their attention to finishing the castle as soon as possible. Eamonn was in the training yard with those who were working and Bran, who had shown up again.

Sorcha grinned. The Unseelie continued to say he didn't like them all that much, and that they were more work than they were worth. Yet, here he was. This time training with the dwarves and teaching them all the ways to fight dirty.

A voice whispered in her ear, "The Unseelie throws them to the dirt and laughs."

"He's teaching them how to fight his way."

"The Seelie are honorable in their battles. This dark newcomer is not."

"Is war honorable?" Sorcha turned down a dark hallway. She picked her way over the cracks and craters left by a battle long ago. "I have never seen a battle where the soldiers took the time to be polite."

"There is an etiquette to fighting."

"And I'm supposed to place a napkin in my lap before eating, yet I rarely do."

Sorcha didn't have time for the druids to whisper their opinions in her ear. She didn't want to be distracted while wandering the castle. The Sword of Light was far more important than debating the properties of war.

"Is the treasury this way?" she asked.

"Yes."

"How far?"

"To the right and down the stairs."

"It's in the dungeon?" She had only seen the dark underbelly of the castle once. The memories of screaming victims left imprints. She had left when their screams became too much for her.

"It is beneath the dungeon."

"There's further to go?"

The voice chuckled. "The castle stretches deep into the heart of the mountain. You will find much within its belly."

"Well that's not ominous at all," she muttered.

The ragged edges of ripped vines hung in front of the dungeon. Plants were already taking back the areas where Eamonn and his men had slipped through. Moss covered the footprints they left behind, only the faintest hint of a divot revealing she was still in the same doorway.

Mist curled out of the opening. Sluggish and thick, it was more magic and ghostly essence than water.

A blast of cold air rushed from the bowels of the dungeons, bringing with it the echoing call of screams.

"I don't want to go down there," she said.

"It's the only way."

"Why would Eamonn put the sword in the most terrifying place?"

"No one goes into the dungeons."

"No one but foolish women who want to help," Sorcha corrected. "After all, why else would any sane person walk through this haunted place?"

"You traveled through the Unseelie court."

She shuddered. "Yes, I did. And it was eerily similar to this place."

"The Unseelie gather souls like gemstones. They let them wander through their dark castle hallways so they never truly die. They like to watch the specters relive their death over and over again."

"Of course they do. That fits with all the things I remember," she said as she brushed aside a vine and started down the long stairwell.

Each step squelched underneath her booted feet. The moss covered steps were dangerously slippery, but no railing guided her way. Instead, Sorcha placed her hands on the walls and made her way while holding her breath.

Slipping and falling would end poorly. No one would know where she was, other than Cian and Oona. She didn't see them often enough for them to raise the alarm.

She repeated all the ways she could help a head injury to herself. "Check the pupils to ensure they are not dilated. If they are, keep the patient awake for as long as possible. Wrap the wound with white fabric so the bleeding will stem, and to create an easy way to monitor any potential wound. Pack with yarrow and mugwort to stem the bleeding and prevent internal bleeding."

She recited another directive on how to help injured people with each step. It calmed her. She remembered how to heal, and that meant she had not changed. Druid blood ran through her veins, faeries worked around her, but Sorcha was still the same person.

She could say it over and over again, but she wasn't certain how true the thought was.

Reaching the bottom, she pressed a hand against her chest in relief.

"There. Now where do we go?"

A druid soul wrapped around her bicep. "Past the cells."

"Really?" Sorcha groaned. "I don't want to go all the way back there."

"You want to go to the treasury?"

"Yes."

"Do you want to climb the cliffs?"

"I don't think I know how to do that."

"Then you go forward."

Sighing, she started forward with her shoulders set. If she had to walk by all those deranged souls, she would. But she refused to look as if she was afraid.

A clanging started up as soon as she moved. The souls liked to throw stones, rattled their cages, anything they could do to get her to look at them.

Sorcha wasn't sure if the others could see them. Eamonn hadn't reacted when a faerie soul who's jaw hung limp from its socket billowed through him. She had seen it, gasping in shock and horror.

He had looked at her as if she had gone insane. Sorcha knew what she had seen, the green glowing light of the dead man hadn't been magic. It was the fiber of what made him live.

Souls shouldn't pass through solid bodies.

She told herself not to look. The cells weren't filled with real people, these were the last remaining pieces of souls that replayed over and over again. She could do nothing to help them.

But she looked. Sorcha glanced over at the nearest cell and immediately regretted her decision. A dryad, masculine and covered in bark, grinned at her. There was a gaping hole where his heart should be and sap oozed down his skin in tiny rivers.

"Hello, pretty girl," he said, the muscles on his face twitching. "Want to help a man out?"

"You're dead," she told him. "You have no place in the land of the living."

"It is my job to remind people like you what waits for them at the end of the dying light. Join me. Share your beauty and I will save you from the darkness."

"Be gone."

A druid pressed its ghostly against her spine, smelling like pine and earth. "Weaver, use your magic."

Could she? She looked over at the spirit of the faerie and wondered just how far her power stretched. She could compel him to keep his mouth shut.

But there were better things to do.

The ghostly guidance of her ancestors helped pull thread from her flaxen magic. She spun it in her mind and wove it around the thread of the dryad spirit. Tugging lightly, her fingers danced in the air.

His eyes widened. "What are you doing?"

Sorcha didn't know. Her magic and everything she was capable of felt new and shiny. Fingers gracefully swaying in the air, she mimicked sewing a thread through a tapestry.

"I release you from this realm," she said. The magic needle between her fingers dipped. "Go home to your ancestors and family. Tell them of your journey and adventures, feel peace in the comfort of their arms."

"How?" The spirit looked down at his arms which were slowly losing form. "This is impossible."

"You have earned the right to death, warrior. Find your eternity."

"What have you done?" He looked her in the eye, horror and fear glimmering in their depths.

"I have released you."

"Thank you."

He dissolved into thin air. She felt the pull of his soul disappearing even as the energy left her own body. Every time she controlled a faerie, she felt it deep in her gut.

"You did well," the druid whispered in her ear. "Far better than expected."

Sorcha didn't respond. Controlling even the remnants of a soul felt wrong. It was the reason she was in this dungeon. Preventing others from controlling the free will and mind of faeries meant more to her than life itself.

And then she used such power herself.

The floor grew slick with moss and algae. The souls shook the bars of their prisons, screaming their rage and anger into the air until Sorcha's headache blossomed again. She did not stop and help any of the others.

"There," the voice proclaimed. "The treasure room is ahead."

She saw the door now. Gemstone encrusted hinges fairly glowed in the dim light. A sweeping movement had recently disturbed the dust on the floor.

The door handle was molded into the shape of a snake. It reared up with an open mouth, waiting for her to place a hand upon its metal surface. Gritting her teeth, Sorcha tentatively grasped the silver metal and pulled the door open.

Faint light filtered through slits on the walls which let salty air stir the room beyond. Roots hung from the ceiling, tangled and gnarled. Bats squeaked above her. Sorcha could just barely make out their small, fuzzy forms.

Graceful archways were carved with legends and myths, Tuatha dé Danann battling back beasts. Hallways split off from the main chamber, suggesting rooms upon rooms of ancient knowledge and treasure.

She was not here for the riches.

"Where is it?" she asked the druid souls.

"Clasped in the hands of the most ancient king."

"Which king?"

"Walk towards the center."

Movement in the shadows caught her eye. She glanced over to see the ghostly specter of her grandfather. Beads embellished his full beard and a sparkle in his eye made her worried.

"Grandfather," she acknowledged.

"Are you certain this is the path you wish to take?"

"There are many ways to alter the future. I wish to walk the path with the least death."

"Then you have chosen correctly. Towards the back of the room is my own tomb. You will find the sword in my corpse's hands."

"You really are dead?" Balor seemed like he was impossible to kill.

"Even the most ancient of beings must die, my dear child."

A stiff breeze passed through him, and he faded away into green light. Sorcha took a deep steadying breath and made her way across the wide antechamber.

The tomb was relatively simple for a god who had made such an impact. A rectangular stone with a plain cover. No carvings marked him as anything other than one of many soldiers who had died in this land.

For that, Sorcha felt her heart soften towards Balor the great. She ran her hand over the top, noting the crumbled stone at her feet.

"You chose a plain coffin?" she asked.

"It is not my place to ask for grandeur in death."

"You made a good choice."

"I like to think so."

Perhaps she was more similar to her grandfather than she gave herself credit for. Sorcha leaned her weight into the cover and pushed hard. It groaned, scraped, screamed in her ears until it fell from its base and crashed upon the floor. The heavy stone cracked in two.

King Balor lay with hands crossed over his chest. A golden crown circled his skull while all the flesh had withered away long ago. Skeletal hands clutched the hilt of the Sword of Light.

"Why would he put it with you?" she asked. "This is not your sword and giving it to you would anger Nuada."

"Nuada does not know. And if someone was searching for the Sword of Light, they would not look in my grave."

He had a point. She wouldn't have looked in Balor's tomb for it was far more likely he would raise from the grave than hold the legendary Sword of Light. His brittle fingers wrapped around the hilt, gemstones glittering on each skeletal finger.

"Do I—" she hesitated and gestured towards his corpse, "pull it out?"

"It won't hurt." Amusement warmed her grandfather's voice.

"I don't want to break anything."

"What harm could you possibly do to my body? I'm dead."

"Good point."

It still felt wrong to touch his corpse. Swallowing hard, she reached out to touch the dust covered hands. Mummified skin slid off the smooth bones at her touch, sloughing off like parchment paper piled too high. She gagged.

"I didn't expect you to have such a weak stomach, grand-daughter."

"Have you touched a corpse before?"

"Many times."

"I don't want to know why."

His bones creaked as she pulled back the fingers, snapping and cracking until one hand released its hold. She gently set it aside while her stomach muscles clenched.

"Don't think about the corpse moving," she said. "The body is dead, the soul is what makes it move."

"Are you reassuring yourself?"

"Hush."

She peeled back the second hand, wincing when one of the fingers broke off between hers. This was not how she wanted to find the sword. Why had Eamonn hidden it so thoroughly?

The wolf's mouth gleamed in the dim light, rubies dripping like blood from its jaws. Magic swirled around the blade. Tendrils of mist too thick to be water coiled around it like snakes.

She didn't want to touch the cursed blade. Nuada may have been a strong enough faerie to handle such magic, but she had no desire for it to touch her life. Steeling herself, she grasped the hilt and pulled it from the tomb.

It was heavier than she expected. The sheer power of the

sword weighed her down until her arms shook and the tip touched the ground.

Her biceps quaked. Did she want to throw the sword over the edge of the cliff? She could take it with her instead, force them all to bend a knee to Eamonn and stop the war now. There didn't need to be any more fighting. It could end with her.

"The future hangs in the balance," Balor mumbled. "It is your choice now. Destroy the sword, use it, or throw it away for later generations."

She saw the threads of magic wrapping around her. Unlike her own woolen threads, these were coarse and improperly spun. They weren't right, and they couldn't control her.

She snapped the threads hanging onto her mind and straightened. "Where is the cliff where Ethniu waits?"

"There is an opening to the waters below." Balor pointed down a hall near her. "Do not fall."

"I don't plan on it."

The sword suddenly felt much heavier. It dragged on the ground, sharp tip sparking red hot embers as it screeched across the stone. She did not stop even though the sound made her ears bleed.

"I don't care if you want to stay," she growled at the blade. "You've caused enough trouble for me and mine. Wait for the next desperate generation."

Sorcha swore the sword grew even heavier. Gripping the hilt with two hands, she threw her back into carrying it and pulled it down the hall where light filtered into the cave.

Salt spray coated her skin long before she reached the edge. The salt stung the scrapes on her arms from the thorns she battled in the garden and filled her mouth with the bitter taste. Waves crashed and foam flooded the front of the cave.

Sorcha did not hesitate this time, flexed her arms, and heaved the sword over the edge. It spun wildly in the air, rubies shining sunlight in her eyes.

Just before it hit the surf, an arm shot out of the waves.

Graceful fingers caught the hilt of the sword, holding it aloft for a few moments before sinking back into the depths.

"And good riddance," she muttered, kicking a stone into the surf for good measure.

She froze when Eamonn's voice rang out behind her.

"What have you done?"

The Invitation

Eamonn watched her heave the sword over the edge and felt his resolve shatter into a thousand pieces. His grandfather's sword, his legacy, now gone.

He'd seen the hand raise from the waves to grasp the blade. If she had simply thrown it into the sea, he might have recovered it. But he knew the claw-tipped fingers. A Fomorian had swayed her and taken the relic for itself.

"What have you done?" he asked.

"What you should have done a long time ago."

"That sword was the only assurance we had at winning this war!"

"Do you really believe that?" She spun on him, the cloud of her red hair billowing in her anger. Her cheeks stained red as she glared him down.

His woman was a fearsome creature when she grew angry. Almost enough that he didn't want to scold her, to shake her hard enough that her teeth rattled. Why had she done this? Now of all times?

"Sorcha, that was a relic of the Tuatha dé Danann! It can force Fionn to his knees. We will win with that blade on our side!"

"And you were using it against your own people. I will not stand for it!"

Her words flew at him, tearing at his heart and shoving him a step backwards. "You think I used that against our people?"

"Perhaps you were not aware that you use it, I told Cait that—"

"Cait?" He shook his head, running his fingers through the loose crop of his hair. "Sorcha, Cait doesn't want to be here!"

"None of them do!"

"Is this what you think of me?"

It all made sense now. He had been busy, there were too many things for him to oversee. He understood that she wanted to be with him. Eamonn missed her with every fiber of his being, but he could not allow his focus to wander.

Every time he was near her, his soul drifted. He wanted to touch the beloved locks of her hair, trace the outline of her stubborn pout, ease the nightmares he knew plagued her.

But he couldn't. He saw his mistake in pulling away.

Eamonn went to her, clutching her cold hands and pressing them against his heart.

"A chuisle mo chroí," he breathed. "Pulse of my heart, the folly is mine. I have done nothing to control the dwarves. They wish to be deep within their mountain halls with no one to tell them what to do. There are plenty of soldiers who wish to fight Fionn, and those who do not. I would never force a soldier onto a battlefield. That is a certain way to kill them."

"Then why did you fight Fionn when I asked you not to?"

He smoothed the tangled curls away from her face. "I am a general, and I make mistakes. I thought a small war party would convince him that I was not retreating. I was wrong."

"What did you plan to do with the sword?"

"I would have forced Fionn to abdicate the throne. He would have no choice when the sword of Nuada commanded him."

Her green eyes searched his, questions forming within their emerald depths. He knew her well enough to expect the question before she voiced it. "Is that really how you want to win?"

No. He wanted to battle until his brother fell onto his knees. He wanted to shred Fionn's face, strip everything from him and send him out to the wilds.

"I can't hurt him," he admitted. "He is my brother. My blood."

She tucked herself into his embrace, her tiny cold hands pressed against his chest. "I couldn't harm my siblings either."

"And now I have no choice."

"You still do. Eamonn, we can do this together. He doesn't have to fight us!"

He shook his head. "You don't want to get involved with faerie politics, Sorcha. Trust me."

"Why not? You were raised among them! You must be able to prepare us for what might come."

"That is what you want?"

He didn't want it. A part of his wounded soul never wished to return to the castle where they had stripped him of all rights. They despised him, feared him, hated him because he was no longer the handsome man he had once been.

Eamonn knew the dangers of the court. They would latch onto Sorcha with sharp teeth and claws, desperately trying to drag her down into their bitter anger at the world. His pure sunshine would slowly be corrupted.

He squeezed her tighter, holding her against his heart where she belonged. He wouldn't lose her. They wouldn't get their greedy hands on her as long as he drew breath.

She looked up at him, green eyes shimmering with tears. "Eamonn?"

"If this is the path you wish to walk, then I will walk beside you mo chroí."

"Then what do we do?"

"The correct way to address the king is to request an audience."

"That doesn't sound like something Fionn would respond to." Tiny wrinkles gathered between her eyes. "He seems more likely to ignore it, or deny that it ever reached him."

"Especially if it comes from me."

"What do you suggest?"

He arched a crystal brow. "Are you asking me for advice on how to approach this difficult situation?"

"Of course I am."

"You threw away the only relic which could have taken the throne from Fionn with no blood."

"Eamonn," she bit her lip. "I can control the Fae."

"You are the most beguiling creature I have ever met, but you cannot control everyone."

"I am a Weaver. I never told you what that meant. There is a particular kind of druid which can reach into a faerie's mind and order them to do whatever it is they please."

His mind raced through the old tales, the reasoning behind why they cast the druids from the Otherworld. "That is true?"

"Yes."

"And you can do it?"

"I can."

"You won't do it to me?" He only halfheartedly meant the words, although it was a slight concern. Sorcha had never shown any tendency to cajole faeries into doing what they didn't want to do.

"Eamonn," she scolded.

"I had to ask, mo chroí. Are you saying you can control Fionn?"

"If I'm close enough, I believe I might be able to. I tried in the dream when he visited me, but I wasn't fantastic at it. I did overpower him though."

"I imagine younger faeries are easier." Eamonn shook his head. "We are trained from a young age to shield our minds. Faeries do it naturally by the time we are adults. Too many of our kind can peek into others thoughts, it's easier to ensure that no one can pick up on what you're thinking."

"So that's why he was more capable than I."

"Have you practiced?"

"No."

"Not at all?" He could taste her lie upon the air. "Sorcha."

"Only a little! With Cait, who insisted I prove to her that I was actually a druid. That's all I've done."

"You need to practice far more than that if you plan to walk the halls of the Castle of Light."

He already knew the tactics he wished to take. Though he was still angry over the loss of the sword, this was no longer the end of all he knew. Sorcha was a hidden power in her own right, and one his brother might not suspect.

He would make her stronger than she ever imagined. They would train noon and night until she could control even him. Then, he would know for certain she was ready.

Sorcha must have recognized the calculating expression on his face. She shook her head and said, "No. Eamonn, whatever you are thinking, no. I will not be used as a tool to end this war."

"How else are we going to defeat him?"

"We will exhaust all other options before we force him to his knees."

He couldn't think of any other way which would seat him on the throne.

Eamonn knew she believed that faeries were good. He saw it every day as she healed their scrapes, ignored their quips and predisposed fear of her people. Even the dwarves, for all they had grown to tolerate her, whispered stories about her behind her back.

Sorcha didn't let any of it bother her. She went about her day giving and giving until she fell exhausted into bed. It was one thing he loved dearly about her and hated at the same time.

He wanted her safe and happy. The only way that would happen, was if he were king.

"What do you suggest?" he asked with a sigh.

"Let us speak to him first. What harm could there be?"

"Then I will send a missive." He released her from his arms and shook his head. "I cannot believe I'm allowing you to convince me to do such a thing."

"Why wouldn't we at least try?"

"He will ignore it. And then we will be back to sneaking you into the castle."

"If he ignores it, then I will train." The troubled wrinkles returned to her brow. "Though I would not choose such a course."

"Swear it."

"What?" She stared at him in shock.

"Give me your vow that if this fails, you will agree to do what I say to overthrow Fionn."

He held his breath, knowing without a doubt that she would argue. She always did.

But sometimes, Sorcha surprised him.

"I vow it."

❧

COOL NIGHT AIR DRIFTED OVER SORCHA'S SHOULDERS AS SHE made her way down the stairs. She awoke to an empty bed with the sheets thrown back and the sheets cold. He had left, and she wasn't certain why.

Although, that wasn't entirely true. They had mended their ways after she threw the Sword of Light into the ocean. So she thought.

But he was still distant. She often caught him wrapped up in his own thoughts, staring off into the air even as the dwarves shouted and lifted their glasses to toasts.

As more faeries joined them, Eamonn retreated further and further into his own mind. It worried her. Was this partly Sorcha's fault? Had she unknowingly made all of this worse?

Her nightgown swished around her ankles, the white fabric fluttering in the wind as she stepped out of the stairwell and into the wide expanse of the great hall.

Moonlight streamed through the stained glass. The giant sun reflected on the stone, silver and cold thought it should have been warm.

Eamonn sat in the dark throne, his head resting on his fist.

She paused. How many times had she seen him sitting exactly the same way? He liked to be where people expected the most of him, even when no one was around.

Her stomach rolled with nerves, and she blew out a breath.

"It is late," she said, breaking the still quiet. "What plagues your thoughts?"

"Many things." His deep voice rumbled through her, sending shivers down her spine.

Eamonn never ceased to be both a sensual and terrifying creature at every turn. He wasn't like the other Fae. He moved in an otherworldly way, but he did not show the natural, lithe grace the others had.

It was why she loved him so much.

Love. It seemed strange that her heart had called out to him almost immediately upon meeting him. She didn't know if it was normal, perhaps not, but there had never been a question in her mind.

Once her stubborn heart decided it wanted him, she had no other road to travel. Where he went, so did she.

His fingers twitched, beckoning her to his side. Sorcha's footsteps made soft shushing sounds as she glided across the stone floors.

"It is late," she said with a soft smile. "We should be resting."

"I find it difficult to rest these days."

"Your mind is busy."

"Among other things." He patted his knee for her to perch upon.

She was so tiny, she could sit on his thigh and not worry about her weight or his discomfort. Sorcha found it easier to forget his size now that she was in his presence so much. But he was incredibly large compared to her.

His massive hand smoothed down her spine. "Nightmares have plagued my sleep."

"About?"

"I worry you did not make the correct choice. Fionn will come, ravage this land and these people, and I will lose again."

"We must have faith, my love." She rested her head against his shoulder. "I still believe there is a better way. That we can still change the path towards something more kind. We shape the future with our actions. I would have it be a good future."

He sighed. "You are right, but that does not mean I do not worry."

"No, I imagine it doesn't."

She worried about them as well. War put people on edge, forcing them to realize that their time walking the earth was limited.

No one was ready to die. Many years stretched out into their future. Years which could be filled with happiness and life. Family, animals, a small house where one might farm or grow crops. To have those years be questioned was no easy thing.

Sorcha lifted a hand, tucked it underneath the loose lapels of his shirt and rubbed his smooth chest. "You have gathered a capable group of people. It is admirable that you worry for them, but I believe they can take care of themselves."

"It is not just my people I worry about."

She heard the warble in his voice. "You're worried about me."

"I do not know what I would do if I lost you again."

"Would you fight for me?" She leaned back with a mischievous glint in her eye. "If Fionn stormed the castle and stole me away, my knight in shining armor?"

Eamonn did not want to tease. His brows furrowed, and he reached forward to stroke the high peak of her cheekbone. "If Fionn captures you, he will not keep you alive for long. You are one human, with a life that is unnecessary for his plans."

"He will not kill me."

"He will do much to get back at me."

"Eamonn!" She sighed in exasperation. "When are you going to put an end to this foolish battle? You're brothers, you should be able to work this out."

"Faeries do not work the same way as humans."

"No, but they should."

He chuckled. "Ah, my fierce love. You see the world with such a light in your heart. I wish I could."

"You can," she vehemently declared. "You just have to try."

"I am, mo chroí. I am."

He drew her into his arms and tucked her head underneath her chin. Crickets chirped their midnight song, and the air was no longer cool with him touching her. Sorcha dipped her fingers into a crevice of stone, chewing her lip as thoughts danced through her mind.

"You're thinking," he grumbled in her ear.

"I don't know how to help you."

"This is not something you can heal. Worry and anxiety are not physical wounds."

"I don't like it that I can't help you."

His heart beat against her ear, steady and strong. Each thump reminded her that he was alive, but their time was limited. That of all the things they had survived together, all the things they had suffered, they might still be cut short.

His fingers stroked through her hair. Sorcha smiled at the slight tugging, for she knew he was coiling individual strands around his fingers and unraveling them again.

"Why do you do that?" she asked.

"What?"

"You wrap my hair around your fingers over and over again."

"It helps me think."

"Does it?" Sorcha tucked her face into the hollow of his collarbone, grinning from ear to ear.

"Why, does it make you uncomfortable?"

"Not at all."

"Good," he rumbled. "I don't want to stop."

Sorcha would never forget moments like this. She didn't need wondrous declarations of love, romantic scenes in front of other faeries. She wanted a quiet evening hidden away from others where they could privately enjoy each other.

But there was much left unsaid.

"Are you mad at me?" she asked. "For the sword?"

"Mo chroí, there is too much going on in the world to say mad for long."

"Is that a yes?"

"I will always be a little angry about that. But I will never let it stand between us."

She swallowed hard and nodded. "If you say so."

"Sorcha," he groaned while rubbing her back. "What must I do? I will not let this stand between us, not when I know what life is like without it."

"Like a piece of you is missing?"

"I wasn't myself without you at my side. I do not wish to ever repeat that again."

"I wasn't the same either," she admitted. "I am far more giving when I know you will be there to stop me should I go too far. I didn't know what I could or not do while I was home. Even my father commented on it. That part of me was something I left here."

"I was cold," he replied. "Losing pieces of myself over and over again as a kind of punishment. I forgot there were people out there who loved me, who cared whether I lived or died."

"I've never felt this way about anyone before."

"The Tuatha dé Danann believe in soulmates. Do humans?"

"My mother did," Sorcha said with a soft smile. "She used to say I would meet someone who meant more to me than my own life."

"A wise woman."

"A good woman who died far too soon."

She felt the hitch in his breath as she mentioned death. Perhaps it was too soon, he was still worried about her. She shouldn't have said anything so dark.

His hands clenched on her shoulders. "The Tuatha dé Danann

are not like humans. We do not have priests to marry us, nor chapels to ring bells."

"You know of that?" She tilted her head on his shoulder so she could stare up at his severe profile, outlined by moonlight. "Why were you gathering information about human marriages?"

"I tried to find a priest who we could safely bring into the Otherworld, but there were none near faerie circles for the past week. They do not seem to support the old ways."

"No, they avidly stay away from anything of the old religion. They don't believe in it." Sorcha wrinkled her nose. "Eamonn?"

"I want to keep you safe. If I die, you should have everything of mine without question."

Everything clicked into place. She lunged back, slapping her hands on his shoulders. "Are you asking me to marry you?"

"In a rather awful way, I suppose I am."

"You suppose?"

"Is this not the right way to do it?"

She groaned and tossed her head back to stare at the ceiling. "No, this is a horrible way to do it."

"What should I do?"

"Men get on their knees! They plan accordingly to ask a woman in a romantic way! They don't ask in the middle of the night because she happened to find him."

"I would have asked tomorrow morning, but now seemed like an opportune time."

"Did you even get me a ring?"

"A ring?" His brows furrowed. "Did I need one of those?"

"Generally."

"Then I ask we postpone this until I may ask in a more appropriate way."

Sorcha huffed out a breath, half laugh, half frustrated sigh. "Well, I already know what you're going to do now."

He reared back in shock. "Is this usually a surprise for women?"

"Sometimes we have an inclination that it may happen soon."

"You do not talk about marriage beforehand?"

"Some do, but many women are surprised when the man proposes."

"That sounds horrible," he scoffed. "Such a decision should be a mutual agreement. If it's a surprise, then how can the man ever be certain she didn't make her choice under duress?"

"I don't know."

"I will not do that to you." His lips set in a thin line of determination. "You know of my intentions now. I would like to marry you, and I apologize you were not aware of my thoughts. Please, take all the time you need to make your decision."

This man would be the death of her. She shook her head. "I know how I want to answer."

The alarm in his wide eyes nearly made her laugh in his face. "Well I'm uncertain I wish to know what such a quick response is."

"Do you think I will say no?"

"I never have any idea what you might say."

"Yes," she said immediately. "A thousand times yes."

"That I don't know what you'll say, or that you wish to marry me?"

"I will marry you in whatever way you wish. I do not need a priest, I am satisfied with the Fae tradition."

"That's much easier."

He sank his hand in her hair and pulled her forward for a kiss that rocked her soul. She gasped as his lips smoothed over hers, teeth and crystals nipping.

"I pledge my soul to you," he growled. "My heart, my mind, my life are now yours."

Somehow, she knew she was supposed to say the words. "I pledge my soul to you, my heart, my mind, and my life are now yours."

⚜

"Good," Eamonn called out. "Again!"

The young dwarves all stood in formation, squaring their shoulders and attempting to stand like he did. It was the sincerest form of flattery and one that did not escape his notice. The boys were learning fast. He wouldn't put them in a war soon, but they didn't need to know that.

Dwarves were talented in many areas of war. Their arms were strong from manual labor and lifting stone. Their punches were enough to cause Eamonn's teeth to crack. The right handed hook a few of them dealt made him see stars.

They were a better army than he remembered the Tuatha dé Danann being. Perhaps it was because they were so eager to learn.

Sorcha had forgiven him in the eyes of their people. She ate with him every night, scooped food from his bowl and stoked his arm when the others were looking. Although they were still learning their way around each other, the dwarves had relaxed.

When the king and queen were happy, so were their people.

"Raise arms!"

The dwarven boys and girls held their swords horizontal over their heads, freezing in place while waiting for his next order.

He held out just long enough for the weakest few to tremble. "Attack!"

He paired them off in twos and threes. Individual sparring for those who were not confident in their abilities, and larger groups for those who had fought with him longer. Their parents trained in the afternoon.

He was slowly turning this castle into an army full of legendary warriors. Untried, but capable in every way he could make them.

Ghosts of the past haunted his steps. Eamonn couldn't shake the feeling that something bad would happen. He wanted to be present for as long as he could.

"Again!" he shouted.

They didn't need to train even more than they already did. These men and women were no longer children. They could step onto the battlefield confidently and know they could protect themselves.

"You work them too hard," Sorcha's soft voice echoed through his being. A shiver trailed down his spine, and he reminded himself to pay attention to his pupils.

"They need it."

"They need water and food."

The amusement he heard made him glance over his shoulder.

She wore a plain linen dress that hugged her arms and waist while leaving her legs free to move. The style was far more dwarven than he liked. But on her? It was magical.

Sorcha had taken to wearing her long curls free. They waved in the breeze and stretched towards him as if begging for his touch.

He groaned. "You are distracting me."

"That was precisely the point. Come, mo chroí. It's far past time for us to take our lunch."

"Our lunch?" He lifted a brow. "We do not have a lunch."

"We do now."

She lifted a small wicker basket. The lid was closed, revealing nothing but a small corner of red fabric.

"You brought me food?"

"I brought *us* a picnic. I thought we might disappear for the afternoon."

"I need to train the adults."

"They know how to fight, Eamonn." She ducked underneath the training ground fence and waltzed towards him. Her hand brushed against his chest, sending shivers down his spine once more. "They can practice without you for one day. Let us go and enjoy ourselves."

"Have we heard any response from Fionn?" The letter hung over him like a dark cloud.

"No, not yet."

"How much longer are we waiting until you begin your training?"

"Enough talk of work! Let us go and enjoy ourselves for the afternoon. It is the last warm day of the summer before the rains catch us. And then it will be winter, and we'll be stuck inside the castle all day!"

He felt time bearing down on his shoulders. He should be a king. His people needed him to drive them until they were better fighters than he.

But she wanted to play in the fields. The smile on her face was as tempting as a warm summer breeze.

Finally, he relented. "All right. Get out of the training yard while I finish up here."

"Hurry, please. I have plans for us."

"Plans?" He didn't like the wicked glint in her eyes. "Sorcha, what plans?"

"They're a surprise!"

"I don't like surprises."

He tried to catch the tail end of her dress as she whirled from him, but she was already gone. The woman was likely to be as much pixie as druid.

Eamonn growled in frustration, torn between duty and desire.

"Enough!" he shouted to his students. "We are done for the day!"

He expected complaints and worried noises. That was what he was used to from the soldiers in his previous company. The children did not make any sound he recognized.

Casting a calculating glance over them all, he saw how tired they were. Their shoulders slumped forward and they let their swords hang in the dirt if they hadn't dropped them entirely. Their eyes were drooping, a few even listing to the side.

Not a single one had complained throughout the entire training.

His heart warmed. "You've all done well today! You've earned your supper. Enjoy your afternoon with your family and forget training for the time."

"Are you going off with your lady friend?" One of the boys called out.

"I am."

The boy was nearing his teenage years. He might even travel with Eamonn's company if the war came to that. For a dwarf, he was tall and broad. His face was handsome, beard already thick and lush.

While the others left the training yard in a hurry, this handsome child stayed behind. Eamonn recognized a youngling who wished to speak. He lingered and waited for the dwarf to come to him.

Like a wild horse he wished to break, he remembered Sorcha proclaiming.

"My king?" the boy asked.

Eamonn glanced at him but did not speak.

"I have a question for you that I did not want to ask my Pa."

This had already gotten off to a bad start. Eamonn propped himself up against the fence, crossed his arms firmly over his chest, and tried not to appear worried. "Go on with it."

"It's just..." The boy scuffed his feet in the dirt. "There's a girl I like, you see. She's one of the peat faeries that comes in here now and then. I thoughts, seeing as you and your lady aren't the same species, that maybe you'd be able to help. I don't even know how to talk to her."

The tips of Eamonn's ears heated. Was the boy asking him for relationship advice? Him?

Years ago he might have been capable of giving the dwarf good advice. Women had flocked to him just because he would be king and was as handsome as his twin. For some, the fact that they were twins had been most of the appeal.

Now? It had been centuries since he had even thought about a healthy relationship with a woman. Not until Sorcha came along.

Clearing his throat, he shifted his weight onto the opposite leg and gave the question good thought. "You like this girl already?"

"Yes?"

"Is that a question or do you know you're interested in her?"

"I know, sir."

"How do you know if you haven't talked to her yet?"

"Well," the dwarf scuffed a path of grass with his toe. "She's awful pretty."

Eamonn nodded wisely. "That is why most of us find ourselves enamored."

"And she's smart!" The boy appeared insulted to be categorized with all the other men who found themselves infatuated. "I've seen her figure out problems that none of the other dwarves could figure out."

"She sounds like a good catch."

"She is."

"You must talk to her."

That blew all the wind out of the dwarf's sails. His shoulders sagged and his chin dipped towards his chest. "I don't know how."

"I didn't know how with Sorcha either."

"You didn't?"

"Not at all. The first few times we spoke, I picked fights with her. Every time I opened my mouth, something rude would come out. I didn't know if my tongue was broken or if I would become a mute."

The boy snickered. "So what did you do?"

"I forced myself to keep talking. I figured that eventually, something nice would come out."

"Did it?"

"It did. And once that first sentence was said, I could talk to her without hesitating."

The boy's lips screwed to the side as he pondered the revelation. "So you're saying I should just talk to her?"

"It's a good place to start."

"What if she doesn't like me?"

"Then you keep talking. Be polite, listen to what she has to say, and she'll come around. If she still doesn't like you, then respect that. We can't win them all, boy."

Eamonn watched as the boy's face turned bright red. He stammered something about needing to find his friends and bolted from the training yard. Small puffs of dust kicked up underneath his heels.

He felt her gaze on his back, the cause of his own trials and tribulations. Sighing, he turned. "How much did you hear?"

"Enough," she said with a soft smile. "Just keep talking?"

"That's how I won you over."

"I don't remember you talking much at all."

She had a point. Eamonn pointed to his crystal eye with exaggerated care. "I talk with my eyes."

"Sure you do." Her laughter was music to his ears.

It was why he had to stay away from her so much. He would give anything to hear her laugh over and over again until the world ended.

Eamonn swung his leg over the fence and landed lightly on his feet. "So, where are we going for this surprise?"

"I can't tell you, that would ruin it."

"I don't like surprises."

Her eyes sparkled. "So you've said."

She was a siren, calling him to crash upon her rocks. And he fully intended to.

Eamonn followed her as if in a dream. He was a lucky man, for all that she annoyed him or overstep her bounds. Few women would walk into the Otherworld and not grow to despise the strange creatures or their world.

Sorcha thrived here. She stood straighter than she had when she first arrived to the isle. Her eyes sparkled with life and a vivacity that he knew were from helping his people. She showed love to everyone she passed with bright smiles, blown kisses, and a gentle touch that shook the foundation of his being.

She was a gift he did not deserve.

They walked out of the castle onto the cliffs at the back. The sun was weak this time of year, the usually unbearable heat tempered by a crisp autumn breeze.

Salt spray stung his cheeks, but invigorated his soul. Eamonn had always loved the ocean. It was the only part of his banishment to Hy-brasil that made it slightly tolerable.

Seagulls soared overhead, their screaming cries quiet compared to the hush of waves crashing against the shore far below them. He hadn't realized the cliff on the other edge of the castle was so dangerous.

"Here we are!" she exclaimed. "Isn't it lovely?"

"It is."

He was no longer looking at the surf or the stunning cloud formations. He was staring at her.

The wind brushed her curls over her cheeks, her full lips parted in appreciation of the beauty all around them. The half smile he so loved quirked her lips to the side. He'd seen them frown, grin, speak rapidly, everything that a person could do. And he would never stop watching her until the day she died.

Her linen dress fluttered in the delicate breeze. She had to be cold, but she didn't shiver at all. Instead, she caught him staring and laughed.

Sorcha lifted her arms to the side, dropped her head back, and let the sun play across her face. The wind scooped underneath her arms, trailing along the length of her sides. She was beautiful, wild, and all his.

Unable to resist, he stepped behind her and followed the path the wind had taken. The dip of her waist was so intriguing although he could not understand why. His fingers spread over her belly and he stooped to breathe in her scent.

Strawberries and sunshine. She always smelled the same, no matter what she had gotten into that day. How was it possible for a woman to work all day and still smell like sugar?

She spread her fingers over his. Each tiny imprint seared through the back of his hand and deep through the crystals that spread throughout his body like wildfire.

They were growing again. He wasn't certain to tell her or if he even should. She would only worry.

Eamonn had always known that the crystals would continue to harm him. He had never truly thought about how they worked. They pieced him back together when he was injured and that was enough.

Now, he wondered just how far they would heal. A poisoned blade would sink into his bloodstream and spread throughout his entire body. Would the crystals follow that path? Would he be reduced to little more than a statue?

He rested his head atop hers, stooping slightly to accommodate for her small size, and focused on what was around him. There were so many things to be thankful for. He would be a fool to not appreciate them while he had them.

He sighed, stirring the sprigs of red curls. "What did you have planned?"

"A lunch with just the two of us."

"It sounds wonderful."

"I had hoped it would be." She looked up and caught him with her gaze. "You'll have to let go of me."

He didn't want to. She belonged within his embrace and nowhere else. But he also understood these weren't rational thoughts. With a sigh, he released her.

She sank onto her knees and opened her woven basket. The scrap of red fabric was a blanket she spread across the ground, patting gently to remind him that he could also sit.

It all seemed strange.

Eamonn frowned, but sat down next to her. "We're eating on the ground?"

"Yes."

"There are perfectly good tables within the castles."

"Don't you remember taking women out into the wilds? To eat among the birds?"

"Vaguely." He leaned back on an elbow and hooked his ankles. "That was back when I thought I could woo a woman with pretty words."

"Really?" Sorcha made herself busy sorting through the basket, but he could see she was intrigued. "Were you quite dashing?"

"All faerie men think they are poets."

"I cannot imagine you as a poet," she said with a chuckle.

He was almost insulted. Plucking a blade of grass from nearby, he stuck it between his lips and stared her down. "Why's that?"

"You don't seem the kind of man who would take the time to string together words. You're more the type to back a woman into a corner and kiss her senseless."

"It's what I did with you."

"Precisely."

She thought she knew him so well. He almost wanted to let her believe it of him, for that was who he was now. Eamonn had become that man after three hundred years in faerie courts. His father once said that men had to sow their wild oats long before they became intelligent royals.

"I trained as a general my entire life, but I was not always on the battlefield."

"You weren't?" Her jaw dropped. "I thought you weren't like your brother."

"We both went through similar training when we were children and young men."

"How young?"

"Three or four hundred years, give or take a few centuries I cannot remember."

"What did you do then?" She gave up on the basket and turned completely towards him. Her legs crossed, skirts akimbo as she leaned forward for a story. "Tell me, Stone King, what kinds of poetry would you use to woo a woman?"

"I have no use for those words any longer."

"Of course you do! I want to hear them Eamonn."

He didn't want to speak them. His ears heated, turning bright red under her scrutiny. "You'd laugh."

She clapped her hands on her thighs in disappointment. "So you aren't good with words then. You'd wax on about her corn-flower eyes and laughter that sounds of bells, wouldn't you? The same poetry every man thinks will win a woman's heart."

"You know these tricks?"

"Every man has tried to use them on my sisters or I." Sorcha rolled her eyes. "They never work."

"You compare me to human men?"

"What else should I compare you to? I haven't heard any faerie men recite poetry."

He pursed his lips. She thought he was similar to any man she had ever had before? It was a pity these humans were so pathetic.

Eamonn grabbed her hand so quickly that she gasped. Her eyes wide, she stared at him as he brought her knuckles to his lips.

"When I was young, I would have told you that I heard your voice in the song of the sea. That in your absence, the scent of strawberries filled me with yearning for your hair, your lips, the white moons of your fingertips." He stared down at her hand in his, stroked her palm gently with his nails.

"Eamonn—"

"I am no longer the faerie prince with soft words. My poetry for you is a vow. The world may burn down around us, but nary a flame shall touch thy beloved flesh. The ocean may swallow the land, but I shall be your ship and feed you sweet air. A sword may try to cut you down, but I will bear all your wounds. I have lived a thousand years in the dark, waiting for the rays of your sunlight."

Her ragged breaths filled his heart with a longing he could not explain. He desired her, but not her body. He wanted her thoughts, her dreams, her wishes, her future. Every bit of her was his, and he wanted to mark it all.

"That was beautiful," she murmured.

"I told you all faerie men are poets at heart."

"That was not poetry. That was *you*."

Their gazes caught, and he forgot what they were even speaking of. Her eyes blazed, singing her love. He wished he was as good as the best faerie poet.

She deserved every sonnet he could write. Those days were long gone, but Eamonn wished he could go back. Even for a few moments.

Clearing his throat, he nodded towards the basket. "What did you bring, mo chroí?"

"Oh." She dragged it towards her. "A little something I thought you'd appreciate."

Sorcha pulled out a loaf of bread, warm steam still puffing from its surface. A small jar of honey and cream, more for him than her. He knew she didn't like the sweet gold. And finally, she pulled out a small wrapped bundle that she revealed to hold fresh strawberries.

He leaned forward and pulled one out of her hand. "Where did you get these?"

"I asked Cian for a favor."

"He grew you strawberries out of season?"

She shrugged. "I might have pushed for them."

"You wicked thing." He bit into the soft flesh, savoring the sweet taste that danced over his tongue. Nearly as lovely as her, but not quite so satisfying.

He felt her eyes on him. The memories they shared lit a fire deep in his belly.

"Are you not eating?" he asked.

"I was enjoying the view."

It was almost too easy to pluck a strawberry from her grasp and hold it to her lips. "Bite."

For once in her life, she did not argue. He nearly groaned as her white teeth bit into the red flesh, soft lips barely touching his fingertips.

As the first time, a small trickle of wine red juice trickled from her mouth and traveled over her chin. It ran down the long column of her neck to nestle in the hollow of her collarbone.

"I thought I would die the first time you ate strawberries," he groaned. "Now I am certain of it."

"Why is that?"

She knew. She had to know why he was so enamored with a woman covered in his favorite taste. Woman and forbidden fruit.

A growl vibrated in his throat. He pushed her until she lay on her back, hair splayed out like a sunset. Leaning down, he licked from the valley of her neck to the base of her chin.

"You are a dangerous woman."

"Am I?"

"You consume my thoughts."

"You poor man."

"I cannot even train my soldiers without wondering what you are doing, who you are with—" He fisted his hand in her linen skirt, tugging hard enough to make her gasp. "What you are wearing."

"Likely hand-me-downs."

"The most tantalizing clothes I have ever seen on a woman."

"I borrowed them."

"As long as you wear them, I don't care," he moaned. His fingers moved, bunching the fabric in his palm so that it rose higher and higher over her milky white thighs. "You could wear a blood soaked cloak and I would still want you."

"Oh, don't say that my love, I may test you."

"Test all you want, but not today."

He pressed his lips against her shoulder, moving the fabric of her dress as he went. He knew she enjoyed the way his crystals scraped against her skin. The tiny movements she made were the ultimate victory.

Eamonn had always thought a woman in the throes of passion to be a wondrous sight. He spent centuries learning every inch, every trick to pleasure them. But each one was a unique pearl. A book that must be read, correctly and frequently to fully understand. He was a very attentive student.

Letting the rough edge of his lower lip drag just below the rise of her collarbone, he breathed onto the damp trail he had made.

She whimpered.

"I love how sensitive you are," he said while pressing kisses lower and lower. "No matter what I do, you react."

"You've done little to disappoint."

"I am flattered."

He trailed his hand up the rise of her hip, pressed his palm flat against her belly, and slid between her breasts. Front ties held her dress together. He sent a prayer to whatever god had looked out for him.

"Eamonn," she gasped. "What if someone sees?"

"Let them look, mo chroí. They will not bother us on the one afternoon we have together."

She must have planned this the entire time. The knots were loose at the front and came free easily. He parted the fabric and bared her to his eyes.

"Exquisite," he said. "It was the first thing I noticed about you."

"My breasts?" She sounded almost angry.

Eamonn shook his head and bit his lip. "No, mo chroí."

He smoothed his hands over the pale, smooth skin of her shoulders. He dug in just enough to squeeze her muscles. The fine bones captivated him.

"You are a storm of a soul contained in a glass bottle. So fragile and easily harmed, yet powerful in every other way." His shoulders rocked in a shudder. "You take my breath away."

She clutched at his biceps, tiny nails digging into his skin with sudden fervor. "Eamonn, do *something*."

"As my lady commands."

He dipped down, nibbling at the delicate swells laid out before him like a banquet. She writhed beneath him. He knew she was ready, but he was not done tormenting his own little prize. Not just yet.

Reaching for the woven basket, he uncorked the bottle of honey. She gasped as the soft liquid spilled over her chest.

"What are you doing?"

"Enjoying the meal you've provided."

"What?" Her voice sounded hazy. "I didn't—"

"Hush, Sorcha."

His tongue swirled through the golden elixir, coating his tongue with sugar and woman. She had no way of knowing what honey meant to the Fae. That this substance was as much an aphrodisiac as it was food.

He sucked a rosy bud into his mouth, spreading the honey until he couldn't tell where she began and where the sweet started. It didn't matter in the end. She shivered underneath him. Her thighs dropped open, and he filled the void with a surge of motion that brought her tighter against him.

Releasing his prize, he turned to the other with a growl that rivaled an animal. He could hardly believe how much he desired her. His heart throbbed his chest, lungs heaved with movement, and he strained against the tight fabric of his breeches. It had never been this way with a woman before.

Only her.

She arched her back, demanding his attention with a subtle movement he understood. Her body was a language he was dedicated to learning.

He brushed her skirts to the side and slid a hand between them. Her core throbbed, slick and satin soft as he had always remembered it. His entire body shook with the force holding him in check. Groaning, he released her and shook his head.

"You turn me into little more than an untrained boy! I should torment you for hours."

"I would surely die!"

They were the words he had hoped to hear. Eamonn fumbled desperately with the ties of his breeches, freeing himself with a relieved sigh.

He would need to be mindful of his crystals. He reminded himself every time that she was delicate, her skin easily breakable, her bones fragile. But she dug her nails into his shoulders and moaned for him to hurry.

How was a man to keep his head?

He flexed his hips and eased into the slick heat of her. They both threw their heads back in ecstasy. She moaned his name, and he clenched the muscles of his jaw so hard he heard his teeth creak.

Sorcha was home. Every inch of her, whether he was inside her, beside her, or so far away that he could no longer catch the scent of her on the wind. Home had been a place he had fought and searched for. Centuries had passed with many people and places passing by.

Eamonn had never realized home could be a person. He hadn't known how a single smile, a curl wrapped his finger, a graceful arch of a foot could change his life forever.

He moved, slowly drawing them both closer and closer to the peak. But it wasn't right, not yet.

He leaned down and smoothed the hair away from her forehead. Her beautiful eyes opened, meeting his stern gaze without fear.

"I pledge myself to you." His breath fanned across her lips as the tempo of their bodies quickened. "Everywhere you go, I shall follow. You are the only light in my life, the beacon at the end of a long and winding road. Together we will be more than lovers, husband and wife, king and queen. We are a thousand years of want and desire and love. So much love."

"Together," she repeated and pressed a delicate kiss upon his lips.

A jolt of fire and lightning raced through his body until he pressed his forehead against hers and joined her as they burst into a thousand stars. He imagined that in the wild rush of passion that he sewed her stars into his own to create a cloak of midnight that would forever keep him warm.

"Mo chroí." He pressed a kiss against her lips, her cheeks, her eyes. "My heart beats for you."

THEY LOUNGED ON THE CLIFF EDGE UNTIL THE SUN SET AND THE stars blinked to life above them. Sorcha didn't want to leave. Every second that they had together was infinitely precious.

She shivered. Cold air sank through the thin fabric of her dress and dug claws into her bones. She tucked herself deeper into his embrace and sighed.

"Do we need to go inside?" he rumbled.

"It is growing cold."

"Delicate little human."

"Druid," she reminded him. He rolled her onto her back, smiling down at her with a soft expression she never tired of seeing.

"Druid," he agreed. "How could I ever forget?"

"It's rather easy when you're so distracted."

"Am I?"

She followed the ragged edge of a crystal fissure from his forehead down to his lip. "Perhaps not as distracted as you were this afternoon."

He nipped at her fingers. "Don't tempt me."

Temptation was the definition of him. Her heart throbbed every time she looked at him. They were different here in this castle than they had been on Hy-brasil. Responsibilities filled their lives and finding time together was difficult.

The time they found was rare, and therefore all the more special.

She shivered again and laughed. "I'm sorry, mo chroí. I need to warm up. Unless you magically have a jacket?"

"No jacket."

He rolled to his feet and held out a hand for her. "Then let us find you a fire."

"Or a bed with blankets."

"Not yet satisfied?"

"Thoroughly satisfied, but finding myself still hungry."

He scooped her up into his arms and carried her back through the castle. She laughed as he struck the door like a battering ram. The sheer power of his body was impressive, yet he was infinitely gentle with her.

They raced through the halls, hiding in the shadows when a faerie passed them. His hearing was far stronger than hers. He listened for their footsteps, for the sound of their breath, and ducked behind drapes to avoid them.

He hushed her when she giggled. "We're hiding!"

"Why?"

The glint in his eye suggested he was enjoying himself.

She was so glad to see him happy. Bubbles of incandescent joy lifted through her being and spilled out in waves. She stroked whatever bit of him she could reach. His jaw, his hair, his shoulders, the ragged edges of his throat.

"Master!" Oona's scolding shout made them freeze.

They had just reached the stairs, so close to freedom. Eamonn's sigh stirred her hair. Responsibility called.

She stroked the back of his neck and smiled. "We had an afternoon."

"And a lovely afternoon it was."

He let her legs swing down onto the ground. Sorcha kept hold of his shoulder as they turned towards the pixie, wanting to stay connected to him as long as possible.

Oona's brows furrowed and the tips of her elongated ears drooped. "Master?"

"Yes, go ahead Oona."

"It's..." She swallowed and held out a small square of parchment. "A letter arrived."

"A letter?"

Sorcha's stomach dropped to her feed. Nerves traveled through her veins in electric currents as she stared at the too white paper. She knew what it was, what it had to be, and couldn't force her feet to step forward.

Eamonn released her hand and walked forward as if in a trance. She watched his expression, the crestfallen way he stumbled and gently took the letter in his hand.

He smoothed his fingertips over the edges but did not open the envelope.

She didn't notice she had moved until she placed her hands over his. "We'll open it together."

"It is the first time I have spoken to them in centuries."

"Them?"

He turned the letter over and revealed gold wax stamped with the curled lines of a tree. "It is the royal marker. This is not just from Fionn."

It was from his entire family. Tears stung her eyes until she could hardly see the sigil. They had condemned him, hung him, banished him, and still he desperately wanted to speak with them.

"Give it to me," she said.

He handed it over without complaint.

Sorcha slid her nail underneath the wax. It popped open with no magical seal or warning sign. At least they weren't trying to poison him.

She slid the letter out and ran her eyes over it, reading through the note with disappointment. This wasn't handwritten by anyone in his family. She suspected they hadn't even looked it over.

"All it says is that our formal request has been accepted. In three moon's time we are to arrive at the palace where rooms will be prepared for us to meet with the king and his court." Sorcha looked up. "What is this? We asked for a private audience, not an assembly."

"So that is how he will play this," Eamonn growled. "So be it."

"What does it mean?"

"Oona, prepare the dwarves. They will need to create court acceptable outfits for the both of us. We leave tomorrow afternoon."

The pixie shifted. "Is that enough time to reach the castle?"

"We will ride all night if we have to."

Oona raced down the hall towards the servants quarters. They would need to be up all night to piece together outfits that Eamonn deemed acceptable.

Worried, she grabbed his arm as he started away from her. "Eamonn! What is going on?"

"We're going to court." Pity filled his eyes. "We will need to prepare ourselves for the worst, and hope that my brother has not completely lost his mind."

The Seelie Court

They left the castle just as the sun kissed the horizon the next day. Oona and her faeries worked until their fingertips bled. The clothing they made was stunning, golden threads running throughout the black cloth that looked like starlight.

Eamonn grunted when he saw them, but Sorcha saw the appreciation in his gaze. Oona did as well. The pixie's cheeks flushed bright red in pleasure.

They decided that only a limited amount of their people would travel with them to Cathair Solais. They had no way of determining what Fionn was up to, and in the end, it wasn't worth risking the lives of their people.

The army would remain behind. Only Oona, Cian, and a few select dwarves travelled with Sorcha and Eamonn.

Eamonn wanted to leave her behind, saying that the castle required a queen. She argued that he required a queen far more than the dwarves, who had never had a queen before.

She won.

Eamonn set a grueling pace that quickly made everyone regret going. He lashed the faeries to their horses so they could sleep while they travelled. Rather than tie her down, Eamonn held Sorcha on his own horse and allowed her to sleep against his chest.

They did not rest until the castle was in their sights.

She blinked her eyes at the golden light that nearly blinded her. "Are we here?"

"We'll get a good night's sleep first. We'll all need our wits about us when we enter the palace."

She wouldn't argue with that. Sorcha waited for him to slide off his horse before following him on rubbery legs. He caught her against his chest, giving her time to find her footing before stepping away to untie the faeries. Sorcha started on Oona's ties first.

"We're stopping?" Oona slurred her words, exhaustion tying her tongue. "Why aren't we continuing? We're so close."

"Eamonn wants us all to have a clear mind when we arrive at the castle."

"Oh," Oona slid down and braced her hands on Sorcha's shoulders. "That's probably a good idea."

"Can you get yourself settled?"

"I'll help the others."

"No. Get your bedroll and lay down. We'll get the others."

It only took a few minutes to free the rest of the faeries who piled on top of each other and fell asleep in a giant heap. They were so tired that they were silent and still.

Eamonn spread a blanket out on the hard ground and sighed. "It's not the luxury we're used to."

"We're used to luxury? And here I was thinking we were living in a haunted, crumbling castle." She placed a hand on his arm, gentle and kind. "It will suffice."

They lay down together, his arm curved over her waist, her hands tucked against his chest. He was warm enough that she didn't ask for a fire.

She breathed in his woody scent and sighed. "Are you ready for tomorrow?"

"No."

"We can turn around now. There is no need to take back your family's throne now that you have your own."

"Nuada's old throne is not real," he replied. "There is no substance to the claim, and the faeries will eventually remember that. If I am to save our people and change the old ways, then I must take back the Seelie throne."

Sorcha understood his desire to take it back. She had seen in the Unseelie mirror all that Fionn was capable of. The Lesser Fae deserved a life equal to that of the Tuatha dé Danann. Eamonn saw that when others did not.

But she worried what they were walking into. The tense way Eamonn held her suggested he was also troubled by the possibilities. Fionn had never been a man to trust before.

What horrors awaited them?

She sighed and tucked her head underneath his chin. Of them all, she would need her wits about her. A human was little more than a plaything to these creatures. The others would watch her back, yet they all remembered what she really was. A druid was capable of far more than a simple human.

Sleep claimed her until the early morning light. Her arms were freezing and held close to her chest. He had left her some time ago without waking.

Oona crouched in front of Sorcha, holding out her hand. "It's time to wake up, dearie."

"Thank you." She rolled onto her side, shaking out the long mane of her hair and yawning. "How much longer do we have?"

"Not long. I'm to get you ready and then we will ride into court."

"We? Are you coming with us?"

"We're to be your court."

"Do we have a name?" Sorcha stood up and stretched her spine, loud cracks easing her tension. "The Seelie, the Unseelie, who are we?"

Oona did not respond.

Sorcha glanced at her and caught the haunted expression in the pixie's eyes. "Oona?" she asked. "Are you all right?"

"It's the first time I've been back."

"Oh." Sorcha didn't know how to help the kind woman. Pixie deserved the world laid at her feet for her giving nature and her sweet disposition. These people had not cared that she existed at all, and then Eamonn had dragged her to an isle far away.

Sorcha cleared her throat, "Oona, I realize I have been remiss in getting to know you. I don't even know if you have family here."

"No, dearie. I never had the opportunity. Pixie families are rather small, and my parents left this world a long time ago." She gestured to the bundle in her hands. "Let's get this dress on you and I'll see what I can do with your hair."

"Did you want children?" Sorcha couldn't help but ask.

"Yes."

"Why didn't you have them?"

"Lesser Fae in the service of Tuatha dé Danann cannot have children unless their masters permit them."

"Who was your master back then?"

Oona glanced over her shoulder as Eamonn strode towards them. "His father."

"We have little time," Eamonn called out. "Get her ready!"

"Yes, master."

Sorcha's heart clenched. She reached out and caught Oona's hand that held the glimmering fabric. "You don't have to call him master anymore."

"I do. That is what he is."

"He doesn't want that to be the reality for Lesser Fae anymore."

"I know, dearie. But I won't stop calling him that until that becomes truth for us all."

This was why she was here. Sorcha stepped away from the men and hid between the horses as Oona stripped her of clothing. She let the silken fabric slide over her skin, barely noticing the fine quality and cool touch.

Nerves made her stomach clench. She stared off into the distance as her mind wandered. Would they be as cruel as Fionn? Was she walking into a court where they would all attack?

Would she lose the people she loved today?

"Worrying will get you nowhere," Oona soothed. "Clear your mind and show them you are more than just a weak human."

"Humans are not weak."

"They are compared to us. But you are a druid priestess, a Weaver who is capable of great things. The granddaughter of Ethniu, Fomorian and mother of the druid race. You have nothing to fear."

"And everything to lose."

"Arms up."

She lifted her eyes for Oona to clasp delicate gold mesh over the top of the sleeves. The entire gown was made of yellow silk that clung to every inch of her body. Oona affixed bands around her arms, her waist, and her collar.

"This is uncomfortable," Sorcha complained.

"Beauty is not comfortable. Can you breathe?"

"Yes."

Oona synched the metal corset tighter. "And now?"

"No," Sorcha wheezed.

"That's perfect then. Let me see what I can do with your hair."

"Leave it down."

"It's not in style."

"I don't care if it's in style. I want them to remember that I am not Fae. Even if I'm trying to look like one."

It felt important to remind the Seelie Court that Eamonn and his consort were not the creatures they expected. He had grown much in the years since leaving them. She was an unknown creature they would underestimate. She wanted to use that to their advantage.

Rounding the horses, she carefully picked her way across the ground, avoiding mud puddles as she went.

"I'm ready."

Eamonn had donned his armor. Clean and oiled, it still bore the marks of war. Dents and cracks turned the metal chest plate into a dimpled mess. Crystals poked out where swords had crushed the armor against his skin and shattered the plates.

He looked every inch the warlord, and she was thoroughly pleased.

"You are beautiful," he said. "They won't know what to think of you."

"Ideally nothing at all. I would prefer to stay in the shadows. I'm better at listening then I am at politics."

"No, we have not had the time to train you." He tucked a strand of her hair behind her ear. "Let me do the talking while we are there."

She didn't argue.

Eamonn lifted onto his own horse rather than letting her ride separately. He swung up behind her, wrapping an arm firmly around her waist and pulling her back against him.

They were all quiet on their ride to the castle. The few dwarves who had traveled with them were on high alert. They scanned the distance as if waiting for an army to appear out of thin air.

Sorcha assumed it wasn't such a far-fetched idea. She held her breath, waiting.

They reached the main road without incident. The buildings around the castle were just as splendid. Gold poured from the roofs as if the rain were molten metal. Filigreed pieces so fine they must have been made with magic decorated the outsides of building like the finest of wallpaper.

Faeries milled through the streets, far more beautiful and impossible than Sorcha had ever seen. A woman with ebony skin walked by their horses, a red cloak covered her head and tiny dots of gold flecked over her cheekbones and forehead. She bought a strand of gemstones from a man covered in so much jewelry that Sorcha couldn't tell where he began. Perhaps he was made entirely out of gold and gems.

No one even glanced at them as they rode by.

Sorcha leaned back and whispered, "Why aren't they looking at us?"

"We are the banished. We do not exist."

"They *can* see us, can't they?"

"If they cared to look up, yes, they could see us. It is forbidden to acknowledge that any of the banished exist."

"How do they know we were banished?" she asked.

"They were warned."

So this was how Fionn would tear at Eamonn's confidence before he even reached the castle. Not soldiers. Not bloodshed.

Sorcha had forgotten how painfully intelligent Fionn was. The king wouldn't take the risk of making Eamonn angry. His pride could be wounded long before anyone needed to fight. A man with no surety in himself would fall without Fionn lifting a finger.

She lifted her chin. "Let them know we are not ashamed then. They may not remember our faces, but they will remember we walked through this crowd without fear."

The dwarves lifted their chins with her and Oona's ears tipped up. Sorcha refused to allow any of them to feel unwanted. They were dearly wanted by *her*, and if the Seelie Fae could not appreciate them, then she would.

"Sing the stones," she whispered.

One of the dwarves glanced at her in surprise. "M'lady?"

"Sing the stones. Let them hear us coming, we have nothing to hide."

Eamonn's arm tightened around her waist, but he did not silence the dwarves. They lifted their deep voices high into the air and let the wind carry their ancient song. Faeries flinched all around them, some lifting startled eye towards the newcomers before violently turning away.

Good, Sorcha thought. Let them know the high king traveled among them.

The dwarven song echoed through the streets, bouncing off stone and statues. Fionn's people scattered. Soon, the streets were empty of all but a brave few who refused to budge or look.

Sorcha watched them as they ducked their heads and kept their eyes trained on the ground.

"They look as though they are bowing," she observed.

"They are not."

"Do your kind not realize that looking a leader in the eyes is the greatest show of defiance?" A faerie nearby lifted his green-haired head. But he still did not meet her gaze. "It is a shame there is so little bravery amongst your people."

At that, the faerie looked up and meet her gaze. She smiled, cold and sharp edged, until he looked back at the ground.

They reached the steps of the castle and Eamonn did not hesitate. He clucked his tongue, urging the horse to continue. Sorcha leaned forward, gripped Eamonn's forearms tight, and took a deep breath.

The large doors opened.

Cathair Solais was as beautiful as she remembered. Polished floors, open ceilings that filtered the sky through emerald green leaves, tall columns made of the whitest marble with no veins to speak of.

This time, faeries filled the castle. They lined either side of the great hall which lead to a massive throne. Three stories high, billowing red fabric stretched as far as the eye could see. A great tree grew behind it, nearly as tall as the castle. And seated in the center, Fionn the Wise watched them approach.

Eamonn leaned down and said, "So it begins."

The crowd remained silent, their eyes staring towards the throne and not the newcomers who dared parade horses through the hallowed halls of the king. Sorcha nearly gasped in shock as they grew close enough to see the throne in detail.

There were two chairs on lower levels, upon which the previous king and queen sat.

"Eamonn." Her nails dug into his arms.

She felt the moment he saw them. His body tensed, his spine straightening and his breath sawing unevenly.

What torment he must feel! She wanted to close her eyes to

banish the image of Eamonn's parents who did not even look at him. They too, kept their eyes on the floor. Fionn was the only person in the entire room who met Eamonn's gaze.

Stone hands gripped the reins and tugged hard. The horse chuffed, tossing its head in discomfort.

"So," Fionn's voice echoed through the great hall. "The banished prince returns."

"I have come to take back what is rightfully mine."

Eamonn's powerful message sent a ripple of shudders through the crowd. Sorcha hadn't expected him to declare his intent immediately, but she agreed with his decision. They needed to be strong because Fionn expected them to be weak.

"It is a shame I must disappoint you." Fionn leaned back in his throne, crossed his legs, and gestured at the hall. "None of this is yours."

"This is when we dismount." He leaned down so only Sorcha would hear him. "Get down before me, mo chroí."

She swung her leg over the horse's side. Her skirts rode up her smooth thighs, but she didn't cover herself. No one was looking.

Eamonn followed, standing powerfully behind her. She could feel the electric power of his anger and disappointment in his brother.

"Fionn," he projected through the great hall. "You have ruled in my stead for long enough."

"Have I? If there is any faerie in this court who wishes to desert and go with my brother, please, make yourself known."

Sorcha stared at the crowd who remained silent and still. Not even a cough echoed, nor the shuffle of feet against stone.

She wanted to scream at them. Were they all cowards? Was this the faerie court she had dreamed about as a child? Nothing more than meek followers of a king who wasn't even frightening.

A smile spread across Fionn's face. "So you see? No one wants to go with the banished prince who returned uninvited."

"They would not state their opinions in so public a setting."

"Why not?"

"They are afraid of you, brother."

"Stop calling me that."

Eamonn patted his horse, the soft sounds startling a few of the faeries nearby. Their fearful gazes lifted to the high king. "That is what we are, whether you choose to admit it or not."

"You have no place here."

"You are sitting on my throne."

Gasps echoed again. The audacity of a man to walk into a king's court and level such a bold taunt! Sorcha could feel their horror, curiosity, and wonder growing with every second.

Fionn stood, his great height nearly as imposing as his brother. But he lacked the muscular build that suggested a hard life. Instead, Fionn was lean and tall. His body was everything Eamonn's might have been. Smooth lines, gentle curves, graceful hands that made women beg for a single touch.

He floated from the throne like a feather on the wind. Waist-length gold hair shimmered in a perfect swath of color. Fionn walked directly to Eamonn and stared him in the eyes.

Sorcha winced at the similarities between the twins. She had seen them both individually, but together they were a sight to behold.

They were mirror reflections of each other. She knew the stubborn set of Eamonn's chin, the curve of his jaw, the tiny marks at the edge of his eyes when he smiled. They were all on Fionn's face, right down to the exact wrinkles caused by worry between their eyes.

Where Fionn was stunning, Eamonn was not. Crystals and geodes ruined the beauty he might have born. Handsome couldn't begin describe the grace with which they moved, the whispered sounds of their body shifting even as they stood still, and the gentle inhalations that lifted their chests and flared their nostrils.

"You have no right to be here," Fionn growled.

"You had no right to banish me."

Fionn tilted his head to the side, lips curled in a snarl and eyes flashing hatred. What had caused such a rift? Sorcha refused to believe it was jealousy, for that was an emotion that dulled with time. Eamonn had nothing left. What more could Fionn find to hate him for?

The Seelie King's face wiped of all emotion and he turned towards Sorcha with a smile that made her shiver. "Sorcha of Ui Neill, it is a pleasure to be in your presence again."

He reached for her hand and she had no choice but to allow him to kiss her fingers. "I wish I could say the same."

"Are you not pleased to see me? Your king?"

"You are not my king."

Eamonn and the crowd stiffened, but Fionn laughed. "No, but no man is your king. Are they, little druid?"

"You do not know me, Fionn the Wise." His hand clenched around hers at the mention of his name. "You sit upon a stolen throne, and as such you have no right to it."

"And just what are you going to do?"

She leaned forward so the crowd could not overhear her words. "I argued for a peaceful treaty rather than an army at your doorstep. You should be grateful."

"You think I'm afraid of a dwarven army?"

"Have you not yet learned that underestimating a druid is dangerous?"

"Oh, I remember that very well." He leaned close, trying to intimidate her with his body. Sorcha did not back way even though she could feel his breath against her forehead. "But now you are in my court, and I have a thousand guards who would like nothing more than to run a sword through your chest."

"Careful, brother," Eamonn growled.

"And what will you do? Banished prince that you are?"

"You know what you made me."

"Immortal?" Fionn shook his head. "No, it is possible to kill you."

Sorcha's eyes widened at the revelation. What did Fionn know that they did not? She looked over at Eamonn who's troubled expression only made her more nervous.

Throughout it all, the dowager queen and king remained silent on their thrones. Fionn walked up the steps and gently touched the arms of their thrones. They did not speak, they hardly even moved but to acknowledge the son they had chosen.

Anger planted a seed in her chest that burned. Sorcha rubbed her throat and told herself to remain silent. This was not her battle.

Not yet.

Fionn sat back down and lifted a hand. "I granted you an audience, banished prince, not a scene. As you can tell, there are already many who wish to speak with me. Your antics and dramatics are not appreciated by those who already have waited for days to voice their pleas. You will remain in your quarters which I have graciously provided until the time of your audience. My guards will see you there."

Clanking armor echoed as a veritable army of golden soldiers advanced upon them. Sorcha's pulse jumped as the army separated her and Oona from the others.

"Eamonn!" she shouted.

He did not respond, only glared at his brother as the guards shoved his chest and pushed him out of the great hall.

"Fionn!" her voice carried through the hall so loudly that the king had to look at her. "Where are you taking me?"

"It wouldn't be proper to allow an unwed couple to stay in the same quarters, now would it?"

She couldn't tell him they were married, and Fionn knew he had her cornered. He was up to something, and she refused to play along with this game.

❧❧❧

"THEY DIDN'T EVEN LOOK AT HIM!" SORCHA SHOUTED AS SHE ripped the golden bangles from her arms. "Did you see that? They're his parents and they didn't even have the decency to glance at their son whom they have not seen for centuries!"

"It is the faerie way," Oona said in a quiet voice.

"It is a *stupid* way!"

Sorcha threw the bangles at the wall. The crashing sound only made her feel slightly better.

"They will not look upon his visage until he is no longer banished," Oona said.

"And who can do that?"

"Only the king."

"Right." Sorcha balled her hands into fists. "He will never do that."

"No, Fionn is unlikely to choose that path. He wants Eamonn to remained banished for as long as he reigns."

"Do we have no other recourse?" she asked. "How are we supposed to do this?"

She slumped down on the bed and put her head in her hands. Fionn already had them by the throat. Eamonn's plan had been ironclad. He was so certain he could waltz in and his people would support him.

They hadn't. They wanted nothing to do with the banished king, especially when his own parents wouldn't even look at him.

How cruel were these Fae?

She couldn't imagine forsaking her own child. No matter what they did, they would be in her heart for the rest of her life. But these people didn't hesitate to disown a child for merely being different. Ugly. Strange.

Eamonn wasn't any of those. He was a kind and capable man, one who saw the differences in others and accepted them for those differences. He understood that what made these people strong were their differences.

Oona knelt in front of Sorcha, her knees creaking. "My sweet girl, all is not yet lost."

"What else is there?"

"The audience with the king may go differently than we expect."

"How could it?"

"We cannot know the future." Oona reached up and brushed a strand of hair behind Sorcha's ear. "We can only hope that the future remains bright."

"We cannot even see the men, Oona."

"Then we shall plan on our own, we have no need of men."

"He will banish Eamonn again, or worse."

A rustling from the window broke through their conversation. "He's already banished me, he cannot do it again."

Sorcha lifted her head so quickly her vision spun. Eamonn threw one leg over her windowsill, the other dangling over the sheer drop towards certain death.

"How did you get there?" she shouted as she stood. She raced to his side and gripped his arm, terror coursing through her veins. "Get inside you foolish man! You'll tumble to your death!"

"Mo chroí, have a little more faith than that."

He grinned, and she lost her breath. Had she ever seen him this happy? The wild abandon of joy that danced across his features with the breathless excitement of near death. She kept finding new sides of him, new stories that his body told, new whispers of the man he used to be.

She squeezed the hard edges of his bicep. "What are you doing here?"

"I didn't like Fionn keeping us apart."

"Why didn't you use the door?"

"There are guards posted outside both our rooms. He wasn't making it easy on us, mostly just to spite me."

Sorcha shook her head. "How would that spite you? He doesn't think highly enough of me to consider my thoughts or plans a threat."

"He knows I will worry about you, and not about my audience." Eamonn swung his leg over the edge of the window and slid into her room. "Now, I can focus."

He pulled her into his arms and cupped the back of her head. She felt a sigh lift his chest as he tucked her further into his embrace.

Oona cleared her throat. "I'll find us some food then."

"A bath as well, Oona."

"Master?"

"We've been traveling for a very long time. I'd like to be clean when I stride into that faerie pit again."

"As you wish, Master."

Sorcha grinned and rested her head against his chest. "You don't want the bath just to clean, do you?"

"It's your first night in Cathair Solais. You should enjoy all the pleasures of faerie life."

"Which are?"

"The bath water here is mixed with ambrosia straight from the enchanted flowers. If I know Fionn, he will have too much added to the bath water Oona requests."

"What will that do?" Her brow wrinkled with worry as she leaned back to stare at his face. "Why don't you seem concerned about that?"

"Ambrosia in small amounts relaxes the body. In large amounts, it acts as an aphrodisiac."

"Ah." Her cheeks flamed red. "You said you didn't want to be distracted."

"I am in my childhood home for the first time in centuries, with the woman I love more than life itself. A man would have to be insane to not wish for distractions at a time like this."

"You may regret that come morning."

"I shall never regret a single moment of your time." His hands smoothed down her ribs to the dip in her waist. "If this is our last night, then I wish it to be a night our souls remember in the ancestral halls."

Eamonn swept down and claimed her lips. He pressed his body against hers, delved into her heart with his tongue, whispered promises against her skin all night. Promises they both worried he couldn't keep.

"ARE YOU READY?" EAMONN ASKED.

Sorcha watched Oona tighten the remaining straps of his armor, checking each one to make certain she had gotten them all. He could have worn the regalia of faerie royalty. It was the chosen outfit laid out for him by Fionn's men.

Eamonn had refused. Instead, he pulled out the armor which he wore like a second skin. Sorcha didn't know whether she approved. On one hand, giving his people a chance to see him as something other than a warlord was potentially good. On the other, he shouldn't change simply because they were used to a king who did not fight by their side.

She would be soft for the both of them. Oona had dressed her in an ephemeral dress that floated like a cloud. Green as sea-foam, it pooled around her legs and moved on its own. The sleeves were so fine, they appeared as if made of smoke. Gems dripped from her throat and wrapped around her arms in coiled chains.

"No," Sorcha replied. "I am not ready. My stomach is in knots, and I can't stop thinking something horrible is going to happen."

"We cannot plan for what might happen."

"What did he mean when he said you weren't immortal?" Sorcha stared at him with wide eyes. "The crystals stop every blade. What does he know?"

"I cannot fathom what he might be up to. He will not kill me, Sorcha."

Oona finished tightening the straps and Eamonn strode towards Sorcha. Confidence echoed in each step. He took her hands and pressed his lips against the backs.

"How can you be so sure?"

"He is as much a part of me as I am of him. Twins are two sides of a coin. To kill me would be to kill himself."

"You want to kill him," she said.

"And I am prepared to kill myself to end this war. Fionn has never been so selfless."

As he turned, she reached out and grasped his hand. "Do not kill yourself for this. There are other ways."

He looked back, emotions dancing in his eyes like the flipping pages of a book. "I have much to live for. I have no intentions of letting him take that from me."

She followed him out of the room, into the safekeeping of twenty guards, and back to the great hall.

For all Fionn's blustering when they first arrived, he had not made them wait long. A single night in the golden rooms of the Seelie castle could hardly be considered an extended stay. He had wanted to throw them off, make them uncomfortable, and then force them to return.

He showed them that his word was law by simply making them go away and then he would see them on his own terms. Their plans were foiled that easily.

It made her worried.

Every inch of this castle spread fear throughout her mind and soul. What would Fionn do? What madness could he bring to life?

Eamonn's square shoulders did not waver as he stepped into the throne room. Sorcha locked her eyes on his form, the only rock that grounded her. He did not let fear rule him. Neither should she.

Faeries filled the hall again. Why? Fionn had made it seem as though they were waiting to speak with him, but she recognized many of their faces. These were the same faeries as before. Beauty, so powerful that it hurt her eyes, spread across his court.

She glanced at Oona. "They are faerie nobility, aren't they?"

"They are."

"Why are they here?"

Eamonn strode towards the throne, halting mere feet from his parents. "My petition was for a private audience."

Fionn reclined on his throne, rings glittering on his fingers. "And it is within my right to deny that request. Your petition will be public."

"Are you certain you wish to do this, brother?"

"You have nothing to say."

Eamonn bowed his head. "Then I shall address both you and your court."

"You may begin."

The faeries looked up as one and met the gaze of the high king. The firstborn son who should have ruled them, but had fallen from grace.

Sorcha's throat clenched. They *looked* at him. All it took was a few words from Fionn and suddenly Eamonn existed again. But why? Why now would he allow it?

Her beloved hesitated for a brief moment as he met individual gazes.

"My people, you have suffered long enough. The throne has always passed to the firstborn of the king and queen, never the second unless the first dies. I am not dead. Many of you have fought beside me on the battlefield, some have saved my life. Others, I have saved.

"You knew me from when I was a little boy. You watched me grow with confidence and honor, you loved me as one of your own.

"This deformity was not my choice, but neither was beauty yours. Your king caused this wound and all others you see upon my face. What you look upon is your own face, your fears, your temptations, your nightmares. I may be ugly, but I am far more worthy a king than the one who sits upon your throne.

"Faeries should not be slaves. We have a chance in this moment, to change our world. To live with tolerance of each other, to grow stronger together. I will not rest until I sit upon that throne and bring our people together once and for all."

His words were beautiful. They brought tears to Sorcha's eyes and were spoken like a true king. One who would take the burdens of his people and carry them upon his shoulders.

But did they see it?

She looked over the crowd of people and her heart fell. They did not care for his words. No one moved, blinked, or breathed as they stared him down.

Fionn scoffed. "And so you have had your petition, banished prince. Your people have given their answer."

Eamonn did not respond. He kept his gaze locked upon the men and women who scorned him so easily. His expression did not change, the set of his shoulders did not move. He watched them and waited.

She sucked in a wavering breath, telling herself not to cry.

The king sighed. "Yours is not the only petition I accepted."

Eamonn turned and stared. "What?"

"You sent a request with two names, and I accepted both."

"Whose?"

"Mine," Sorcha said. Her voice carried line the peal of a bell. "I signed my name on the letter."

He twisted towards her. "Why would you do that?"

"I don't know."

Hundreds of faerie gazes burned. They waited for the druid woman to say something that might change their minds. Something that would rock the very foundation of their world.

And she couldn't find a single word.

Fionn gestured for her to step forward. "Come here, Sorcha."

Her feet carried her without her knowledge. She watched the faces as she passed by and wondered what she could say that would change their minds. They already knew what decision they would make. They had condemned him years ago and didn't want to alter their thoughts.

She stopped next to Eamonn and brushed her pinky against his. She wouldn't disgrace him by taking his hand.

"Not there," Fionn said. "Approach the throne."

What games did he play now? She looked up at Eamonn who stared down at her with worry in his eyes. But she had no choice. The king had summoned her to his side.

Each step felt strange. The stairs weren't right to walk upon. A king should be level with his people, should eat at their table, fight by their side. He shouldn't sit above them and cast his judgment throughout a crowd.

The dowager queen made the slightest of sounds as she passed. A hum, a hymn, a whispered prayer that skittered down Sorcha's spine.

"There you are." Fionn licked his lips. "You're such a pretty little thing for a human."

"Thank you." Her words slid between her clenched teeth.

"So polite! Since when do you curb your tongue?"

"I have been learning self-control."

"I bet you have." He leaned forward and stroked a finger down her arm. She felt the heat of him burn through the fabric, her body's confused response to a man who was Eamonn but not. "Why don't you tell us why Eamonn is more worthy of this throne than I?"

"It is not my place to suggest such a thing. Faerie politics are beyond me."

"Even you shall not stand beside my brother? If his own lover will not claim him worthy then why should we?"

She swallowed. "I care little whether he sits upon this throne or the one he has already claimed. The name of the castle or seat means little, it is the people who decide where their allegiance lies. I have watched all those who seek shelter from your mistreatment arrive at our doorstep.

"And we have taken care of them. Each faerie who was neglected, whose family hungers for food. We cared for their wounds, filled their bellies, provided a warm place to sleep. Whether you continue on as Seelie king or not, matters little to me. We will continue to save those you have wronged. And you will continue to wrong them."

Fionn's brows lifted. "Banished prince, your lover speaks quite well for a gutter rat."

"She is a queen. You would do well to show her respect."

"A queen?" Fionn burst into laughter along with a few of the faerie court. "She is a druid. We ran them out of the Otherworld long ago, and for good reason. I should send her back to the human realm now."

"She would only find another way to return. She already has once."

"Then you choose him?" Fionn asked her directly. "There are many gifts I can give you. Many wonders you might behold in this court without the presence of a faerie prince that will amount to nothing."

"He is your brother," she said with a hitched breath. "How can you be so cruel? He is a part of you."

A shadow passed across his face. The same sadness she had seen on his face when he looked at Elva. "I cut out that part when I stuck a dagger in his back, little midwife. There is no mending that wound."

She didn't think anyone but her had heard his admission of guilt. Regret rang in his voice, saturated his words with heavy oil. He hated himself for what he had done. But he was not willing to back down.

They were so much alike. Eamonn would never let his brother rule at his side, and Fionn would never apologize. They were two pillars of hatred and jealousy which had grown so solid they could never break.

"You have this moment to change the future," she whispered. "You can take this step towards mending your life and his. It will not belittle you, nor will it make you appear weak. Two great men are stronger than one."

"Your words are so pretty." He reached forward and touched her cheek. "And your soul is so bright. He does not deserve your devotion."

"He has earned it wholeheartedly. Again and again."

"If only the world was filled with more women like you."

"Where is Elva?" she asked quietly.

He shut down, his expression smoothing into porcelain and hands gripping the arms of his throne so tightly that they groaned. "You have made your plea, midwife. Return to your lover's side for my judgment."

"Judgment?" her voice rang out. "We are not here for punishment. We came to you for an audience, king to king."

"I do not recognize another king in the Seelie Court. Nor will my people."

"They already have!" She backed down the steps, her soul screaming for justice. "They flock to us by the hundreds, and thousands more will come."

"You have fled from Hy-brasil in clear defiance of banishment."

"You have no right!" Sorcha screamed even as she reached Eamonn's side. "Your judgment means nothing!"

"I find you guilty of breaking the laws of our people and treason."

Sorcha clenched her fists. "You are not their king! The true High King of the Seelie Court stands before you, and you are blind to see it!"

"Sorcha," Eamonn caught hold of her shoulders. "Silence."

"I will not be silent while these fools call him king!"

"Mo chroí," he leaned down and pressed his forehead against hers. "We have failed."

"I will not accept that."

Fionn's voice boomed. "Guards, remove the midwife."

Hands grabbed her arms and yanked her from Eamonn's hold. He growled, palming the blades at his side and jerking forward. Two other guards held him in place.

She watched the blood drain from his face as he was forced to stare at his brother.

Fionn shook his head. "Release him."

The gold clad hands fell from Eamonn's shoulders. Sorcha twisted and turned, trying to break the solid hold upon her. One of the guards wrapped his arm firmly around her waist.

"You knew what the punishment for such blatant disregard for our rules was, and still you came here," Fionn said.

"Hang me again, brother. I will swing from the cord for as long as you wish, but I will come back here when that rope breaks."

Again, the darkened expression Sorcha recognized crossed Fionn's features.

"No," she breathed. Her gut clenched, her hands shook, her eyes watered. She didn't know what Fionn was going to do, but she could see his heart breaking.

"You forced my hand, brother." It was the first time Fionn admitted his familial ties to Eamonn. "And now you will remain here, for all to remember what happens when they defy their king."

"I am to be a prisoner then?" Eamonn scoffed. "You truly are a fool. Eventually, they will hear what I have to say as truth. Abdicate the throne. End this."

"You are not the only one to find the old relics."

Time slowed as Sorcha watched the scene unfold before her. Eamonn's eyes widened and for the first she saw fear. Raw and ragged, it shredded his quiet visage, and he gripped the sword at his side.

But Fionn was faster. He reached through the folds of his robe and pulled out a bejeweled handle. At the press of a finger, it extended into a wicked spear with an edge so sharp it was blinding.

Fionn turned so quietly her eyes could not track his movements and sank the blade through Eamonn's armor, between his ribs.

He couldn't die, the crystals would stop it. She waited for the telltale clink and shattering sound of metal breaking against earth. It did not come.

A choked sound echoed through the hall which was suddenly silent as the grave. Eamonn coughed again and Fionn twisted the spear. He pushed until the tip split through Eamonn's back and gleamed in the light. No blood tainted its tip.

Rattling breath mirrored her own. Fionn stepped back, wiped a hand across his mouth, and ascended the stairs to his throne.

Eamonn fell onto his knees and would have sprawled onto the floor if the spear had not caught on the stairs. It held him up, balanced on the very thing which plunged through his heart.

A wail split through her head, screaming and crying in pain. It was the scream of a bean sidhe, the thundering of a heart breaking, the shattering of a soul.

She made that sound. Screaming out her rage and fear until her throat vibrated, and she tasted blood. Sorcha wasn't certain if she said words, or if the sound was merely the raw, violent edge of agony.

The guard loosened his hold just enough for her to break free. She ran towards Eamonn and cupped his face, tilting his head until she could look into his eyes.

Crystals spread from the wound on his chest. They climbed down his arms, solidifying his stomach until he couldn't move.

Tears slid down her cheeks and her hands trembled.

"No," she moaned. "No, my love. You will not leave me!"

"I—" The crystals traveled up his throat and locked his words within his body. His eyes tried to say what his lungs could not. But all she saw was the fear and sadness. Their life had been taken from them. It was always taken from them.

"Mo chroí, fight for me."

His lips moved but crystal sprouted from his tongue. They rose out of his mouth and spilled into her hands. His eyes roved, sightless, until they too stilled.

She no longer held a man in her hands. No heart beat, no lungs drew breath, no eyes spoke of his love. He was nothing more than a man made of crystal, a symbol of all those who fought against Fionn.

Sorcha drew air into her lungs, threw her head back, and screamed. Her agony was so great it cracked the surrounding stone. Great fissures that spread like spider legs across the floor towards the hated faeries who had condemned him to this fate.

She would kill them all. They would die a thousand deaths for taking him from her.

One brave soul linked an arm through her waist but she would not let Eamonn go. She refused to leave him here where so many hated people would look upon him and laugh. They had no right to keep him.

"Sorcha!" Cian shouted in her ear. "Sorcha, we must leave!"

"I will make them regret ever drawing breath!"

"We will, love. But we must go!"

She opened her eyes and saw that the throne room was in shambles. Faeries tore at each other and the guards. Screams and shouts echoed her own though she did not recognize those who fought.

Fionn fled from the room with a small army of guards trailing behind him. They ushered the dowager queen away who stared at Sorcha with pain in her eyes.

Sorcha pointed directly at her. "You have no right to mourn him."

The queen flinched and fled.

"Now, Sorcha! We cannot risk being caught in the dungeon! All our work will be for nothing!"

"I cannot leave him."

"He doesn't know anymore." She heard the anguish in Cian's voice. "He doesn't know, Sorcha. We have to go."

Trembling, she pressed a kiss against Eamonn's cold, stone lips. "I will find you again. In this life or the next."

Heart numb, she stood and left with what remained of Eamonn's people. Her soul screamed out a vow.

She would destroy his house and pity the fool who tried to stop her.

The Druid Queen

"The king is dead."

The words rang throughout Nuada's stolen castle. The dwarves and Seelie Fae who found shelter in the ancient walls watched with wide eyes.

They had arrived two weeks ago. Broken, bleeding, and dragging Sorcha as she screamed and fought their hold. Once calm, she told the others to still their tongues. She would tell their people once the words no longer stuck in her throat.

She hadn't known it would take this long. Madness danced at the edges of her vision for longer than she cared to admit. Sorcha had not thought herself so weak.

Bran's words danced in her mind. Find something else to fill her time, to give her purpose, to force her life in another direction. She had survived without him before. She could do again.

But she hadn't thought losing him a second time would destroy her.

Now, she stood before the crowds of people with a clear mind. She had a purpose, and it was to provide a home for every faerie that sought shelter from the bitter storms of Fionn's wrath.

Sorcha said it again, forcing herself and them to realize the truth. "The king is dead. Fionn plunged the Spear of Lugh through his chest, the only weapon that could kill our crystal king."

"Where is his body?" A dwarf called out.

"Fionn kept him as a symbol of what would happen to all those who defy him."

Murmurs lifted into the air. The faeries' minds grew troubled, wondering what would happen next. They had defied the king. Living in this castle, following Sorcha and Eamonn's people, all decisions that went against the king's orders.

"We will prevail," Sorcha called out. "This place is our home. The people next to you are your family, by blood and by choice. Our lives remain as he would have wished them to. Free."

She buried her hands in the folds of her dress. Tears pricked the edges of her vision, but she couldn't let them fall. How many tears could a single person have?

"We will stay in this castle. We will continue to build our people."

"Will we go to war?" A peat faerie shouted.

"No," Sorcha shook her head. All her energy drained and her posture sagged. "I have no intention of leading our people to war. I make these decisions based on what he would have wanted. You were more important to him than his own life. We could not have known what Fionn planned, but we do know Eamonn's intention. We will not fight until we are forced to."

She left the great hall as the murmur of the faeries lifted into the air. They could think what they wished, but she was done fighting.

Her hands shook as she pushed the door open. Her stomach tensed as she walked down the hall. Her knees quaked until she pushed into one of the rooms and slammed the door shut behind her.

He is gone.

A sob shook her shoulders, rocking her body back and forth. *He is gone.*

What was she supposed to do when her ribs were cracking

open, exposing her heart to the frigid expanse of her soul? She had lost everything, over and over again. And now she was alone.

She slid to her knees and pressed her forehead against the door. Their people needed her to lead them, to guide them forward and all she could do was fall into thousands of pieces.

Eamonn had never failed them. Even the loss of their love had driven him forward. His own family hung him, and still he found the strength to lead the people on Hy-brasil, the courage to return home and look them in the eye.

She couldn't even stand.

Hands pulled at her shoulders, ghostly hands that chilled her skin.

"Sorcha," they whispered. "Let us comfort you."

"I do not want comfort. I want to feel the pain."

"You should not have to bear this weight alone."

"He shouldered my burdens. He comforted my worries and lifted my soul. Who am I without him?"

"You are Sorcha of Ui Neill."

"No longer. I left that life behind when I abandoned my family."

"You are the Druid Queen of the Seelie Fae."

"What is a queen without a king?" She licked her lips and turned into the green mist of her ancestors.

"A dark, powerful creature with no man to temper her steel. You shall wield a sword as your crown, a whip as your jewels, and armor as your gown."

"I have no more wish to fight."

The mist stirred and parted. Dark hair and billowing clothing covered Ethniu's graceful body, but her feet were bare. She had cloven hooves, tiny goat-like feet that tapped against the stone floor.

"Granddaughter," she said and opened her arms wide. "My girl, I am so sorry."

Sorcha scrambled to her feet, launching herself into the waiting embrace. Ethniu smelled like a rose garden. She breathed in her grandmother's sweet scent and sobbed into her shoulder. "I don't know what to do."

"Let us help you, child. You are not alone."

"I am. I have no family, no lover, no one but people who expect me to lead them when all I wish to do is curl up in bed."

"You have us," Ethniu said with a smile.

A deep voice echoed the words. "You have always had us."

Sorcha turned her face against Ethniu's shoulder and stared at her grandfather. Balor, Torin, the unnamed druid who had helped her through so much. "What can you do? Can you bring a man back from the dead?"

"I warned you," he said with a sad shake of his head. "Without the sword, the story changed. Sacrifices have to be made, and that is not always easy."

"I didn't know I would lose him. I didn't know that was what I traded."

"Your heart is so big. If I had known it would hurt you thusly, I would have prevented you from throwing it away."

Ethniu squeezed her. "All is not yet lost. You have found your people, and they deserve a leader like you. One who is kind, good, honest; who cares for them."

"He did," she replied. "He cared for them as no one else ever did. He understood them in ways I never will be able to."

Balor and Ethniu shared a troubled glance over her head. Ethniu guided Sorcha deeper into the mist. "My sweet girl, let me tell you a story."

"I have no need for a story, grandmother. I have need of a miracle."

"Stories can be that." A bench materialized before them. Ethniu sank onto it, skirts puffed around her. "You know that Nuada and I were married?"

"It is a legend I know well."

"The human stories never do it justice. Nuada and my father had battled for centuries. They ravaged this land, and all who lived in it. The Fomorians did not want to give up the Otherworld, and the Tuatha dé Danann refused to allow them to remain.

"The easy solution was to unite our people through marriage. I had seen Nuada before. He was handsome and powerful and everything I had ever desired in a man. Even to the Fomorians, the Tuatha dé Danann are beautiful creatures. I desired him like no other, and it blinded me to all his faults.

"I married him on a cold spring day. He pleased me for a time, and I gave him many sons. There were other women far more beautiful than me. Not cursed with animal features, but gifted with beauty that only the Tuatha dé Danann have."

Sorcha swallowed. "Are you saying his attentions wandered?"

"Wandered is the kind way to say it. I might use such a term if it were but a handful of women. He found pleasure in the arms of many before I discovered his infidelity."

"Why are you telling me this story?"

"You cannot trust the Tuatha dé Danann. They are a strange lot who see themselves as lords above all. You have seen it with your lover, how he refused to see reason even when his people were fighting to the death."

"He explained that to me. It was their choice."

"The fires of war can be fanned with the slightest of breaths."

Sorcha stood and shook her head. "No. I will not think ill of him. He was a kind man, he wanted the best for his people, and though I did not always agree with his decisions, the motives behind them were pure."

"No one can know the intentions of a faerie."

"I will not let you twist my mind!" she shouted. "I love him!"

Ethniu reared back. "We're not try to twist your mind, Sorcha. We're trying to ground you."

"By insulting him?"

"By telling you his lineage. Even the greatest of them all had his faults. That is why I left Nuada. That is how you were created. There are a great many things in this world you do not know."

"I know that I trusted him and he was far more capable than any other to rule his people."

"Would he have been alone?" Balor asked. "Or was he great because you stood at this side?"

"Both. The answer you seek is that we were both better when we were together."

The two Fomorians shared a glance and Ethniu smiled. "She sounds so much like me."

"She is more than you were, more than you are."

"She believes in him, where I did not believe in Nuada."

"Then we will help you." Balor turned to Sorcha. "Your lover is not a man easily liked, nor do I respect his family line. But I do respect you. If he has earned your trust, then he has earned mine as well."

"Thank you," she said. "I did not know I was trying to win your approval with the haunting memories of my dead husband."

"You weren't. We came here because your soul cried out for help, and you must forgive us for blaming him. We have not had good experiences with those of Fae blood."

She slowly sank back onto the bench. "It seems that not many have. Even their own people are distrustful of each other."

"With full right. Fionn the Wise sits upon a throne he has built from lies and rivers of blood. His twin would have helped for a small amount of time before he too turned towards the wickedness existing in his soul."

Sorcha recognized the words of a prophet. Balor could see the future, or perhaps he knew one who could. Her mind whirled, and she said, "That is what the Unseelie Queen saw in my future."

"Your path has always dripped blood."

"What would have happened if I hadn't thrown away the sword?" The Fomorians did not even blink at her question. "Balor, what would have happened?"

He hesitated for a brief moment before relenting. "What dripped blood would become a river. A war unlike any other would spread across Tir na nOg. The Unseelie would join the battle after fifty years when the refugees spilled into their lands."

"And Eamonn?"

"He would be known as the Bloody King. His armies would win the war after you died of old age."

Sorcha's mouth went dry. "The Unseelie Queen was right. The fate of the Fae rested upon my decisions."

"It always has."

"What now? Nothing has changed. Eamonn is dead, Fionn sits upon the throne, and the Seelie Fae have seen no positive change."

Ethniu leaned forward and grasped her hands. "They have seen change. They have seen *you*."

"I am not Fae."

"The Fae do not need a faerie leader. They need someone who will guide them through this difficult time, who will right the wrongs, and fight on their behalf."

"I don't want to fight anymore."

"Sometimes that is not a choice," Ethniu said. "We must do what is right for our people. And your people are still spread across Tir na nOg with no one to bring them together."

Sorcha's hands shook. She did not want to be the person who did this. Eamonn's dream was to lead his people. Hers was to be a healer, not a queen.

"I am not ready to lead the Fae."

"We will help."

She couldn't help but feel suspicious of the druid souls swarming around her. "Why would you want to help? All your lives you have tried to control the Fae. I wonder if you are just trying to fulfill that desire."

Balor scoffed. "We are dead. Even if we control the Fae through you, what good will it do? We want to see one of our lineage repair the rift between our species. A single person has a difficult time healing old wounds throughout all the Fae. But a queen? A queen could convince all the Fae that Druids are worthy to return."

"I ask again, grandfather. How many Druids still breathe?"

He pondered her question for a few moments as though he were reaching out to the remaining souls that still flared bright with life. "Many. Although most do not know they are Druid."

"Where are they?"

"Spread across the lands, handling magic as much as they can without humans growing suspicious."

A plan laid out in her mind. She wanted to help Eamonn's people, but she desired her own as well. "If I do this, if I lead these people, you think they will become more tolerant towards druids?"

"Yes."

"I need you to guide me. To help me in every choice I make because I desire to bring our people together. Both druid and Fae."

"That will take a long time."

"Then I suggest you bring me more water from Dagda's Cauldron."

Resolve settled into her soul like a sword sliding free of its scabbard. She had a purpose again. A reason for living. Even if Eamonn was gone, she could continue his work.

Balor shifted. "You wish to become immortal? Even though your lover is gone?"

"I will not share my body with another, and I trust no one other than my own line to continue my destiny. Bring me the waters, Balor, and I will devote my life to bringing home our kind. I will see these halls filled with Druids once more."

Ethniu lifted her hand and souls tangled around them. Sorcha saw their faces in the green hued smoke. Men, women, even children staring at her with approval or fear.

Her grandmother smiled. "Then we will whisper in your ear and guide your hand as you lead your people. But first, you must gather your armies. Spread word that though Eamonn is dead, you remain.

⚜

THE CROWD TEEMED WITH FAERIES. DWARVES, PIXIES, WILL-O'-

the-wisps, and countless others who feared for their lives. They did not know whether they should stay when the king had disappeared.

A month had passed, then another. One entire year since Eamonn had lost his life, and they became leaderless. Their queen remained in the castle, her wails carrying on the wind. They mourned with her, shrouding their bodies and homes in black. But the time for mourning had ended.

The queen called for them.

Sorcha stood on the ramparts. The wind whipped her hair, creating a swirling mass of red like a cloud of blood. She waited for them to quiet. Their jostling ceased, their whispers ended, and they all stared up at the woman they knew to be sweet, kind, and giving.

"The king is dead." Her voice lashed across the crowd, carried by magic and souls of Druids who repeated her words to the far reaches of the crowd. "But his work is unfinished. A usurper sits upon the throne of the Seelie Fae while his people toil and die. We will not stand for this."

She felt the excitement of the crowd like an electric current. They stared up at her with hope in their eyes, and she finally understood what Eamonn felt when he walked into battle. This was a heady feeling, one which could run away with her senses.

"We have spent one month in mourning. A full moon of regret, sadness, and fear. No more! Now is the time for action, and we will not let this attack upon our people go without response."

A few will-o'-the-wisps trilled, dwarven hums joining their approving song.

"Let it be known, I call for war."

Her people began to shout. They lifted their hands into the air, some brandishing swords already. They desired revenge just as much as she.

Sorcha curled her hands into fists and the druid magic grew stronger as they lifted her voice even louder.

"I call for blood. I call for vengeance. Fionn the Wise shall know our names and feel the ground tremble beneath his feet as our armies march towards his city. We will destroy the nobility and replace them with our own!"

They screamed unlike anything she had ever heard before. The resounding shout of a people who'd suffered their entire lives.

Sorcha understood their desire; she felt it boiling in her own breast. She needed them to feel it too, and then she needed them to understand the truth of their situation.

"But we will make smart, calculated decisions in every step we take. I will not lose a single one of you to men and women who do not care we exist." She stared at all her people and sighed. "You follow a druid. I know many of you personally, and some I do not. I say to you now, I am not human."

Ethniu had suggested a show of power, and Sorcha had not been pleased with the idea of it. The faeries needed to trust her, not be frightened. In the end, all the druids had agreed. Sorcha was not one of them, and they would fear only what they did not know.

The crowd silenced again, staring up at her in expectation of something great.

She breathed in and pulled on the threads she could see connecting them all. It was the slightest of tugs, the kind they wouldn't even feel. And then she tied all their threads to herself.

Sorcha argued this was the gravest of insults. She took all their names, all their memories, all their dreams and threaded them through herself. Weaving them into her very soul, knotting the tapestries of time. All without their knowledge.

Now, she saw that it wasn't harming them at all. The warm glow from her own soul, the part that still wanted to heal, spread throughout the crowd. It lifted their hearts, eased the torment and fear, breathing life into faeries who were very much afraid of the future.

They felt it. The crowd stirred, spines straightening, faces lifting to look at the woman who stood apart from them. The same place she had judged Fionn for taking.

"I cannot do this alone," she said. "I am a midwife from the human world who has no experience in war or battle. Ordering you without such knowledge would lead to devastation. I ask two things of this crowd.

"First, any of your leaders who wish to join my council are welcome in my great hall. For the rest of this moon I shall plan our attack upon Fionn and his castle. All who come to advise will be heard, fed, and housed.

"Second, all others must spread the word. Our army is already great, but I wish for it to be a thunderous wave crashing down upon the golden army. We will snuff out every inch of the Castle of Light and fill it with our magic. Tell others there is a haven for them here. The wounded and the weak shall be healed. The old shall find a safe place to rest their heads. All others will train for war."

Exhaustion sank nails into her bones. She stood strong and regal on the ramparts as her soul crumbled even further.

Eamonn would have loved to see this. The crowd screaming out as their champion spoke for them. As they took steps towards reclaiming what was theirs.

She had led him wrong. These creatures didn't want political talks. They wanted blood, gore, and death.

Sorcha felt more distant from them than she ever had before.

Turning from the crowd, she descended the stairs and made her way towards the great hall. She would remain there for as long as it took.

Oona and Cian waited for her. Their faces wrinkled with worry, for they knew what this meant.

The pixie held out a cup of tea. "Here, dearie. For your nerves."

"Thank you," Sorcha took the offered drink and drank it in one fell gulp. It burned her tongue and the roof of her mouth, but the pain was welcome. "Will they come?"

"I believe so. They desire retribution from the king who took Eamonn's life."

"Have I made a grave mistake? I do not wish for them to think me weak, but I cannot do this without them."

"They will decide upon your character once they have met in your war council. If you appear weak there, then they will believe you weak. If you do not, then they will support your decisions."

"Wonderful," Sorcha sank onto a table. "There is little I can do to control that outcome. If their suggestions are overly cruel, I will not support them."

"And if you do not support them, then they will fight without you."

"There are many factions of Fae," Sorcha said with a sigh. "They do not all fight together very well."

"No, they do not." Oona agreed.

Cian stepped up onto the bench seat and then onto the table. He sank down beside her, short legs dangling. "It's the first step towards doing anything at all. They are likely to be feral. And will want to test you."

"I expect that."

"Do not give in to all of their whims. They are good people at their core, but they wish for their people to be safe."

"Did I agree to another century-long war?" she asked.

"I do not know. You won't last for more than a century, so for your sake I hope you are not an old woman fighting a battle that may never be won."

Sorcha reached into her pocket and palmed the small vial of liquid the druids had left at her bedside. She had never thought she would drink it. It could heal thousands.

Drawing it out, she lifted it to the light and watched the rainbow reflections of the milky moon. "What if I didn't have to worry about age?"

"Is that–?" Oona gasped.

Cian gaped at the bottle. "Where did you get that?"

"Does it matter?"

"The relics of the Tuatha dé Danann disappeared before we even had the second generation of kings. When the first generation disappeared, they took their relics with them. Dagda was very careful where he hid that cauldron."

"The druids have it. I suspect they always have."

"Why?" Cian shook his head forcefully. "Why would he give it to the druids?"

"Maybe he trusted them. They've kept it secret for all these years, and no one knew they had it."

"Now they give it to you? For what purpose?"

Sorcha palmed the bottle, squeezing gently. "The first time they gave it to me, it was to cure the blood beetle plague. They told me it would heal thousands, or make one person immortal."

"Immortal?" Cian blinked rapidly. "You could become long lived? Like us?"

"I think it's more than that."

"Why would Dagda give that to the druids? Foolish faerie, they would only use that against us! They would become all powerful!"

"They didn't." Sorcha breathed out a long sigh. "They didn't use it all. Only in gifts to those who would alter the future in a positive way. There is so much mending needed between our people."

She stared into the glass for a moment, popped the cork, and drank deeply. Like the first time in the druid hallucination, it bubbled in her throat and settled cold in her belly. She didn't feel any different. The world looked the same through her eyes.

But she wasn't the same anymore.

Cian cleared his throat. "My apologies, m'lady. I don't mean to speak ill of you or your people."

"I will help in whatever way I can to restore this world to its original purpose. Kindness, honor, respect. All the laws that Seelie Fae live by have been twisted to suit Fionn's vision. I want to see it go back to the way it was originally intended."

A new voice joined them, booming and deep. "Bravo. I couldn't have said it better myself."

Sorcha leapt to her feet. The newcomer was handsome, tall for a dwarf although still not quite to her shoulder. Beads decorated his fashionably short beard. A golden crown sat atop his head.

She nodded. "Master dwarf, it is a pleasure to meet you. Have you come to join the war council?"

"Indeed I have. If you are to lead my people into battle, then I would have a say."

"Your people?" She glanced at the crown. "You are the dwarven king?"

"I am. But you, pretty thing, may call me Angus."

"And you may call me Sorcha."

He raised his eyebrows. "I've never met a human who so willingly gives her name to a faerie. You know that might cause trouble in the wrong hands."

She tugged on his thread, enough that he lurched forward in surprise. "I have my own tricks up my sleeve."

"Weaver," he breathed. "I thought all of your kind were dead."

"Many thought the same. It is not so."

"And glad I am of it. My father had many friends among your kind. We were frightened of them, but always pleased when they fought on our side."

She inclined her head and gestured towards the tables. "Shall we?"

"Are the others here yet?"

"I was unaware there were others." She tucked her hands behind her back as they made their way towards the makeshift war council. "Has there already been talk?"

"I profess, I do not know. It is my assumption that many will wish to have their hands in such a declaration of war. We have been waiting for a very long time to take on Fionn."

"Strange, I heard you did not wish to send your troops."

"Not to Eamonn." He cleared his throat. "My apologies, m'lady. I understand you were close. However, I fought next to him on the battlefield and I know how he fights. The man was reckless, without care for his own life. It served him well, but I had no wish to pledge my people to one who cared little for their lives."

"He changed. Eamonn was focused far more on the lives of his people than his own in the end. It's why he took the risk to visit Fionn."

"Ah," Angus nodded. "Then sorry I am to have judged him wrongly. What is your plan?"

"There are many, and I would have the opinion of my war council before I decide."

"I think you'll find there are many opinions."

The dwarf sat himself down, braced his elbows on the table, and looked her in the eye. "Shall we begin?"

⁂

THOUGH SHE APPRECIATED THEIR CANDOR, SORCHA WOULD never have anticipated the faerie leaders to be so vocal.

She held her head in her hands and stared at the worn wood of the table while the men and women shouted over each other. A headache pounded between her eyes, racing down the long column of her neck with every heartbeat.

They couldn't agree on anything. Each leader had their own opinion on how to attack, what to do with the armies, where to come from, what day to fight.

And there were more leaders every day. Sorcha hadn't expected the swarm of faeries who rushed to the castle. The cooks grew overwhelmed, the fields wilted, fights broke out in the bars nearly every night.

She tried to tie them all to her, but there were too many to keep track of. Every time she broke free from the war council to wander the streets, she would find yet another who she hadn't attached to her expanding web of faeries.

She breathed out a slow, controlled sigh. Every moment was another second to remind herself that she had asked for them. These people were here on her request, and she owed them respect.

They had led their people for a very long time. They knew

these lands as she could not. Yet, she still wondered just how much they actually knew.

Druids voices whispered in her ear.

"We could have made these decisions hours ago."

"Let us guide you, Sorcha. The Fae are only slowing down the process."

"It takes longer as more arrive. Make your choices now and tell the others they were too late."

She squeezed her temples. "I cannot do that. They deserve to have a choice in their future."

"This will only end poorly, Sorcha. You must control them."

"I will not use my powers to sway their opinions."

"Then you will be long dead before they agree!"

"So be it!" Sorcha stood and slammed her fists down on the table. The faerie leaders fell silent, staring at her in surprise. "We have argued enough."

"We still have not decided," the brownie hissed.

"Then I urge you to decide soon, or I decide for us all."

"You have no right," the pixie grumbled. "You are not a faerie, merely the catalyst for a war which has been in the making for centuries."

Sorcha rolled her eyes.

One of the peat faeries clawed at the table. "I did not agree to follow the whims of a Druid!"

"You agreed to that the moment you walked through those doors and sat down at *my* war council!"

"How dare you!"

The shouts started again. Some argued that Sorcha was the only reason they were there. Others agreed that she had no right to be their leader.

Sitting back down with a hard thump, she watched the proceedings and wondered where she had gone wrong. Was she not supposed to assume these creatures were capable of rational thought?

"They aren't," a druid angrily said in her ear. "Why do you think they banished us all those years ago?"

She ached for Eamonn. He would have known what to do. Worse, they never would have become unruly when he was here. They would fear for their lives and what torture he would force them to live through.

"M'lady!" Oona's shout echoed through the outside halls before the doors burst open. "I tried to stop her, but she would not listen!"

"Who?" Sorcha stood and placed her palm on the knife at her hip.

The woman who entered the room was so painfully beautiful that she was difficult to look at. Hair, so golden it rivaled the sun, spilled down her shoulders to her waist. Sunlight blossomed from her skin, making her glow with an otherworldly light.

Sorcha glanced down at the woman's fingertips, pleased to see the stains had turned gray. Elva had shaken the addiction, so it seemed. Or at least had not partaken in such activities while she traveled.

"Royal consort," Sorcha greeted her. "I did not expect to see you here."

"I ask for a private audience."

The faeries stared at her, and Angus chuckled loudly. "Sorry, we're not able to afford you that. Not when we asked for the same and you killed our king."

"I did not kill him, and I request you respect my station, dwarf."

"What station? That of a sheath for our bastard of a king?"

A pink blush spread across Elva's cheekbones, and Sorcha knew it wasn't from embarrassment. There was a certain sense of panic radiating around the faerie. She was here without permission, Sorcha guessed.

"Go," she said to the faeries. "Leave us."

"M'lady, I cannot agree to such folly."

"Out, Angus. All of you, get out."

She half expected them to refuse. But they stood as one, reluctantly filing out of the room. Angus was the only one to remain.

"You too," Sorcha ordered.

"With all due respect, m'lady, I intend to stay. Someone should remain as your guard."

"Oona will stay."

"A pixie?"

"They are surprisingly capable of protecting those they love. Please, inquire with the pixie leader and see if she disagrees."

He grumbled, but left the room. She caught the way he hesitated to close the door. He watched them for as long as he could before the doors boomed shut.

Oona shook in the corner, her body locked tight as she stared at the woman she had helped raise. Sorcha caught her gaze and nodded.

The pixie launched herself forward and wrapped her arms around Elva's waist. Tears dripped down her cheeks, and her lavender wings beat so hard the wind knocked a cup off the table.

"Oh dearie! I never thought I'd see your face again!"

"Hello again," Elva hesitantly said. Her hand hesitantly pressed against Oona's back. "It is good to see you."

"I am so sorry. I should have kept you. I should have run away with you and never looked back. But that mother of yours was so certain you would become queen! She didn't let you be a child, and she certainly didn't want me around you too much. I should have tried harder!"

"Oona, there was nothing you could do to alter my future." Elva gently set the pixie aside, grimacing at the tears streaking Oona's cheeks. "I dislike being touched."

Sorcha watched from her seat at the head of the table, elbows propped up and her chin on a fist. "Yours is a story I would very much like to hear. But not now."

"No, there is little time for reliving the past," Elva agreed. "Thank you for offering a private audience."

"As private as one might get in such times. Please, have a seat. I would offer you food and drink, but I suspect you would not take it."

Elva sank into the chair across from Sorcha, arranging her skirts neatly. "The others did not?"

"Many choose not to eat until they have become invested in the cause. Once they realize we are talking about war, they are more likely to gorge themselves on my gardens."

"I did not realize midwives were capable of such greatness."

Sorcha's grin was feral. "I did not realize consorts traveled without permission."

"I see your tongue is quicker than I remember." Elva ducked her head. "It is true, Fionn does not know I am here."

"How long will it take him to realize where you have gone?"

"I imagine he already knows I have left, but he will never suspect I came here."

"Why not?"

"He still believes I love him."

Sorcha leaned forward, steepled her fingers, and pressed them against her lips. "Did you ever?"

"Love him? No."

It was a shame. Sorcha had seen how attached Fionn was to the beautiful faerie. Though it hadn't seemed possible, he was gentle with his consort. Almost kind.

Elva saw the emotions flicker across Sorcha's face. "It is true, he loves me."

"How is that possible?"

"Did you think him incapable of it? He is just a man, like the others."

"He admitted his guilt to me before he killed Eamonn."

Elva nodded. "He has nightmares about that night. He dreams of the blade plunging between his own shoulders and everything being taken from him while Eamonn watches."

"That was his plan."

"I suspected it was. They gave each other no choice."

"They could not see past their own differences."

"Both were set in their ways."

Sorcha felt a kindred spirit in the Tuatha dé Danann before her. They both knew the dangers of meeting, but both understood why the events had unfolded the way they had. They both mourned for the pain the twins had inflicted upon each other.

"Why have you come?" Sorcha asked.

"To offer my aid."

"You wish to go against the king? To help build an army which will defeat him?"

"I wish for my freedom," Elva corrected. "I wish to make decisions for myself, which I have never done before."

Freedom. It was a concept they all fought to possess. Sorcha wanted nothing more than her own freedom as well, yet she was now queen of a people who were not her own. At the very least, she could help Elva.

"Then you are welcome within my walls. I'm certain you will understand my hesitation at having you here, and that I will assign a personal guard."

"Understood."

Sorcha leaned back in her chair. "All right Angus, you can come back in."

The doors immediately burst open, and the dwarf sauntered into the room. "I knew you'd have need of me, m'lady."

"You were listening at the door. I don't take kindly to those who do not know when they are needed and when they are not."

"I wanted to be sure you would not be harmed. The queen needs a protector."

Sorcha forced her eyes to remain still. "This queen does not. You will assign a personal guard to attend to Elva. Please, remind the others she is here as a guest, not as a prisoner."

"It will be my pleasure."

"Take care of her and keep her safe."

Elva stood, brushed her hands down her skirt, and hesitated.

"Yes?" Sorcha asked. "Is there more?"

"I thought you would like to know. He keeps Eamonn next to the throne, a crystal figured twisted in pain and anguish."

"As a reminder to his people what happens when they go against the King."

"No." Elva shook her head. "I think it is a reminder for himself."

"Of what?" Sorcha asked.

"I do not know."

The thought was unsettling, and the last piece of information Sorcha needed to hear. She wished that Fionn was one of the evil characters of old. The man who wanted nothing more than to maim and torture, who needed to be put down.

He simply followed the old ways and trusted that they were the right decision for his people. Blind and foolish, he made decisions he might not agree with because they should be the right ones. Fionn was a complicated man.

Almost as complicated as his brother.

Sorcha nodded. "Angus, please show her to one of the guest rooms. Send Oona to attend to her and post two guards outside her door. She is to have whatever she wishes. Tomorrow morning, bring her to the war council."

"Understood."

The door closed behind them with a final bang that eased the tension from her neck. She lifted her hands and massaged the muscles, sighing as the headache faded away.

Balor appeared in one of the seats, leaning forward to grab a goblet of wine. "You did well today."

"Did I? I cannot say anything was accomplished."

"No, but you're earning their trust."

"By letting them scream and shout?"

"They need to get out their frustrations. The future is tenuous, and that makes people nervous."

Sorcha nodded. "And nervous faeries seem to have knee jerk reactions."

"That they do."

She leaned back and watched as he inhaled the sweet scent. She had yet to see him or Ethniu eat, and suspected they couldn't, but he still enjoyed smelling the food and drink.

"What would you do?" she asked him.

"I would have gone to war long ago."

"How many people would die?"

"Thousands. The land would be decimated, crops ruined, ground burned, grass trampled underneath the feet of my armies. We'd have cut down all the trees for lumber, killed all the animals for food, destroyed the mines so the other army couldn't get more resources."

"So, you would have killed Tir na nOg along with Fionn?"

Balor nodded. "The old ways were cruel."

"Are they the only ways?"

"That is up to you, my dear. These people deserve at least one battle. See how you like that first and then make your judgment."

She leaned back in her chair and stared at the ceiling. It was a large decision to make and one she did not anticipate would end well.

<hr />

FREE FROM THE WAR COUNCIL FOR A FEW HOURS, SORCHA STOOD on the edge of the cliff where Eamonn had recited poetry. Her soul ached. It was a bruise she did not know how to heal.

"There are so many people here," she said to the wind, hoping it would carry her words to his soul. "Dozens of leaders, hundreds of clans, thousands of warriors all ready to stand in your name. I wish you were here to see it, my husband."

He would have been proud. He would have stood at the top of the mountain with her and stared down at the sea. Likely made a joke about how they could still run away and leave this place.

She smiled. He would have trailed a hand down her head and tangled curls around his fingers. He had always loved her hair.

Stones crunched from the crack in the wall behind her. It was almost completely fixed when she asked them to let it remain cracked. Though it was a weakness should an army climb the cliffs, she couldn't let them take this place away from her.

"Oona," she sighed. "I asked to left alone."

"Then it is a good thing I am not Oona." The deep voice sounded like the stamp of hooves. The fresh scent of grass drifted to her nose.

Sorcha stiffened. "Macha."

"Yes."

"You have not spoken to me in a very long time."

Why did the faerie come now? Of all times, why did the Tuatha dé Danann arrive just as the battle was about to begin?

Stones shifted back on her heels. Macha stood beside her, staring out over the crashing waves with her hands clasped behind her back. Their red hair tangled together until Sorcha could no longer tell whose curls were whose.

"You have done well," Macha said. "Far better than I expected from a human girl."

"Druid."

"As you wish. Druid."

Sorcha licked her lips, refusing to glance up at Macha. "I did not uphold our deal. Have you come to collect my debt?"

"No. You have exceeded my expectations and done the impossible. While Eamonn was not returned to my children, the outcome was exactly what I hoped."

Sorcha looked at her then, eyebrows lifted in surprise. "You wished Eamonn to start a war?"

"That was the intent of bringing him home. I expected he would fight my children for a time, but then he would agree that returning to Tir na nOg was the only way to save his people. I did not anticipate he would fall in love with you and wish to take back the throne on his own."

"He didn't really want the throne," Sorcha hesitated, "he wanted a home."

"Yet, he found that with you."

"I believe he realized that too late." She looked back out to sea. "And because of that, he paid dearly."

"It is always sad when we lose one of our own. I am sorry you must bear the weight of his loss."

"I bear more than that," Sorcha whispered.

"An army waits outside these walls for your orders. It is strange how time changes. I remember when we ran the druids out of the Otherworld for fear they would destroy us. Now, we all wait with bated breath as a druid determines whether or not she will catapult us into a time of blood and fear."

"You gave me this power."

"No," Macha shook her head. "I would love to take that credit, but you took this power all on your own."

Sorcha supposed she was right. If she had gone to Hy-brasil and done what she was told, then she would likely be back home with her father and sisters.

She sighed. "Did your children ever have the cure?"

"No."

"Did they know of it?"

"They knew ways to prevent a person from contracting the beetle plague, but not any way to cure those who were already ill. They also knew the druids had it, but with no way to contact them, they would not have told you."

"Could they have killed the beetles?"

"No."

Sorcha nodded. "Then you and your children misled me."

"We needed you to get Eamonn, and I knew he would follow you."

"Why?"

"He always had a weakness for pretty girls. Even more so for humans. I remember when he was a child, he used to watch your people through that mirror of his. He was fascinated by the choices you made, the stories you told, and the world you had built."

She could believe it. Eamonn had been too comfortable with

her, too easily swayed when the others still did not trust her. They respected her, but they would not allow her to stay in their homes.

"Why did you lie about the cure?" Sorcha asked.

"It was not a lie. We would have given you whatever we could and then told you that there was no true cure. Only bandages to wrap around a gushing wound."

"You were wrong."

Macha curled her hands into fists. "I could not have known the druids hid a relic."

"They didn't hide it. They kept it safe for all these years because your brother asked them to."

"My brother has much to answer for, but that is not why I am here."

Sorcha spun, her feet confident and sure on the edge of the cliff. "Then why are you here? The great Macha, one of the trinity which makes up the Morrighan, stands upon a cliff side with a midwife. What could you possibly have to say to me?"

"That I am proud of you."

"I do not want your pride!" she screamed. "You and your people took everything from me. My life is in ruins, and you say you are proud? Do not be proud that I have discarded all sense of self."

"I have watched you grow from a child, to a woman, to a queen." Macha reached out, her hand hovering in front of Sorcha and then closing into a fist. "You are more than the midwife I found in a glen with honey on her hands and rosemary in her hair. Look at you!"

Sorcha hated it that the Tuatha dé Danann was right. She wasn't the same person she had been at the beginning of this journey. She had changed so much that she barely recognized herself.

And she expected that. Who wouldn't? Making a deal with a faerie was bound to affect the way she saw the world. The way she saw herself.

She could never have seen this future for herself. If she was being truthful, she had dreamed of a quiet cabin on the edge of the forest. A family who loved her, a tiny baby that bounced on her husband's knee.

Macha looked at her with pity. "You wanted a family."

"I wanted a life."

"Is being queen not a life?"

"No," she shook her head. "It is living a life for others. And while I do not resent them, I wish to be selfish, to live by my own choices without affecting so many others."

"There is no such life."

"Yes, you are right," Sorcha said with a sigh. "I didn't think I would walk this path alone."

"Are you alone? There are hundreds of souls standing around you, even now."

"The support of the dead is not the same as a loving touch, nor can they warm my bed at night."

She missed him with every breath she took. Though he would have been proud to see her accomplishments, Eamonn could not.

And now he stood as a trophy at his brother's throne. She wanted to bury him. To plant roses on his grave and tend to them every day. Sorcha would gently guide them into blooming all year, through snow and sun. She could do the impossible for him.

Tears pricked her eyes, and she cleared her throat. "It does not matter now. I have no choice."

"I cannot gift you a relic of the Tuatha dé Danann," Macha said. "I cannot even fight beside you on the battlefield as I am not supposed to alter faerie lives. But, if you will accept my final gift, I would give you all the knowledge I have."

"How is that possible?"

"I have watched thousands of battles, killed more men and women than those that walk this earth. It is my penance and my desire to see you win."

It could only help, although she did not want more screams of the dying in her head. She sighed. "It is another choice I make for others. Yes, Macha, I accept your gift."

The red haired woman reached out, tapped a finger to Sorcha's forehead, and all her battle knowledge flowed between Sorcha's eyes.

She understood the formations which worked and those that didn't. She saw through the eyes of the dying and the victors. Blades formed as red hot hammers struck them. Shields dented before her great strength, and blood flowed like a waterfall from her palms.

Sorcha landed on her knees with her hands outstretched. "Take it back," she cried out. "Take it back, I do not want it!"

"You will need it to protect yourself and your people. No matter how hard it is to bear."

She hated it. She hated the screams, the guilt, the wonder if the warriors had families. Macha didn't feel this worry. She saw the cold, hard truth of war and filtered it away.

How did the Tuatha dé Danann carry all this within her?

Macha knelt and took Sorcha's hands. "You must not let it overwhelm you. War is dark and dangerous, there are many who fall prey to its nightmares. But you will not let it devour you. That is not your destiny."

"I do not want to know all this."

"You must know it and use the knowledge well. You will carry your people into battle and you will fight by their side as a leader should."

"I will only slow them down."

"Not with this knowledge. You will wield a sword, you will fight with a shield that will drip with blood, and you will make your next decisions knowing you have done it their way."

Sorcha heard the hidden words in Macha's speech. She looked up through eyes ringed red with tears. "You do not want us to go to war."

"I have seen the outcomes of countless battles. I have seen what the Fae are capable of. I believe you need to see it too."

"Are the memories not enough?"

"You may share my memories, but you still have not experienced it for yourself. War tears at the strongest of creatures and breaks them into raw materials. You will only find your true self once you are in the heat of battle."

Sorcha searched her gaze for an answer. "And if I don't like what I find?"

"No one likes what they find at the end of a blade. But it will help you decide for yourself what the future of the Seelie Fae must be."

Macha stood, dusted her skirts, and held out a hand for Sorcha to take.

She wanted no more of the faerie's help, but realized she was being petty. Sighing, she reached out and let Macha lift her to her feet.

The scent of grass was overwhelming this close. It smelled of home, of kind things, of summer days that never ended. These were not memories Sorcha had the time to dwell upon.

"Are you ready, child?" Macha asked.

"No."

"But you will be."

"Yes."

"When will you give your army the answer they wait for?"

Sorcha looked up at the sky and saw the sun was already dipping below the horizon. "Tonight, at the feast they have prepared. They will expect such news to be announced then."

Macha nodded and released her. "And so the Druid Queen begins her war."

The Battle To End The War

"**O**h, dearie," Oona said as she tightened a strap of Sorcha's armor. "Are you certain of this?"

No. She wasn't certain of anything. But Sorcha knew she could not stand by while her people fought. She refused to stand atop a hill and watch people die when she should fight with them.

She was a queen now. That was her duty.

"Yes," she finally said. "I will fight by their sides."

"He wouldn't have wanted this."

Sorcha chuckled. "No, he would've tucked me in a corner and told me to wait until the screaming stopped. That isn't me, Oona. And you know that even if he were alive, I would have found a way to go."

"But you would have been healing people, not fighting with them."

"I will admit that is the difficult part of this. I wish very much to heal, not harm. However, this is my only choice. I took these people as my family, as my wards, and I will not be a coward in their eyes."

Oona smoothed her hands down the ornate breastplate covering Sorcha's chest. They had chosen an armor to rival all others. Hammered swirls created a pattern on the flat plate covering her chest and belly. Interlocking pieces lay smooth over her arms, shoulders, and thighs.

It did not hinder her movement, the most important part of a good piece of armor. They found the set hidden deep within the bowels of the castle, and Oona claimed to remember it from long ago. It was not faerie made, but the Druids had worn such armor long ago.

"Dearie, someone has come to see you."

Sorcha glanced over her shoulder, expecting to see a member of the war council. Instead, Elva stood in the shadows of the doorway.

"Enter."

She gracefully stepped into the light, and Sorcha locked her jaw. Elven armor covered Elva in gold from head to toe. She remembered it well from the attack upon Hy-brasil.

"Are you joining us then?" Sorcha wanted to ask if she were joining Fionn's army, wearing their symbol so blatantly.

"I am. I wanted to send a message to my beloved consort."

"Which is?"

"I may bear his name, his marks, and his love, but I am not his."

The fire blazing in Elva's eyes was enough to set an answering flame crackling in Sorcha's own breast. She nodded firmly. "Then select your weapon."

"Thank you Oona, I can prepare her from here on."

The pixie ducked her head and left the room.

Sorcha watched the elf circle the room, testing the weight and balance of sword after sword. "My council has warned me not to be alone with you. They do not believe you are to be trusted."

"I am certain they believe I am here to assassinate you."

"Could you?"

"Easily." Elva selected a rapier thin blade and tied the strap over her shoulder so the sword hung between her shoulders. "I have no wish to kill you."

"You say you are here to gain your freedom. How does starting a war with Fionn gain you that?"

"I am not starting a war. I am ending a war." Elva's gaze locked with hers. "Eamonn and I were very close in our youth. He protected me even though I didn't want him to. He was like an older brother, and then someone I could put a pedestal and fall in love with."

"And then Bran showed up." Sorcha said, thoroughly pleased with the shocked expression on Elva's face.

"How do you know that?"

"Eamonn mentioned something of your back story, and I pieced it together. Bran was here, you know."

Elva nodded slowly, ducking her head until shadows blanketed her expression. "A long time ago, he and I would have made a powerful pair."

"A long time ago?"

"I am weary of men. Their hands are grasping, their needs are great, and my mind no longer wishes to bend to their will."

"I do not believe Bran would ask that of you," Sorcha declared. "He seems an honorable man for all he is Unseelie and his family is unsavory."

"It is a good word for them." A small smile spread across Elva's face. "I wish I had become a different person as I aged, but I did not. The woman residing inside this physical form no longer wishes for the attentions of any man. Even one I might have loved."

Sorcha vividly remembered the state Elva had been in. The opium stains on her fingers, the glassy eyed expression, her fear when she thought Fionn might return. Although Fionn loved her, she had still been abused.

Stepping forward, Sorcha reached out an armored hand and

grasped Elva's. Metal scraped against leather in a harsh grind. "When I was little, a woman on the street told me that women were created to suffer. It was the card life dealt us, no matter our station or purpose. I never believed it, and I see now we make our own path in life."

"If we choose to."

"You have made that choice, Elva. I will fight at your side for your freedom. I will support your choices after this war is over and will let no one stand in your way."

Sorcha meant every word with a power that vibrated through her body.

Elva nodded firmly, squeezed her fingers once more, and stepped back towards the weapons. "Have you selected a weapon, Your Majesty?"

It was the first time someone had addressed her as queen. Sorcha's spine straightened. "No. My skills lie with the bow, but my war council has advised I must also adorn myself with a sword."

"It is good advice. A bow is superb for long range combat, but a sword is the only thing that can protect you once his armies reach ours." Elva pulled a small sword from the rack. "This will suit you well."

It was much smaller than the sword Elva had chosen, but it felt good in Sorcha's hand. It was not too heavy as many of them were. She slashed through the air.

"I like this one."

"As I expected you would. It is a Druid blade."

Sorcha tested the weight in her hand again. "It feels right."

"That's what you want in battle."

"Have you fought in many?"

"Every Tuatha dé Danann has fought in many battles. We are a warring society. It is what we are good at."

"That's sad," Sorcha said.

"Is it? Our men test their worth through blood and fire. Our women learn kindness through small acts of kindness."

"Do any of you know how to love without the need to harm?" Sorcha shook her head. "I count my blessings that Eamonn was banished to that isle. For all the harm it did, he is a better man for it." She caught herself. "*Was*. He was a better man, but no longer."

Elva winced. "I envy you. At the very least, you carry him with you wherever you go."

"Love is like that."

"No," Elva shook her head. "I didn't plan to fight with you until I walked past you in the hall. There are two heartbeats inside you."

Sorcha blinked, not quite comprehending what Elva said. "Excuse me? Are you suggesting magic is at work?"

"Magic in the most earthly way. You are a midwife, Sorcha. I thought you would have recognized the signs before I did."

It wasn't possible. She couldn't be carrying his babe, could she?

She tried remembering the past few months, but all she could think of was the stress and fear. Her spells of nausea were brought about by the yelling of the war council, the memories of Eamonn's death, the responsibilities that rested on her shoulders. Not from a child.

"How is that possible?" she asked, pressing a hand against her armored belly.

"I suspect much in the same way my child happened."

"But I am not Fae."

"That has never stopped children from being born. There are plenty of half breeds, even in the Otherworld. Eamonn comes from a lineage of Fomorian and Tuatha dé Danann, as do you."

A dizzy spell made Sorcha's head spin. "I need a few moments."

"Of course, Your Majesty." Elva paused as she walked by and placed a hand on her shoulder. "I will fight by your side, to protect both you and the babe. Nothing will touch you. You have my word."

Her hand slid from Sorcha's shoulder and the door closed quietly behind her.

Sorcha stared at the racks of swords, the hanging crossbows, the shields leaning against the wall. A loud sob echoed through the weaponry, and she pressed a hand against her mouth to hold in any further sound.

A child? She was to bring a child into this life?

Still, it was the last bit of him she had left. She stumbled backwards and leaned against the wall.

"I am so sorry," she sobbed as she pressed her fingers to her belly once more. "You deserve so much more than this life. So much more than war and violence. You deserve a father who loves you and a mother who will kiss your bruises."

She couldn't fight now. She couldn't go into battle with thin armor and expect her child to live. What kind of mother would do that?

Rustling caught her attention, slicing through her fear and anguish. Looking up, her tear streaked cheeks turned cold as she saw a glimmering portal open on the ceiling.

A long, bristled leg reached through. It held a small clay pot in its claws, which it let drop onto the nearest hay bale.

The Unseelie Queen's voice boomed through the portal. "A queen makes many hard decisions, and you will not be the first pregnant woman to march into battle. We fight many wars. With our bodies, with our minds, with our words. Go and be safe, Druid Queen."

Sorcha watched the leg withdraw and the portal disappear.

Scrubbing her cheeks free of tears, she lurched towards the pot and wrenched off the top. Blue powder coated the inside. She recognized this, although she did not remember why. Sorcha dipped a finger into the substance and rubbed her index finger and thumb together. They both stained bright blue.

A druid voice sighed in her ear. "It is the symbol of our people."

"Why did the Unseelie Queen have it?"

"None know the reasons why the Unseelie Queen collects anything. Woad has always been a druid symbol of anger and war. Our women and men paint their faces and bodies before battle. It brings the ancestors with them."

"You will come with me to war?"

"We will guide your hand."

Sorcha blew out a quiet breath.

She could make the choice in this instant to fight. Her people would charge towards Fionn's and meet with them fierce pride, with or without her at their side.

But they would fight powerfully if she was with them. She would lift her blade and champion their injustices. The offending armies would fear the Druid Queen, rumored to control the whims and minds of the Fae.

She couldn't force them to do anything. She hadn't been able to since Eamonn left.

Sorcha dipped her fingers into the pot and swiped one across the high peak of her forehead. She glimpsed herself in the reflection of a shield. Each pass of blue paint made her anger grow stronger, louder, and all the more fierce.

Her hair tied up, swinging at her shoulders, she lifted a helm and placed it on her head.

As she stepped from the armory, all who saw her felt fear in their hearts. Gone was their healer queen. A warrior stood before them, hair like a waving banner of blood, and war in her heart.

⚅⚇⚅

THEIR BANNERS SNAPPED AS LOUD AS A DRUM. SORCHA'S HORSE shifted beneath her, restless for the battle to begin. It wanted to paw at the air, to crush skulls beneath its hooves, to race down the hill towards Fionn's army and begin.

She sat and stared down at the golden army, measuring each breath, forcing her movements to remain calm and still.

"M'lady," Angus said from behind her. "It is too late to turn back now."

"I have no wish to turn back, dwarf king. I am merely allowing them to look at us as we look at them."

"Why?"

"I want them to see our faces. To see the sheer number of faeries who disagree with their king."

"It will not change their opinion of him."

She shook her head. "I am not yet ready to believe these are not intelligent men and women. If they are not courageous enough to leave their king, then I want them to see those who were brave enough to do so. I want them to quake with fear before we even begin."

Angus fell silent and stared down at the army with her. This would be a bloody battle. Each army had sent a massive amount of soldiers. Fionn's was clearly well armed, but she knew they did not fight for the right reasons. They would falter because they were not angry enough.

The white stallion next to her huffed out a breath. Elva tightened her grip on the reins. "Will you give a motivational speech?"

"Is that necessary?"

"It is tradition for the leader to scream out a cry for their warriors."

"Then I shall."

Sorcha kicked her heels against the horse's side, moving out from the army and riding parallel to their ranks. She racked her brain for something to say, anything which would give these men and women a reason to be here. A reason to lose their lives.

There was none. There was never a reason to take a life or give their own, nothing worthy of their soul.

She drew her horse still and looked out over the people she loved. The last of her family, the last of Eamonn's great ambition.

The wind picked up, catching her hair and snapping it out like the red banners they all held. The Druid Queen—the Rose Queen —sat atop her mighty steed. She knew how small she looked, how small she felt.

In the end, the words came to her without the hard edge of steel, the metallic taste of battle, or the bitterness of war.

"Be safe!" she shouted. "Be well! And if you are not, I shall meet you in the halls of our ancestors with wine and stories to tell. We fight to take back what is ours, and we will not rest until we scream victorious in the halls of Cathair Solais!"

A cheer lifted into the air. Not enough, not nearly enough to strike fear into the hearts of the army behind her. Sorcha was too soft, too weak, too much a healer. She hardened her tender heart and screamed out a battle cry.

She was not a weak human. She was not faerie to hide behind armor and steel. The woad was her message, and it had been heard.

She reached up and pulled off her helm as green smoke swirled around her arms. The souls of druids dipped into her armor and would guide her hands as she fought.

The faeries fell silent as they stared. Blue woad covered one side of her face, patterns drawn across the other. She was an otherworldly creature, now. A being from their history who stepped out of time itself.

Her feral grin split the paint. "Let our swords feast this day! May your shields hold, your arrows fly true, and your battle cry resound through the Seelie courts from this day forth!"

The faeries screamed out. They lifted weapons into the air and cried out, for the Druid Queen rode with them.

Sorcha wheeled her horse around and stared down at the golden army readying themselves for war. Elva and Angus urged their steeds forward, their legs pressing against hers.

She could hear each breath she took, each beat of her heart thumping loudly against her ribs. The castle gleamed behind the army, so bright it burned her eyes. That was her goal, her destiny, where this would all end. Sorcha lifted her runic blade, inhaled, and shrieked, "Faugh A Ballagh! Clear the way!"

The horse's hooves sounded like thunder as they raced down the mountain. Clanging armor beat against her ears and her thighs gripped tight to her mount.

Fionn's army raised spears, ready to catch the horses the moment they reached them. But Angus had planned for that.

"Dwarves! Ready yourselves!"

They lifted great maces above their heads, swinging them wildly and releasing them at Angus's command. The spiked weapons bashed through the lifted spears, shattering the staffs into thousands of shards. The faeries only had a moment to stare at their broken weapons before the horses struck them.

She heard nothing at first. Then, the ringing in her ears dimmed.

They were screaming. Men, women, and horses all screaming as their lives drained from their bodies.

Dwarves lifted heavy hammers and brought them down on the heads of those who were not riding horses. The great thuds sounded like gongs as the Tuatha dé Danann dropped to the ground. Pixies threw knives into the air, catching underneath armor and digging into flesh.

She flinched as a golden soldier swung his massive sword and cleaved a peat faerie's head from its shoulders. He advanced towards her only to meet Elva's double blades.

"Sorcha!" she screamed. "Behind!"

She whipped around at the last moment and lifted her sword. The blades locked, vibrations jolting down her arm and zinging through her nerves. The soldier staring back at her knew exactly who she was. A grin spread across his lips as he swung the sword back again.

A spray of blood splattered across her face. Sorcha cried out, but the soldier slumped forward on his horse which raced away.

Angus lifted his hammer in salute and turned to swing at yet another man.

There were so many people. All she could hear were the screams of the dying, the aching pain and agony that stretched throughout the battlefield.

This was only the start.

She lifted a hand and touched the blood on her cheek. None of it hers, her people wouldn't allow that.

Elva screamed her rage into the air. She wielded dual blades, said she didn't need a shield, and Sorcha could see why.

The fair woman was not just stunning in person. She used her body like a weapon. Leaping and striking out from the air. Her horse was long gone, groaning on the ground and kicking its legs to kill any who came near it.

Sorcha was infinitely glad she had forced Cian and Oona to stay at the castle. They did not need to see this.

A soldier fell to his knees beside her horse. He reached for her ankle and she flinched, but the golden soldier did not try to pull her off.

She looked down and lost herself in his eyes. He was dying, he knew, and wanted a small bit of comfort as his soul leaked out of the gaping hole in his chest. She reached out a hand for him to take.

Cold metal met her fingertips for a brief moment before he fell onto his side. The final sigh of his breath echoed so loudly that she swore it was the wind.

On and on it went, the dying screaming out for mercy, for help, for anyone to hear their pleas. Both her people and Fionn's, all the same and yet infinitely different.

The Lesser Fae were brutal. They had so much anger built up over centuries and they showed no pity. The High Fae grew more and more angry that those who they believed beneath them would dare rise up.

She watched the ground grow slick with blood. Her heart beat slower and slower even as she refused to lift a blade.

A large man broke through her personal guard's ranks. His chest heaved, and he rushed towards her with his sword lifted. She heard the angry cry of the dwarves, the sad wail of Elva as they all watched him charge forward.

Sorcha was so tired of death. She lifted a hand towards the great man and called out, "Enough."

He stumbled but his sword remained in the air.

"Enough," she cried out. "There has been enough death!"

He took one more step towards her and let the blade dip towards the ground.

Sorcha slid from her mount, armored feet touching the ground so lightly they did not make a sound. She walked towards him with her hands at her sides.

The fighting slowed in the small pocket around them. Lesser Fae watching in fear as Sorcha risked her life. The High Fae staring with stunned expressions, horrified their largest soldier was hesitating to kill such a small girl.

"Be at peace," she said calmly. "You are not my enemy, and I am not yours. We did not choose this destiny, but we can change it. I do not wish to harm you."

In the blink of an eye, he lifted his sword and jabbed it towards her. Sorcha cried out, her voice mingling with his shout, and waited for the pain. It did not come.

A sword split through the front of his armor and he staggered to the side.

"No," she sobbed. "No more of this."

Sorcha reached out and caught him as he fell to his knees. She pulled off his helmet and smoothed her hands over his handsome face.

Shock reflected in his eyes even as blood dripped over his cheek.

"You did not deserve this," she said. "I am sorry."

He lifted a shaking hand lifted even as Elva cried out a warning. "You are not what I expected."

"Rest easy warrior."

"You should not be in war."

The life drained from his eyes as tears slid from her own. She smoothed her hand down his face, closing the vacant stare.

"M'lady!" Angus shouted as the Tuatha dé Danann advanced upon them. "Get back on your horse."

"No," she growled as anger sparked in her veins.

The green smoke of her ancestors swirled through her armor. They knew what she wanted to do. That she would no longer lift a blade towards these men and women who should be her people as well. They were Eamonn's family, and they would be hers.

"Enough."

The word carried across the battlefield. A druid tugged hard on her armor, "More, Sorcha. You must do more."

She imagined a distaff in her hand and remembered in startling clarity her mother's voice as she taught Sorcha how to weave.

"No, Sorcha, be patient. You'll create bumps in the wool!"

"We're just going to knit it anyways!"

"Silly girl, weave the flax around the distaff so it doesn't get tangled as we work. That's it, hold it like that, all the unspun fibers will keep still and then you can spin them into thread. Good. See? You were capable of it all along."

A tear slid down her cheek and Sorcha wove all the unspun magic and souls in the air into a fine thread strong as steel. She wove it into the air, knotting and untangling until she had created a tapestry of this moment in time.

"Sleep," she told the faeries on the battlefield. "Rest until this is done."

Releasing her hold on the thread, she heard every Fae drop to the ground. Their breathing was even and synchronized, creating a hushed wind that brushed against her ears.

She was so tired. She wanted to sleep with them, to curl up with the dead soldier and let her mind wander. It had been a long day. And she had spent so much energy to calm their minds.

"No, Sorcha. Our work is not yet finished," druids whispered in her ears. "You cannot sleep yet."

She had to go to *him*. Once Eamonn was put to rest, she could finally sleep in peace.

A quiet chuff blew on her face. When had she closed her eyes?

The air puffed again, brushing against her cheeks and reminding her of a time when a selkie had awoken her on a beach. Was she back there? Would he still be alive if she opened her eyes? Had this all been a bad dream?

Sorcha lifted her gaze and flinched at the sight of red fields. The stench of death filled the air and clogged her lungs.

Breath washed over her and brought with it the salty scent of the sea. Sorcha inhaled deeply, clearing her mind and lungs of war.

A kelpie stood before her. His dark eyes spoke of pity and forgiveness.

"You," she said in wonder and reached up to touch his velvet soft nose. A drop of water splattered on her forehead. "I remember you."

He bounced his head in agreement.

"You were at the waterfall on Hy-brasil. How did you get free?"

His eyes seemed to say that kelpies could were wild creatures. The waters of the earth wove together like her magic, and he had come because she needed him.

The kelpie shifted, slowly getting to its knees and waiting for her to pull herself onto his back.

She stood, her knees crying out in pain and her back aching. Her hands glided over his seaweed mane and the bumps of his spine.

"Eamonn said you would drag me down into the depths and drown me if I tried to ride you."

The kelpie's eyes said otherwise, the same as they had at the waterfall.

She swung a leg over its side and pressed herself against the cool wet skin. "Bring me to the castle, faithful friend."

፠

THE GUARDS AT THE GATE DID NOT HESITATE TO OPEN THEM FOR the warrior queen who rode alone into Cathair Solais. They could see the army laying on the field and wondered if they were dead. What had this witch woman done? What powers did this druid possess?

She balanced herself on the kelpie's back and planned what she would say. She would call for peace, she wouldn't give Fionn an option, she would force him to understand.

But then she rode directly into the palace and all words drifted from her mind.

They were having a ball. Gorgeous men and women swirled in colors she could not comprehend. Wine flowed from statues and laughter bubbled towards the ceiling.

The faeries wore fine masks, the metal so thin it looked like wire. Their dresses were pristine and their movements graceful.

They were so drunk they didn't notice she had arrived.

Anger burned so hot that Sorcha couldn't control herself. She leaned down, stuck her hand under a plate a passing waiter carried, and upended all the glasses onto the floor. The shattering made even the musicians shriek to a halt.

They saw her now.

The crowd parted, and she locked eyes with Fionn who relaxed on his throne.

"There is a war on your doorstep, Wise King," she mocked. "Or had you not noticed the blood coating your stairs?"

"Kings do not fight in wars."

"No, but apparently Queens do." She swiped at the blood on her cheek and pointed at him with a hand that dripped seawater. "I have come to claim what is mine."

"You think to take this throne?" he said, chuckling. "You are a mere human."

"I care little for a chair. The crystal man beside you is mine, and I intend to take him back."

"No." Fionn stood and gestured with the glass of wine in his hand. "Guards, remove this woman."

None moved.

"Guards! Take this human from my sight!"

Sorcha growled. "Sit down, Fionn."

"You cannot order me, midwife."

"I said, sit down."

"No!" Anger mottled his face with red splotches. "You have no right to be here, to interfere with anything! You should be on your knees when you greet me!"

"It is you, false king, who will *kneel*!"

Her scream echoed through the great hall. The threads in her mind flared bright, and she tugged them hard, grabbing them in her fist and twisting cruelly. She wanted them to feel the pain and torment in her soul.

Each and every Fae dropped to their hands and knees.

Breathing hard, Sorcha clenched her hands into fists and slid from the kelpie's back. Her armored boots clacked against the stone as she advanced towards Fionn. Anger, so vivid and raw it blew hot breaths against her neck, beat through her mind and screamed for release.

There was so much pain inside her that thunder echoed in her ears. She walked up the stairs to Fionn and fisted a hand around his throat. Souls tangled around her arm, giving her inhuman strength. She slammed him against the back of the throne and squeezed.

"Your time is up," she growled.

"Never," he croaked.

Not releasing her grasp on his neck, she reached over her head and pulled out an arrow from the quiver at her back.

"You have been tried and found guilty, Fionn the Wise. Your crimes are slavery." She sank the arrow into the throne next to his head, reached for another, and continued. "Brutality." This one just missed his ear. "And lies."

She whipped the crown from his head and sank the last arrow so close that it cut through his hair.

Sorcha met his gaze with burning eyes and held the crown up for him to see. "This is not yours."

Turning to the crowd of faeries behind them, she brought the crown down on her knee and broke it in half. The two pieces fell to the floor and tumbled down the stairs. She met the gaze of each guard, saw the fear in their eyes, and felt it resound in her own chest.

Sorcha snapped her fingers and yanked hard on the threads of their existence. "Bring your king to the dungeon and wrap him in iron chains."

"No!" Fionn shouted. "Do not listen to this woman!"

"If he screams overly loud, tell me. I will ply him with herbs that will swell his tongue until he can hardly breathe."

The guards linked their hands underneath Fionn's armpits and dragged him from the room. His protests were ignored.

But then the faeries couldn't do anything other than ignore him, could they? She hadn't given them a choice.

Sorcha dropped into Fionn's throne with a heavy sigh. "Get out. All of you."

The faeries scrambled to their feet and left in such a rush that in three heartbeats she was alone.

A sob cut through the silence. Her agony rushed to the forefront.

"I have become everything I did not want to be," she cried out.

Her hands shook, and she stopped breathing as she finally turned her head and stared into Eamonn's cold, vacant eyes.

"My love," she sobbed. "I have come for you."

Pulling herself from the chair, she wrapped her arms around his shoulders and pressed her lips to his. Cold crystal bit at her flesh. So familiar and yet not at all. His chest did not move, his heart did not beat, and his eyes did not fill with the tenderness she had grown to expect.

Sorcha pressed her mouth against his again, "Would that I could save you. My love. My heart."

Tears dripped from her eyes and splattered against the cold stone.

Rage poured through her again. It wasn't fair. It wasn't right that she was so close to him, and yet so far. He would never look at her with love again. Never touch her shoulder, wrap her curls around his finger.

It was a cruel and angry jest that the world played on her.

She whipped around and cleared the food and wine from Fionn's side table. Screaming out her rage she fell to her knees beside him and gripped the Spear of Lugh.

"This does not belong here," she cried.

As if the spear understood what she wanted, the staff short-ened, no longer propping Eamonn up. Yanking with her entire weight, she pulled the spear out of Eamonn's heart.

It clattered to the floor and all her anger drained, leaking from her eyes as tears slid from her cheeks. What was she to do with him? Bury him in the earth? Place him at the front of the castle like a watchful gargoyle?

She whimpered and wrapped herself around him once more. "Please, mo chroí. I want to hear your voice one last time. I love you."

At first, she didn't notice that her lips were pressed against silken hair. Then she heard the cracking of crystal as his fingertips moved.

Stumbling back, she landed on her behind and watched with wide eyes as the crystal shattered. It fell from his body in great shards, leaving behind warm caramel skin. He shook the stones from his shoulders, twisting away from her to rip off his armor and lift his hands to his face.

A chunk of crystal fell to the ground, the piece which had covered his face. Cold, blank eyes stared back at her, as if he had simply taken off a mask. Sorcha gasped and pressed her hand to her lips, watching with wide eyes as he stared down at his hands, then turned to face her.

He was perfect. Ragged and tired, but free from all blemishes. His face was smooth, his throat unmarked. Not a single crystal remained, not even a small one poking through his shredded shirt.

She watched his throat work as he swallowed.

"Sorcha?"

She moaned and scrambled to her feet. Launching herself in his arms, she tucked her face against his now smooth neck and breathed in his scent. "I thought I'd lost you."

"I thought I was dead." Eamonn pressed his lips against her shoulder and crushed her in his embrace. "How is this possible?"

"I do not know, but I thank every god who ever existed that they brought you back to me." She leaned back and traced her fingers down his face, foreign now but just as beloved. "It's really you."

He said nothing. Eamonn palmed the back of her head and pressed their lips together. Warm and safe and wondrous, she framed his face with her palms and counted each of her many blessings.

The Coronation

Sorcha couldn't let go of him. She had to feel the smooth skin to believe he was really here, that somehow, some way, the disfiguring marks were magically gone. A god must have smiled upon them and healed all their wounds.

It was difficult to believe.

As they stumbled from the throne room, arms wrapped around each other, she realized how weak he was. His muscles trembled, legs quaked, and he leaned on her for support. This was not the king she remembered, but he would be.

He stepped out of the palace and lifted a hand to block the sun.

Faeries spread out on the grounds before them. All having stayed to see what the Druid Queen might do next. They gasped when they realized she wasn't alone.

"Fionn?" Someone called out.

"No," Eamonn replied. "Your high king."

Sorcha felt the tremble run through his body at the name. He glanced down at her.

"What happened?"

"Your crystals, Eamonn. They're gone."

"Gone?" He ran a hand down his face, shaking as he touched his throat. "Are they truly gone?"

"I don't know how, or why, but you are reborn a new man."

He swallowed, and Sorcha didn't know whether she would get used to see his Adam's apple move. How strange it was to see so much skin after all this time.

She linked her arm through his and pulled him through the crowd. There was more for him to see, more that needed to be explained, and all these Fae didn't deserve to see him at his weakest. They had condemned him long ago. They would now wait to hear what their fate would be.

They paused at the gate to the castle. His eyes widened in shock as he stared out over a battlefield of thousands all lying on the ground.

"You went to war?"

"And I ended it."

"You?" He tore his gaze away from the bodies and met her gaze. "You killed them all?"

"They're not dead, just sleeping."

"Do they know what happened?"

"No."

He blew out a breath. "I will confess, mo chroí. I can hardly handle this right now."

"We can wait to wake them."

"We shouldn't. Where is your horse?"

"No horse," she said with a smile. The wet suction of feet pattered on the ground behind them. "Just a kelpie."

His expression was almost comical. "You rode that? Alone?"

"I told you he didn't want to hurt me."

"The kelpie from the waterfall?"

"Not everything is black and white," she said as she stroked the kelpie's forehead. "I don't know why he helped me, but I know I'm forever grateful. I'm not sure I would have made it here otherwise."

Her own legs were trembling now. They both desperately needed to lie down in each other's arms and rest.

How long had it been since she'd slept in his embrace? Too long. Months, weeks, days, even hours were too long for Sorcha to bear.

He nodded. "Let's get this over then. Thank you, my friend. You have earned honor for the race of kelpies."

The sea horse bent to its knees and waited until both Sorcha and Eamonn were safely on its back. It surged forward and raced towards the battlefield. She could smell the sea air, hear the cries of seagulls, and the whispering crash of the waves.

Gods, how she missed the sea.

His arms tightened around her. She traced her fingertips over his forearms and realized she would have to learn him all over again. The sway of his body, the sparse spray of chest hair, the taste of skin rather than stone.

Breath stirred the curls at her temple. "How was I blessed with such a woman?"

"Is there an answer for that?"

"The gods smiled on me when they created you. I am a well-loved man."

"You are." Sorcha dug her nails into his arms and sent a silent prayer towards the sky.

But she knew it wasn't the gods who had helped. Whatever deity was out there had only set the wheel in motion.

The kelpie picked through fallen bodies as Eamonn guided it towards a rise which would give them the highest peak to call out to the armies. As they walked, she saw the faces of her ancestors hovering above the Fae. Each woad painted face smiled at her. They kept the faeries still and quiet.

Macha stood at the edge of the battlefield, her sword lifted in greeting. Beside her, Balor and Ethniu held their arms around each other and grinned.

Sorcha nodded to them and leaned further back against the wall of strength behind her. She finally had him. The only thing she'd wanted since starting this journey was a place to call home, a family who loved her, and to feel as though she belonged.

She would never have guessed she'd find it all in a single person.

The kelpie's feet touched the highest rise and shook its head. She jostled forward with a gasp, Eamonn pressing against her spine.

He groaned and pressed a kiss between her shoulder blades. "Just a little longer, mo chroí."

They moved like ancients, sliding from the kelpie's back while wincing. A headache throbbed between her eyes. It was over and yet not... for her.

Eamonn caught her as her knees gave out. He pulled her against his chest and smoothed the hair back from her face.

No crystals caught her hair.

"Let them go. Let them awaken and we shall greet our people."

She sighed, tucked her head against his chest, and released her grip on the threads. She could feel the druid souls disappear into the mist. A great weight she hadn't realized pressed down upon her lifted. She sagged against Eamonn, her head lolling to the side in relief.

"Good." He pressed a kiss against her temple, breath tickling her neck. "You've done remarkably well, mo chroí."

Sorcha nodded, incapable of responding in any other way.

He held her against his side and stepped forward to watch as the faeries rolled to their sides, some to their knees. Soldiers pulled their helms off to shake their heads in confusion.

Eamonn waited only a heartbeat before he called out, "Faeries of the Seelie Court! Behold! Your new king and queen!"

The golden army froze. A few looked up at the couple, torn clothing, blood splattered, and strangely alive.

No one could mistake Eamonn for Fionn on a battlefield. He stood with his legs spread wide, his chest rounded and spine straight. This was his domain.

"What did she do to us?" someone called out.

"I made you sleep," she said. "No more fighting, no more battle, just dreams."

"And our king?"

"He stands before you," Eamonn growled. "The Usurper sits in my dungeon until I decide what I wish to do with him."

Those who supported Fionn fell silent. Sorcha's people grabbed their weapons and corralled them until they stood in a great mass before their new king and queen. He squeezed her shoulders, tilted her chin, so she met his gaze.

"What shall we do with them?"

"If they wish to join our family, to support us, then they may."

"And if they don't?"

A spark of anger fired in her mind. "Then they can join their king who forced so many into slavery and more into starvation."

The armies heard her words loud and clear as druid souls echoed her words. One by one, the golden soldiers bent a knee. Not a single one remained standing.

Sorcha smiled. "I think they are afraid of me."

"In truth, so am I." But he lifted her hand and pressed his lips against her fingers. "My Druid Queen, I am sorry I could not battle beside you."

"I hope we will never have the chance."

"Angus!" Eamonn shouted. "Take care of things for me! I'm taking my queen home."

The dwarf saluted. "My pleasure!"

Eamonn swung her onto the back of the kelpie and they raced away from the Castle of Light. The kelpie swung his head, huffing out a breath, and mist formed beneath its feet. Faster and faster they rode until Sorcha threw her head back against Eamonn's shoulder.

"What is happening?"

"A kelpie can travel anywhere they wish, so longer as the water hears them."

"Then where are we going?"

"Home."

They sank into the earth and raced on rivers of magic to the small crevice in the back of Nuada's castle which Sorcha refused to fix. They carefully dismounted as the moon laved them with silver light.

Eamonn swung her into his arms and turned to the kelpie. "Thank you, my friend."

It bowed and leapt from the cliff into the sea.

He carried her through the shadows to give them a few moments of peace. The castle was silent, its residents sleeping with quiet dreams.

He tucked them into bed and wrapped himself around her. Just before she shut her eyes, she watched as he lifted her hand and stared at it in the moonlight. "You are a miracle, mo chroí."

"I am yours," she whispered.

They slept tangled up in each other, alive and finally at peace.

❧

FEATHER LIGHT TOUCHES PRESSED ACROSS HER CHEEKS AND LIPS. She furrowed her brow, desperately trying to hold onto the warm grasp of sleep.

"Stop," she murmured. "It's not time yet."

"Mo chroí, if we wait any longer they will fear we died. Again."

Her eyes snapped open at the deep baritone so familiar it made her heart hurt. She blew out a breath as her gaze met bright blue eyes.

"Eamonn?" She lunged forward and wrapped her arms around his neck. Yanking him down on top of her, she breathed in his woodsy scent while tears trickled down her cheeks. "I feared I dreamt it all."

"I am here."

"You are *here!*"

He chuckled against her throat. "Yes, I am. Although I'm uncertain how much longer if you keep choking me."

"You're too stubborn to die by my hand. Let me hold you for a few moments longer. Please."

"A man cannot deny such a tempting argument." He rolled them over and wrapped his arms and legs around her. "Be at ease. We survived."

She couldn't stop crying. Tears splattered onto his chest, mingling with the short hair there. *Hair!*

Sorcha tugged on it. "Since when did you have chest hair?"

"Eh?" He ran a hand down his chest, craning his neck to look down at himself. "I didn't. Or I haven't, for a very long time."

She sucked in a breath and traced a circle around a hole she hadn't noticed before. A star shaped wound over his heart Tiny crystals scattered around it, hardly comparable to his previous crevices and cracks, but still there.

"Look," she said.

He held his hand over hers. "I'm pleased to keep it. It's a good reminder of how precious life is."

"It is." Sorcha leaned up and pressed her lips against his, making a face when she pulled back. "You have morning breath."

"I have *what?*"

"Morning breath!"

"I've never had morning breath in my life."

"You have now." Still, she kissed him again just to enjoy it. "Eamonn, there's something I have to tell you."

A fist pounded on the door, Cian's angry voice shouting through the wood, "Ain't no servants meant to be in those rooms at this time of day! If you're canoodling in the master's chambers, I'll flay you myself!"

Sorcha bit her lip and shook her head. "It can wait."

"I don't mind telling him where he can find the whip."

"Eamonn," she giggled. "We have to tell them sooner or later."

"A few more hours alone couldn't hurt." He ran his hand suggestively down her spine.

"You were the one waking me up and saying we needed to go."

"I changed my mind."

"Are you certain you're up to it?" She winced as her hip popped when she moved.

"Ah, we're both still aching. Perhaps we should wait."

She didn't want to, but knew she would regret it if they found time for each other. She wanted to run her hands over this new body of his and rediscover every piece of him. But her body creaked when she moved and trembled at the mere thought of stretching.

It would have to wait, as he said, but she wasn't happy about it.

"Shout for him then," she grumbled. "I hadn't thought to reintroduce you in our bedroom. But so be it."

Eamonn cleared his throat. "Cian! You mangy bastard open the door!"

The gnome's bellow echoed through the hall nearly as loud as the banging door which slammed off its hinges. There was so much hope in Cian's eyes as he looked at them, wrapped up in the cream sheets with gossamer curtains all around them.

And then rage so red it burned turned the gnome to stone.

"So that's how you're repaying him?" he growled. "The master's only been dead for three months and you crawl into bed with his brother?"

Eamonn moved, a sword flinging through the air so swiftly that it embedded halfway through the door just above Cian's head. "You'll be careful talking to my queen that way, gnome. We might have a history, but I won't stand for that."

"I won't have the false king in this castle."

"Then it's a good thing you don't have him."

Cian crossed his arms firmly over his lumpy chest. "You aren't the master."

Sorcha pulled the sheets up to her chest and sat up. "I appreciate your loyalty, but you must be blind if you cannot see this is Eamonn."

"Have you been tricked girl?"

Clattering steps echoed up the hall and Oona shouted, "What is it Cian? Did one of the will-o'-the-wisps get stuck again?"

She burst into the room, froze when she saw them, and crumpled into tears. "Oh my stars! Master!"

She threw her arms wide and leapt onto the bed. Sorcha choked as Oona's elbow hooked over her throat and dragged her back down to Eamonn's side.

Oona blubbered, "Oh my dearies! I never thought to see your faces again! And Master! You're so handsome, not that you weren't before, but look at you!"

She pulled back enough to pat his face with her violet hands.

"Oona!" Cian scolded. "That isn't the master! That's his brother, Fionn. Look at his face!"

"You dolt! Don't you recognize our boy when you see him?"

Cian's face paled. "Eamonn?"

"I tried to tell you," he grunted. "Instead you made me put my sword through a perfectly good door."

The gnome launched himself across the room and wrapped his arms around Eamonn's shoulders. "You're alive!"

They all laughed and held onto Eamonn until he turned bright red and attempted to shove them away. Neither Oona nor Cian would let go. He looked over their heads at Sorcha with wide eyes.

"They're in our bed."

"They missed you."

He sighed. "Ah well, we'll have a new bed soon."

Oona pulled back and stared at Sorcha. "You succeeded?"

"We conquered Cathair Solais and its previous king now rots in the dungeon until we decide what to do with him."

"Dearie, that is wonderful. And now the true king can take the throne."

Eamonn grinned, but Sorcha winced.

"They won't like me with you, Eamonn. You may wish for me to step aside for a while, just until you are comfortably king."

"Why would I want that?"

"There's a reason my people were cast aside. They fear me, even more so now that I proved what I can do. I can control them so easily. They are right to be afraid."

He reached out and took her hand. "They fear what they do not know. You've already captured the love of half the Seelie Court, and that's far more than any king has ever managed."

Sorcha lost herself in his gaze. He believed in her so much, it made her heart swell. She could do anything with him by her side.

Oona cleared her throat. "Then we go back to the Castle of Light?"

"As soon as possible."

⚜

CATHAIR SOLAIS WAS ABUZZ WITH MOVEMENT. FOR THE FIRST time in hundreds of years, a new coronation was being held. No one knew much about the mysterious king and queen who had fought through the golden army and won.

But all were curious. And all were invited to see the momentous crowning.

Servants rushed through the halls, Lesser Fae and High Fae alike. Some of the High Fae enjoyed their new lives. Working gave a purpose rather than constant balls, drugs, and alcohol.

Others chose not to have a respectable life, and they had the right to that choice. Old money would sustain them for a time, but eventually, they too would need to earn their keep.

"M'lady!" A shout echoed down the hall. "That's for the ceremony!"

"Oh it'll be fine, Ada! Shh."

Sorcha giggled at the startled expressions. The servants had yet to grow used to her strange behavior. They expected her to be like the countless other queens and princess they had seen. Stoic, demure, kind to a fault.

She stuffed the sweet pastry in her mouth and waved her fingers at them. Someday she might act like a queen, but certainly not within her own quarters.

Wiping sticky fingers on her skirts, she wiggled away from the wall of servants and rushed towards her room.

She still couldn't believe that an entire wing of the castle was dedicated to her. She had looked at the woman who ran the castle with wide eyes and asked why on earth she would need an entire wing.

Apparently, most queens thought they needed that much room.

Sorcha wanted a painting of the woman's expression when she had said to give the servants the bottom three floors. It was as if she'd suggested keeping farm animals inside her rooms.

"Sorcha!" Oona called out. "If you aren't in your coronation gown, I will come and stuff you in it myself!"

Her eyes went wide. Right, she needed to get into her dress, and wait patiently for the hairdresser.

She heard the tell-tale whoosh of Oona's wings and spun on her heel to race up the stairs.

"I can see your skirts!" Oona shouted. "Get dressed!"

The servants had to get used to their relationship as well. No one would dare speak in such a way to any previous queen. But Oona was nearly a mother to Sorcha, she could say anything she wanted.

Feet flying up the spiral stairwell, she made her way to the highest tower. Why had she insisted on this room? Her breath sawed out of her lungs and dizziness threatened to throw off her balance.

She slipped through the door, screeching when arms wrapped around her waist and lifted her off her feet.

This was why she had insisted on a tower room. Eamonn yanked her back against his chest and peppered kisses over her shoulders.

"You're supposed to be in a gown made of sunlight," he growled and bit down on her neck. "I don't see a gown, I see a milkmaid hiding from the scolding fishwife."

"Did you just call Oona a fishwife?" she laughed.

"She shrieks loud enough to have earned the name."

"Did you call me a milkmaid?"

"Oh, is that only in my fantasies?" He spun her around to capture her lips.

Sorcha shook her head, laughter bubbling through her lips. "You have fantasies about me as a milkmaid? Of all things, Eamonn!"

"What? There's something rather entertaining about the idea of returning from war, hungry, aching, tired. And there you are, on a hillside among the heather with your hair down and a smile on your face." He tugged at her dress. "And skirts that aren't too tight to toss."

She rolled her eyes. "That's more what I expected. Are you trying to distract me? We have a coronation to go to."

"And we're the king and queen! We can make them wait." He backed her towards the bed, tugging at the laces of her bodice.

Sorcha laughed again, slapping at his hands. "Stop that! You're only tangling them further!"

"I'm helping."

"You are not!"

"Sorcha, I've undressed more women in my lifetime than you have yourself. Stand still!"

It was to this playful scene that Oona barged in on. She pressed a hand to her mouth and blushed bright red, but Sorcha knew she had seen far worse.

"I see the master has taken it upon himself to get you into the coronation gown."

Sorcha shrugged and yanked the strings out of Eamonn's hands again. "It seems as though everyone is working against me."

"Into the gown with you." Oona pointed at Eamonn with a severe expression. "And if you delay her any longer, I will take a switch to your backside, boy."

"You haven't done that for centuries."

"Don't think I won't!"

She left the room and Eamonn glowered at the empty space. "We shouldn't have given her so many airs. She speaks to us as if we're children!"

"We are to her," Sorcha said with a chuckle. "More than that, we're her children. So don't take it away from her."

"Hm. Maybe just a little?"

"No!"

She let him spin her around and start on the clasps at the back of her dress. There was something quiet and sweet about the way he undressed her. Whether he had a particular goal in mind, or was helping after a long day.

Eamonn was always so gentle with her. And she still had a hard time believing this was her life.

Such a short time ago she was a peasant girl living in a brothel. The old religion was her escape from the mundane world of her life. And now? She sat on a throne with a man she would have claimed a god.

One of the Fair Folk loved her. How was she so lucky?

"I'm the lucky one," he said against her shoulder as he let her outer layers drop to the floor.

"Was I speaking out loud?"

"No, I could read it in your expression, mo chroí."

"Then we shall both be the lucky ones, for we have surely been blessed in this life." She spun around, shoved her hands against his shoulders, and forced him to sit on the bed. "Eamonn, I've been wanting to tell you something for a while now, and I refuse to have a crown placed on my head without you knowing."

"You were married before you came here."

"What? No!"

"You killed a man on the battlefield."

"No."

"You've been cursed to shout 'toad' whenever you see my twin?"

She burst into laughter again. "No! You foolish man, none of that."

He palmed her hips and dragged her forward until she stood between his thighs. Pressing a kiss against her collarbone, he breathed, "Then what is it? It surely will not make me love you any less."

"No I suspect it will make you love me quite a bit more."

The words were hard to find, and nothing would do it justice. Instead, she took his hand and guided it over her lower belly where the slightest of bumps had formed.

He took a moment to understand what she meant.

Sorcha watched as each emotion danced over his features. His brows drew down in stubborn concentration as he worked thoughts through the feel of her belly. His eyes widened as he realized what she meant. Then, his hand flexed ever so gently over their child.

She had never seen Eamonn so stunned, or so moved. Tears filled his eyes and a rapid exhale took all the air from his lungs.

"Ours?"

Tears pricked her own eyes as she laughed. "Could it be anyone else's?"

Beside himself and without words, Eamonn slid from the bed onto his knees before her. He pulled her close and pressed his forehead against her belly. She felt the slow glide of his nose as he nuzzled closer.

"You are loved," he growled, both to her and the child. "You will be great and honorable and good. You will have your mother's flaming hair and your father's stubborn chin. I will rock to sleep at night, and your mother will kiss you awake every morning."

She pressed one hand to her trembling lips and the other to Eamonn's head. She held him against her, close to their child who seemed so much a miracle in the midst of such darkness.

Voice choked, Eamonn looked up at her. "How long?"

"I can't be so certain. Six moons, maybe a little longer."

"Is it a girl?"

"I don't know," she chuckled. "Don't you want a son?"

"I want anything you can give me and hundreds more." He lurched to his feet and drew her so gently into his arms she wondered if he thought she were now made of glass.

"Hundreds?" she chuckled. "That's too much to ask, high king."

"Not enough. I can't ever have enough of you."

She lost herself in his kiss, in his embrace, as he held her against his heart.

⁂

"ARE YOU READY?" EAMONN ASKED.

They stood just outside the throne room, fully garbed in the most uncomfortable clothing Sorcha had ever seen. He looked wonderful. Dressed all in white and gold, the long tail of his braid left free to swing as he moved. Ocras swung from his hip and a large starburst pendant from his neck.

Sorcha's high necked dress made her want to scratch. It splayed out around her chin like a wave from the ocean, and in theory was stunning. The bell sleeves touched the floor if she let her arms dip too far. Gemstones studded the metal corset and sprayed down the heavy skirt in fine, embroidered stitches. Her hair piled heavy on top of her head, braided so tight she could feel the skin at her temples pulling back.

It was too bad the whole thing made her feel as if she were an antique on display.

"Sorcha?" Eamonn asked again.

"Yes, yes I'm ready."

"Are you certain?" He reached out and touched a hand to her belly. "We can always postpone if you wish."

"I'm no different than I was before, and you didn't treat me like glass then. Besides, we've already made them wait too long."

"It will be overwhelming."

"Why should it be? They will be silent as the grave and wondering just how much we will change."

He smirked. "You'll see. Guards, open the doors."

The two men in silver armor, Eamonn had insisted the uniform change no matter how much Sorcha argued it was wasteful, swung open the doors to reveal the crowd of faeries.

They saw their king and queen and burst into boisterous cheers. She forced her mouth to remain shut at their enthusiasm. She had thought they would remain reserved, unsure of their new rulers who had taken the kingdom by storm.

They were not. Some faces she recognized, dwarves from the battlefield, pixies in the air, peat faeries in the shadows with bright smiles on their faces. But others, she did not. Tuatha dé Danann, dryads, brownies, those who had remained faithful to Fionn until the bitter end.

Even they were pleased to see Eamonn and Sorcha at last.

She gripped his forearm tighter and glanced up at him. "I had not expected this."

"The Fae are much used to changes in their lives. The royalty moves, pieces changing, switching as the game is played. They hope we shall be better than the last, and if we are not, that we will be overthrown just as quickly."

Sorcha blew out a breath. "That is a lot of pressure."

"It is, but we will be a good king and queen."

"How can you be so certain?"

He looked out over his people, a soft smile on his face. She was struck by the ease he stood among them. The simple way he could switch from warlord to king seamlessly.

"This is what I was raised to do, Sorcha. I saw the injustices our people were forced to bear, but it was you who convinced me they could truly be changed. We will make a great difference in this world, unite our people, and give this land much needed peace."

She looked up at Eamonn and smiled. They made their way up the steps towards their thrones. One jagged edged, burned, and foreboding. The other with roses blooming over every inch.

A voice shouted, "Thus ends the era of Fionn the Wise and so begins the reign of the Stag King and the Rose Queen!"

Two of the oldest Tuatha dé Danann stood, carrying gilded crowns that made Sorcha's heart pound. Was she ready for this? Could she ever be ready to be Queen?

She looked out over the crowd and saw faces she loved, people she trusted, and she knew that if it were her destiny to become queen, then she would wear such a destiny with pride.

The strange creatures were a myriad of color and textures. Wings, horns, glittery appendages, all blended together to creature a patchwork of magic and wonder.

Except one single person, who stood out like a sore thumb.

She gasped out a wrenching sob. "Papa?"

Eamonn squeezed her hand and nudged her back towards the crowd. "The crowning can wait."

She didn't care what her people thought of a queen who fled from her throne and burst into the crowd. She threw her arms around her father's shoulders and sobbed into his neck.

"Oh, Papa! I didn't think I would ever see you again!"

"Neither did I, my sweet girl." He held her close, laughing in her ear. "But your husband found me far too easily, and here I stand."

"And my sisters?"

"Waiting in our room. I'm afraid they were much overwhelmed by the Otherworld."

"And you are not?"

"No, I'm too ornery to fear these creatures." But he looked around them and gulped. "Besides, it's not every day a father gets to watch his child crowned queen."

Sorcha tightened her hold around his neck. "I must go and do that, father. But I wish to speak with you immediately afterwards."

"Aren't you supposed to be having some kind of ceremony?"

"They can wait. My family is far more important than stuffy old traditions."

He chuckled. "I believe your husband feels the same way."

"He does."

It took quite a bit of effort to release her hold on her father's neck. She missed him terribly and hadn't realized the hole in her heart that came from him not being here. Sliding from his embrace, she smiled brilliantly before turning back to her husband.

Eamonn. The man who had not only saved her life and convinced her to become something far more than a midwife, but who catered to her every whim and desire.

She walked back up the steps and reached her hands out to him. "You did this."

"I knew you wouldn't want to go through it without at least one of your family members."

"I would never have asked. I don't even know what you must have done to bring him here."

"You don't want to." He pulled her close to him and feathered a kiss over her lips. "But I would do anything for you, mo chroí."

"Then let us be crowned and get this over as soon as possible. I wish you to meet them."

He whirled her around so her skirts flew in a bell shape around her knees. The faeries cheered, and he sat her down in her throne, taking his beside her.

The herald cleared his throat and began again. "We crown thee the Stag King! May you rule with honor, confidence, and a sure hand."

The faerie behind Eamonn lowered a crown which twisted and turned, pockmarked like the tines of an antler.

"We crown thee the Rose Queen! May you rule with kindness, nobility, and forgiveness."

She felt the thin gold crown nestle in her hair. She knew without looking that delicate roses had been crafted by the finest artisans in all the land. Looking out over the crowd of her subjects, she smiled at them and prayed she would never let them down.

Eamonn reached for her hand and squeezed it. "Together."

She looked over at him and felt her heart swell. "Together."

⚜

"ARE YOU CERTAIN YOU'RE UP TO THIS?" EAMONN ASKED.

"Would you stop asking me that question today?"

"It's just in your delicate condition—"

"If you say one more word about me being pregnant and fragile, I will set the drapes on fire."

"You wouldn't dare."

Sorcha glared up at him. "I most certainly would."

"Your sisters sound..." He glanced at the door as shrieks of laughter blast through the thick wood. "Exhausting."

"They are. But they are very kind and have good heads on their shoulders. I think you'll find that they are wonderful women who love me very much."

"They let you go."

"Because it was what I wanted." She put her hand on the doorknob and grinned. "You'll be all right, won't you?"

"Just open the door."

Sorcha turned the knob and threw her arms wide. "Sisters!"

"Sorcha!"

The shrieking group of thirteen women surrounded her. They passed her around for hugs, tears, and blubbering words incapable of being understood. They didn't need to know what the others had said, the love was already in the air.

Each woman had missed Sorcha so much that it boiled over into a cloud of happiness that tasted of salt and relief.

Eamonn leaned against the door with his arms crossed. Sorcha's father walked over to him and stood watching the teeming mass of females.

"It's rather intimidating, isn't it?"

Eamonn glanced down. "That's one way to put it."

"Her family loves her very much."

"It is a rare gift. She appreciates it."

"Do you?" Papa glanced up with a stern expression. "I won't have my daughter taken away from me by the Fair Folk."

Eamonn found it strange that such a small man was threatening him. Humans were tiny compared to the Tuatha dé Danann, and yet Sorcha's father had no hesitation. He understood what those words meant but did not curb his tongue.

Inclining his head, Eamonn replied, "I have no intention of keeping Sorcha from her family."

"Good, that is good."

Sorcha glanced up and gestured for Eamonn to join them. "Mo chroí! Let me introduce you to my family!"

He shouldn't have to steel himself to manage a group of Sorcha's sisters. But Eamonn found himself more nervous than the eve of battle.

Straightening his waistcoat, he stepped forward. "Ladies."

They tittered. *Tittered* and giggled like little schoolgirls and ducked their heads to whisper to each other.

Gods help him.

Eamonn glanced behind him, hoping Sorcha's father would provide some much needed guidance. The old man simply shrugged.

Some use he was. Eamonn clenched his fists and lowered himself onto a tiny couch with women flocking all around him.

"Sorcha! I thought he was supposed to be beastly! That's what all the stories say."

"Stories?" Sorcha blinked at them. "What stories?"

"Well once we knew you went to Hy-brasil, we searched for any rumors! Everyone was talking about the ugly brute on the isle, but this man... Oh, he's not ugly at all."

He wanted to remind them that he could hear them. But the ladies were enjoying themselves, and he hadn't had a crowd of women admiring him for a very long time. What harm could find him from allowing himself to find peace?

Sorcha's eyes flashed with jealous anger.

Right. That's where the harm could come from. Sighing, he wrapped an arm around her shoulders and pressed a kiss against her temple. "It's been a pleasure, ladies. But I have other business to attend to. I trust you will take care of my life?"

"Your wife, you mean?"

"No," he corrected. "My life. She is the very reason I draw breath and is worth far more than just a title."

One of the sisters listed to the side with her hands pressed against her heart.

He stood immediately, catching Sorcha's eyes to make sure she was all right. She nodded with more glee in her expression than he had ever seen. If all it took to make her happy was having her family around, then he would keep them.

What would the old Tuatha dé Danann say to that?

Grinning, he strode from the room. He did not run. No one would dare say that the new king of the Seelie Fae would ever run from a group of women.

But he may have rushed.

The servants bowed as he walked by, and Eamonn didn't have the heart to tell them to stop. So many things were already changing. They needed something to remain the same so their world didn't completely upend.

He looked just like his brother. Some of them still slipped and called him by Fionn's name, turning white as a bean sidhe when they realized what they had done.

He wouldn't hurt them for the small slip. He understood why they were concerned, but didn't have the heart to punish them. These people had suffered enough.

Or perhaps they hadn't. Some of them had liked having Fionn has their king. Eamonn didn't know what to make of that.

The dungeon was a dank, dark place. Water dripped from the ceiling in a never ending stream of sound that would have driven him mad. Some of the prisoners had already lost their minds.

Eamonn had personally reviewed their records. Some he let go, Lesser Fae who had broken the law only to feed their families. Others stayed where they were. Just because the king changed didn't mean murder was acceptable.

At the far end of the dungeon, far away from the others, Fionn waited. His arms stretched out at his sides, chains digging into the skin. His beautiful hair dripped water and hung lank to the ground. They removed most of his clothing, leaving him in nothing more than dirty breeches.

Eamonn nodded at the guard who opened the door.

Fionn did not even look up.

He knelt beside his fallen brother and sighed.

"You told me I forced your hand when you plunged the Lugh's spear through my heart."

The chains rattled, but Fionn remained silent.

"So I say to now, you have also forced my hand. I wish it could have been different between us, brother. I would have liked to rule with you by my side."

Eamonn tipped Fionn's face up, staring at his sunken eyes and the bruises on his jaw. It was like looking at a mirror image of himself. And so painful that Eamonn forgot how to breathe.

"Are you going to kill me?" Fionn croaked.

"No. I'm banishing you to the human lands and denying you all ties to the Otherworld. No faerie shall speak with you, no Wild Hunt shall find you. I gift you life, brother, but nothing else."

"It's a fate worse than death."

"Perhaps you think so now. But I promise you, someday you'll realize these people are capable of love in a way we never imagined. You have never been alone, Fionn. Now you will be." Eamonn stood. "I look forward to watching you, and how you change your story. Or how you don't."

As he walked out of the cell, Fionn lifted his voice once more.

"And Elva?"

"She doesn't love you, brother."

"It doesn't matter. I love her, and I would know she is safe."

"Elva has taken her life into her own hands." Eamonn clasped his hands behind his back and turned towards Fionn. "She travels to an isle far north, dedicating her life to the art of war. No man may step foot on those lands. I would be surprised if she ever leaves it."

He turned away from the tragic expression on Fionn's face. The fallen king was more affected by the loss of his consort than he was his own fate. A shame, because his brother didn't know what real love was.

The chains rattled, and Eamonn blew out a breath. The head of his army waited at the top of the stairs. The tall elf worked closely with Angus who had returned to his home under the mountain.

"Your Majesty?"

"You heard my judgment?"

"Yes. Do you wish to wait and speak with the queen?"

Eamonn shook his head and clapped a hand on the elf's shoulder. "No. She need not be a part of this. Keep the information from the dowager king and queen, they are to be confined to their quarters for the remainder of their lives. Banish Fionn, take care of the gates, and ensure all faerie rings reject him. I want no chance that he will ever return to the Otherworld."

"Consider it done."

He already did. And perhaps that was why his heart ached.

෴

MUCH LATER, EAMONN AWOKE FROM HIS DREAMS. THE WIND brushed through the windows of the high tower, cooling his skin. Groggy and half awake, he reached for Sorcha only to find her spot cold.

He grumbled as he rolled over to stare at their balcony.

The moon silhouetted her figure, sheer white fabric billowing over her body as the wind kissed her curves. How he loved her.

A man's legs shifted, perched on the railing. Eamonn also knew who that would be. Damned Unseelie, they never knew when to stop meddling.

He swung his legs over the edge of the bed and strode towards her. Shirtless, he pulled her back against his chest and pressed a kiss to the top of her head.

"Bran," he grumbled.

"Your Majesty." A distinct tone of mockery was in the Unseelie prince's voice.

"Jealous?"

"Never. The throne is not my destiny."

"Don't say that. The ancestors have a way of meddling in our lives."

"I wish they'd stick to humans."

Sorcha scoffed. "Keep your bad luck to yourself, thank you."

She was warm and soft, everything he had always desired his wife would be. He couldn't remember ever seeing a Tuatha dé Danann woman quite like her. They were always regal, put together, tall and broad shouldered. Sorcha was tiny and so hot she burned like a furnace.

He spread a hand wide over their child and the ever growing bump of her belly. "What were you two talking about?"

"The future," Sorcha replied.

"And?"

"We think it will be very good."

"Is it? Why do you think that?"

Bran chuckled. "My mother said so."

"Ah. Then it will be."

Eamonn felt the last chip of his soul slide back into place. His life had never been blessed with love, family, friends. He'd always been alone.

Now, with this woman who was never alone, he found himself and a future filled with laughter and love.

Sorcha's hands pressed against his, and a firm kick pressed against his palm.

"Was that—?"

"Your daughter is restless, Athair," Sorcha said with a smile.

He didn't care that Bran was watching. Eamonn spun her around and dropped to his knees. He pressed his lips against her belly and felt the slow roll of his child between her hips.

"Just a little while longer, nighean, daughter. Soon our family shall be together at last."

Sorcha threaded her fingers through his loose hair, and Eamonn suddenly realized what it was like for all to be right in the world.

Afterword

And thus ends the second part of Socha and eamonn's story.

What a journey with these two! I thoroughly enjoyed writing this book, and I hope you enjoyed reading it as well!

The series of the Otherworld will continue in another character's story, with a new fairytale. I think it's safe to say, I can tease you that the story will be the Swan Princess!

Please make sure to keep in touch on my social media (Facebook, email, etc) as I will continue to update you on all the exciting new stories and books!

Well met, and blessed be.

Acknowledgments

There are so many people to thank for this book that I couldn't possibly write them all down. If I forget you, I am sincerely sorry and yell at me later.

NATA - Again, the cover. I mean SERIOUSLY I am so lucky to have found you and your wonderful talent. This artwork embodies everything I want people to see in these characters. Their strength, their virtue, and their ability to overcome all odds. I can't thank you enough.

AMY - The fearless editor who has no problem telling me when something is stupid, or just not up to my usual standards. You're a saint.

RENEE AND EMILY - The fearless duo who have helped me get through writing in general. Thank you for never letting me get too far down in the dumps, and for taking the time to listen. It means the world.

MOM AND DAD - Is there any way to thank you? For all the bruises, scrapes, nights crying, headaches, and crap you put up with, I love you and appreciate you more than words can express.

TO MY READERS - Every book you buy, every review you leave,

every message you send means the world. (Didn't that sound like it was going towards a Police song? Everything breath you taaaake)

This is for you.

About the Author

Emma Hamm is a small town girl on a blueberry field in Maine. She writes stories that remind her of home, of fairytales, and of myths and legends that make her mind wander.

She can be found by the fireplace with a cup of tea and her two Maine Coon cats dipping their paws into the water without her knowing.

To stay in touch

www.emmahamm.com

authoremmahamm@gmail.com